Praise for Ma

DON'T LOOK NOW
"With plenty of possible suspects, Burton's latest will appeal to readers who want light romance and heavy suspense."

—*Library Journal*

BURN YOU TWICE
"Burton does a good job balancing gentle romance with high-tension suspense."

—*Publishers Weekly*

"Scorching action. The twists and turns keep the reader on the edge of their seat as they will not want to put the novel down."

—*Crimespree Magazine*

HIDE AND SEEK
"Burton delivers an irresistible, tension-filled plot with plenty of twists . . . Lovers of romantic thrillers won't be disappointed."

—*Publishers Weekly*

CUT AND RUN
"Burton can always be counted on for her smart heroines and tightly woven plots."

—*For the Love of Books*

"Must-read romantic suspense . . . Burton is a bona fide suspense superstar. And her books may be peppered with enough twists and turns to give you whiplash, but the simmering romance she builds makes for such a compelling, well-rounded story."

—*USA Today's Happy Ever After*

THE SHARK
"This romantic thriller is tense, sexy, and pleasingly complex."
—*Publishers Weekly*

"Precise storytelling complete with strong conflict and heightened tension are the highlights of Burton's latest. With a tough, vulnerable heroine in Riley at the story's center, Burton's novel is a well-crafted, suspenseful mystery with a ruthless villain who would put any reader on edge. A thrilling read."
—*RT Book Reviews* (4 stars)

BEFORE SHE DIES
"Will keep readers sleeping with the lights on."
—*Publishers Weekly* (starred review)

MERCILESS
"Burton keeps getting better!"
—*RT Book Reviews*

YOU'RE NOT SAFE
"Burton once again demonstrates her romantic-suspense chops with this taut novel. Burton plays cat and mouse with the reader through a tight plot, credible suspects, and romantic spice keeping it real."
—*Publishers Weekly*

BE AFRAID
"Mary Burton [is] the modern-day queen of romantic suspense."
—Bookreporter

The House Beyond the Dunes

The House Beyond the Dunes

MARY BURTON

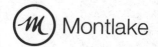

Published by Montlake, Seattle

www.apub.com

Amazon, the Amazon logo, and Montlake are trademarks of Amazon.com, Inc., or its affiliates.

ISBN-13: 9781542038676 (paperback)
ISBN-13: 9781542038683 (digital)

Cover design by Ploy Siripant
Cover image: © Silas Manhood / ArcAngel

Printed in the United States of America

The House
Beyond
the Dunes

STEVIE PALMER'S DIARY

Friday, July 7, 2023

This diary is an account of what happened last week. I've written it all down because, well, life always goes sideways, and I've learned to hedge my bets. Trouble and I know each other well. Hell, we're almost besties after all these years. But everything is changing. The ground under my feet is steady today, but that never lasts. Not sure how long I can hold it together, but I'll fight the good fight while I can. No one gets out of here alive, right?

Chapter One

LANE

Friday, December 29, 2023
Norfolk, Virginia
7:00 p.m.

The fall began with a small slip on a marble step. Any other time, I'd have caught myself, adjusted, and found a way to hold steady. But not this time.

That misstep sent both of us tumbling down twenty-one stairs. *Us.* Kyle and I weren't really an *us*. We'd known each other three and a half weeks, technically twenty-five days.

He'd first approached me in the coffee shop I manage. I was refilling the whole milk and creamer containers at the self-serve station when he slid in beside me. The soft scent of his aftershave snagged my attention. Sandalwood. He said something charming. I thought he was talking to someone else. But his gaze pinned me. I was flattered, and even blushed.

Almost immediately, the floodgates between us opened. He began showering me with enchanting texts, fragrant flowers, and mouthwatering kisses. He didn't push sex, and I was wooed by his patience. In a few short weeks, *we* were on the path to *something*.

This weekend was supposed to be our big, romantic beach getaway. Our first sleepover. We were going to ring in the New Year alone, wrapped in each other's arms. A big step toward figuring out if this thing between us might be real. So much anticipation. Excitement. I've no free time between school and managing the coffee shop, so for Kyle to have lured me away for a long weekend was saying something.

However, within an hour of arriving at his glittering North Carolina cottage overlooking the dunes of the northern Outer Banks and the Atlantic Ocean, we fell. The weight of our bodies sent us hurtling through the air so fast, adrenaline didn't catch up until the last microsecond, when we hit the marble floor.

Now I'm in the hospital, my left hip is banged up and bruised, and my body is so stiff, it's hard to turn my head to the right. I feel as if I've gone three rounds with a boxer. But my injuries aren't critical. I'll heal.

Kyle wasn't so lucky.

He's dead.

"You're fortunate to be alive." Dr. Jackson sounds cheerful, a little too upbeat, as he closes the curtain to my room. He's tall, lean, and keeps his hair cut short. Dark circles smudge under his eyes. Emergency room sounds swirl around us. Gurneys. Machines beeping. Hushed conversations.

I shift, doing my best to sit up. The muscles in my gut and along my ribs scream in protest. The guy I liked is dead, and I can barely move without my body crying. I was supposed to be sipping wine while sitting in a hot tub with Kyle, making out, and taking another step toward *us*. "Yes, lucky."

Dr. Jackson holds a light up to my eyes and waves it over my pupils. I stiffen. "Just look at the light."

"How long have I been here?" I ask.

"About six hours."

"How did I get here?"

"You were airlifted from the Outer Banks to Norfolk."

The Outer Banks is a 170-mile barrier island chain, and Kyle's house is in the northernmost section, tucked against the Virginia line.

As the crow flies, Kyle's cottage is thirty minutes from Norfolk, where I live. But there's no quick way to get from here to there. This remote stretch of land requires a trip around Norfolk's beltway, followed by a few secondary highways in North Carolina, crossing the three-mile-long Wright Memorial Bridge, and then another twenty-mile drive north. All that travel is rewarded with an eleven-mile four-wheel drive on an untamed beach. Basically, over the river and through the woods takes two and a half hours.

Memories of the trip and the house are vague. My mind is trapped in a loop, replaying the crack of Kyle's skull on marble, the pool of his blood oozing toward me, and the pain rocketing through my body.

I'm only vaguely aware of a man trying to rouse me and then being placed on a stretcher. I was out cold during the med flight ride to Norfolk. Most of this entire day tangles like a bad dream.

"Kyle is really dead?" I ask.

"Yes," Dr. Jackson says. "He was pronounced dead at the scene."

I brace for a rush of sadness. Grief, despondency, and sorrow are all natural responses for someone who's lost the other half of a potential *us*.

Kyle and I weren't married or even sleeping together, but we'd had a connection. I didn't fully understand what tethered us so tightly, but it had been very real. Yet no emotions charge or encircle me. There's only numbness. Must be shock.

"Are you taking any medications?" Dr. Jackson asks.

"For sleepwalking. I can't remember the name."

"That might explain the drugs we found in your system."

"What drugs?"

"A sedative."

"I don't take anything other than the pills to hold off the sleepwalking."

"Okay." He regards me and then says, "The head scan tells me you suffered no damage to your brain or spine, which is excellent news. But

I'd like to do an MRI of your left hip. X-rays tell me it's not broken, but I suspect you've torn muscles or tendons, or maybe separated the labrum."

My head is good. A win. "What's a labrum?"

Dr. Jackson tucks his penlight in his front pocket and runs calloused hands up and down my neck. I brace. "It's the cartilage cushioning the hip joint. Any pain in the neck?"

"A little stiff, but okay." I angle my neck away from him and feel the muscles resisting. "The hip aches."

Dr. Jackson nods. "Then we should do the MRI."

I look around the curtained-off emergency room cubicle. How much is all this going to cost me? "MRIs are expensive."

"Clear images give me a good look inside your body. You don't want to risk more damage."

As I shift, the back folds of my hospital gown open, and a cold breeze fingers up my spine. I can live with a stiff hip, which in all likelihood just needs rest. "My head is good, right?"

Dr. Jackson sighs. "Yes. But the hip correlates with long-term mobility."

"I'll rest it. See how it goes. If it's an issue, I'll call you. When can I leave the hospital? I'll take it easy. Take aspirin. Ice, heat, ice. Chill out." This place is suffocating, and I want to go home, where I'll try not to think about the fall, the sound of Kyle's head exploding, or sticky, warm blood.

Dr. Jackson shakes his head. "I'd like to admit you overnight for observation."

"No," I insist. "I'd rather be in my own bed. It's paid for."

His brow furrows. "Do you have insurance?"

"I do if you can call it that. My plan is stitched together with high copays and ridiculous deductibles. I'll take a pass on the tests and the overnight."

"I don't advise this, Ms. McCord," Dr. Jackson says carefully.

"I get it. Liability. Lawyers. I'll sign whatever I need to." I shift, wince. Seven hours ago, Kyle and I were driving up the beach toward his house. The day was warm, the sun bright, and the ocean calm. I was nervous, in an excited kind of way.

Now Kyle's blood smears my arm. "Are you sure about Kyle?"

"Yes. I'm sorry." He clears his throat. "What do you remember?"

"Arriving at the cottage." It's a stunning place and unexpectedly elegant on such a remote stretch of beach. Vaulted ceilings, large plush couches, floor-to-ceiling windows overlooking the dunes and ocean, white granite kitchen counters, dazzling stainless-steel appliances, and modern art on the walls. Fresh red roses filled a crystal vase on the living room coffee table. I remember almost teasing it was a no-one-can-hear-you-scream kind of place but thinking better of the joke. My dark sense of humor is best reserved for people who've known me more than three and a half weeks.

"The EMTs responded to the house at one fifteen p.m. today. When did you arrive at the cottage?"

"About noon. I don't remember much after we arrived."

Doubts crease his brow. "It's okay. Those memories should come back in time."

I know better than anyone, the power of positive thinking is faulty at best. "I want to leave. Where are my clothes, purse, and phone?"

"I really would like you to stay overnight for observation."

"No." Panic constricts my chest. "I hate hospitals."

"Most people do."

I sit up straighter, wince as my hip protests. My head is clear. "I'll call if something goes wrong."

Dr. Jackson's frown deepens as he shakes his head. "I'm going to hold you to that, Lane."

I cross my chest. Hope not to die. "Promise."

"Any signs of dizziness, nausea, or headaches, call me. No running, cycling, or jumping. If you don't heed my advice, you'll really screw up your hip and be in surgery by Valentine's Day."

"You don't have to tell me twice." A few days ago, I'd toyed with spending Valentine's Day with Kyle. He might have come out of nowhere, but our relationship was headed somewhere. He was so into me. And now he's dead.

"Are you sure you're feeling okay?" Dr. Jackson asks.

"I'm fine, Doctor." In an hour, Dr. Jackson will have seen five or six more patients, and I'll recede into his distant memory. I'll enter the hospital's digital archives and reside alongside my foster care records, student loan debt accounts, college transcripts, and credit card scores. I've lived between the cracks all my life, and I'm comfortable with obscurity. "I just need to get out of here."

"I'll send in someone from administration to help you check out."

I glance over the side rails to a small table outfitted with a phone. "Where are my purse and clothes? My pills are in my purse. I'll show you the prescription bottle."

"Let me check with the nurse." He's trying to care, but it won't last long. At least I have his attention right now. "I'll be right back."

"Great. Thanks." I lean my head back against the pillow. I breathe in deeply and slowly exhale. I feel light-headed. This small room feels as if it's shrinking by the moment, and the hospital's antiseptic smell makes deep breathing unsatisfying.

When I close my eyes, I hear the pop of Kyle's skull as it splits like a melon. My stomach tumbles, and I think I'm going to get sick. The bathroom is across the room, but I'm hooked up to an IV, and my hip cries every time I move. *Please, I cannot get sick. They'll never let me out of here if I barf.*

The curtain opens and closes, and Dr. Jackson reappears. "The nurse said your purse didn't come with you."

"What do you mean it didn't come with me?" It contains my cell, my medications, and basically my life.

"The nurse contacted the EMTs, and they said your belongings were left behind at the beach house."

"Are they still there?" I shift and grimace. "I remember setting my overnight bag and purse by the bed in the main bedroom."

"The EMTs say the house was closed up," Dr. Jackson says. "It must still be where you left it."

Shit. I must get my phone and the pills that keep my insomnia and sleepwalking in check. "Where are my clothes?"

"The nurses bagged them. I understand they were badly stained. We also had to cut your pants off to examine your hip."

"Stained with blood," I say more to myself. My hands tremble. Blood stains forever, right?

"Let me talk to the nurse. She can get you a set of scrubs."

"That's not necessary. I'll call my neighbor." I reach for the hospital phone.

"No running or long walks at all, Lane," he warns. "I'm serious. Take it easy for a few months, or that small rip will go full-blown and will require surgery."

"I'm not doing surgery." The idea of a surgeon's blade cutting my skin terrifies me.

"Then take care of yourself. Call me if you need me. I can also put you in touch with a psychologist."

Kyle was a psychologist. I'm also a semester away from being one. "Thanks."

He leaves, and I dial my neighbor Shelly's landline. I remember it because it's only two digits higher than my phone number when I was a kid. She's not going to recognize the hospital number and won't answer, but she has an old-school answering machine. The phone rings six times before the machine picks up. *This is Shelly. Don't leave a message.*

"Shelly, this is Lane. I'm in the hospital. I need you to go by my place, use your spare key, and get a few things." I rattle off a list and tell her where I am.

I hang up, shift my weight off my left hip, and lie back on the bed. My body aches, and I still can't believe Kyle is gone. Kyle. Is. Dead. I should be doing something for him. Calling someone. But my eyes drift closed.

"It's going to be a great weekend," Kyle says. We've stopped at the redbrick Currituck Lighthouse Historic Park, and we're parked next to a row of air tire pumps in the shadow of the lighthouse. He reaches across me, removes an air gauge from the glove box, and kisses me on the lips. "Can't wait to get you alone. Be right back."

"What are you doing?"

"Letting air out of the tires. It's called airing down," he explains. "You can only drive on the beach with deflated tires. Better traction. Don't want us getting stuck in the sand."

"We're leaving the hard surface road?"

"Only way to get where we're going."

My nerves ripple, but I can't tell if it's with worry or anticipation. Maybe both. This is going to be our big weekend. "I've never driven on sand before."

"It's a sight to see." He gets out of the car, and I follow, mostly because I like being close to him.

"Are we headed to the middle of nowhere?" The wind is brisk, but the sun is warm as I watch him kneel by the front driver's-side tire. Kyle has a long, lean body earned in a gym and by consuming two protein shakes a day. He's always careful with his appearance. He's a far cry from the underpaid social workers I've worked with as part of my dissertation. Social workers and grad students favor faded jeans, graphic T-shirts, and hiking boots. Court days mean a wardrobe upgrade to khakis and a slightly rumpled button-down shirt.

"It feels like that sometimes. But the isolation is what I like about it." He brushes a thick lock of dark-brown hair away from his gray eyes. "Wait until we get to my place. It'll just be us. Total privacy." When he smiles, his eyes warm.

"I like it when you look at me like that," I say.

He rises, stands so close I must crane my neck to meet his gaze. "And how do I look at you?"

"Like I'm the only person in the world."

He kisses me gently on the lips. "Right now, you are."

Voices from the hospital hallway reach through the curtain and pull me away from the memory. My eyes flutter open. I roll my head to the left and glance at the digital clock: 9:30 p.m. I sit up, suddenly alert. I've fallen asleep for almost two hours. Shit. I must get out of here.

Where are you, Shelly? Without my phone, wallet, pills, or clothes, I'm dead in the water. I can't Uber my way home without a phone or walk out with a bad hip. And ticking clocks in a hospital mean dollars leaking from my paltry bank account.

There's a knock on my doorframe. I run a hand over my short hair. "Yes?"

The curtains rustle, and a pale face peeks in the room. It's my neighbor, Shelly. She's a midfifties woman who likes her tattoos, bourbon, and her three cats—Wink, Blink, and Nod. We've lived in the dilapidated building in the Ghent district for a couple of years. We're not close, but we did exchange numbers and keys in case one of us gets locked out or disappears. Nice having someone who'll notice if I vanish.

Shelly's sweatshirt swallows her thin frame, and faded bell-bottom jeans graze blue flip-flops. My neighbor doesn't wear socks, or really shoes, no matter how cold it is outside, and most days her bare feet are splashed with the green, yellow, and blue acrylics she uses in her paintings. She's a starving artist.

"Lane." Shelly twirls a gray strand between her fingers. She has a cigarette tucked behind her ear.

I've never been so glad to see anyone in my life. Tears pool in my eyes, and it takes effort to keep them from spilling. "Shelly, thanks for coming. I was afraid you wouldn't get the message."

Shelly clutches a paper grocery bag. "What happened?"

"Long story. I just want to get out of here." I realize one of the nurses has removed my IV, so I swing my legs around and ease off the bed. The nerves in my left leg scream only a little. Not perfect. But manageable. *Slow and steady.*

Shelly approaches, smelling of cigarettes and turpentine. I've warned her about the combination, but she tells me not to worry. I have five smoke detectors in my apartment now. "Funny, I never play back messages."

I smooth my hands over the gown's thin cotton. "Maybe you felt my desperation."

"No, I didn't feel anything. I accidentally hit 'Play' instead of 'Delete.'" Shelly is literal. Sarcasm and expressions of speech go over her head.

Accepting the grocery bag, I peer inside and see my clothes. I did laundry before my big weekend, so at least the garments are clean. "Thank you."

"I didn't know what to get, so I grabbed a few tops and a couple of pairs of jeans. There's just one pair of shoes."

"It's perfect."

"Do you need help getting dressed?" Shelly hovers, but she looks ready to bolt. She's a recovering addict who has enjoyed moderate success with sobriety. From what she told me last week, she's been clean an entire month. Baby steps. I've worked with enough addicts to know the struggle is intense.

"No, I think I can manage," I say.

"Okay, good. I'll meet you in the lobby. You could use some privacy."

"You'll wait, right? I can't get home without my wallet and phone. They're still at the beach cottage."

"Yeah, yeah, sure, I'll wait right outside the front entrance." She pulls the cigarette from behind her ear, rolls it between her fingers before vanishing.

I test my hip with a little weight. It aches, but the pain is more manageable. I shrug off the hospital gown and glance at the bruises already darkening my entire left side.

Fishing panties from the paper bag, I try to lift my left leg, but it complains bitterly. I back up, regroup, and refocus. As I gingerly pull on the panties, I catch my reflection in the mirror over the sink. Deep blues and purples skid down my left side. Carefully, I touch some of the darkest spots near my hip.

A memory sputters and tries to fire. I close my eyes, coaxing it forward. Unexpectedly, I feel the floor go out from under my feet. I'm facing Kyle. He's gripping my arms as he falls backward, pulling me with him. There's anger in his eyes. And then we're flying. *Whack!*

My stomach twists. I shrug on the flannel shirt and then carefully work on the jeans. Shoes are slip-ons. No jacket, but I don't plan on spending a lot of time outside.

As I cross the room, I concentrate on each small step. It burns like hell, but my ability to absorb hardship and pain makes me a good candidate for a PhD in psychology. The plan is to eventually counsel broken, lost girls who live in society's cracks.

Kyle had wondered why I didn't want to work with clients with money. I'd tried to explain that that world is not mine. I thrive in the forgotten places. Who knows, maybe I can teach a few of the misplaced that there's life beyond now.

I smile at the nurse when she arrives, sign hospital papers that commit me to massive debt, and promise to call if I need anything else. Hospital protocol means leaving in a wheelchair, so with my grocery bag clutched in my arms, a nurse pushes me across the lobby to the hospital's main front door. Outside, the cold, dark air chills my overheated skin, now damp with sweat.

Shelly is standing under a light smoking, inhaling deeply. "Ready?"

"Yeah." Carefully, I rise, and we cross the lot toward the parked cars. The cold, salty wind off the waterfront is brisk and quickly robs me of the heat I banked in the hospital.

Shelly's car is a fifteen-year-old Toyota Corolla. Rust rings the front door and the back wheel well. The hinges on the front passenger door squeak when I open it. I brush the fast-food wrappers onto the floor and ignore Blink's white cat hairs clinging to the seat. Cigarette smoke mingles with the smells of something that desperately needs to be tossed.

"I should've cleaned the car up." Shelly slides behind the wheel, takes a last drag on her cigarette, and tosses the butt into the lot.

"It's fine." A fading Christmas tree air freshener dangles from the rearview mirror, fighting the good fight but losing.

"I'm surprised you called me," Shelly says. "No one ever calls me."

I click my seat belt. "I thought we were our own support team." Shifting, I struggle to get my left hip comfortable.

"I'm not exactly reliable."

The chill outside leaks into the car. "You're here now. That counts for a lot." My backup bench is so shallow. I'd thought maybe Kyle would join Team Lane. He was rigid, but so is steel, and it's dependable.

Shelly tucks a gray strand behind her ear. "I thought you were a telemarketer at first. They always call around dinnertime when I've just heated up pizza in the microwave."

The engine starts, Shelly turns on the heat, and I close my eyes. Warmth skims over the gooseflesh puckering my skin. Shelly switches on the radio, and the grainy sound system crackles "Riptide" by the Chainsmokers. The bass pulses in my chest.

"So, what the hell happened at the beach house? The nurse said that guy you went away with is dead." Shelly rarely minces words.

"Yes, he's dead." The word *dead* overwhelms the simple sentence. "We fell down the stairs."

"How?"

"I've no idea."

Shelly's gaze narrows. "How do you not know? It's been less than eight or nine hours."

I stare into the darkness broken by the glare of overhead parking lot lights. "I remember right up until we reached the top of the stairs. I don't know what triggered the fall. I guess my brain is rattled."

Bracelets jangle on Shelly's wrists as she turns up the heat. "That's super weird. I didn't think people really lose their memory."

"It's in there somewhere, and it'll come back." This conversation sounds like it belongs to someone else. Kyle and I still feel like an almost couple. My heart pinches.

A hard knock on the car door startles me. I look to my right and see a man standing inches away. I never saw or heard him coming, and it's unnerving to realize my guard has dropped so low.

The man is tall with wide shoulders. *Country boy strong*, as one of my foster mothers used to say. His short hair shifts between black and silver depending on how the light hits it. Blue eyes are arrow sharp, his jaw is square, and his nose hooks as if it's been broken a few times before.

He's staring at me with a combination of intense curiosity and challenge. Quickly, a deliberate grin softens his features, but not his eyes. They're dissecting me.

"Do you know that guy?" Shelly asks.

I turn my face away from him. "I've no idea who he is."

"I bet he's a reporter." Shelly's speaking in a stage whisper.

I don't want to be in the news. I don't want to be noticed. I'm the girl who lives between the cracks. "The accident can't be that newsworthy."

"Lane McCord, open up." The stranger's voice is deep, insistent. "We need to talk."

"Anything?" Shelly asks. "Does the sound of his voice ring any bells?"

"Nothing."

"Lane, we have to talk," the man says. "I know you've been through a lot."

The stranger's voice stirs panic. "Let's get out of here."

"He's probably a bill collector," Shelly says.

"I've only been out of the hospital ten minutes."

"Let's face it, girl. Neither one of us looks like we're good for the money."

Shelly puts the car in reverse, backing up quickly and forcing the stranger to step back. I glance toward him, fearing she's hit him, but he's standing strong, staring at me with a mixture of frustration and interest. I feel like I should apologize, but I have no words.

Shelly guns the engine, cranks the radio, and we're out of the lot and on the road headed east. She races toward a red light, ready to run it when a pickup truck in front of us stops. She slams on the brakes, stopping inches from the bumper. I grip my door. The light turns green, and she punches the accelerator, tailgating the truck for a couple of blocks before it turns. Thankfully, the town house is just a few miles away from the hospital.

Kyle was a smooth driver. *Was.* Kyle now lives in the past tense.

My kind-of-boyfriend *was* comfortable behind the wheel of a car. Sunglasses on, hand resting easily on the steering wheel, he was a picture of confidence. And when I sat in his polished black Range Rover, the plush leather seats and music gently wrapped around me. With him, my cares vanished. When we left for our beach weekend this morning, the moment was very *Pretty Woman.* Granted, I'm not a sex worker, and he wasn't a billionaire, but he was richer than me and could afford some of the nice things. And I felt taken care of. A first. As he pulled out onto the highway toward North Carolina, I remember it felt so good not to worry.

Neither Kyle nor I saw each other over Christmas. He was on call, and because I'm between semesters, I picked up all the shifts I could at the coffee shop. I also took a few turns at the suicide hotline. Holidays and crisis can be as tough for the poor as the rich.

But New Year's we were both off the clock, and it was going to be our time. Our holiday. I'd even fantasized that it might be a tradition. I'm surprised when I think about all the expectations I heaped on a not-quite boyfriend.

Shelly drives down tree-lined streets, past small shops, row houses butted close together, and an old brick schoolhouse now converted into condos. The drive from the hospital to the town house takes us fifteen minutes. Holidays, vacations, and half days have thinned Friday traffic down to nothing.

Shelly races to her parking space in the alley beside our town house and parks next to my Jeep. She slams on the brakes hard, and though my seat belt holds me in place, the pressure hurts places on my body that I didn't realize were injured. It's a miracle she hasn't worn down the brake shoes.

As I climb out of the car, my left hip sends nerve pain jolting down my left side. *Reaching too high. Should've stayed with your own kind.* My foster mother's smug voice extends from the past. It's weird I'd remember that about Frances. She wasn't a bad person, just overworked and afraid of poverty.

"Thanks again, Shelly," I say.

She hands me my front door key but is careful not to touch me. She's not a fan of personal contact. "No prob. Go inside and rest."

That's about all I can do. All my strength is gone. "Will do."

"Hey, how's your Wednesday night group? I saw you carrying the decorations."

My Wednesday night crowd, which meets at the YMCA multipurpose room, is a collection of teens who are homeless, or who have one foot out the front door. I normally arrange orange plastic chairs in a circle, make a pot of coffee, and serve up a sleeve of grocery store doughnuts. Last week I was feeling more festive and draped silver garland from the walls, and I sprang for hazelnut roast coffee from my store. When I arrived at the meeting room, Kyle was there arranging carefully gift-wrapped boxes under an artificial tree. Inside each box was a collection of chocolates. Nothing fancy. But I was so touched. He left before group, but all seven girls seemed grateful for their gifts.

"It was good," I say.

"We all have to look out for each other. If I can help sometime with your group," she says, "let me know. I won't go to a meeting, but I can do something."

We've had this conversation before. So far, "something" hasn't materialized. But I appreciate her good vibes. "Thanks."

My apartment is the second floor of a town house split into four apartments. It's a tall brick building with a slate, gabled roof and peeling gray paint. Shelly follows me past her first-floor apartment to the second level, where I live. I unlock the door. I've never been so glad to be home.

"Thank you."

"Yeah, sure. I'm home if you need me."

"You're the best."

My apartment is one thousand square feet with wall-to-wall wood floors coated in layers of shiny polyurethane. The furniture is secondhand, as is the shag rug. A small kitchen sports white cabinets and appliances that date back at least two decades.

In the living room I've hung colorful posters ordered off the internet that not only cover peeling paint but feature all the places I'd like to see for real one day: Muir Woods, Paris, Rome, and London. *Dream big,* I always tell the girls in my circle.

In the corner there's a browning Christmas tree I put up four weeks ago. I've celebrated Christmas since I left foster care. The tree represents hope, kindness, a goodwill-to-all kind of thing. I even go so far as to wrap a present from me to me and set it under the tree. This year, I gifted myself a new knit hat and matching gloves.

I glance toward a tall bookshelf filled with books from school and library sales. There's also a repurposed dining room table that doubles as my study desk. A lot of my dissertation research is done on the street, but the bulk of the writing happens here.

I'd budgeted the long weekend off, so I don't have to be anywhere. Most days I'm robbing Peter to pay Paul timewise, and I'm not sure what to do with the free time. I head to the shower and turn on the hot spray.

Stripping, I pile my clothes on the bathroom floor and step into liquid heat. The water pulses my skin, washing away hospital smells, and the last remnants of Kyle's blood swirl around my feet and down the drain.

From the outset, I was punching above my weight with Kyle. He was smart and sophisticated, and what he saw in a would-be social worker who worked as a barista was beyond me. But we'd clicked. Opposites do attract, I guess.

I shut off the tap, towel dry my forgettable shortish, light brown hair. I gingerly re-dress in the clothes Shelly brought me, finger comb my curling hair, and limp into the kitchen. I set up the coffeepot. As I hit "Brew," a fist pounds against my front door.

Shelly. What has she forgotten? I don't think twice as I cross to the door and open it. Standing outside my door is the man from the hospital parking lot. Mild annoyance furrows his brow as he stares at me. Did he follow Shelly and me here?

"That was rude," he says.

Chapter Two

LANE

It was one thing to have this guy beating on a car window in a public parking lot, but it's another level of creepy to find him standing on my doorstep. The ick factor hits a dangerous level. "I don't know what you want, mister, but I don't have it." I move to close the door.

He stops the door with his foot. "Not yet, Lane. We need to talk."

That large, broad frame has grown exponentially since the parking lot. And he's staring at me like I have a third eye. He hesitates, waiting for something. If it's an invitation, he's out of luck. "I'm with the sheriff's department."

I didn't see that coming. "What?"

"Your accident happened in my jurisdiction. I was hoping to catch you in the hospital so we could talk, but you left so quickly. Dr. Jackson asked me to remind you to take it easy."

It's standard advice any doctor might dole out to a woman who's had a fall. If he thinks that tidbit is going to ease the unsettling feeling he's stirring, he's wrong. My grip on the door tightens. "Do you have a badge?"

He fishes one from his pocket, holds it up in front of my face, and then quickly tucks it back. The credentials look real enough. "I'm Detective Becker. I want to talk to you, Ms. McCord. I have questions about the fall."

"This isn't a good time, Detective."

"There's never going to be a good time, Lane. I know you've been through a lot. May I come in? You look like you need to sit down."

I shift my stance, dropping more weight on my right side. I'm braced to slam the door as soon as that size-thirteen foot moves. "There's not much I can tell you, Detective Becker. I don't remember the fall."

"I'm afraid I'm going to need more. A man died, and you were the only witness to his death. I need to know what happened at the top of those stairs."

"I don't remember." Tears well in my eyes. Shit. I never cry. Now twice in one hour. "I remember arriving at the cottage. Dr. Iverson and I were upstairs. He was giving me a tour. We returned to the top of the stairs, and then . . . nothing."

"You met Kyle Iverson a few weeks ago, correct?" His voice softens a little.

"Yes, how did you know that?"

"I spoke to Devon." When the name doesn't ring a bell, he adds, "She manages Kyle Iverson's beach house. She keeps it clean, stocked with supplies, etc. According to her, Kyle told her about you."

Kyle had given me a number to call in case of an emergency. That must be Devon. Unsettling to have strangers discussing me. "Oh. I didn't see her today."

"How did you meet Iverson?"

My pulse throbs along my left side. "Why does this matter?"

"Humor me."

"We met in the coffee shop where I work," I say. "He quickly became a regular and asked me out. We've been dating casually for a few weeks, but this weekend was supposed to be . . ."

"I get it." Detective Becker drops his gaze briefly as a muscle tenses in his jaw. When he looks up, his arrow-like gaze hasn't softened. "How long were you at the house?"

"We arrived about noon. I understand we fell around one."

"The rescue squad arrived about one fifteen."

Such a remote stretch of beach, yet word traveled so fast. "Who called for help?"

"There's a contractor working across the street. He dialed 9-1-1."

"Working over the holidays?"

"Apparently, a pipe burst in the house. It was an emergency, and seeing as he owns the company and everyone was on holiday, he took the call."

"Right." Kyle had received a call when we were driving across the bridge, and as we pulled into his driveway, he had glanced toward the black truck parked across the street. He'd looked slightly annoyed. "I suppose I'm lucky he was around. How did he know we fell?"

"The contractor said he heard you and Kyle fighting." The statement dangles between a question and an accusation.

"What would we have been fighting about? We'd only been on the property an hour."

He's staring, as if he's trying to peel back layers. "I don't know. Again, you tell me."

I press fingers to my temple. Suddenly, I'm so exhausted. "We weren't fighting. We'd just arrived. Maybe he heard a radio or television. Why would we fight?" The last question is more for me.

He shrugs, but his foot doesn't move off the threshold. "You're the witness, not me."

My shoulders slump with fatigue. "I've no idea."

He draws in a breath. "How are you doing, Lane?"

Each time he says my name, there's extra weight behind it, as if he's testing its strength. "I'm banged up, but I'm fine. Like the doctor said, I need rest."

"No one at the hospital was willing to discuss your injuries with me. Even my badge didn't sway Dr. Jackson."

"Good. I'm none of your business." My voice rises with each word. I don't have the reserves for this now. "Please, remove your foot."

It doesn't budge. "When you were with Kyle, did the name Stevie Palmer come up?"

"Who?"

"Stevie Palmer."

"No. I never heard of him or her."

"Her." He's watching me more closely. "What about Nikki Kane?"

"No. Who are these women?"

"Nikki's been missing since early July of this year. Stevie vanished shortly after Nikki."

Suddenly, I feel off balance, uncomfortable. "What do these women have to do with Kyle and me?"

"That's what I'm trying to figure out." That jaw pulses again. "Did Kyle try to hurt you at the beach house?"

"What? No, no. He never once raised his hand or said anything that was a red flag." I feel a need to defend Kyle. "I can't help you, Detective Becker. I don't know either woman. Do you have a picture?"

"No. Both women used fake IDs and have been difficult to identify beyond the names they were using."

"Girls on the street often make up names, especially if they don't want family, cops, or pimps to find them."

His fingers grip the door's edge. One hard shove, and he could thrust inside. "Are you sure you haven't heard the names Stevie Palmer or Nikki Kane?"

The adrenaline fueling me dips closer to empty. "I can't help you. If I knew, I'd tell you."

"You work with kids like Nikki and Stevie, right?"

"'Work with' isn't exactly right. I have a Wednesday-night care group. The girls gather for advice, support, and/or companionship. I'm getting my PhD in psychology and counseling. The group is part of my training."

"PhD?" He sounds impressed, but not surprised. He's been asking around about me.

"Almost. I graduate in May."

"And then what?"

"I don't know. Start looking for a job in social work."

"Kyle Iverson was a psychologist, too, right?"

"Yes. He had a successful private practice."

"Dr. Iverson did well from what I know about him."

"You've been busy," I say. "You learn all this in the last eight hours?"

His gaze doesn't waver. "I'm good at my job, Lane."

"Do you work this hard on all accidents, Detective Becker?"

"Doing my due diligence." He looks as if he'll leave, but then he says, "Stevie was looking for Nikki Kane. They'd worked together at Joey's Bar on the Outer Banks. Stevie's a bit of a mother hen. Always looking out for lost souls. A little like you. Anyway, I can't find either woman."

"Why do you think there's a connection to Kyle?"

"He was seen flirting with Nikki in Joey's Bar in early July."

"Did you talk to him about it?"

"I did. He denied seeing her beyond the bar flirtation. But he's been on my radar since then." He searches my eyes as if he'll glean more.

Kyle never said a word about being questioned by the police. "We never once discussed other women."

His grip eases on the door. He reaches into his pocket and removes a card. "Take it. If you think of something, call me. 24-7."

I accept the card, barely glancing at the plain black lettering. DETECTIVE DONALD S. BECKER. The paper quality isn't the best. I shift my stance and almost don't wince. "Don't hitch any hopes to me. I really don't know anything about these women."

"You're in pain," he says. "Exhausted and traumatized. Give it time. There might be answers swirling in your subconscious. I hear the subconscious mind makes up ninety-two percent of our brain."

"It's where we store emotions. Unfortunately, it requires the remaining eight percent to translate the images and feelings."

He looks impressed. "Putting that degree to work."

"The fall messed up my hip, not my brain, or so says Dr. Jackson."

Detective Becker appears in no rush to wrap this meeting up. "EMTs tell me Kyle hit first. Broke his neck and smashed his skull. You landed on top of him. It's a miracle the fall didn't kill you, too."

My mind replays the *thwack* of splintering bone against marble. "That's what Dr. Jackson told me."

"You said Kyle was giving you a tour of the upstairs."

I rewind through the minutes of that last hour, but the tape keeps skipping over the fall. "That's right. But I don't remember."

"Why is that?"

"I remember feeling tired. We'd had champagne and I'm not used to it. It hit me like a ton of bricks. I was counting the stairs as we climbed. Twenty-one total."

Thinking about Kyle hurts. It takes effort to distance myself from the pain. I'm tempted to walk away from the door, climb into bed, and pull the covers over my head. If the detective wants to keep talking, he can follow. However, I don't move.

"Dr. Jackson did tell me there were traces of a sedative in your system."

"I don't take drugs."

"Except the sleepwalking pills."

"I don't take sedatives during the day." I think back to this morning. Maybe I'd taken my pills late last night, and traces remained in my system.

"I'm sorry . . . that you were hurt, Lane."

The detective's foot slides back, but I don't slam the door. He jams his hands into the pockets of his black jacket. The fabric shifts as if he's fingering more business cards, a receipt, or change. Faint traces of cigarettes drift toward me. Unlike Shelly's heavy smoky scent, his reminds me of the occasional cigarette bummed from a pal. He wants to quit but can't quite give it up.

"Are you doing PT?" Is he as interested as he sounds?

"No."

"PT's important. When I rehabbed my shoulder, I didn't miss a session." He rolls his, as if to prove it still works. Removing a packet of gum from that pocket, he offers me a piece. I decline. He carefully unfolds the silver wrapper as if he has something on his mind.

A fleeting smile crosses my lips. "My insurance works great as long as I don't need it."

"Tough break." He scores the wrapper's crease with his fingers.

"Life, right?"

"Kyle Iverson's autopsy just concluded an hour ago." He drops the statement like a grenade.

And it lands right at my feet, explodes, and rocks me back on my heels. "It was an accident. Why was an autopsy ordered so quickly?"

"Unless you're very old and die in bed, the cops want to know the details. The exact cause of death is important. I've seen murders packaged and delivered like they were accidents."

Murder. "The autopsy happened so fast?"

"I made a few calls."

Kyle was vibrant and alive this morning, and now he's cut up on a stainless-steel table. "It was an accident."

"Interested in knowing the autopsy results?" He speaks to me like we're mystery-solving pals. Only we're not. This is clearly a cop technique. Lure them in. Get them to trust you.

"It was an accident." If I keep repeating the words, maybe all this will feel less tragic.

"Shattered C-4 disc. The fall severed his spine immediately. Death was instantaneous. He felt no pain." He rubs the side of his neck. "If he'd landed a little differently, he might have survived with bruises, or he could've spent the rest of his life in a wheelchair. Damage to that part of the spine is measured in millimeters."

"The ER doctor said my clothes were soaked in his blood," I say quietly.

"Head wounds bleed a lot. Doesn't mean they're serious. But a broken neck . . . well, it's usually game over."

I cringe. "Oh."

He's still watching, testing. "The medical examiner ruled the cause of death *undetermined*."

"What does that mean?"

Creases run across his forehead. They're the wrinkles of someone who worries. "There are three manners of death. Natural. Homicide. Undetermined."

"Accidents are natural."

"They can be, but I'm not totally convinced."

"Are you accusing me of murder?"

He shakes his head slowly. "You said yourself, you don't remember. And the neighbor heard you fighting. I need to fill in the missing pieces."

"The neighbor is wrong. I was excited to see the beach and spend time with Kyle."

"You'd been drinking, and there were drugs in your system."

"A glass of champagne. Prescription meds taken the night before." Frustration warms my cheeks.

"Don't get upset with me, Lane. I'm only telling you what I know."

This guy is holding too many cards close to his vest. "You're suggesting I had something to do with his death."

"I'm not."

Then why are we having this conversation? "I can't do this right now."

"Get a coffee with me, Lane. My treat. Seeing as you sell the stuff, I bet you know the best places to get it." When I don't respond, he adds in a lighter tone, "You look like you could use a good meal."

Eating hasn't been on my priority list for months. "No. I think that the next time we talk, I should have a lawyer."

"You can't afford PT, Lane. The retainer is twenty-five grand for a case involving a death." A smile teases his lips. "Can you afford a lawyer?"

No, I can't. Still, none of this feels right. There are layers under layers that I'm not privy to, and I know for a fact that the brain requires two sleep cycles to fully process a trauma. "There are lawyers that don't require money up front. They take a portion of the settlement."

"There's no lawsuit. This would be a criminal case. You'll be racking up billable hours with whomever you hire."

"I don't need this now."

His grin widens, and he holds up his hands. He seems pleased I'm rattled. "Okay. Backing off, Lane. For now."

I don't slam the door when he steps back. I watch him turn and walk down the front steps. Hands in pockets, Detective Becker moves easily, casually, as if insinuating I've committed murder is just another Friday. He walks past all the cars parked at the curb and vanishes around the corner.

I don't know when he's coming back, but I suspect Detective Becker is a man of his word. He's not done with me yet.

Chapter Three

LANE

Saturday, December 30, 2023
7:00 a.m.

The fall replays in small, broken sound bites. *We're on the top landing. Kyle has his back to the stairs as he's looking at me. He's smiling. But am I? My hands raise to his chest. I feel his racing heartbeat. He grips my forearm. Is he losing his balance? There's no time to process because a second later there's air under our feet.*

I sit up on the couch. My pulse pounds fast, and my palms are slick with sweat. What happened? How did we go from him smiling to dying? Was he reaching out in desperation because he felt his balance teeter? Those missing milliseconds hover in a hazy darkness.

Swinging my legs over the side of the couch, I glance toward my Christmas tree. Needles fall, joining the others in a green ring around the base. I'll take the tree down after the New Year because it's bad luck to do it before then.

What am I doing here? I was supposed to be waking up beside Kyle now. I should be nestled close to him, filled with hope and contentment.

But I'm home. And alone. Cinderella has left the ball. And she's not only lost her slipper, but she's battered and bruised, and a cop thinks she might have killed the prince. "How did I get here, Kyle?"

When Kyle pulls off the main road, the dazzling sun is almost too warm. I crack a window and drink in the cold ocean breeze as he crosses over the cattle guard where Route 12 terminates into soft sand. Waves roll up onto the beach, and the ocean is as smooth as glass. Immediately, we pass a small four-door car that's mired in the sand and a tow truck driver attaching a strap to the vehicle's underside. Beside the car stand two young men wearing jeans and puffer jackets.

"All-wheel drive doesn't cut it on a day like today," Kyle says.

"It's bright and sunny. And the beach looks so smooth."

"Can't be fooled by this place. It rained hard last night, and the sand is extra soft. If I hadn't driven this so many times, I'd be nervous."

"Are you going to stop and help?" I ask.

"Naw. That truck driver has it. Hate to take away any of his holiday revenue. And those two guys will never forget this expensive lesson."

The side mirror again catches the mired car and its helpless occupants. Raised in the city, I've only had concrete and asphalt under my feet. I've had flats before, but I can fix those. But a car mired in quicksand is beyond my skill set.

The Range Rover bucks as the front tire slams through a patch of soft sand. I grip the door, and my seat belt keeps me from pitching forward. For an instant, I'm certain we are now stuck. "Are we stuck?"

Kyle grins and presses hard on the accelerator. "We're fine."

"What's the weekend weather like?"

"We've got weather coming in, so we might be trapped at the cottage for a few days. When do you have to be back?"

I grip the door tighter. "Wednesday."

"What if we're stuck here for weeks or months?"

His teasing is unsettling. "We'll just have to walk out."

Laughing, he lobs an amused glance my way. "You aren't scared, are you, baby?"

"Of course not," I lie.

He speeds up, zooming past tree stumps that are echoes of a migrating shoreline and a long-lost forest. The sand smooths out for a stretch, and he drives close to the ocean. Waves glistening with sunlight crash within feet of the Range Rover.

The beach is deserted. I've read that in the summer it's filled with tourists and parked four-wheel-drive vehicles. I've also read that the 4x4 beach, as it's called, is home to over one hundred wild horses who come with nonnegotiable no feeding or touching rules. The horses were brought to the Outer Banks by the Spanish four hundred years ago and now live in a fenced-off sanctuary in the woodlands behind the dunes.

I open my window more and reach out into the cool air. Driving this close to the water is exciting. "This day is perfect."

Kyle turns toward me. His dark eyes spark as if he's devouring a delicious morsel. My skin warms knowing soon after we arrive at his cottage, we'll be naked and in his bed.

"The weather doesn't get any better than this," he says. "It won't last. Heavy rains tomorrow afternoon, but we'll be inside."

Four or five miles up the beach, there's a house on stilts that stands almost dead center on the beach. The hurricane fencing along the dunes is broken like snapped twigs in several sections.

Kyle angles his car close to the water and around the house. He keeps driving, and when I glance in the rearview mirror, there's nothing but empty beach for as far as I can see. We drive for another ten or fifteen minutes. There's no traffic on the beach, and the cottages beyond the barren dunes are dark.

In the distance, I see a fence that stretches from the water, along the beach and over the dunes. According to my research, this fence marks the Virginia and North Carolina border. It's designed to keep the horses from wandering north.

When it seems that we are running out of beach, Kyle takes a sharp left and arrows the Range Rover directly toward a channel cutting through the dunes. My heartbeat ramps up in a fight-or-flight leap, and I hold my breath. The front wheel hits a rut, and the vehicle tosses me against the door. Finally, we break through to the other side of the dunes and roll onto hard-packed sand.

The breath trapped in my lungs leaks out. "Feels like we're leaving the world behind."

Kyle looks at me and grins. "Sure you aren't afraid?"

I scoff. "What's there to be afraid of?"

He arches a brow. "Can't fool me, Lane. I know you too well."

I learned at a young age to guard my thoughts. Safer not to put all the cards on the table. I've revealed more to Kyle than anyone else, but my jokers and aces remain tucked up my sleeve. Ingrained habits don't die easily.

"Maybe I'm a little nervous," I concede. "This is a first for me."

His hand shifts from the steering wheel to my thigh. He squeezes. "Don't worry, baby. I got you."

When he calls me baby*, I feel protected. Ex–foster kids tend to like their security. How did I get so lucky with Kyle?*

Lucky.

I don't feel lucky now.

Mine has been a long, hard journey from foster care, but I've made it. My life is on track, I'm making a difference. And until yesterday at 1:00 p.m., I wasn't alone anymore.

Rising, I move to the kitchen, pour cold coffee from the urn, and put it in the microwave. The bell dings, and the coffee is hot, but also bitter. Outside, the mailman's keys rattle as he opens the mailboxes. I wait until his footsteps recede before I grab my extra key and move slowly down the stairs and out my front door. As I open my box, I glance up and notice a manila envelope resting on top of the boxes. It's addressed to me. No return address. A mystery. I hate mysteries. I'm a Leo. We like having answers.

Back in my apartment, I curl up on the couch, cup in hand, and sip hot bitterness. I stare at the envelope.

A knock on the door startles me out of my melancholy. I'm in no mood to deal with the detective. A fist raps against the door again. Drawing in a breath, I open it and am surprised to see Shelly.

"Shelly. Everything all right?" I ask.

She nibbles her lip. "I should be asking you that."

It's not like her to hover or wonder how I'm doing. "I'm okay."

"Checking in," she says. "It's not the kind of thing I do, and tomorrow I might forget about you altogether, but I'm remembering now."

Her fleeting kindness is touching. "Thanks, Shelly."

"That guy that was here last night . . . was he the one from the parking lot?"

No sense getting into a story she won't remember tomorrow. "He's gone, and that's all that matters."

She frowns. "He's not the type that gives up."

"How do you know that?" I ask.

Shelly's eyes spark with wisdom and mischief. "I've been around enough to know when a man won't go away. I'm guessing he's not a stalker, but he's trouble."

"He's a cop."

Her eyes narrow. "Did you see his badge?"

"Yes. I asked." When she looks more worried, I add, "He's gone. He asked a few questions and was satisfied."

"If you say so."

"Are you doing okay?" The few times we've passed on the front porch, I'm the one reaching out.

"It's going to be a good day. I have a painting in mind."

"That's great." Shelly has lots of paintings in her head. She starts many of them, but few make it fully to the canvas. The one I've seen was stunning, which makes me wonder what other works of art are trapped inside her. "Want to come in for coffee?"

"No, thanks." She rubs her palms over her jeans. "Just checking in."

"Thanks, Shelly."

"Our kind needs to stick together."

Her expression is serious, touching. "Right. Thank you."

Shelly chews her bottom lip again. "Anyone can get a badge, Lane. Anyone."

"Why would you say that?"

"I don't know. Just came to me."

She has a point, and it's not the least bit comforting. "I'll keep that in mind."

"Be careful, Lane. The world is full of crazy people."

"Will do."

Back in my apartment, I gulp coffee and reach for the manila envelope.

Threading my finger under the flap, I tear it open and remove a collection of handwritten notes. I don't recognize the handwriting.

A yellow sticky is pasted on the top page. The thick, bold script reads, *Don't say I never gave you anything.*

I thumb through the diary pages and read the first and last lines of the note attached to the journal. *July 7, 2023. Stevie Palmer.*

Stevie Palmer is the woman Detective Becker mentioned. The woman I swore I didn't know. Is this a cop trick? Could Becker be testing me?

My gaze drops to the first line. *I've written it all down because, well, life always goes sideways, and I've learned to hedge my bets. Trouble and I know each other well. Hell, we're almost besties after all these years. But everything is changing. The ground under my feet is steady today, but that never lasts. Not sure how long I can hold it together, but I'll fight the good fight while I can. No one gets out of here alive, right?*

I thumb through the ten or so pages. It looks like Stevie Palmer's journal. Reading another person's diary, even if it's a Detective Becker fakeout, feels like a terrible invasion of privacy. Stevie is none of my business. We don't know each other, despite the subtext humming under Detective Becker's words.

The handwriting is bold and creases the yellow paper, and that kind of intensity fits with Detective Becker. But the loops and swirls feel slightly feminine. I can't tell if the writer is a man or woman.

Normally, I wouldn't read anything so personal. I don't want people poking in my life, so I extend the courtesy. I kept a diary as a teenager, but those filled spiral notebooks have long been lost.

Tracing the handwriting with my fingertip, I think about the missing women. Beyond Detective Becker, is anyone else asking about them?

If I'd gotten a better vibe from Detective Becker, I might call and give this to him.

But I don't have a good feeling about him. He gets under my skin. Makes me nervous, even a little anxious.

Drawing in a breath, I reread the date. Stevie wrote this note six months ago, right before she vanished.

Not sure how long I can hold it together, but I'll fight the good fight while I can. No one gets out of here alive, right?

I start reading the diary.

Chapter Four

STEVIE PALMER'S DIARY

Saturday, July 1, 2023
8:00 p.m.

When I wake up, I realize I'm in my car. It's hot, and I'm sweating. My back aches, and my head is spinning. I blink, look around, and realize I'm parked in an alley. The car's passenger side is inches from a cinder block wall. The engine is dead, and the windows are open. The smell of trash floats up from a nearby dumpster.

"Shit. What have I done this time?" I push a thick shock of muddy-brown hair out of my eyes. I do a quick check. My jeans and T-shirt are dusted with dirt, but otherwise intact. I have both shoes and my small wallet. No cell phone, but I don't own one. Jackpot. At least I wasn't rolled or raped this time.

As I sit up straighter, my head spins. I blink. Bright orange drains over the side of the building and splashes on the hood of my car. Sunset. Must be about 8:00 or 8:15. Leaning against the steering wheel, I give my mind time to settle.

In my rearview mirror, I notice a parked truck and see a couple in the back seat. The woman sits up, and the flat of her palm presses against the rear window's glass as she raises her head. For an instant our gazes meet. Her panic pins me. A man rises behind her, puts his hand over her mouth, and pulls her backward. She grips the back of the seat, like a drowning woman reaching for a life preserver.

I blink again, look around, and seeing no one, grab the baseball bat I keep on the passenger-side floor. Gripping it tight, I get out and stride toward the truck's back taillight. I note the plates are Virginia but don't register the numbers as I raise the baseball bat like a major league player and hit the truck's red plastic light. It cracks. I draw back again, and the second blow breaks it. As I move to the next light, the man jerks his head up. I'd have thought the first blow would've gotten his attention, but he's clearly focused on what he's doing. The woman screams for help.

As I draw back the bat, the back driver's-side door opens and a tall, lean man scrambles out. He's reaching for the fly on his pants, zipping and cussing.

The passenger-side door opens, and a girl tumbles out. She's young, maybe midtwenties, and has curly light-brown hair and a mascara-smudged face. She's wearing a purple sequined top, a short skirt, and one silver ankle boot with rhinestone accents. She might have gotten into the truck willingly, but it's clear she doesn't like what's happening now.

"What the fuck are you doing?" the man yells at me.

I keep the bat cocked. It doesn't take much pressure to break a knee, but you've got to be dead-on with the aim. "Looks like the lady is telling you no."

He glowers at the young woman. "You don't get to say no after I've paid."

The woman hovers in my side vision. She's straightening her skirt and wiping the smudges from under her eyes. The other boot is now in hand.

"You okay?" My question is directed to the woman.

"Yeah."

"Is he hurting you?" I ask.

"Yes." She glances toward the guy. "I mean no."

"No?" I don't ease up on my grip. "Want me to walk away and mind my own business?"

"No," she says quickly. "I have to get to work."

"You haven't finished with me," the man complains.

"Where's work?" I ask.

"Next door. Joey's Bar."

I smile. "Sorry, pal. Lady said she's got to go. Time to move on."

"You busted my taillight," he rages. "This is bullshit."

"I had to get your attention somehow, didn't I?"

He lurches toward me. So predictable. I let the bat swing, and the end catches the side of his knee. He goes down hard.

I might have come looking for trouble, but I wasn't expecting it this fast. It usually takes an hour or two.

The young woman moves to my side as the man grips his knee. "Be careful. He can be mean."

"I swear to God, I'm going to kill you both," the man shouts.

Tensing, I stand my ground and ask the woman beside me, "Are you okay?"

"I'm fine, thanks. You okay?"

"I'm good. What do we do with him?"

"You'll leave, won't you, Pete?" the woman asks. "He doesn't want trouble with Joey."

"The bar owner?" I ask.

"Yeah."

I look at Pete. "Joey sounds like a badass. That true?"

Pete glowers.

"We can get Joey, if you're not sure," I offer. I can finish him off myself, but if someone else will do the work, let 'em.

Pete rubs his knee, winces. "Never mind."

I watch as he limps toward the driver's door and slides behind the wheel. Wounded animals can be very dangerous, so I keep a close eye on him.

"Come inside," the woman says. "You look like you could use a drink."

"I don't need a drink."

No one does anything for free, and certainly not out of the goodness of their heart. Everyone has an agenda. Even me. Best to know what it is.

Pete fires up his engine. The one working taillight blinks, signaling he's shifted into drive. I stand ready to fight, but Pete pulls out of the alley and onto the main road. I glimpse his license plate and commit the numbers and letters to memory.

I'm tempted to ask the young woman where I am but don't. Salt air suggests near the ocean, indicating I've likely returned to my favorite place. And when I say favorite, I mean most hated.

"My name is Nikki," the young woman says as she rubs her arms, a sign adrenaline is rocketing through her body. I also feel jittery and flushed.

"I'm Stevie."

"Where did you come from?" Nikki asks.

"Just happened by." My voice is rough, forcing me to clear my throat.

"I saw your car parked in that spot an hour ago. You were sleeping, and I didn't want to bother you."

"Don't worry about me." The last words sound awkward, rusty. "What are you doing here?"

"I'm a bartender at Joey's."

An engine revs, tires screech, and a truck with a broken taillight races past the alley. "Who was your friend, Pete?"

Nikki drags shaking fingers through her hair. "A really big mistake."

"You make a lot of mistakes like that?" I lower the bat but decide to keep it close.

"Sometimes. Not all the time. I only said yes because rent is due in four days. Well, technically rent is due today, but I get a four-day grace period."

"Sometimes is all it takes, Nikki."

"I know. I know. You really saved my ass. Pete was in a mood." She leans forward as if sharing a secret. "He had a big fight with his wife."

"Doesn't bartending pay the bills?"

"I haven't been here long, and I'm still learning, so the tips aren't great. And sometimes I need extra cash."

"Stick to bartending."

"Joey says I'll get a handle on the drinks eventually." She rolls her eyes, grins. "I'm not sure he means that."

"How long have you worked here?"

"A couple of weeks."

A man and a woman walking arm in arm pass by on the street. They're laughing and leaning heavily into each other. I'm a little jealous of their connection. It looks nice. But self-contained is safer. "Take care of yourself, Nikki."

"Thank you, thank you, Stevie. Like I said, Pete isn't always so rough."

Pete likely wouldn't have killed Nikki, but he'd have made her wish she was dead. It's such an old story, and it's replayed too many times.

Nikki's smile wanes. "Get a coffee or soda. Seriously, you look dead on your feet. No charge. Joey would be pissed if I didn't offer you one."

I shove my hands in my pockets. The heat is now catching up to me, and I could use a cold soda. "Why is Joey so giving?"

Nikki rolls her eyes. "He's not exactly. But he comes around if I ask nice. He's a teddy bear."

A cold soda might chase off the headache starting to pound behind my eyes. "Sure. But I'll pay."

"Let's get you inside." She reaches for me, but I tense so her hands drop. "Follow me."

"Sure."

I'm expecting my legs to work, but I misstep on the broken asphalt. Without chaos fueling me, my muscles lock. Drawing in a breath, I steady myself, and like a baby learning to walk, I master movement and follow Nikki to the back door. She opens it, and I'm hit with a rush of light and movement from a bar kitchen. There's a tall, burly guy wearing a red bandanna on a bald head by the griddle. Beside him is a younger kid with dark hair and a wiry frame who's working the fryer. My stomach grumbles, and I realize I'm hungry. When was the last time I ate? In Elizabeth City? I can't remember.

Nikki points to a red plastic chair in the corner, and I sit, bat still in hand. The chair legs are uneven, forcing me to steady my balance. As the seconds tick by, I'm feeling more like myself, but I'm still shaky as I watch the buzz of activity in the kitchen. A door swings open, and I glimpse the bar on the other side. It's dimly lit, and the glow of a red neon BEER sign flashes before the door swings closed.

The man who pushes through the door is tall and has broad shoulders. He's wearing a blue JOEY's T-shirt, jeans, a bar apron, and boots I bet are steel toed. Shoulder-length dark hair frames a square face etched with frown lines. Fading tattoos cover his arms.

Big Boy is no teddy bear, and he's the kind of guy that scares most people. He glowers, and they back off. He's capable of violence, but I sense he keeps it leashed. Tough, but no monster. And believe me, I know monsters.

Big Boy glares at me and then Nikki. "Who's this?"

Nikki shoves a glass of soda into my hands. "I just met her outside. She's a friend."

"You said you just met her."

"She's a friend," Nikki insists.

The cola is cold, and I can almost hear the steam when the cool liquid hits my stomach. "I'm Stevie. And Nikki is being kind. We met five minutes ago."

"Is there a baseball game I'm missing?" Joey asks.

"No," I say.

"You're high." His perfectly etched frown finds a way to deepen.

I sip more soda, drawing in coolness, which quickly leaves me chilled. It's summer, and yet I'm now cold. Go figure. "No. I generally have a lot more fun when I'm high."

Big Boy appears torn between amusement and outrage. "You don't know if you're high?"

"I know. I'm not," I say honestly. I could admit that I lose time. I could tell him that a doctor once theorized the missing hours are caused by mini seizures. But showing anyone your weak underbelly is foolish.

Big Boy glares at me. "You said your name is Stevie?"

"Palmer. Stevie Palmer." I finish the soda and rise. Thankfully, I'm feeling steadier. "Thanks for the soda. What do I owe you, Big Boy?"

Big Boy shakes his head. "Nothing."

I set the cup in the sink next to other unwashed dishes. "Thanks." I glance toward Nikki. She's grinning, but it's strained with a nervous vibe. Most would be more rattled by what happened in the alley, but I sense she's used to that kind of treatment. "Thank you."

"Sure, no worries," she says. "There's no rush for you to leave, right, Joey?"

"Orders are backing up, Nikki," Big Boy, a.k.a. Joey, says.

Nikki's attention shifts to the door leading to the bar. She looks like she's waltzing into the lion's den. "Right. I'm on it."

I watch Nikki push through the swinging door. Again, red neon flashes. "Thanks again, Big Boy."

He raises a brow. "Name's Joey, Stevie."

We're on a first-name basis. "Good to meet you, Joey."

His gaze slides up and down me. His energy radiates calculated assessment, and maybe a hint of attraction that has him wishing he were thirty years younger. "You have a job, Stevie?"

"Not at the moment." I'm not even sure what town I'm in. I think it's Nags Head, but I wouldn't bet on anything right now. But I'll figure that out quickly.

"What are you doing tonight?" Joey asks.

Some might have heard a loaded question, but I hear hints of desperation. The labor market is hungry for workers, and that gap in the employment landscape has worked well for me. It allows me to jump from job to job on a whim. "Not much. And before you ask, I have experience bartending."

Short of exposing my breasts, I don't think I could've done anything sexier. "Do you?"

"I work for tips. I don't do applications and official offers. Cash and carry."

"Works for me."

"If there's a restroom, I'll wash up. Give me five minutes."

Joey looks toward the cooks, who haven't bothered to glance in our direction. "Cookie, make her a sandwich." He doesn't ask what I like because he must figure food is food.

"Restroom?" I ask.

"Through the door to your left."

"Back in five."

The bar is packed, as are the two dozen round tables on the floor. The decor has a *The Old Man and the Sea* vibe that's reinforced by dozens of framed black-and-white pictures on the walls. Most look like fishermen holding up big catches or shipwrecks buried in the sand. A few are images captioned in Nags Head, North Carolina. Okay. I'm in Nags Head. I'm not familiar with Joey's, but places come and go down here all the time.

Judging by the crowd, I'd say these aren't your family beach vacationers. This crew is working class. Construction, electricians, plumbers, military, or ex-military. The room's noise level tells me everyone is at least two to three drinks into the night.

I find the restroom and push inside. I lock the door behind me. It's a tad quieter in here, and I'm grateful for a moment to hide and regroup.

The wood-paneled space is small but clean. The walls are covered in framed photographs featuring people standing on the beach over the last thirty years. I scan the photos, half expecting to recognize one of the sun-weathered faces. I don't.

I pee, and then I step in front of the sink and turn on the hot tap. As steam rises, I pump soap on my hands and wash vigorously. *Clean your hands. Clean your hands!* Even to this day my dead mother's voice still echoes. Despite all efforts to resist, I scrub harder. Logic is no match for ingrained past punishments.

I wash my face, grab a handful of paper towels, and press them to my cheeks. I'm not wearing makeup, which isn't my norm, but I don't analyze my appearance. I operate better if I don't dwell on my features. I'm attractive enough, and when I smile, or show a little cleavage, the tip jar on the bar fills. That's all I need to know. My balled-up paper towel lands dead center in the trash can. Score. I feel better.

As I cross the room, I glance at the black-and-white pictures, the fishnet draped from the ceiling, and the ship captain's wheel on the wall, all of which have a familiar vibe. If I haven't been here before, I've been in a place just like it.

I glance toward a frazzled Nikki and step into the kitchen long enough to grab an apron from a hook and half of the sandwich Cookie has left for me beside the six-burner gas stove. The white bread is toasted and cut on a diagonal. Lettuce and tomato peek out along with turkey. I take a bite.

"Fancy," I say. "Really good, Cookie."

Cookie grunts.

I take two more bites and then make my way back into the chaos. Behind the bar, I finish up the last of the sandwich and put on the apron. A guy catches my gaze. He looks annoyed as he raises an empty beer mug. I nod toward him, smile. "What can I get you?"

He relaxes a little. "Another one of these."

"On tap?"

"Yeah."

I fill a sparkling mug to the brim and set it in front of him along with a fresh napkin. I collect the empty and the discarded peanut shells littering his bit of real estate at the bar. "Holler if you need another. I'm Stevie."

"Sully."

"Good to meet you, Sully."

"You're new here," Sully says.

"I am indeed." There is always a limit to how much TLC I dish out. I flirt, and I listen to sob stories, but I keep a professional distance. Leave them thinking they might get more the next time. I'm good at pretending I care when I don't.

On to the next customer, I'm refilling a beer mug. The following hour is basically a wash and repeat. Despite my faults, I have terrific recall and can remember a dozen drink orders at a clip. Memory is my superpower and curse. I pocket a few hundred bucks in tips. It's summertime, and everyone here just wants to relax and kick back.

Nikki also calms. Having a wingwoman who can serve three times as fast makes her night easier. She moves behind me, flashes a genuine smile. "You're a natural."

"I like tips," I say.

"How do you remember all the orders?" Nikki asks.

I shrug. "I've a photographic memory."

"Really? That's fantastic."

"Sometimes I wish I could forget." I smile to soften the emotions swirling under the words.

"You can remember everything?" she asks.

"Just about."

"What if I recite a bunch of numbers?"

I've won a few bets with this little trick. "Shoot."

She raises her notepad, and as she writes she recites, "12, 19, 2, 232, 106, 5,001, 17, and 12."

I fill a bowl of peanuts and swap it for an empty. "That's the best you've got?"

Nikki giggles. "Can you do it?"

I sigh, almost bored. "12, 19, 2, 232, 106, 5,001, 17, and 12."

"Wow. Exactly right."

"I know." I see a man sit at the end of the bar. "You've got a customer."

Nikki moves toward the guy. This one doesn't fit with the Joey's Bar working-class crowd. I suspect he's dressing down tonight, but his shirt looks tailored, and his short hair is neatly cut. More polished than anyone else here. Likely this place isn't on his normal glide path. Can't tell if he's local or from out of town. Wonder what he's hiding from? Trolling for? Nikki fills a tumbler with a top-shelf bourbon and sets it in front of him.

Bourbon smiles at Nikki and says something that makes her laugh. I roll my shoulders, shrugging off tension pinching my muscles. I just dragged her ass out of the frying pan, and now she's flirting with it again. She tucks a strand of hair behind her ear. Whatever he's said, she's grabbed on to it hook, line, and sinker. I can already tell, she's too soft. Far too trusting. Not a good thing in this world, Nikki. Not a good thing.

Chapter Five

LANE

Saturday, December 30, 2023
8:00 a.m.

I know this sounds boring, Lane. But this night is important to me and you.

My name jumps off the page as I stare at the note in the margin. The script is bold, darker than the diary entry, as if made later with a different pen. The room suddenly feels too small for me. Have the walls shifted in five feet?

Surprised? Yep, I know your name, Lane.

I try to picture her, but she's said precious little about herself, as if who she is doesn't matter to this story. I imagine her standing behind the bar, brow furrowed, a tumbler half-full of scotch as she writes.

I drop the sheets and stare around my apartment, half expecting to find someone watching me. Why am I upset? Is it seeing my name scrawled in a stranger's handwriting? If this is a play engineered by Detective Becker, it's odd.

I walk to the window, open it, and suck in a cold blast of air. I was honest with Detective Becker when I told him I don't know Stevie Palmer. But clearly, she knows me. I've run a lot of group sessions over the last few years. She might have sat in one of my circle sessions, met me at a mental health awareness expo, or passed me at the university. There have been so many people in these groups over the years. So many lost souls.

The words on the page trace my spine like cold fingers. *Yep, I know your name, Lane.*

Being known by a stranger is unsettling. I have a social media account, but I never post. The account is strictly for checking up on gals who want to join my group. Social media posts are as good as, maybe better than, any personality test.

A local paper did a piece on the homeless a few months ago. I declined to be interviewed but got caught up in a group picture the reporter took of my fellow grad students. Even if Stevie saw the article, she wouldn't have seen my name attached to the piece.

I reread Stevie's journal entry three more times. There's nothing about her that really stands out. Stevie and Nikki seem to have their own issues. Stevie, or whoever gave me these pages, seems to want me to know that.

Suddenly, my hip throbs, or maybe I finally notice the discomfort. I walk to the refrigerator and reach past a few random beers for a cola.

Cracking the top, I take a liberal drink. My skin is chilled, but my insides feel hot, as if there's a fire burning in my belly. The cool liquid does little to tamp down the flames.

I grab a second cola, even as the beer calls, open my laptop, and search Stevie Palmer. After clicking through several pages, no female matching her approximate description appears in the search engine. There's a guy in Scotland going by that name. He's a folk singer. Not a very likely candidate.

Next, I dig into social media.

A dozen Stevie Palmers pop up on several platforms. I scan each profile, searching for anything in their pictures or entries that matches the words I've read. Of all the Stevie Palmers I find, none live in the areas of Nags Head, North Carolina, or Norfolk, Virginia. Many have full-time jobs. None mention part-time bartending. Nothing jumps out at me, but it's impossible to tell who these people really are. Even looking past the exaggerated half truths and embellishments, I don't see anyone that fits my Stevie Palmer.

I look for Nikki Kane, the girl both Stevie and Detective Becker mentioned. There are dozens of Nikki Kanes, but none fit Detective Becker's description. But hadn't he also said he thought both women were using fake identities? There's a good chance they both appear on other pages, but without their real names it'll be impossible for me to find them.

Next, I search Joey's Bar in Nags Head. There's a web page filled with pictures taken in the bar last summer. I scan the images for anyone who could look like Stevie or Nikki but see no one. The current post announces that the bar closes after New Year's until March 1.

Kyle did have social media. I know because I cyberstalked him when he started flirting in the coffee shop. There are photos of him sailing, playing tennis, driving his Range Rover, and volunteering at a church Thanksgiving meal giveaway. Even if he'd been exaggerating a little, he'd looked good from the start.

I open his page, wondering if anyone has posted something about his death. Nothing. His last post is a picture of him at a holiday crisis hotline. There are no traces of us.

A wider search lands me on the page of an online newspaper that covers the Outer Banks. I find a small article mentioning that Dr. Kyle Iverson of Norfolk, Virginia, expired yesterday in a tragic home accident. There are no details about how he died, but there's a mention of an unknown woman having been airlifted to a Norfolk hospital.

Great. Just what I need.

Before I can do anything, I need to get my phone, meds, and purse from the beach cottage. The phone is not only brand new, but I use it for everything. It's my traveling office.

I also want to scroll through the images on my phone and look again at the pictures I took as Kyle and I drove up the beach. There are also a few selfies of us. In the last, Kyle was hugging me close, grinning, clearly happy to mug for the camera.

My Jeep has four-wheel drive, but riding off the main road onto the beach is a daunting idea. It's colder today, and Kyle said weather was moving in this weekend. That means that the surf will be rough, and there'll be few if any people on the beach or in the rental cottages. If I get stuck without my cell, I'm screwed.

Chills roll up my arms. I don't want to go back. I don't want to see the place where we landed, where Kyle died. Will his blood still be there? I remember so much blood.

But not having my cell and wallet is like walking around naked. And if I don't get those meds, I'll be sleepwalking all over town. I can get in quickly, get my things, and be back on the road in minutes. If I hurry, this can all be over for me by this evening.

I crush the empty soda can, consider another, and then reject going for a third. Over caffeination never makes the world turn more smoothly. I walk into my bathroom, turn on the shower, strip, and step into the water. It'll be a long while before I wash away yesterday.

Kyle came in and out of my life in twenty-five days, but he's left a mark on me. The trauma of the fall still reverberates and likely will for years. And his death has infected my blood and saturated my marrow. Like it or not, we are connected forever.

Returning to the beach house could help with my memories. Maybe not like a light switch flipping on, but brain neurons might spark images that will coalesce into a recognizable picture.

The remote Carova Beach location feels as if it's a million miles away. I could call the property manager and ask her to collect my things.

That would save me a trip to the house. But I realize now that I need to see it.

If Detective Becker can be believed, Kyle's death has been ruled *undetermined*. Which I suppose means the house technically is not a crime scene. It's been only a day since I was there, so hopefully the front door keycode hasn't been changed. This is going to be a quick operation. Grab my things, look around the house, and face what happened.

Kyle's death was a senseless accident. People die unexpectedly all the time.

It was no one's fault, right?

Chapter Six

LANE

Saturday, December 30, 2023
11:00 a.m.

Second thoughts catch up to me as I'm driving toward the interstate. I swing by the coffee shop where I work and enter through the back entrance. The rear space is small, filled with boxes of cups and napkins, and a couple of chairs. It's the place employees retreat to when they want a quick bite to eat or a coffee.

In the back room, there's also a landline. It's a throwback, but the owner keeps it because there's always an employee who didn't or forgot to pay their phone bill. The receiver feels like a heavy relic, but it has a dial tone. And beggars can't be choosers.

I'm calling the number Kyle gave me if something went wrong, and I'm assuming it's for the property manager, Devon.

I'd rather not tell Devon I'm coming, but with Detective Becker lurking around, it's wise to warn her. All I need is for someone to see me enter the house and alert the cops. Detective Becker could spin my return in any number of bad ways.

The smell of roasted coffee winds its way toward me as I dial the number. A woman answers on the first ring.

"Vacation Home Management. This is Devon."

"Devon, this is Lane McCord." I fumble for a familiar point of reference. How do I describe myself?

"Ms. McCord. How are you?" There's a pregnant pause, suggesting the woman is aware of what happened. Likely everyone on the island has heard about Kyle's death by now. "What can I do for you?"

"I need to return to the cottage today and collect my things."

Devon pauses again. "I can get whatever you left. It's not necessary for you to make the trip."

"I'd like to return. I want to see the house again and make sense of what happened." Auditory, visual, and sensory cues are powerful memory stimulants.

"Sure, sure. I get it."

"I'm leaving Norfolk now."

"Of course. Are you staying the night?"

"I wasn't planning on it. I want to collect my things and leave."

"We've got weather coming in, which will drive the tide close to the dunes. You should be able to get in and out easily as long as you don't delay."

"I'll leave now."

"I'll be on the lookout for you. I live close to Dr. Iverson's cottage. I answer this number day or night."

"Thank you, Devon. I appreciate it." I search for words that don't sound insensitive. "What's the status of the place?"

"The main entryway is put back as it was before yesterday. I planned to stop by tomorrow to strip the beds and clean out the refrigerator."

"So, there's no . . ."

"No," she says quietly. "All taken care of."

Kyle's head cracks, blood sprays my face, and pain rakes over my body. He's so still, and his vacant eyes stare toward the ceiling. I reach for him, and my fingers brush warm skin that still feels alive. He doesn't move, and his chest is not rising and falling. I can barely breathe through the pain. I want to call for help, but I can't move as his warm blood oozes toward my face.

The blood is gone. I can do this. "The entry code numbers are still 674510, correct?" I suspect the property management company doesn't give that number out easily.

"That's correct. I'll change it after you leave."

"Thank you."

"Sure. You take care."

In my car, I start the engine and turn up the radio. My gas gauge registers a little less than half a tank. That should cover the trip, assuming I don't get lost. Once I find my purse and credit cards, I can fill up before the return trip.

I follow the signs around the beltway and then south toward the Nags Head exit.

"Demons chasing you back from the underworld, Lane?"

I blink, break my lingering gaze on the rolling dunes beyond the cottage. "No, monsters."

Kyle tosses me a grin, and I catch my startled expression in the reflection of his sunglasses. "Where did you go?"

Nowhere. "I was thinking about you."

He chuckles as he runs his hand over my shoulder and traces the underside of my chin. "Liar."

Yes, but I stick to my story. "It's true. You're my dream come true."

His hand moves to my breast. "I can't wait to get you to the cottage."

I really like Kyle, but it's been a long time since I was in bed with a man, and I don't want to disappoint him. The fact that I'm willing to sleep with him says something about him, but it also makes a bolder statement about me. I'm ready for a normal life. I'm tired of being alone.

I downshift and take the exit toward 168 South. Within an hour, I reach the Wright Memorial Bridge and cross over the gray-green Currituck Sound dotted with whitecaps. A gust of wind catches my car, forcing me to grip the wheel tighter.

The sky is gray and thick with rain as I take a left onto Route 12 and drive north past closed shops and restaurants. It feels as if I'm the only one crazy enough to be here now. When the brick Currituck lighthouse comes into view on my left, I pull off and drive toward the air-down station.

Air gauge in hand, I get out of the car, then glance up at the gray overcast sky. The weather app is calling for wind and rain. As a way of a greeting, an icy wind whips among the live oak trees bent and twisted by the constant sea winds.

I quickly kneel by the driver's-side front tire and press the metal edge of the gauge into the air valve. Air hisses out as an ocean breeze swirls around me. The airing-down process takes ten minutes, and by the time I get into the car, my skin is ice-cold and my teeth are chattering. I crank the heater and glance at the gas gauge. One-quarter of a tank. Not a lot to spare, but enough.

Back on Route 12, I drive to the end of the paved road to a set of cattle guards. Pausing, I switch to four-wheel drive, and then I roll over the rails onto the sand. The engine strains, and the back end of the car fishtails slightly as I hit a moist patch of sand. Gripping the steering wheel, I'm tempted to slow or stop, but as Kyle did, I press the accelerator and power toward the waves.

The water is churning today, and the foamy waves are crashing higher up on the beach. Ahead, hardened tree stumps jut up from the sand, forcing me to arrow the Jeep toward the dunes. The wheels catch in the thicker sand, slow, and the engine strains. Most of the blackened stumps are tall and easy to see, but there are several that are short and nestled close to the sand. A few are marked with reflectors, but several could be missed. If I hit one, I'm liable to tear into the underside of the Jeep. I glance in my rearview mirror, catching the barren beach behind me.

The houses on the other side of the dunes are dark. I have no phone and a dwindling gas gauge, and rain is looming. This trip suddenly doesn't make a lot of sense. It's cold and wet, and if I get stuck, it could be hours before I can walk out and find someone to tow me.

"What the hell was I thinking?" I mutter as I lean toward the steering wheel.

When I finally notice the wire fence dividing North Carolina from Virginia in the distance, I remember my turn is up ahead. Finally, I spot fading tire tracks cutting over the path between the dunes. I gear down and nose the car west over the dunes.

Again, the temptation is to go slow over the rising mound of sand, but I press the accelerator like Kyle did. The Jeep fishtails, and the wheels slow to a crawl as the engine strains through wet, thick sand. I jam the accelerator to the floor, and after seconds of spinning in place, the vehicle lurches through the squishy wet sand and up over the dune.

My heart jackhammers against my chest as I descend toward the hard-packed sand road. I've left the modern world and entered no-man's-land.

I notice a street sign that reads SANDFIDDLER ROAD, and I'm oddly relieved. No-man's-land surely doesn't require street signs.

After a right turn, the Jeep's wheels roll north past dark and deserted cottages. The house numbers tick down. Finally, I spot 123. It's the last in line and closest to the thick woods to the north.

Kyle's house isn't like the other homes. Its stark lines are an outlier among the homey beach cottages painted in whites, grays, and even bright blues. The cottage's blunt angles are stunning and could easily adorn the cover of an architectural magazine, but it doesn't quite mesh with the rolling dunes or the sea oats bending in the wind. The dwelling was designed to catch attention.

Pulling into the driveway, I park next to Kyle's Range Rover. As the engine rumbles, I lean over the wheel and allow the first deep breath I've taken in the last half hour.

When I look over at the Range Rover, I picture us both smiling as we sat in the front seat yesterday morning. *"Can't wait to get you inside,"* he says as he kisses me. I guess the Range Rover will be a detail for Kyle's estate or Devon.

I shut off the engine and stare up at the three-story house with a wraparound porch and tall windows. It's a house designed to catch the light, and on a cloudy day with the windows covered, it loses almost all its charm. It's now just an unwelcoming four-thousand-square-foot box.

Out of the car, the cold wind slaps. I slam the car door and look up the stairs to the porch. I might not remember the fall, but it's stored in my mind somewhere, and it's screaming danger. I hurry up the stairs. My fingers are numb when I press in the code. 674510. When the lock turns, I'm relieved, grateful, and a little worried. I rush inside into warmth and close the door.

Drawn shades cast deep shadows that telegraph this house is unwilling to receive visitors. Only the hum of the heating system echoes out of the darkness. I flip on the entryway light, but the glow does little to dispel the gloom looming in the house. The air is ripe with pine-scented cleaner.

I've heard stories of spirits lingering near the spot of their death, especially when it's a violent, sudden passing. I understand how a soul would get confused. Breathing one second, gone the next.

I had lain at the bottom of the stairs, unconscious, close to Kyle's dead body for five, maybe ten minutes. Does that mean his spirit is now attached to me? Will he always be lurking close, wondering how we fell?

"Shit, Lane," I mutter. "Don't go there. Stick to what you know."

My first memory after I regained consciousness is of a voice reaching into the darkness and reverberating around me.

"Ma'am, can you hear me?" The man's voice echoes in the distance. "Ma'am!" Cutting, direct, all business.

"Yes." My whisper is hoarse. My first instinct is to sit up.

Strong hands roll me on my back against a body board. All my muscles scream. "Do you know where you are?"

If he'll let me sit up, I'll figure it out and tell him, but he's holding me flat on my back. "No. Yes. Maybe."

"Where are you?" he demands.

I scramble to piece together the bits of information floating in my head. Kyle . . . "Beach house. Kyle?"

"Can you move your arms and legs?" the man asks.

I wiggle fingers and toes, but when I try to move my left leg, a searing fire radiates up and down the nerves. "My hip."

Hands move over my body in a clinical way. "It took the brunt of your fall. But I don't think you broke any bones."

"She's been unconscious since I arrived," another man says. I don't recognize the voice. "That was about fifteen minutes ago."

Those missing minutes are my first reference to time. I focus on the face looming over me. Deep wrinkles circle blue eyes. White hair. Tanned skin. "Kyle?"

Red and blue lights flash on the walls, but there's no sound of a siren.

"What's your name?" the white-haired man asks.

"Lane. Lane McCord."

"Lane, my name is Barry. Can you tell me what day it is?"

"Is Kyle okay?"

"What day is it, Lane?" He's pressing to determine if I have a head injury.

"Friday." I've answered a question, now it's his turn. "Kyle?"

"Ma'am, he's dead."

I turn my head to the right. The slight move shoots lightning down my spine. When I refocus, I see Kyle lying in a crimson lake. I close my eyes, regroup before opening them again.

There's a tremendous gash in his head, and his neck contorts at an odd angle. His arm is bent backward. The gold of his college ring winks in the sun. Beyond his neck and arm, his body looks whole, intact. I almost don't believe Barry, and then my gaze settles on Kyle's glassy stare. I reach for Kyle, but he's now out of range. My voice is barely a whisper. "Kyle?"

"Lane, we need to focus on you," the man says as he wraps a brace around my neck.

Panic claws its way through my body, dragging its old pal terror with it. Both surround me and squeeze my heart in a stranglehold.

I kneel on the clean floor at the base of the stairs and smooth my hand over the cool stone. Swallowing, I draw in a deep breath. As Devon said, all traces of blood have been removed from the floor and stairs. Even the grout is a pristine white. Also gone are the discarded bandages, rubber gloves, and paper wrappers littering the bloody floor.

My memories of the fall begin at the end, but I need a beginning. It's as if a switch flipped. On and then off.

I look up the staircase toward the iron railing that bands the second-floor landing. My purse, phone, and pills are up there. I need to get my things, but as I look up each step, my head swims. The sensations of weightlessness, panic, and fear line up and land a punch. I'm not ready to climb the stairs.

A few extra minutes to collect myself won't make a difference. Just a little time and I'll settle, get my things, and leave.

Rising, I move to the kitchen, flipping on each light switch as I pass and then finding the switch that controls the shades. They all rise slowly, but the overcast sunlight that eases into the house does little to chase the gloom. Beyond windows that sparkled yesterday, dark, bloated clouds dangle over the ocean. A thick, cold mist shrouds the crashing ocean waves that roll almost up to the dunes. The weather and this house are both colluding against me.

"Not going anywhere until I'm ready." The whispered declaration is as much for me as it is for the house and lingering spirits. I need reinforcing like a crumbling brick wall requires props.

I move past the stairs and take a long look at the main room. Its vaulted ceiling stretches up past the landing on the second floor to the pitched roof. All the furnishings and carpeting are white. Not the kind of place where you kick off your shoes and curl up with a book.

There's a large modern painting mounted over a cold stone fireplace. It's a black-and-white charcoal sketch of a naked woman. She's facing away from the artist, her wrists crossed over her head. Her hands aren't bound, but as I stare at the image, I get the feeling the artist wants me to believe the subject is trapped.

There are no personal pictures, and the accessories in the room are as blunt as the exterior. There's a small gray statue of a naked woman leaning against a tree, and a small oil painting of a young woman's face. She looks sad, lost.

The bloodred roses in a crystal vase on the coffee table are the one bright spot of color in the room. Yesterday, I was dazzled by the sun and barely glanced beyond the expensive furnishings. However, the longer I stare at the hard angles, the art choices, and the clouds shrouding the house, the more uneasy I become.

Beyond the living room, I find the laundry room, a bedroom, a home gym, and finally double doors leading to an office.

I enter the office and flip on the light. My gaze is drawn first to metal bookshelves that line the east wall. Every square inch of shelving is filled with books on psychology, the human brain, and anatomy.

Hanging on the light-gray walls are diplomas from Georgetown, Harvard, and Yale framed in sleek pewter. Several service awards sit on a credenza, along with a few pictures: Kyle with the Virginia governor, Kyle with law enforcement officers, and Kyle playing golf at a lush country club course.

The desk is made of teak with straight, balanced lines. There's a gray handwoven carpet on top of beige wall-to-wall carpet, and in front of the desk are two chrome chairs with thick metal armrests. I sit behind the desk.

There's a paper calendar to my right. It's for the upcoming year, and the only notation in January is a neat pencil line drawn through Monday. Kyle expected to be at the beach with me into the New Year. That slim pencil line hits me hard. We all like to think that when death comes, we'll see it first. Not so.

There's no mention of me in his calendar. Kyle knew what the simple line meant, but no one else looking at it would.

I flip the pages and travel back through last year. He's made notes in ink about contractors scheduled here at the house for the septic maintenance, roof repair, and window cleaning. There were several weekends also blocked off with a simple pencil line drawn from Friday to Sunday.

No names. Funny that a man who was so exact would use pencil and skip specific notations for certain dates.

Everything in this space reminds me of Kyle. Stark, modern. Attractive but slightly unapproachable.

On the desk, there's an amber paperweight that encases a yellow butterfly. I hold it up to the light, marveling that the creature was so perfect and beautiful at the time of its death.

I smooth my hands over the glistening desktop, which still smells faintly of lemon polish. I tug the front center drawer, but it's locked, as are the side drawers. He surely kept a spare key somewhere. I run my hands along the underside of the desk. Nothing. Kyle's life is none of my business, but that doesn't temper my curiosity. I need to know more about the man who died inches from me.

Pivoting in the chair toward a closet behind the desk, I open the door. Inside are two sweaters dangling from wooden hangers. They're both navy blue, and the seams are carefully arranged. I raise one sleeve to my nose and inhale. The power of scent is a potent memory trigger, and I've used it from time to time with some of the girls in my circle group. The soft scents of Kyle's sandalwood aftershave invade me, and I can imagine him standing beside me.

I'm immediately transported back to a moment when Kyle is laughing at a comment I made about politics and then to another when he's frowning after I refused his offer of financial assistance.

Blending with his fragrance are traces of fresh paint, lingering in the small space. I touch the wall and discover the paint is so tacky my fingerprint impression remains.

Who paints the walls of a closet in the wake of a terrible accident? Paint masks memories, hides a multitude of sins, and destroys forensic material.

I will the drywall to whisper its secrets. I wait, but these walls are as standoffish as the rest of the house.

The longer I linger in the space, a feeling of déjà vu tightens around me. I don't recall any detail of the closet, but it feels familiar. Odd.

Claustrophobia constricts my chest, making breathing difficult. Suddenly, I'm fearful someone will shove me inside and lock the door. All I can imagine is oppressive darkness. I immediately step out and slam the door closed.

My phone dings with a text.

Keep reading, Lane.

Attached is a PDF file.

Chapter Seven

STEVIE PALMER'S DIARY

Sunday, July 2, 2023
2:00 a.m.

If Joey had an employee-of-the-day vote right now, I'd win. His two waitresses leave at closing, and Nikki is minutes behind them. Judging by Nikki's extra lipstick and perfume, she has a date. My bet is Bourbon. He seemed as into her as she him.

Nikki's a big girl and must know trouble like Pete always awaits. Still, as I tuck my tips in my back pocket, I say, "Bourbon?"

"Yeah." Her grin is broad. "He's kind of cute. And he's rich."

Rich? That's a stretch. "Does he have a name?" I arch, stretching the tension from my lower back.

She smiles. "I'll let you know when I show up for tonight's evening shift," she says.

"Be careful?"

Nikki laughs. "That a question or advice, *Mom*?"

"A friendly reminder."

Joey flips on the overhead lights, which cast a glare on the empty bar. The intimate, cool vibe vanishes, and what's left is a careworn room with full trash cans, discarded clusters of beer bottles, and glasses with boozy residue. Joey grabs a large green trash bag.

I remove a band from my wrist and gather up my thick hair. I tie it up, snag a tray, and start moving from table to table picking up glasses and trash.

"You're off the clock," Joey says.

"Roger that," I say.

I don't love downtime as a rule because it leaves me restless, even anxious. Better to be busy, even on the worst shifts, than to be over-thinking existential bullshit questions like do any of us really exist or when will we die? Nope, mopping a sticky bar floor at 2:00 a.m. beats that hands down.

When I leave the bar at three, Joey hollers, "Back tonight?"

"Sure," I say. "Five?"

"Works for me."

"Will do."

"Don't worry about Pete," he says. "I texted him a warning, and he's a lot of things, but he's not stupid."

"Is he a regular?"

"Not anymore." He frowns. "Nikki told me what you did for her."

"How long have you known Nikki?"

"A couple of weeks. Like you, she wandered into my life."

And he is one kind soul, but I won't tease him. Kind gestures are rare, and it's nice to see Joey trying to help Nikki. I grab my baseball bat from behind the bar. "Takes a village, right?"

Outside, the hot summer air has cooled, but the air remains thick and humid. I pause, looking left and right, fearful one of the patrons— or maybe even Pete, who might not be as smart as Joey thinks—is waiting for me. A salty breeze skims over my skin, carrying the sounds of cars and drunken laughter.

When I see no one waiting for me, I cross to my car and slip behind the wheel. Starting the engine, I drive down the two-lane beach road until I find a dark corner of a crowded hotel parking lot and slide into a shadowed spot.

Baseball bat in hand, I settle into the back seat, lock the doors, and cover myself with a blanket. I should have at least four or five hours before the sun comes up and someone notices me.

The parking lot is busy, but it's summer in Nags Head. The intoxicated men and women who are wandering around, looking to squeeze a little more out of a vacation or long weekend. Male laughter is followed by a collection of women chatting about looking for their car. One tries the driver's-side door of my car but discovers it's locked. Burrowing under the blanket, I hope they don't notice me.

"Renee, that piece-of-shit car isn't yours," a woman says.

"Oops," another woman says.

A couple of others laugh. Thankfully, they move on. Soon the world around me is silent.

This time of year, stillness summons the old demons. Anything I've buried deep bubbles to the surface during the Fourth of July weekend.

Fourteen years ago, I'd hitchhiked to Nags Head when I was fifteen. I'd snuck out of my foster home determined to prove to myself and my foster mother that I didn't need anyone. I thought adventure was waiting.

Well, something *was* waiting, but it wasn't adventure.

A carload of gals who'd picked me up in Norfolk drop me off on the beach road at the ice cream shop at Milepost Six. The bleach-blond driver asks, "Are you meeting someone?"

"Yeah, yeah," I lie. "My cousin is going to meet me here. We've got it all figured out."

She eyes me an extra second. "You sure?"

"Yeah." I smile. "It's all good."

The driver finally nods and drives off.

At the ice cream shop, I order double scoops of chocolate. I'm licking my cone outside the shop, wondering where I'll go next, when I spot the neon signs of a bar. A place like that won't hire me to work the front end, but maybe I can wash dishes. I'm licking my way through the second scoop when an old truck pulls up beside me.

The driver has a thick beard, his dark hair skims his torn T-shirt, and a gold earring stud winks in the lamppost light. The other bearded guy is harder to see, but he kind of looks like he might be a brother or cousin.

"Hey," Mr. Earring says.

I shift my gaze away from them.

"Chocolate Cone Girl, don't look away." His friendly tone sharpens with tension. "We just want to talk."

I rise and toss the ice cream in the trash can. "No thanks."

A door opens, and I hear boots moving toward me. When I turn, the driver is only feet away. He smells of construction dust and sweat. "I'm just trying to be friendly."

"I don't need any friends."

If he's realized how young I am, he doesn't seem to care. "Can't have enough friends."

I dash into the bar and stand in the shadows. When a waitress eyes me, I hurry to the ladies' room, where I linger for at least a half hour. When I'm sure the guys are gone, I slip out the back door. I'm proud of myself. I've made it to the beach, ditched a few losers, and even had ice cream. Who says I can't take care of myself?

Headlights flash, and when I turn, the truck is at the end of the alley. I grip my backpack and take a step back. Time to get to the street and vanish into crowds.

As I turn to run, the truck's passenger is blocking my path. He's grinning. "Are you ditching us?"

My heart pounds in my chest. "No."

"Liar."

He grabs my arm as the truck pulls up beside us. He opens the back seat door. "Get in."

I know the score. If I get in the truck, I'm screwed. It's not going to end well. The alley opens onto the beach road on the east end and a small side street to the west. I'm smaller than this guy, and I can run fast. And that's what I do. I twist free of his grip, turn, and run.

My heart pounds in my chest as my feet hammer the pavement. I've no idea where I'm going, but away from here—them—is the goal.

I make it until the end of the alley when strong arms band around my waist, and a hand clamps over my mouth. I'm kicking as I try to bite thick, dusty fingers. He drags me back to the truck, tosses me onto the back seat, slides in beside me, and slams the door. The other guy puts the truck in gear and drives.

Scrambling toward the other door, I'm ready to jump out of a moving vehicle, but the guy grabs my arm and sandwiches my body between his and the worn seat.

I bite his hand. He grabs a fistful of my hair and smashes my face several times against the seat. "That wasn't very nice."

Blood trickles from my nose. "Let me go."

"Not yet. We got a party to get to."

What comes next is a forty-minute drive up the beach road until the tires leave the hard surface for rough sand. The truck rocks and jolts, and the longer we drive, the deeper I draw within myself. I'm not afraid. I can't afford fear.

When the truck finally stops, I am sick to my stomach. If I can just get a second or two break, I can run. This time I'll be faster.

I get that second, and I am faster, but not quick enough. Strong arms again band around my waist, and a calloused hand clamps over my mouth. They drag me to a ramshackle beach cottage, up the stairs, and through the front door.

"I can do whatever I want to you. I own you," one of the men says.

When the door slams behind me, I know I'm not escaping. The goal now is to survive.

Moonlight shines through the car windows. I hug my bat closer as I stare at the soft top ceiling.

I haven't forgotten how those two men smelled, the feel of their hands, or the way the big guy laughed at me when I refused to show pain. He did his best to make me cry. He liked hurting me. But I never gave him the satisfaction.

I lost track of time. Finally, they left me tied to a bed. They were hungry. Needed a break before round two.

It took me nearly an hour to free a wrist. When I did, I was able to unknot my bindings. I found my pants, shirt, shoes, and backpack all discarded on the floor.

As I'm leaving the house, a third man appears. My heart catches, and I'm seconds away from begging for freedom.

He turns his back on me. I'm not sure if he understands what's happened, and I don't ask. I run, following a sandy road to the beach, and slip through a small fence opening. I walk toward lights on the horizon for at least ten miles until I get hold of a phone and call my foster mother. She's mad but resolved and tells me to wait in front of the gas station. An hour later, she picks me up south of Norfolk and takes me to the hospital.

***

I arrive at Joey's at 4:30, ready to work and keep busy. Nikki is late, so I prep the bar, and when the doors open at 6:00, I'm ready to work.

The crowd is jazzed, but it's still the holiday weekend. Revelers have arrived with cash and credit cards ready to spend. It's their time to drink too much, eat crap food, or hook up.

Always amusing to see star-crossed, horny lovers lock eyes and slowly migrate closer. What happens on vacation stays, right?

Nikki arrives at 7:00. Her skin is slightly flushed, and she's grinning like a kid. She looks pleased with herself and doesn't seem to care that Joey is pissed. She gets to work, and the Fourth of July weekend is so crazy busy, we don't have time to talk.

"Over under," Nikki says when we finally get a lull around 9:00. "Mr. Blue Button-Down at the end of the bar scores with the redhead three seats down from him."

"Blue Button-Down isn't going for the redhead," I say. "He's got eyes for the blonde. He keeps sneaking peeks at her."

"Maybe." She fills a mug.

No maybes about it. "How did the date go?"

"It went really well. He treated me like a queen."

"Did Bourbon give you his name?" I'm curious about the guy and wonder if I'll recognize the name.

Nikki giggles. "We were too busy to really think about names."

"Where'd you go?" Not sure why I'm pressing, but I can't shake the fear that the kid is walking into a bear trap.

"A hotel down the street." She grabs a bowl of peanut shells and dumps it. "He wants to see me again."

"Do you not hear the warning bells?" I ask. "They're clanging in my ears."

"Why are you so worried about this guy? He treated me well."

I can't explain why I don't like Bourbon. But I can smell trouble. "I have a soft spot for people who need protecting."

Nikki laughs. "I can take care of myself."

I'd said the same once. And that lesson gave me real appreciation for pain, so I try to steer others away from it if I can. In Nikki's case, I sense it's a never-ending job.

Nikki fills five iced mugs and loads them on a tray. "Bet you five bucks Blue Button-Down goes for the redhead."

I smile. "Sure, I'll take your money."

Nikki chuckles as she hefts the tray and moves toward a collection of guys sitting in a corner booth.

To my surprise, Bourbon returns to the bar and takes the same seat he had last night. While Nikki lingers at one of the booths, I grab a tumbler and the top-shelf bourbon. Without saying anything, I set the glass down and fill it.

"Good memory." He's staring at me when he speaks.

His vibe is still off, and there's something worrisome about him. Can't nail down the feeling, so I smile. "The best."

More customers pull me away, but my thoughts never linger far from Bourbon. Nikki flirts with him every chance she gets. Maybe the kid will be fine. Lying in the back seat of my car all night while hugging a baseball bat tends to make a person paranoid.

Each time Nikki moves toward Bourbon, he smiles. He seems to enjoy it when she laughs. However, when she turns away, his smile vanishes, and his jaw pulses. Something has changed. A switch has flipped.

While Nikki closes out a tab, I hold up the bourbon bottle, and when he nods, I refill it. "Any plans for the holiday?" I ask.

He grins. "Maybe fireworks, you?"

"Behind the bar until closing time and then rinse and repeat."

"No family gatherings?"

"Nope."

He regards me as if being a solo is a good thing. I hold his gaze, letting him know this lone deer knows how to fight. "What about you? Family?"

"No family. Just vacation for a few days. Then back to work on Wednesday."

I nod. "No rest for the wicked, right?"

His smile doesn't reach his eyes. "Exactly."

Another guy raises his beer mug and I take it, smiling as I refill it from the tap. He was here last night. Didn't say much. Name's Sully.

Tonight, I've found a rhythm, so I have time to really look at Sully. He's in his late thirties, salt-and-pepper hair, collared shirt, rolled-up sleeves revealing muscled forearms and the bottom edge of a sleeve tattoo. He's some variation of a cop because, remember, I'm good at spotting trouble. And for me, cops generally mean problems.

"You're back." His conversational tone is sprinkled with a couple of beers' worth of sincerity. It's almost Fourth of July, and everyone—including me on rare occasions—wants to have a good time. Oddly, I don't mind making conversation with him.

"My second night," I say. "You come here often, Sully?"

He smiles. "You remember."

I tap my finger against my temple. "It's a steel trap."

Grinning, he shakes his head. "My second night, too. You going to be working here now?"

"Doubtful. I'm like a cat. Come and go." I grin. "Catch any bad guys lately?"

A brow raises as Sully sips his beer. His eyes are a vivid blue, and his gaze is totally focused on me. A cop would wonder why I stay on the move. Drugs, an abusive ex, or debt?

I lean a fraction closer. "If you're undercover, bro, you're blown."

A smile reveals even white teeth. "I'm like everyone else, hiding out until the holiday weekend storm passes. No agenda. And I'm in construction."

"Right." My eyes narrow. "Everyone has an agenda."

"No agenda. But if I get lucky, I wouldn't complain."

It's my turn to laugh. "There's a redhead at the other end of the bar. She's got 'take me home' written all over her."

He glances at the woman, who's now talking to Blue Button-Down. "She's busy."

"Blue Button-Down is going for a blonde."

"Why do you say that?" He regards me with genuine curiosity.

"Not my first rodeo."

He sips his beer. "The redhead looks a little like my ex-wife, so that'll have to be a hard pass."

"Divorced. Because you're married to your job." There's no hint of a wedding band shadowing his left hand, so it's likely been a while since his divorce. But my guess is that he didn't wear the ring on the job anyway. Maybe it was a noble move, but protective brick by protective brick he constructed a wall between his public and private lives. Finally, that wall grew so thick, the wife left. Maybe that's what he means by construction.

He taps a gold pinkie ring against the mug. He's not the fussy type, so safe bet the ring belonged to a father or grandfather. "That's what she said."

"Maybe you should be talking to her, not me."

He raises his mug, pauses before the glass reaches his lips. "She got remarried last Saturday."

Ah, he's here for a soft shoulder to cry on, but then aren't they all? "Ouch."

"She tried." The bitterness is barely detectable. "I'll always give her credit for that."

"But she couldn't compete with the job, a mistress no wife can beat."

"Balancing two lives rarely ends well." He takes a sip.

"So I've heard."

Nikki passes behind me and catches Bourbon's attention. She refills his glass. Bourbon's gaze lingers on her as he says something that makes her smile. Nikki is eating up the attention.

Sully extends his hand. "You know my name. Remind me of yours again?"

I take his hand. Calloused fingers wrap around mine. "Stevie."

His gaze holds mine for a beat and then shifts to Blue Button-Down, who's now talking to a blonde. "Looks like you know your man."

"Consider me a student of human behavior."

His brow arches. "Or you're playing me, and you know Blue Button-Down?"

"Nope. Never saw the guy before."

He taps the ring on the side of the mug. "What was his tell?"

"He's been secretly ogling that blonde for at least a half hour while talking to the redhead."

"What about the guy flirting with the other bartender? What do you think about him?" Sully asks.

Not a good guy. He looks at Nikki as if judging a prize mare. Sometimes this game isn't fun. "Not for me to say. Joey's is a bit of a summer meat market, and we're all adults."

"But you don't like him." Sully sets down his mug, turning it until the handle is at a right angle to the bar's edge.

"His money is green, and he's not causing any trouble," I say.

Sully nods slowly. "I get it. Can't run down the paying customers."

I set a fresh bowl of peanuts in front of him. "Let me know if you need anything."

"Stevie, I'll kick myself if I don't ask this question."

I grab a tumbler and polish it. "What's that?"

His gaze raises slowly. "What are you doing later tonight?"

"Me? Closing about one a.m., cleaning up, and then dusting off my broomstick and flying home."

He laughs. "Broomstick? Good or bad witch?"

"All in all, I'm not *that* bad. But not exactly *good*, either." There's something about him that lights a fire in me. I sense he's as dangerous as Bourbon, but his kind of danger is controlled, careful, and sexy. You'd think I'd have no interest in men in general, or if I did, I would only go for the betas. Nope. Like Nikki, I've strung together my own brand of Mr. Wrongs.

"It's a shame to be alone on a fine summer night." He sounds like he almost means it.

"Is it?"

"Don't you get tired of the solo act?"

"I don't. But I suspect you do."

"Not usually." Maybe that's what he tells himself, even though he's happy to be alone.

"Chalk this up to the ex-wife's remarriage. That's got to hurt the pride, but this, too, shall pass."

He raises his mug. "Amen."

"What do you build?"

"Restoration work right now. It's part-time." A group of women behind him laugh loudly. "Want to look for a smaller crowd after you get off work?"

He doesn't give up easily. No one likes a quitter. "Like me with you, kind of small?"

He's not pushing, but he's also not backing off. Points for him. I check my watch. Two hours until closing. His offer is tempting. Though temptation is weakness, sometimes I make an exception. "See you around one."

Chapter Eight

LANE

Saturday, December 30, 2023
2:00 p.m.

My stomach grumbles, echoing in the quiet of the empty house. I should retrieve my things and get on the road. The ocean waves are crashing higher up on the shore, the clouds are thickening, and the air is heavy with moisture. But something in me says I'm not finished with this house.

I'm hungry and wish now I'd packed an apple or a peanut butter sandwich. There's a grocery store on the main road in Corolla, but that means a thirty-minute drive. Devon said she planned to clean the refrigerator out tomorrow. Maybe it's still stocked.

In the kitchen I'm still amazed at the large marble island, the stainless-steel appliances, and the herringbone backsplash. When I stepped in here yesterday, the modern beauty of the place stunned me.

As I stand in the kitchen, the large painting featuring the naked woman with crossed wrists catches my attention. I see now her head is slightly dipped as if she's submitting. I know there are no wrong or right choices about art. Personal taste is subjective. But all the choices we make for our home say something about us as individuals. I've never been in Kyle's apartment in Norfolk or his city office, but now I wonder what I'd find.

My stomach growls. I shift my attention to the refrigerator's double doors. To my relief, it's full not only with water but also luncheon meats, bread, apples, grapes, my favorite creamer, and canned seltzer.

"Bless you, Devon." I reach for the packets of sliced ham and cheese as well as a sleeve of bread.

The bread is fresh, and the meat is sliced thin, just how I like it. I remember that Kyle said he called Devon and told her to order our favorites. I didn't have many preferences, but he had plenty.

I dig a white plate out of the cabinet and pile the meat and cheese on the bread, then smear mustard over it. Grabbing a sharp knife from the block, I slide the blade through the sandwich. Immediately, I wash off the knife and replace it in the block because I still feel like an interloper. Crazy that I am so hungry, especially in this house. I should be terrified, creeped out, or at the very least uncomfortable here. But I'm okay. I eat the entire sandwich.

It feels good to have my belly full. When I was with Kyle, I was always a little nervous and was hesitant to eat. I was more worried about making a good impression than satisfying my hunger.

Now he's dead, gone forever, and I'm ravenous.

I grab a water, twist off the top, and drink as I walk toward another set of blinds, press the button that opens them. The clouds in the sky have grown thicker, and the waves break faster. The weather app calls for a 70 percent chance of rain this afternoon. Moving around the room, I turn on more lights, which dispel some of the gloom outside. I need to get moving if I hope to be out of here before the bad weather arrives.

Setting the water bottle on the counter, I walk toward the stairs. Carefully, I run my hand over the smooth black metal banister. I count the twenty-one steps. The pitch isn't extreme, but the angle certainly is sharp enough to kill.

I climb the stairs quickly, anxious to be off them as fast as possible. At the landing I look over my shoulder, hoping for a spark of memory. What were we doing up here? We were standing close. I was smiling, right? He was staring at me with an intensity that seared my skin.

Detective Becker said there were no drugs or alcohol in Kyle's system. But there were traces of a sedative in mine. Sure, I was nervous, but I only took my normal nighttime sleep meds. The lab must have picked up traces of those.

Detective Becker doesn't believe me, and I have no idea why. Maybe the *undetermined* ruling by the medical examiner has satisfied most, but it appears he's not mollified. That would explain the visit.

I move away from the top step down the hallway. I stop at the first guest room. A king-size bed with a white metal bedframe and an aqua coverlet dominates the center. There's a horizontal mirror over the headboard, chunky distressed side tables sporting wooden lamps with round beige shades. Hardback books are neatly stacked in two piles on a rustic bench at the foot of the bed. The top book is a pictorial featuring historic sailor's knots.

The furnishings are lovely. I could outfit several apartments for what they cost.

The next two rooms are similar. It's not until I get to the end of the hallway and reach the largest bedroom that I hesitate. This had been Kyle's room.

The whitewashed four-poster bed is massive. The navy-blue coverlet is rumpled, and the pillows are carefully arranged on a nearby chair. The creases are proof that we lay here, but the covers aren't pulled back, so I guess we couldn't have lingered long. What had happened?

I spot my purse, move toward it, and fish out my phone, wallet, keys, and bottle of pills. Rolling my shoulders, I try to release the heaviness seeping into my bones. I open the wallet, count out the ten one-dollar bills and inventory my two credit cards. All present and accounted for. I shake the pill bottle, but don't hear a familiar rattle. I open it and realize it's empty. "What the hell?"

I filled this prescription last week. I should have plenty. Shit. I've no idea how many people have been in the house since yesterday, but why take the pills and leave the money and credit cards behind?

My phone's battery is dead, so I plug the charger into an outlet by the bed. Opening the curtains, I look out over the dark houses across the street. I'm utterly alone.

My hip aches, so I sit on the edge of the bed and scan the room. There are several lovely sketches of nude women. Nothing graphic, but it's clear Kyle loved the feminine shape.

The bed's softness melts into me as I wait for the phone to charge before I open the photos and search for the pictures I took of Kyle and me. I need to see *us* smiling and enjoying life. I need to prove that we were real. That we were happy.

I blink, rolling my shoulders again. My body is stiffening, and my limbs feel weighted by iron.

There should be selfies of Kyle and me in the driveway in front of this house. When we arrived yesterday, he was wearing a navy-blue quarter-zip pullover, and his dark hair was wind-tousled. He was reluctant to take a picture, but in the end my teasing won him over.

"I didn't think you were the pushy type," he says.

I hold out the camera, feeling playful. "You make that sound like a bad thing."

He wraps his arm around my shoulder and holds me close to his side. "Not at all."

I snap a few pictures, and we both agree the images are flattering. We decide it's a good omen for our new relationship. I like omens and signs. The world is full of messages, but we miss them if we're not paying attention.

But as I scroll, I don't see the images. I find the series of selfies I took Wednesday night with a few of the gals from the circle group. The girls were holding up their presents from Kyle, and all of them were grinning. All great moments.

I go further back in time to last weekend, when we went out to dinner. There are pictures of the food I ate and the sunset off the restaurant's back deck. But all the shots I took of us have vanished. It's as if we never were.

No record of us. What the hell? I know I took those pictures. Did I delete them? And why would I do that?

I yawn, blink back the fatigue soaking into my bones. My eyes feel like sandpaper. Time to summon the energy, get my stuff, and leave. There's no reason to hold on to this place. Whatever I thought I'd find isn't here.

But logic doesn't quiet the feeling that I should remain a little longer. I wonder if lying back on the mattress will trigger a memory. Touch sensation can be effective. Grabbing fistfuls of the coverlet, I stare at the mirrored white ceiling. I barely recognize my pale face and my body that now seems too thin.

This bed is seductive and feels so much better than the lumpy mattress in my apartment. Softness, coupled with the stress of losing Kyle and yesterday's frenetic pace, oozes through me. The adrenaline that's been fueling me for days is suddenly crashing. Getting on the road now feels like a huge task. I was foolish to think I could make this long drive after yesterday's fall. I'm recovering from trauma and should be in my Norfolk apartment. I should get up and leave the place where Kyle died, but before I realize it, it all turns to black.

***

When I startle awake, moonlight drifts through the window. I bolt upright, then regret the sudden move. A headache pounds behind my eyes, and my hip and ribs burn. I grab my phone and glance at the time.

9:02 p.m.

I've slept six hours.

"Damn it."

Darkness hovers outside as rain hits the roof. I rise and walk to the window. I notice several lights are on in the house across the street. A man's shadow passes in front of a window. As if sensing me, he pauses and looks toward this house, this window.

He's as curious about me as I am him. If he's familiar with the neighborhood and this house, he must know what happened here. Does he think I'm staying in the death house because I'm a thrill seeker or simply clueless? Staying here isn't a sane choice. It's one thing to poke around, but another to fall into a dreamless sleep just thirty feet from the spot where my boyfriend fell to his death.

Fat raindrops fall on a black truck parked in the driveway across the street. It has Virginia plates. Common enough here. Still, this feels a little like the outside world has followed me.

I shrink back, sorry now I didn't grab my phone and purse and leave immediately. Whoever lives here must know about Kyle and me.

Rubbing the tension banding the back of my neck, I close the curtains. Crossing to the bed, I smooth the untidy coverlet. There are now no more traces of me being here or in Kyle's life.

I tuck my phone in my pocket and grab my purse and overnight bag. Turning off the lights, I hurry down the hallway, stopping at the top of the stairs. Drawing in a breath, I close my eyes as I grip the railing.

Kyle and I had stood here. My hand had pressed against his chest, his heartbeat pulsing against my fingertips.

And then . . . weightlessness and the crash.

My foot eases toward the edge of the top step. Energy vibrates around me, as if someone is standing behind me. My eyes snap open.

I move down the stairs to the front door and open it. Lightning cracks, and the rain droplets transform into a wall of water. Maneuvering down the beach in the dark would have been dicey at best. But with the rain . . .

I want to go home and forget about this place. But leaving now is not an option. Like it or not, I'm stuck here until morning.

Chapter Nine

LANE

Saturday, December 30, 2023
9:30 p.m.

Dropping my purse and bag by the living room couch, I make my way to the kitchen and open the refrigerator. I'm trapped, nervous, and starving. Why am I so hungry? Kyle had kidded me about my sparse meals. Now he's dead, and my appetite has come roaring back.

Instead of going for luncheon meats, I grab a sleeve of hamburger patties. It's cold outside, and I need something warm. I fish out all the condiments, veggies, and a packet of buns. "Bless you, Devon."

Thunder rumbles in the distance as I'm searching cabinets for a pan. I glance toward the vaulted roof and the trapezoid window. Lightning cracks across the dark sky.

"One. Two. Three." I count as I did as a kid. My mom had a thing about thunderstorms. She'd take me outside, and we'd lie on a blanket as the sky darkened. She loved to watch the flashes of lightning and feel the roar of thunder. The louder the better.

I was terrified. I'd beg her to go inside, but she'd only laugh. *You don't need to be scared until I'm scared.* The problem was my mother was never afraid.

Drawing in a breath, I turn the electric range on and let the pan heat up. Another explosion of lightning flashes bright. One. Two. Thunder booms. Just two miles away now. Getting closer, though the storm system sounds like it is right on top of the house.

I drop the burger in the pan, listen to the sizzle and snap as the meat sears. Choosing one of the bottles of Merlot on the counter, I dig through several drawers before I find a wine opener. I uncork the bottle. Devon has stocked the house with a couple of Kyle's favorite wines. I like them, but these were all his choices. I sip, savoring the mellow flavor, and then flip the burger.

The overhead lights flicker. Once. Twice. And then they stabilize. It never occurred to me that I'd lose power out here, but of course it's very possible in a storm. With no electricity, it not only would be dark but would turn cold very quickly. I've no idea if the house comes equipped with a generator, and if it does, I have no idea how to make it work.

"Just stay on," I say.

I shut off the burner, settle the burger on a bun, and squirt ketchup and mustard. One bite into my burger, the power flickers again, and this time it goes out. The entire house is pitched into darkness.

"Damn it." Setting the burger down, I reach for my cell phone. I'm surprised I only have 25 percent power. It should be fully charged by now. The phone is new, so there should be no issue. Did the house lose power while I was asleep? Still, it's enough juice to power the flashlight. I rummage through the drawers again, this time in search of a battery-operated flashlight. Ten drawers later, still nothing.

Outside, the wind howls, pressing against the glass windows. Kyle had warned me the storms could be fierce up here. He knew I had a thing about thunder, lightning, and darkness.

As I sit in the inky silence, my fingers click against the side of my wineglass. A great glass of wine in a stunning home is certainly not roughing it. I'll be fine, lights or no.

Bam!

I jump at the sound of a fist striking the front door. Wine sloshes onto my hand. *Bam!* The sound reverberates through the house.

Moving to the front door, I wipe my hand on my jeans. Through the locked door, I ask, "Can I help you?"

"I'm staying across the street," the man says. "My name is Reece Trent. I'm a contractor."

"Okay."

"We've all lost power, but I have a generator if you're worried about the dark. It could be up to ten hours before we get power back."

I open the door. Reece Trent is a big man. At least six foot three. His dark hair is cut short, and he's clean shaven. Lines furrow across his brow and feather out from the corners of his eyes. He's not attractive, but he's also not the kind of guy you ignore.

"Hi, I'm Lane." I don't bother with the last name. McCord will mean nothing to him.

He looks me over, his eyes narrowing a fraction. "Are you okay?"

"Excuse me?"

"I'm the one that found you and Kyle." His words are deliberate and careful.

"Oh." He's remembering me from yesterday, lying in a heap surrounded by Kyle's blood. "Thank you. I don't know what I'd have done if you hadn't come by."

Whatever concern I imagine he has for me quickly sours to suspicion. "Why did you come back here?"

"To get my phone and purse. The EMTs left them behind. I meant to be on the road by now."

"You've been here for almost eight hours."

"I sat down on the bed for a second, and then I was out. I just woke up."

That didn't seem to satisfy him. "A miracle you made it up here at all."

"I realize that now. I can't leave until morning."

"Yeah, you're trapped for now. Most likely the cattle guards at the hard surface road are flooded." His eyes reflect distrust and something I can't quite pin down. "Like I said, I have a generator."

"I appreciate that, but I'm okay for now. A little dark never killed anyone."

"You should be stocked up. I saw Devon at the house on Thursday afternoon."

"She's packed the refrigerator. Long as I keep the door closed, I should be able to retain the cold until morning."

"Fair enough. Give me your number, and I'll call you. Then you can call me if you need anything."

"Or I can walk across the street."

"Provided we don't have forty- to fifty-mile-an-hour winds."

"That's in the forecast?"

"It is."

The weather app on my phone shows only curly lines, not exact miles per hour. I suppose if this guy was going to kill me, he'd have tried something by now. I rattle off my number, which he quickly types into his phone. My phone immediately rings, jarring me slightly.

The area code is Virginia. He might live here now but hasn't always. "Got it. Thanks."

He stares at me as if he's wedging together puzzle pieces that don't want to fit. "Call me if you need anything."

"Will do." As he turns, I ask, "Did you know Kyle, the man who owned this place?" I still haven't said *Kyle* and *dead* in the same sentence.

He halts. "Sure. Why do you ask?"

"Just curious."

He drops his gaze. "Lane, you said?"

"That's right."

A wry smile tweaks his lips. "You look different."

"From?"

"Yesterday morning. I saw you and Kyle arrive."

My stomach tumbles. "Why were you here on a holiday?"

"The washing machine hose disconnected from the wall in the house across the street. The water flooded the downstairs. Devon called me."

"Damage from a washer?"

"Owner forgot to turn off the water valve. Water can do a lot of damage if it floods unchecked."

"How did you know that Kyle and I were in trouble?"

"I heard you two arguing, and then it went silent. I stopped by to make sure everyone was okay."

In a blink, I remember our locked gazes. Kyle doesn't look panicked, but annoyed. Pissed even. *You need to take it easy, Lane.* Before I can process the moment, our bodies are falling and slamming into the floor. And then nothing until the rescue squad arrives.

"You called 9-1-1?" I ask.

"Yes."

What did he hear when he came to the house? What were we saying? But asking means revealing I don't remember. "Then I should really thank you."

His brow lines deepen. "Sorry about Kyle."

"Me too."

"You didn't date very long, did you?"

"No. We knew each other only a few weeks. I guess that's part of the reason why I'm here. I'm trying to learn more about him. I saw Kyle die, but I don't know that much about him. Feels like I should know him better."

I can feel his stare burrowing under my skin. "Have you learned anything?"

"Not really."

"He was a private guy."

"He is . . . was."

"Yeah." I kept telling myself we had all the time in the world to get to know each other.

Reece shifts, clears his throat. "Call if you need anything." He fishes in his pocket and hands me a flashlight. "Just in case."

"Thanks. I know there are flashlights here, I just haven't found them yet."

"Well, until you do. Remember to call if you need help."

"You do the same."

That prompts a half smile.

I watch as he jogs across the street toward his house, which is partially lit up. An oasis of light in a sea of darkness.

Clicking on the flashlight, I close and lock the door behind me. As I turn, the beam of light sweeps over the foyer and the stairs. Reece must be the guy Detective Becker spoke to. It makes no sense that Kyle and I were fighting. We never fought. Not once. Why would we have been fighting after an hour in the house?

You need to take it easy, Lane.

Easy over what?

I move to the base of the stairs and sit. The flashlight beam grazes up the marble stairs. Looking up to the landing, I slowly lie down on the cool marble floor. The darkness swirls around me as I roll on my left hip, wince as pain shoots through me, and curl up my legs.

Kyle is staring back at me. His right eye socket is blown. Blood is pooling around his head, staining his navy-blue pullover. His remaining gray eye briefly registers anger and frustration. And then it glazes over.

"What happened to us?" I whisper as if he'll answer.

My left hip is throbbing, and I roll onto my back. The darkness weighs on my chest, and it's tough to pull in a full breath.

I move into the kitchen following the trail of light. My burger is cool now, and my appetite is gone. But there's little to do in the dark, so I eat and then set the plate in the sink when I'm done.

Looking out the front window, I see Reece standing in his own living room. His hands are on his hips, and he's shrugged off his coat and is wearing only a white T-shirt. His gaze rises to mine.

I cut off my flashlight. My phone dings with a text from the number I now know belongs to Reece. Don't forget to call if you need help.

It's a gotcha text. He caught me snooping.

Yep, Lane is a creeper who can't stop staring at strangers. Nothing like making a solid first impression.

I could ignore the text, but what's the point?

No amount of hemming and hawing will make me look less like a stalker. Will do.

Instead of obsessing, I shift my thoughts back to Stevie Palmer's diary.

Chapter Ten

STEVIE PALMER'S DIARY

Monday, July 3, 2023
6:00 a.m.

When I wake up, I'm in a strange bed. Most might panic, but not me. I give it a second, realize there's a man snuggled up behind me with his arm draped over my waist. His erection is pressing against my backside.

How do I untangle myself and get out of here without waking him? He hauls me closer to him. "Good morning."

Sully. Right. We met at Joey's. I like Sully, loved having sex with him. "Good morning."

I roll on my back, and he shifts, grabs a condom from the nightstand, and slips it on. He pulls back the sheets, and I open my legs.

He slides inside me, moving slowly, as if he's in no rush. Last night had a frenzied pace, but not this morning. Now he wants to savor.

I'm not sure how I feel about this version of Sully—the slow, patient lover. There's more emotion, tenderness, and both make me feel uncomfortable. I need to set him on fire and find a quick release for us both.

My hand moves from his shoulders to his butt as I cup my breast with the other. I arch into him and, moaning, wrap a leg around him. His eyes darken and his muscles grow taut. He's trying to maintain control, but I won't have it. I push against his shoulders, and he slides out of me. I coax him onto his back and mount him. He clamps a hand on each hip, and I move faster. My hair spills over my breasts as I arch back.

For his viewing pleasure, I hold his gaze as I lower my fingers to my center and rub. His grip on my hips tightens as I come, and pleasure rockets through me. Unable to hold out now, he flips me on my back again and drives into me faster and faster until his body grows rigid.

When he collapses against me, he says, "You weren't playing fair."

"All's fair."

He chuckles. "I need to shower and get ready for work. Join me."

"You go first. I'm going to make coffee."

He places a lingering kiss on my lips. "Sounds good."

I dress, and when I hear the shower turn on, I leave his house. I'm not interested in chitchat over coffee, and I'd be surprised if he really is as well. It was fun. But time to move on.

After breakfast at a small café, I settle in the lobby of a nice hotel, cup of coffee in hand, and hang out until the manager asks who I'm waiting for. I move to the next hotel. Rinse and repeat until it's time to go to Joey's.

Parking in the alleyway, I'm compelled to walk the ground where the nightmare began. My mind is clever. It's softened the details around the trauma and erased most of the memories. I don't remember exactly where they took me or my walk back toward home. What lingers are fragments and rage. I want to find these men. It's why I return here whenever I can. The universe owes me a small win. And when I find them, I'll kill them both.

Inside the bar, the night kicks off quickly. Nikki is late again, and one of the waitresses doesn't show. It's all hands on deck.

Sully also doesn't return. One part of me hopes he'll return, and the other is glad he's not here. Getting too familiar never ends well. Besides, last night for him was balm for the ex-wife's remarriage. We both gave as good as we got. No harm, no foul.

89

The bar is hopping tonight. Everyone is squeezing as much as they can into this long weekend. Joey is pissed with Nikki, but he doesn't have time to dwell. Neither do I. The tips are good.

"Thanks for coming in, Stevie," Joey says as he sets a hot rack of clean glasses on the bar.

I notice more hints of gray, and those frown lines are etched deeper than normal. "No problem. Any word from Nikki?"

"Nothing. I've called several times." He shakes his head. "I thought a job would help her get her act together, but I guess not. If you hadn't showed, I'd have been screwed tonight."

I unload the warm glasses from the sanitizer tray. "That's not like her, is it?"

Worry furrows his brow. "She's only been here a couple of weeks and been late more often than not, but she's always been good about calling."

"Has anyone gone by her apartment?" Kids like Nikki could be undependable. Most find another job and don't bother to let their current employer know they've left. Nikki is a bit of a flake, so she fits the profile.

"No."

"Maybe someone should."

"Let me get through tonight, okay? I can't turn down the income to chase after another employee that's a no-show." The words rush out on a sigh. Joey's tired, and this is a fight he doesn't want.

Shit. This is not my business. I'm a temp. Work for cash. Make no commitments. But Nikki had given me a soda. "I'll swing by after my shift."

A faint smile tugs at his lips. "Thanks, kid."

"Write down her address."

"Will do."

The night gets rolling quickly, and the bar fills up fast. All those people who'd made it through the week and have overdosed on family barbecues are ready to bust out and ring in the Fourth in style.

It's all Joey and I can do to keep up with the crowd. The joint is hopping. The cash and booze roll. Life is good.

Last call is at 1:00 a.m., but I don't get out of the bar until after 2:00. Nothing like a room full of drunks to screw up a bar. The cleanup is a bitch.

Joey hands me a piece of paper with an address. "It's a trailer about a mile west on the other side of the bridge."

I shove the paper in my pocket. "Got it. See you soon."

"When?" Joey asks.

"Don't know."

"Make it tomorrow, and I'll love you forever."

I smile. "Give it my best shot."

"Let me know if I need to get involved with Nikki."

"Will do."

Bone-deep fatigue doesn't quite measure up to how I feel as I walk to my car. I really need sleep, but I said I'd check on Nikki.

I follow Joey's directions across the bridge and locate the collection of brown trailers lined up in two neat rows on hard-packed dirt. I pull into the lot and park in front of unit 201, which is supposed to be Nikki's.

Rap music pulses out of the trailer at the far end, and there are clusters of young people swaying in time to the music. A few folks glance in my direction, but I'm out of smiles. My attitude is strictly don't-fuck-with-me, which seems to put them off. For now.

I climb the stairs to Nikki's trailer and bang on the door. There's no answer. Shit. Maybe Nikki has flaked and gone off with the next Mr. Wrong. Maybe she's getting laid and savoring the best of what summer has to offer. I could be doing the same if I wasn't here. I wonder what Sully is doing tonight.

Banging on the door again, I still get no answer. This time I turn the doorknob, and surprisingly it twists. As I push open the door, a sense of dread rushes toward me. "Nikki, tell me you aren't this stupid."

I flip up the light switch. Yellowish light spills from an overhead fixture onto what I can only describe as chaos. Several chairs are overturned. There's a stain on the wall, and glass fragments scattered in the carpet wink in the light. A purse is dumped out, and there's a wallet lying on the floor. I carefully poke around. There's twenty bucks in cash, but the driver's license slot is empty. I'm not sure if this bag belongs to Nikki or not.

There are two bedrooms. I move toward the one on the right and carefully push open the door. With the flip of a switch, light peters out over sheets, and the coverlet is rumpled and tossed on the floor. In the center of the graying sheets is a bloodstain bracketed by two strands of rope. Shit. What the hell?

My heart beats faster. I don't have to imagine what happened here. I've lived it.

There's no sign of Nikki near or under the bed. In the bathroom there's an array of beauty products and several half-snorted lines of coke on the counter. The curtain is closed. Palms dampen as I reach for the plastic curtain. Bracing, I yank it back.

The tub is empty. However, the walls and shampoo bottle are splattered with blood.

I grow dizzy, and for a moment it feels as if I'm being pulled from my body. Old memories I work hard to contain push out of their cages and reach out to me.

"You deserved everything you got," he growls. *"Only bleach is going to clean the sin off you."*

Rage bubbles and boils, burning up my throat. I back out of the room, aware that my DNA is sprinkled around this crime scene. I open the other bedroom door. The bedding has been stripped off, and the dresser drawers are open and empty. The walls are bare except for the tiny corner of a poster. Someone ripped it off in a hurry.

A roommate? My guess is he or she knows something about what happened in Nikki's room. Hearing, seeing, or finding evidence of the violence would've been enough to freak anyone out.

I back out of this room and move to the kitchen. The refrigerator is filled with a take-out pizza box, a half carton of milk that hasn't expired, and a bottle of vodka.

I leave the trailer, careful to wipe the edge of my shirt over the doorknobs. Yeah, my DNA is in the apartment, but no sense leaving prints everywhere and making it easy for the cops if or when they show.

In my car, I press into the seat. Chills roll over my skin, and my hands tremble slightly as I grip the wheel. People have gathered and are staring at me.

Out of the car, I move toward the crowd. "Have you seen Nikki?"

A woman wearing a tank top and jean shorts takes a long drag on a cigarette. "Who?"

"Nikki." I jab my thumb toward Nikki's trailer. "The young woman who lives here."

"Don't know a thing about her. Has she lived here long?"

"A couple of weeks." I glance at the group. Most of them are so drunk I doubt they can remember their own names. "Anyone else seen Nikki?"

One guy with thinning shoulder-length brown hair, deeply tanned skin, and a gold front tooth sips a beer. "I saw her Friday night. She was rushing to work."

"Was she with anyone?" I ask.

"Nope," the guy says. "All alone. But she's had guys here before."

"Who hasn't?" the first woman says.

"Any of these guys hurt her?" I press.

The man sips his beer again. "I don't put my nose in anyone's business."

"Did anyone hear screams or shouts coming from the trailer in the last twenty-four hours?"

A few folks shake their head no.

Back in my car, I'm frustrated that it's so easy for any of us to vanish. Women like Nikki go missing all the time, and generally someone has heard something, even if they won't admit it.

I grab my bat and get back out of my car. I call out to the woman I just spoke to. "Hey, is there a manager here?"

She lights a cigarette. "Lois takes the rent for the slots. She's in the first trailer."

"Thanks." I still might get lucky and find someone who's seen her or noticed something.

As I approach the manager's trailer door, music pulses. Sounds like country western. Not my cup of tea, but what the hell. I bang one fist on the door and grip the bat with the other.

The music stops, and footsteps thud across what sounds like a carpeted floor. There's a hesitation, and then the door opens. The woman standing in front of me is tall and heavyset, and she wears her salt-and-pepper hair in an uneven ponytail.

"I'm Stevie Palmer." Attitude is critical. Can't let them get a whiff of nerves or indecision. "I'm here about Nikki."

"Why?" the woman asks.

"She owes me money. I'm looking for her. Trying to collect." If I sound the alarm about the blood in her trailer, this woman's going to lock up.

"Good luck. Haven't seen her in days. Rent is due each week, and this will be the third time she's been late." There's a slight hesitation in her gaze. "Who are you?"

I ignore the question. "Any idea where she went?"

"None."

"Does she have a roommate or a friend who might know where she's gone?"

"She did have a roommate for two weeks. Jana moved out a few days ago."

That was before Nikki went missing. "Were Nikki and Jana having troubles?"

Lois's expression fills with frustration. "As long as the rent arrives on time and I don't have to deal with cops, I don't ask."

"Did Jana leave a forwarding address?" I'm shoving questions at her as fast as possible before she starts firing her own back.

"She did, but I'm not giving that out."

I pull two twenties from my back pocket. "Just a little hint. I'm not looking for trouble. Just what's owed me."

The woman looks at the rumpled bills before taking them. "She works at a gift shop in Corolla. It's called Sea Change or something like that."

"Jana at Sea Change. In Corolla." I haven't been up that way in a long time. As I'm turning, I pause. "Anyone else ask about Nikki?"

"No."

"Did she have any regular visitors?"

The woman shoves the bills in her back pocket and starts to push the door shut. "I'm not a den mother, lady. Ask Jana. She should know." She shakes her head. "I've seen too many kids like Nikki. Think they can get out of this life if they can just find the right man. I've never seen that work."

"Right."

I walk back to my car, knowing if the cops ever show and see the blood in the rooms, that woman is going to mention me, the gal with muddy-brown hair. The one who was looking for money from Nikki.

That description fits dozens, if not hundreds, of people. And most never remember as well as they think. Facts, descriptions, and details all fade or get jumbled by emotions or life experiences.

But if she does remember me, the cops will be looking for Stevie Palmer. And guess what, they aren't going to find her. Why am I so sure? Because Stevie Palmer doesn't exist on paper. She's a figment of my imagination, and when the time comes, I'll retire her and create a new identity.

I'm not ready to call the cops. They might send a squad car eventually, but a girl like Nikki isn't on anyone's priority list. So, for now, I'll find a quiet spot, sleep for a few hours, and maybe Nikki will find her common sense and show up to work tonight.

Chapter Eleven

LANE

Sunday, December 31, 2023
7:00 a.m.

I wake to the beep of the microwave and the hum of the heating system powering up. The lights in the living room blink on. I spent the night on the couch, reading Stevie's diary while huddled under blankets, willing my dying phone to hang on. I don't remember when the phone finally died. I'm not sure how long I stared at the lightning flashing over the ocean or listened to thunder cracking as winds howled before I fell asleep.

My eyes burn with fatigue. Without my pills, I don't wake up as rested. Without the pills, I live in a constant state of fatigue. I keep telling myself when I get a job with benefits, I'll see a doctor who can dig deeper, but for now I've made do with the urgent care prescription. I'd love to know who the hell took my pills.

Pushing off the sofa, I move toward the kitchen and a stainless-steel coffee maker. Kyle loved his cup of morning brew and was a snob when it came to his brand. I don't care about, nor can I afford, fancy labels. If not for my job at the coffee shop, I'd always be drinking the grocery store brand. I just need caffeine, energy, juice to power me through the day.

I rummage through cabinets, find the coffee beans and the grinder. I've done this so much at work, the process is automatic.

When the machine is set and brewing coffee, the smell fills the room with scents that I always associate with hope. Hope for more energy. Hope for the next day that is a step closer to my degree. Hope that I might make a difference in someone's life.

The heating system is now humming, but the air remains cool. I fill my mug and then splash my favorite hazelnut creamer (thank you, Kyle, for remembering) and take a long sip. Cradling the cup, I absorb its warmth.

I look through the kitchen toward the base of the stairs. This house has an energy that leaves me uneasy.

Shifting from the stairs toward the sliding deck doors, I glance up at turbulent, blue-black clouds, plump with more rain. The ocean is unsettled, choppy, and hurls water over the beach up to the base of the dunes. The shoreline is littered with clumps of seaweed and shattered pieces of fencing cracked like matchsticks. It's going to be a few more hours before the tide recedes enough for me to leave.

As I turn from the window, I catch a flash of bright yellow off to my right. A closer look reveals a woman walking along the beach. She's wearing a lemony jacket, a black knit hat, leggings, and hiking boots. Seems odd to see the lone figure out there this early on such a cold day.

As she passes in front of the house, she looks up and waves. Automatically, I raise my hand and wave back.

She takes this as an invitation and moves toward the house. I'm torn between panic at having to make conversation and hunger for a little human contact.

Gulping another sip of coffee, I set the mug down and grab my coat, then unlock the back door. Outside a cold blast of air strikes me in the face. My eyes water, and I blink before I burrow my hands into my pockets and move across the back deck toward the stairs. The woman and I reach the bottom step at the same time.

"I see you made it." She's a little taller than me, but her frame is slighter. "I'm Devon."

I extend my hand, and she easily captures my fingers in warm leather gloves. "I'm Lane."

"You didn't get out in time."

"I fell asleep, and then it was too dark to drive out."

She chuckles. "That's the way it is this far from the city."

I'm used to the constant light from office buildings, navy yards, cars, streetlamps, and twenty-four-hour drugstores. "Thanks for letting me return to the house. I'll be out of here as soon as the tide recedes."

She glances toward the roaring waves rolling to within feet of us. "That may or may not happen today. There's more rain on the way, and the cattle guard is flooded."

Another night in the house shrouded in cold darkness and restless energy. "Are you sure I can't get out?"

"Yep."

"Right."

"Stay as long as you need. There's no rush."

"Thanks."

"Are you doing okay?" She meets my gaze.

"Bruised and banged up, but nothing that won't heal." My neck isn't broken, and my skull isn't shattered. "How about you?"

"Don't worry about me." She regards me for a beat. "You know the fall isn't your fault, right?"

Why would she feel the need to say that? "I know. Are people saying otherwise?"

"People gossip."

It's not people I'm worried about but Detective Becker. If he's fishing for a crime, he might scoop up enough to mold into a case. "I suppose I can't stop the gossip."

"If it's worth anything, Kyle would hate anyone talking badly about you. He really liked you. When he called and said he was bringing a guest, I could hear the joy in his voice."

I'm glad I made him happy, even for a few weeks. "Thank you for saying that."

Devon brushes a damp curl from her face. "I imagine this is the last place you want to be right now. I'd have brought your things to you."

"I appreciate it. But I needed to be here. The fall didn't seem real until I walked back through the front door."

"TV doctors call it closure, right?"

"I suppose." Nothing feels closed. In fact, it feels wide open, even more uncertain.

Her chest inflates with a deep inhale, and her eyes seem to look deep within me. "Do you have everything you need?"

My stomach clenches at the idea of staying here another night. "I have more than enough. Thank you."

"Kyle was always particular about his must-haves. But he was always like that when we were growing up."

"You've known him a long time?"

She grins. "Since we were little kids. We both grew up around here."

That's new information. Why didn't I know that? Seems like Kyle would have mentioned that fact at some point over the last few weeks. "He always claimed the Norfolk and Virginia Beach area was home base."

Devon's eyes narrow. "I know he said that, but this is where it all started."

"I'm sure he'd have told me sooner or later." The lie slips out easily. "What was he like as a kid?"

"Terrific." She beams when she talks about him. "Smarter than all of us put together. Kind of our leader."

My sadness, grief, or whatever you want to call it, feels paltry. My three-week relationship with Kyle doesn't compare to Devon's thirty-plus years of history with him. "I'm sorry for your loss."

"Thanks."

A gust of wind whips over the beach, sweeping stinging sand against my legs. "Do you know if funeral arrangements have been made?"

"There'll be a service in two weeks. He wanted his body cremated. Never liked the idea of being buried in the ground."

That's a common fear. "Who told you about the funeral?"

"Kyle left me in charge. He said if anything ever happened to him, I was to see him properly cremated."

"Oh, okay."

"Kyle gave me your phone number. I'll be sure to text or call when I have details. You don't mind that I call, right?"

"No. And thank you." A deep breath expands my lungs. Shifting away from Kyle's funeral, I toss a different line in the water. "I met Reece last night. He's an interesting guy. Did he know Kyle, too?"

"He did."

Her tone suggests tension. "Something is swirling under that statement."

Devon laughs. "I've never mastered subtle."

"Did Reece and Kyle not get along?"

"Reece and Kyle had some issues. But Kyle still sent a lot of work Reece's way. They were like brothers. Fight but still look out for each other. In the last few years, Kyle's not been up here as much, so they've been able to avoid each other pretty well."

"Reece was here on Friday fixing a pipe."

"That's right."

"He said he heard Kyle and me arguing right before the fall."

"Then I guess it's true." Devon's face softens a fraction. "Reece is a good guy. He wouldn't repeat a story like that if it wasn't true."

"We weren't fighting," I say, more to myself.

"You were if Reece said you were."

"Does he live up here?"

"He lives on the mainland and only comes these days when I call with a repair job. When I stepped into the house across the street and into two inches of water, I knew the cleanup was going to be big. Reece was my first call."

"You manage that house, too?"

"That one and a half dozen others. I'm the eyes and ears for the owners when they can't be here. When the houses are empty, I walk them all a few times a week."

Wind rolls over the deserted beach like tumbleweeds. Whatever glimpse of beauty I'd seen on Friday is gone. I don't like this place. It's too isolated. Too cold. Kyle said this area represented peace and belonging, but I don't see it.

"How long has Kyle owned this house?" I should know, but I realize all the conversations I had with Kyle didn't reveal much about his life. He always refocused the conversation on me. I never worried about it before now. I thought he was a private man, and I'd learn more during the getting-to-know-you part of our relationship.

Devon's head cocks. "He built this house about three years ago."

The house is stunning and pure luxury, but the route here through rutted sand, past exposed tree trunks, and around the shifting tides doesn't scream welcome. "This is all news to me. I thought Kyle was a city boy."

"He made himself into one. What he loved most about this area was the solitude. He liked breaks from city chaos."

I look around the barren beach, and I try to wrap my head around Kyle growing up in this raw and wild land. He was always so reserved, quiet. Polished. Prided himself on the way he dressed, living well, and making a name for himself. I liked that about him. It was nice to have someone pamper me, if only for a little while. "I can't picture Kyle as a child, much less growing up here."

"He was five when I first met him. He came from a family of three boys. All the Iverson boys ran wild up here. They all loved riding their father's truck up and down the beach and the dunes. They'd head toward the sound with their fishing poles, or they'd hike into the woodlands with their bows and arrows. If they had a tent, they could be gone for days."

I look up and down the beach. "Where are the woodlands?"

"Just west of Kyle's cottage. Follow the road due west. The woods runs along the North Carolina/Virginia border."

There's more to the area beyond the beach. Knowing there's uncharted territory triggers my curiosity. "How far away is it?"

"Less than a mile." Devon smiles. "If you walk up there, be careful. There are folks there that don't like outsiders."

Her warning is unsettling. "Outsiders. Seems odd to call someone that today."

"That's because you live in the city, where everyone is connected."

A faint, unsettled smile tugs the corners of my lips. "Sounds like Kyle was a real Huck Finn."

"If that means he was smart as hell and loved adventure, then yes, that was Kyle. I don't think that guy ever forgot any fact he heard."

"Where are his brothers and parents?"

"His parents died years ago. Cancer. Big smokers. Kyle was the oldest. The middle boy, Jeb, was in jail for years. He was released in July but overdosed within days of getting out in a motel in Elizabeth City. The youngest boy, Zeke, is also dead. Drugs. The summer before Kyle's junior year of college."

"I didn't know that." None of these facts fits the perfect life Kyle projected when we were together. The university diplomas on his walls are a long way from here.

"How did he get from here to Georgetown?" I ask.

"He blew the doors off the SATs," Devon says with pride. "He ended up with scholarships to several colleges."

"You're staring," Kyle says as he stands behind me in his beach cottage.

My attention is drawn to the Georgetown diploma. "That's an impressive education."

"Be proud of your accomplishments." Energy radiates from his body.

"I am." I was. And I wasn't. *Public college is nothing to be ashamed of, but it doesn't open the kind of doors his pedigree does. "I never thought I'd be where I am now."*

"What else do you want to accomplish?"

"After I earn my PhD? Find a job with benefits and pay a few bills. Beyond that, I don't know. There is no grand plan for my life. I stumble from day to day, studying, serving coffee, and telling myself it's all good."

"Don't worry. The future will take care of itself."

"Where did he live when he was growing up?" I ask.

Devon smiles. "His folks had a small place down the road near the forest. His people have been up here for a few generations."

"What did they do? How did they make a living?"

Devon's shoulder raises and drops. "This and that. It's what most folks do up here. Fishing, construction, or hunting guides. His brothers were a lot like Kyle. Smart. Ambitious. All of them were good at hunting and tracking. But the younger boys decided their way out wasn't by using their brains but selling drugs."

"Drugs?"

"All these beaches with no one watching . . ."

I glance out toward the restless ocean. I thought I'd been getting to know Kyle, but now I realize we were virtual strangers.

"Kyle never did anything like that," Devon says. "He was focused on the future."

Kyle had a future until forty-eight hours ago. He was alive, eating, drinking, and anxious to make love to me. And then nothing.

I clear my throat. It's tempting to keep pressing about Kyle, but I suddenly don't want to know any more. "Much appreciated."

"Happy to help. And if you need me to cook for you, let me know."

"Cook?"

"I cooked for Kyle a lot when he was up here. He loved good meals, but he didn't have the patience for the work. I was supposed to cook for you two on Friday night."

"Really?" Seems odd Kyle would have wanted someone else in the house when we were really getting to know each other.

"He was going to surprise you."

"Wow. That's so nice."

"Seriously, if you need me, call. I'm minutes down the road, near the forest and woodlands."

"Will do."

This is Kyle and Devon's world, and I'm the interloper. I need to leave before the afternoon storms. Time to move on, close the door to the past.

A cold wind blows off the water, slithering under my jacket and sliding up my spine. "Thanks, Devon. I'm going back inside to make sure all my things are collected."

"Be prepared to stay longer. The beach isn't letting anyone travel today."

"Right."

"The place is yours for as long as you want it."

"Great."

I toss Devon one last wave before shoving my hands into my pockets and trudging over the dunes toward the house. My head is ducked as I push against the wind's icy hands that shove me forward.

Back at the house, I open the sliding glass doors and step into warmth. I don't feel relieved as I close and lock the door behind me. This house doesn't want me here, but the beach is determined to keep me here for now.

I walk to the base of the stairs, careful not to stand where Kyle's body had lain. The longer I linger, the more questions claw the underside of my skin. "What were we fighting about?"

We couldn't have been fighting. We were only in the house an hour. I was smiling, excited when we stepped in the front door. He showed me the kitchen, then his office, and his hand had pressed against the base of my spine as we climbed the stairs toward the bedrooms. I was sipping from a champagne flute when he flipped on the bedroom light.

I paused when I saw the big bed. I dropped my purse as he set my overnight bag down.

He lays a hand on my shoulder. "Nervous?"

"Sure, a little." I face him. "Aren't you?"

"No." He traces my collarbone with his thumb. I'm nervous about the idea of sex. He knows that and is charmed. "Have another sip of champagne."

Crystal brushes my lips. "I'll be drunk and asleep before you know it."

Smiling, he kisses my lips. "I'll keep you awake."

"I don't want to disappoint you."

"You won't. I've been waiting for this moment for a long time."

And then we were at the top of the stairs. I was annoyed. Agitated, even. Why? What would have upset me in a matter of minutes?

Maybe I brushed past him, slipped, and he grabbed me hoping to stop my fall. Bad, random shit does happen to people.

"Kyle, what happened?"

The persistent uneasiness that has stalked me since I arrived won't release me. I thought coming here would give me closure, but the longer I'm here, the more questions I have.

The house feels small. It has four thousand square feet, vaulted ceilings, and massive windows. But as I stand by the stairs, the air in the house shrinks, tightens around my throat until I don't feel like I can breathe.

"Are you here, Kyle?" I whisper.

The wind blows outside, thumping against the windows. The house sways gently. The ocean roars.

Of course he's not here. He's gone. Dead. We knew each other all of three weeks. Hardly a great love.

Shrugging off my jacket, I snag a water from the refrigerator and climb the main staircase.

"Why do I think you're keeping big secrets, Kyle? Why can't I just leave and forget you?"

Chapter Twelve

LANE

Sunday, December 31, 2023
9:00 a.m.

A hush penetrates the house. I can almost feel Kyle standing behind me, laughing softly in my ear as I move into his bedroom. I open the closet and stare at the jackets, pants, and shirts hanging in a neat row. There's a blazer that's well made and suits his world in Virginia Beach. I open the coat to search the breast pockets, and as I do the faint scent of Kyle reaches out. I press the jacket's sleeve against my nose and inhale more of him.

Kyle wouldn't approve of me searching his pockets or his desk drawers. He'd likely talk very logically about boundaries and minding one's own business.

I'll be a psychologist soon. I'll get paid to root in personal lives. Maybe not literally, but I reason if the shoe was on the other foot, Kyle would wander around my apartment, trying to discover more about me.

Still, I feel disapproval pressing against my shoulders like invisible hands.

"I'm sorry. But I have to." My fingers fish inside the front pocket and skim over a small set of keys tucked in a corner. I pluck them out and hold them up. They're small enough to fit a desk drawer lock.

I move toward the stairs and pause at the top. For a moment, a wave of dizziness swirls around me. Hand on the railing, I draw in a breath and move down the steps. At the bottom, I feel energy gush faster, as if an unhappy Kyle is watching.

Gripping the keys tighter, I hurry into the office and sit at Kyle's desk. My hands shake slightly as I work the key into the lock. It doesn't turn. Pulling the key out, I flip it over and push it in again.

"Please, please, please." I hear the note of begging and wonder why I'm so desperate and determined.

The key turns, and the well-oiled lock releases a latch.

My mouth is dry as I glance forward, expecting to see Devon, Reece, or even Kyle standing there. Of course, I'm alone with only my guilt.

Catching my breath, I whisper, "I'm not stealing. I'm not doing anything wrong." Why am I being so quiet? Because I feel guilty.

I pull open the drawer and discover a thick, black-bound journal. The leather binding is rich, smooth, and I know this style of journal was a favorite of Kyle's. He always had a version of this book (maybe this one) tucked under his arm when we met for morning coffee. I joked about it once, saying, *Dear Diary, I love my life.* A smile had flickered at the edges of his lips, but I sensed he hadn't liked me noticing or mentioning the book.

Heart beating faster, I open it. On page one Kyle has written Dr. Kyle J. Iverson, PhD, and his phone number. I smooth my hands over his bold lettering tucked in the upper left-hand corner.

Carefully, I turn the page. It's blank. I run my fingers over the linen paper and feel the faint, soft impression of a word. I grab a pencil from the leather holder, then snatch a piece of paper from the printer on the credenza behind the desk and place it over the pages. Gently, I lay the side of the pencil on the paper and rub it softly over the impressions. An *S* appears, then a *T* and an *E* before the full word materializes.

Stevie.

"Stevie." I can't be 100 percent certain he's referring to Stevie Palmer, but I'm 99.9 percent there.

Why had Kyle written down Stevie's name?

Kyle knew Stevie. And she clearly knows me. These two facts can't be random.

Did she see me with Kyle? Is she trying to make a point? Maybe the two of them had had a thing before, and she's pissed and messing with me now.

The chair squeaks as I lean back. My face feels hot, likely flushed with color. "Stevie, what's going on here?"

I picture Kyle and me standing at the top of the stairs, but this time a different image flashes in my mind. Kyle is holding my arm tightly, staring down at me with a mixture of mirth and malevolence.

The impression vanishes as quickly as it appeared. But suddenly the house is shrinking again. An invisible rope tightens around my neck. I need fresh air. Space.

Crushing the page in my hand, I grab my coat and hat and head out the front door into the cold. The wind remains strong, biting even, and the sun is trying but failing to breach the clouds.

Hands in my pockets, I walk down the stairs and toward the dirt road that runs west toward the sound and the woodlands and the forest. There are several houses in this area, but they're all dark with no signs of life. Across the street, the lights are on in Reece's house. He didn't mention that he'd grown up with Kyle. It would've been nice to have heard that from him, but he has no obligation to share data with a woman who shouldn't be here anyway.

As I reach the cross street and head west, I spot something from the corner of my eye. I turn and see two black horses. One is a stallion and the other a mare. The stallion snorts and paws at the ground as the mare eyes me. Clearly, they don't want me here. I wait until they move along. This place is raw, wild, and I best not forget it can strike back hard.

I walk in the direction of the sound, the forest, and the place where Kyle grew up. I've no idea where I'm going, but I want to be a little more familiar with the area where Kyle lived as a child.

Kyle left this world far behind, and it's clear he wasn't proud of his roots. One brother dead from an overdose and the other an ex-con who suffered the same fate. Those facts are two pearls on what I suspect now is a strand of misery.

Kyle was always aware of how he dressed, the car he drove, and all forms of personal grooming. On our second date, that perfection obsession set its sights on me. He offered to take me shopping, and when I politely refused, he still bought and gifted me several dresses to choose from for our next date. I could've paid my rent for two months with the cost of those dresses.

I wanted to please him, but I was also thrilled by the soft satins and silks. I wore the indigo-blue dress the next night when we went out to dinner. I felt pretty. Special. No one had ever taken that much interest in me, and after a lifetime of being invisible, I was flattered by the attention.

At dinner, he leans forward, staring at me as if I were the only person in the world.

"Do you like the dress and the restaurant? Far cry from school and the coffee shop."

For a few moments I'd distanced myself from my schoolwork and a difficult day with a patient. I'd wanted this night to be about me. Not about anyone else. But he needs to hear he's swept me away.

"I feel a little like Cinderella. Pretty soon, it's going to strike midnight, and I'll be back in my sweats and sneakers."

He sips his wine, smiles as if sensing I've lied. "How did work go this week?"

"The faces of the women I see change, but the problems are remarkably similar. I want to think I'm making a difference, but I'm not so sure I am."

"It's frustrating to see someone self-select over and over. A patient can be so close to a breakthrough, and then they do something to ruin it all. All that preprogramming in the subconscious mind gets in the way."

"You're right. There are a thousand reasons why many won't be saved."

"Good thing you don't need saving."

I chuckle, and the tension banding my lower back eases. "I'm not so sure about that. There were times when I could've used a rescue."

His gaze sharpens. "Why did you need saving?"

It's frightening I'm falling for a man I barely know. "Don't we all?"

"What's the worst thing that happened to you?" He's watching me closely when the waiter arrives at the table with our dinners. I sit back, folding my hands, and I'm grateful I don't have to answer. I'm hoping he's distracted by the beef tenderloins and sautéed mushrooms.

However, when we're alone again, he says, "You didn't answer."

"Because nothing terrible has happened to me."

He raises a glass of wine and smiles. "If I had you in my office, I'd challenge that statement."

A cold wind teases the edges of my jacket. Now as I look around the desolate land, I shake off my unease. I suppose it makes sense a psychologist would ask a deep question or press for an answer.

"Who are you?"

A man's voice startles me, and I whirl around. I was so lost in thought I didn't hear him approach. He's tall, lean, grizzled. A length of rawhide binds long black hair, accentuating hollow cheeks covered in stubble. His jeans, boots, and old black puffer jacket are worn and dusty.

I clear my throat. "I'm just a tourist. Walking around."

"We don't get tourists up here this time of year." He steps toward me. His eyes narrow as they study me.

It's just the two of us here. No one to hear me scream. "I'm just here for the day."

He steps closer, only a few feet away. "You're staying at Kyle's house, aren't you?"

I stiffen. "Why do you say that?"

"I saw the lights on." A grin draws up the left side of his thin lips. "You're the one that killed him."

My body tenses. "I didn't kill him. It was an accident."

His grin bares uneven, yellow teeth as he angles his head toward me. "That's not how I heard it. Some say you pushed him."

I've walked several blocks away from the beach house. All around me are thick woods. It feels as if I've been transported to another place and time. "No, why would I kill him?"

"Because maybe you figured out what kind of a man he really was." His voice shakes with trepidation, as if saying what he's said out loud could get him into trouble.

"What do you mean by that?" I demand. "What kind of man was Kyle?"

"You know." There's a wariness in his eyes. "You know better than anyone."

Tires crunch on the road behind me, and I step to the edge of the road as my fingers ball into fists. The man sees the truck and his grin widens.

The truck slows and then stops just a few feet to my left. Tinted windows make it difficult to see inside the cab, but I'm very aware that the driver is looking at me.

As the driver's-side window lowers, the man approaches the truck. "Hey, I heard you were back."

"Earl, what're you doing out?"

I recognize Reece's voice and relief washes over me. I don't really know Reece, but he's the closest I have to familiar right now.

"Just talking with the pretty lady," Earl says. "She's trying to get to know Kyle better. I was helping her."

"You're drunk, Earl," Reece growls. "No one needs to hear your drunken craziness."

"Might be crazy and drunk." He taps his index finger against the side of his head. "But I know things."

"We don't need your trouble," Reece cautions.

I'm scared of Earl, but I also want to hear what he has to say. Too many ignore the mentally ill, thinking they can't speak the truth. But without the filters of social propriety, they can be very honest.

"I ain't caused no trouble," Earl says. "Ask her."

"Good," Reece says. "Go on, then."

"Don't know why you want to be up here, girl," Earl says. "Seems this would be the last place anyone would ever find you."

"Go," Reece warns.

Earl moves along the truck, glances at me over the hood, and winks. Without saying another word, he vanishes into the thick, tall grass.

"What are you doing up this way?" Reece doesn't sound happy.

"Exploring, I thought. I needed to get out of the house and walk." Basically true. "Devon told me there are woodlands ahead."

"This is not the place to walk alone. We've got a few residents like Earl who don't like strangers. Up this way you've officially left vacation land."

The sentence dangles and allows me space to fill in several terrible scenarios. "How did you know I was here?"

"I saw you leave the house. You can't be careful enough. Earl isn't a harmless drunk. He has a real violent streak, especially when it comes to women."

My cheeks flush like a scolded child's. Embarrassment washes away the last of relief. "Why are you so interested in my safety?"

The anger flaring in his gaze cools to concern. "Look, you seem nice, Lane. You've had a bad time. I don't want to see you get hurt again."

As I look down the road, I know I'm out of my depth here. The side alleys of Norfolk are familiar territory, but not this untamed place. "Devon told me you both grew up here with Kyle."

Reece draws in a breath. "That's right."

"She said you and Kyle didn't get along."

"Life took us in separate directions, is all. No harm, no foul."

Who was Kyle Iverson? He swept into my life, tried to remake me, died at my side, and knew a missing woman named Stevie Palmer?

As I stand my ground, I feel less like an errant kid. I find a steadier voice. "I can't picture Kyle here."

"Three weeks is hardly enough time to get to know a person."

"True, but—"

Reece is shaking his head and cuts me off. "Get in the truck. I'll drive you back."

"I can walk back."

"Lane, it's not safe. Please, get in the truck."

Hearing his concern, I slide into the passenger-side seat, grateful to be off my hip and inside the truck's warmth, which chases after the chill burrowing in my bones.

"Tell me about Kyle," I say.

He stares out the windshield. "He always talked about getting out. He hated living up here. Didn't want any part of this life. Seemed once he did escape, he'd never look back."

"Escape. Is that how you feel about this place?"

"There's a lot of raw beauty up here. But it's a hard living."

"If Kyle detested this area so much, why build a house up here?"

"Take the boy out of the woodlands . . ."

"But not the woodlands out of the boy," I say.

"He liked his privacy, and it doesn't get much more private than up here." His frown deepens. "We've got more weather coming in. It could be a rough night."

My original plan to grab and go now feels inadequate. Weather aside, I realize, I'm not ready to leave yet.

"Leave as soon as you can," he says. "No good will come of you being here."

"I'm not doing anything wrong."

He shakes his head. "You're better off returning to your regular life. Forget about Kyle and this place. Consider yourself lucky you survived."

"I'm not ready to go." I'm surprised at the force in my voice, so I soften it a little. "Not yet."

"Why? What is here for you?"

"I'm not sure." Seeing Stevie's name in the journal triggered a shift in me. Earl's comments raised fresh questions. He stared at me as if he were looking at a ghost. "Devon said I could stay for a few more days. I think I'll be fine."

He frowns. "If you want a tour of the forest and woodlands, I can take you."

It's just the two of us out here now. I don't know this guy, and my Spidey sense tingles along the back of my neck like it does when I'm crossing a dark Norfolk parking lot. I have my cell, but it's not fully charged, and reception bars are scarce and flickering. I reach for my door handle just in case. "I want to see the house where Kyle grew up."

His hands tighten slightly on the steering wheel before he releases a careful breath. "I'll show you where we grew up. The sooner you're satisfied, the sooner you can leave."

More bait in the water. "Fair enough."

"Our world is very different from the beach cottage where you're staying."

I realize now, I might have come back to the cottage for my phone, pills, and wallet, but even without that excuse, I would have returned to calm an unease that found me when Kyle and I first drove onto the beach.

Reece pauses, as if questioning himself, and then he shifts into drive. Tires roll slowly, carrying us both deeper into the interior. The forest of twisted live oaks and pines lining the road thickens.

Removing my gloves, I hold chilled fingers up to the heating vent before clicking my seat belt. "How close did you live to Kyle?" I ask.

"Everyone is close to everyone up here. It's all walking distance." He smells faintly of sawdust. His hands are deeply tanned, and his skin is rough from construction work in hard weather. So unlike Kyle.

"Did you see each other often?"

"Every day. We went to school together."

"Where is school here?"

"In Kitty Hawk."

"This is Currituck County. Kitty Hawk is in Dare County." I'm not sure where I pull that fact from.

"Currituck had a deal with Dare back then. Dare took kids like us, so we didn't have a two-hour ride to school."

"That's still a hike."

"It was. Enough to encourage anyone who wanted to ditch to skip." He rolls his head from side to side. "Kyle never missed school. He'd check the weather the night before. His mother hated getting up so early, but he'd pester her to do it. Once he got his driver's license, he never let me skip."

"I sensed he was a very motivated man." Intense, driven, focused, and when that attention shifted to me, it was intoxicating. Had I become the next conquest? I'm not sure how long I'd have been comfortable with Kyle's constant texts and calls. "Are your parents still here?" I ask.

"No. Both are dead. Living up here isn't an easy life."

"But you came back."

"For work." He's making this very clear. "Devon called me, and I can't say no to her."

"You didn't return for old times' sake?" My ability to tease is rusty, and I see immediately my words don't land well.

"No."

"Right."

He immediately shifts the conversation back toward me. "Where'd you grow up?"

"Norfolk."

"Family?"

"My mother died when I was young. Foster homes after that."

"That had to be rough. Being alone, I mean."

I swivel my gaze toward the windshield. "It wasn't terrible."

"But not great, right?"

"I'm here now. Still standing." I don't want to talk about me. "How long will it take to fix the flood damage in the house across the street?"

"Weeks, maybe months. My crews will be here in a few days, and then we'll really get moving. I was the only one available to handle the immediate damage control."

"No holidays for you."

"New Year's isn't my favorite holiday. Too many festivities." A smile flicks his lips. "Plus, it's good work in a slow economy. You know Kyle owned that house, right?"

"I didn't know that. How many houses did he own up here?"

"He built just the two, and then there's the house he would've inherited from his brother's estate if it's ever settled. Jeb, his brother, owned the family house, but it's mired in unpaid back taxes."

"I had no idea." I shake my head. "I'm saying that a lot."

His brow furrows. "What were you and Kyle fighting about?"

I'm silent, trying to decide if the truth is the right hand to play. "I still don't remember anything right before the fall. It's like a switch flipped in my head. I think Kyle was annoyed with me, but I don't know why. Did you hear what we were saying?"

Reece is silent before he shakes his head. "I couldn't make out the words."

"You mean mine?"

Again, more silence. "You were shouting, screaming. If Kyle was saying anything, I didn't hear him."

That still doesn't sound right. "Are you sure someone else wasn't in the house? Devon said she was going to cook for us. Maybe she came in early and was the woman you heard."

"There was no one else in the house that I saw," he says.

"How do you know? Did you search it?"

His gaze is steady, but he shifts his grip on the wheel. "I didn't see anyone else. What are you getting at?"

"I still can't believe we could've had a knock-down, drag-out fight within an hour of arriving. We were kissing moments before."

He grimaces, shifts away from me, leaning on the door, as if he doesn't want to know about Kyle and me. "I found you both at the bottom of the stairs. I called 9-1-1, and then I checked on you and Kyle. You were unconscious, but you had a heartbeat. Kyle didn't, so I started chest compressions. He never responded, but given the blood and the angle of his neck, I wasn't surprised. I worked on him for fifteen minutes before the rescue squad and sheriff arrived."

I raise my hands to my lips, stifling a sob. "The rescue squad arrived here that fast? All the way up here?"

"We've a rescue squad a couple of miles from here. They serve this area. Once they arrived, they immediately called the med flight, and you were airlifted to Norfolk. The detective talked to the paramedics on the phone and insisted that Kyle's body stay behind."

"Detective Becker."

"That's right."

"I spoke to him on Friday. How long did it take him to get here?"

"Less than an hour."

"That fast?"

"I guess he was on this side of the bridge when he got the call."

Detective Becker. He's popping up everywhere. "What kind of questions did he ask?"

"He wanted to know about you and Kyle. I told him I heard you two fighting. After that he walked the house and then asked me the questions again. Cops like to see if your answer changes. Mine didn't."

"He said the medical examiner ruled Kyle's death *undetermined*." I let the word hang in the air. "Even if Kyle and I had been squabbling, I still don't understand why Detective Becker would've assumed the fall was anything more than an accident."

"It was more than a squabble. You were very upset. And then there was silence. It didn't feel right, so I checked."

"Upset? Screaming." The words sound distant, disconnected from me. "That's not me. I keep my emotions under a tight lid."

"They weren't on Friday." He glances at me as if trying to reconcile what he's heard with my words.

Kyle's frown flashes, and I'm suddenly clamping down on anger. I can almost feel his fingers tightening on my arms.

Reece slows the truck and turns down a small, rutted dirt road. I grip the door to steady myself and maybe brace a little to jump out if necessary. This is the place a man takes a woman if he wants to kill her.

He stops in front of a small house on pilings. The wood siding is grayed by harsh weather and sun. The windows are shuttered. Tall grass grows up around the pilings, nearly reaching the front porch. There's an old truck covered with a tarp.

"How far are we from the beach?" I ask.

"About a mile."

"It feels light-years away," I say, more to myself.

Seat leather creaks when he leans back. As he looks toward the house, he's tapping his thumb against the steering wheel. "This is the house where Kyle grew up."

I can't reconcile the polished man I knew with this tired, deserted place. There was never a hint of a southern accent to soften his words or any mention of a humble upbringing. He often said he was a city boy. "It looks abandoned."

"It has been since Jeb was sent to prison."

"Was Kyle planning on fixing it up?"

"He never said a word about this place to me."

"He said one of the worst things you can do to a person is ignore them." This place has been disregarded, forgotten, and is literally falling in on itself. It's a slow, painful death.

"It would cost a fortune to fix this place up. It's not worth the land it stands on."

Kyle was so meticulous with everything he touched. He could have tried to keep this place up over the years while Jeb was in prison, but he didn't. "He wanted this place to suffer."

"Suffer?" Reece flinches and then shakes his head. "It's a house, Lane."

"No, it's a symbol, a warning, to where he came from and how far he could fall." I'd come from nothing, and the higher I rise, the more I fear falling backward. "When you have nothing to lose, risk is easy. It's only difficult when you have skin in the game."

"Kyle was never afraid of anything." Awe and disdain intertwine under the words. "This place is just a house."

I stare at an open shutter, a salt-streaked window, and the sinking roof. "Was it so horrible to live here?"

"I don't think it was good," Reece says carefully.

The gray siding is brittle and breaking. The main support beam of the house appears to be caving in on itself. "Kyle never told you what it was like for him here?"

Reece shook his head. "Kyle never told anyone anything. He kept his secrets to himself." He tilts his gaze toward the horizon. "I guess that's why Kyle was good at what he did. No one wants a shrink that talks too much, right?"

I think about the notebook and the traced impression. *Stevie.* "He never talked to you about his patients?"

Reece chuckles as if the question is crazy. "No. We barely saw each other, and when we did, we talked about construction. The next house to build."

"You built Kyle's two houses?"

"I did."

"But you never talked about fixing this place?"

"No." His fingers tighten on the steering wheel.

Reece is a gifted craftsman who might've been able to resurrect this hovel into a rental property. Yet here it sits, abandoned and crumbling.

I look through the tall weeds to the stairs and wonder if they are sturdy enough for me. "Can we walk around the property?"

He glances at my shoes. "No. Athletic shoes won't cut it around here."

"It's all I have."

"We can walk toward the house but not that close. The structure is not safe."

"What's going to happen to the house now?" I ask.

"I don't know. You'll have to ask Kyle's lawyer."

I'm curious about the house, so I tug on my gloves, open my door, and step off the road toward it. I don't wait for Reece to come around his truck and join me. Tall grass brushes the sides of my legs.

As I move closer to the structure, a knot tightens in my chest. If houses have an aura, this one's very dark. My nerves draw tight like a stretching bowstring. I can't reconcile the upbeat Kyle I knew with this place.

"When was the place abandoned?" I ask.

"Fifteen years ago, give or take." I think about Stevie's diary. She was taken to a place like this. Is this house the reason she's reaching out to me?

I angle through the grass along a narrow footpath. The sandy ground is uneven and littered with old, corroded beer cans. This is perfect refuge for anyone looking to drink or do drugs.

I'm drawn to the house. I've always had a soft spot for broken people. I want to fix and rehabilitate them. Maybe houses are no different.

"Stop," Reece says as he reaches out for my arm. His grip is firm but not painful. "There's an abandoned well and septic field on the site. Both are nearby, and with all the grass growth, I'm not exactly sure where they are."

I'm tempted to pull out of his grip and keep moving. I want—need—to know more about Kyle. And I suspect there are more answers in this old, discarded hovel than the pristine beach house.

I turn toward him. Frown lines are deeper around his mouth. "Aren't you curious about the house?"

"No." The tension radiating in him bleeds into me as I stare at the house. "A place like this has nothing good to offer."

I disagree. Leaving this area will be hard without another visit. I'll return alone. When Reece isn't watching.

Chapter Thirteen

LANE

Sunday, December 31, 2023
10:30 a.m.

Reece parks his truck in front of Kyle's house. When I get out, I glance back at him. He's leaning toward the steering wheel, watching me. "Thanks for the tour."

"Sure." He runs fingers through his thick, dark hair. "Remember to stay away from that area. It's not safe."

"Is Earl going to be a problem?"

"Not if you stick to this area. He doesn't like it up this way."

"Okay." I close the truck door.

Reece appeared after the fall and just now. It feels like he's looking out for me. Maybe out of a sense of loyalty to Kyle.

The lines around his eyes and mouth, the strong jaw, and his broad, muscled shoulders create a sexy image. And I like him. Which doesn't say much about me, considering forty-eight hours ago my almost-boyfriend and I had just arrived for a weekend getaway.

The tires of Reece's truck grind against the sand as he turns his vehicle around and drives down the road toward the beach exit. I'm surprised he's leaving.

I climb the stairs and plug in the security code numbers. The lock turns, and I push open the door.

After being in the cold on those deserted side roads, I'm oddly relieved to be back in this house even though it feels as if it still doesn't want me. It might have begrudgingly welcomed me with Kyle, but now I'm the interloper. The trespasser. But it's the closest thing I have to a home base today.

Glancing toward the stairs, I pause, then glower at the scrubbed white floor. Devon is as present in this house as Kyle.

My stomach grumbles, and suddenly I realize I'm starving again. My appetite has returned with a vengeance.

I grab all the luncheon meats, lettuce, condiments, and bread. Within a few minutes, I'm eating. Filling my belly calms the grumbling but doesn't soften the sense of unease burning in my chest. Coming here wasn't a good idea. And still, I'm in no rush to leave.

When I'm finished, I put my plate in the sink, and then I walk into Kyle's office and switch on the lights. I move past his desk to the closet behind it. Door open, I stare into the sterile space, inhale the scent of fresh paint.

When I was a small child, I remember climbing into the closet in my room, burrowing behind the clothes, and closing my eyes. Beyond the closed door, I could hear my mother shouting. She was arguing with a man, a different one each week it seemed. I still don't recall those arguments, but the anger and venom behind them has always lingered like a bad smell you can't clear from your nose.

My mother wasn't an evil person. She didn't choose to be a single mom. She wanted to love me as other moms do. She said often enough, *I should bake cookies for you. Braid your hair.* She loved me. I know she did. Yet loneliness drove her into the arms of men who didn't deserve her.

I never told any of this to Kyle. It was simply too soon in our relationship, though I wonder if time would've made a difference for me.

Maybe I would've told him one day. Maybe he would've opened up to me about whatever life he lived in that small house tucked in the woods.

Maybe not.

I happen to glance at my phone and see Detective Becker's name. I realize the phone has been on mute. I clear my throat. "Detective Becker."

"Lane, you found your phone. Did you lose it again?"

I see now I've missed three of his calls. "What can I do for you?"

"I'm headed your way."

"What do you mean? I'm not at home."

"I know. You're at Kyle Iverson's beach house."

"How do you know?"

"Your phone is pinging up there."

I glance at the phone. Traitor. "Terrific."

"I caught you off guard on Friday. Kind of an ambush. I didn't mean for our first meeting to be so contentious."

I suspect it went exactly as he'd hoped. "What's your point?"

"I want us to talk about the *accident*."

Did he put extra emphasis on the last word, or is my imagination firing out of control?

"I'm hoping since you've been at the house, a few memories have wrestled free," he says.

"I don't remember anything new," I lie.

"Doesn't take twenty-one hours to retrieve a phone."

"The weather has been bad. Driving south on the beach is too dangerous."

"You found your way in."

"Barely, it seems. The beach has changed. It's difficult to navigate now."

"I've driven in worse. Won't be a problem for me. Besides, if you have memories or any reactions to the house, it's my business. In case you forgot, a man died in that house two days ago."

"When I return home, I'll stop by your offices in western Currituck County."

"No need. Turns out, I'm less than ten minutes away from you. Just pulling off the beach now."

I close my eyes. "I don't want to see you."

"But I want to see you." An amused smile radiates behind the words.

"I need to call my attorney."

"Call away. See you in ten minutes."

The line goes dead, but my head pulses with his words. *I want to see you.* Why is he pushing this? What could have changed in a day and a half to redirect him back toward me?

He can't know that Stevie has been sending me her diary entries. Right? I glance at the PDF on my phone, open to the entry I read last night. Maybe she can tell me why Becker has focused his attention on me.

Chapter Fourteen

STEVIE PALMER'S DIARY

Tuesday, July 4, 2023
7:00 p.m.

Happy birthday, America!

The bar is packed. Normally, there's a slowdown on a Tuesday night, but not on the Fourth. Everyone wants to have a good time. Everyone wants to make toasts. Keep the happiness flowing from the beer taps.

I'm on the move from almost the moment I step behind the bar. I got lucky last night and found an unrented cottage, parked in the carport under the house, and slept five whole hours. I also slid into the YMCA and grabbed a shower. It felt good to wash the grime and sweat off my body. As I dried my hair, I could see that the brown rinse had faded a little. Not a big deal, but I do prefer the darker shade. After a big lunch, the heat drove me toward the outlet malls, where I wandered for hours. I bought a new black Graveyard of the Atlantic T-shirt, which I'm now wearing.

Joey carries a tray loaded with sandwiches toward a table of guys as I fill drink order after drink order. I move in a steady rhythm. I guess you could say, I'm in the zone.

I'm two hours into my shift when Bourbon walks into the bar. He looks much like he did days ago, wearing a navy-blue sport jacket, white open-collar shirt, and tan pants. I suspect if he has a tie, it's tucked in his pocket. If there was ever a guy that didn't fit in here, it's him. Not sure what brings him back, but I'm glad he's arrived. He's the last person I saw talking to Nikki.

He takes the same seat he had on his last two visits. Joey hustles behind me, grabs his order, and fills a tumbler with aged bourbon. Bourbon sips his drink slowly as his gaze roams the room.

His body language isn't relaxed or chill. He's tense and very alert. Several times Bourbon stares at a woman separated from her wing women, hesitates, then moves his gaze on to another woman. His fleeting interest suggests he's horny, but he's particular about Ms. Right-for-Now. If he hooked up with Nikki, she's a distant memory.

Over the next half hour, I keep my distance from Bourbon. My nerves tighten when I'm close. Though I'm tempted to shoot questions at him, time and life have taught me to move a little slower.

Joey gets distracted by a group of guys looking to do shots. As he lines up the five glasses and pours, I decide I'm not going to let my nerves keep me away from Bourbon. Run toward trouble, not away from it.

I duck around Joey. Bourbon's glass is half-empty—or half-full if you're an optimist, which I'm not.

"Can I top that off?" I ask.

Bourbon regards me with an intensity that sends a shiver sliding through my body. Even white teeth flash quickly, but not fast enough to blind me. This guy is trouble. He's dangerous.

Nothing like being on the receiving end of evil to know what it smells and tastes like. Pain has a way of honing your instincts and nurturing a sixth sense about bad people.

He slowly pushes his tumbler toward me, but his hand remains on the glass. In this moment, he controls my attention. Yep, control is his thing. His fingers release the glass. "Sure."

My smile widens. I grab the bourbon bottle and fill the glass beyond Joey's limit. I set the glass closer to him. I want him to think I'm into him. "Bottoms up."

He doesn't touch the glass. "What's your name?"

I grab a rag and wipe down the bar. "Stevie."

"You were here Saturday night."

"I was. I'm new here. Are you a regular?"

He raises the glass to his lips and pauses. "I get by a couple of times each summer."

Nothing about him screams local, but he could be a homeowner who visits regularly. "How'd you find us?"

"I've known about this place for years." A muscle pulses in his jaw.

"It's not always been Joey's, has it?"

"Used to be the Salty Dog."

"Okay."

He sips, falls into silence. He's said all he's going to say for now.

I catch the waggle of a glass in my peripheral vision. "Duty calls."

"You're on your own tonight?" he asks.

"Joey has had a hell of a time finding someone. The girl that worked with me ghosted us." I don't say Nikki's name. He sips his drink, and his eyes never waver in the slightest.

He doesn't react to news of a missing woman. But the best predators are successful for a reason. They can hide in plain sight as they sniff out not just the weak but also those willing to do anything to please. That describes Nikki.

The empty glass waiting for me requires a vodka refill. The customer is also ogling me. Yes, he's horny, but he doesn't give off a dangerous vibe. His type wants a drink, attention, and a bendable ear with a pair of tits. That makes me the complete package.

I fill his glass, then chat him up about his summer, the weather, and the song "Born to be Wild" playing on the sound system. He likes the attention, but soon I'm moving on to the next empty glass. It's all a numbers game for me. Drinks equal tips.

A woman approaches Bourbon, and she's smiling as she sips white wine. Bourbon is engaging, but he doesn't seem into her. If I had to guess, and I'm generally spot on, she's too aggressive for him. Her gaze is direct, her entire demeanor too bold. He likes women he can control.

The night drones on, customers get drunker, sloppier. Bourbon continues to chat up White Wine, and they are warming up to each other. She might not be his ideal, but she'll do for tonight.

The conversations get louder, happier, and a few times angrier. Once when two men push away from their table and send chairs toppling, Joey reaches for my bat, which is never far. He stalks toward both and shoves them away from each other. A few of their buddies separate the guys, giving Joey the space to wedge my bat between them. Joey announces they've had their last drink here tonight. Time to leave.

It's close to one in the morning when I collect the empty glasses, accept a few extra tips, smile, and wipe down the bar. Bourbon drains the last of his glass and holds it out for me as White Wine exits the ladies' room. As I take the glass, I let my fingers brush his, but I'm careful not to make eye contact.

"Have a good night, Stevie." A smile rumbles under his deep voice.

My name reverberates in my head as I settle the glass into a tub filled with empties. "You too, Bourbon."

"Bourbon?"

I smile. "In my line of work, you get to know people by their drinks. Easier that way."

An amused brow raises. "That's very efficient. Do you know everyone's drink here tonight?"

For some reason I want to prove I have an excellent memory. "Point to someone, and I'll tell you what they drink."

Bourbon nods toward a man downing the last of a tumbler. "That guy."

I look over my shoulder and see a tall, burly man with a beard and shoulder-length hair. "Gin and tonic."

"Really?"

"He likes a twist of lemon instead of lime. Had a rough Fourth of July. Ordered five, no, six drinks."

"Shouldn't you have cut him off?" Bourbon looks amused.

"His limit is around ten. He was going easy tonight. And he's Ubering back to his cottage."

"What about the short guy walking out of the restroom?" he asks.

"Tequila. Neat."

"Assuming you're right . . ."

"I'm right."

"Then you know your clients well." He rises and fishes a stack of twenties from his pocket.

My battle stance eases. Bourbon might open up if he thinks he's in control. "I like to think that I'm good at my job."

His gaze roams the room, settles briefly on White Wine. She smiles, tucks a strand of blond hair behind her ear. He beams a one-hundred-watt smile in her direction. "I bet you see a lot in this room."

I chuckle. "You would be surprised, Bourbon. Hey, quick question. Do you remember the gal working with me here the other night? Nikki. Cute girl, great figure. The one that ghosted us?"

"Hard to forget a woman who flirts so well."

"Did she say if she was leaving town or not? She owes me money. Be nice to settle up."

"She said something about moving to DC because she wanted to give the big city a try."

Nikki in DC. She can barely handle the bustle of Nags Head. Why would Bourbon lie about Nikki? All he had to say was he didn't remember her. "Thanks."

He lays the bills on the bar. "Take care, Stevie."

"You too, Bourbon."

Bourbon turns, eyes White Wine across the room who is now boldly staring at him. He always pays with cash, but White Wine uses a credit card. When I swipe it, I make a mental note. Jeanne Williams.

After closing, I open Joey's computer in the back room and log in to his Facebook account. I find Jeanne Williams easily. She lives in Chesapeake, Virginia, operates a home health service. There are several recent pictures of her on the Outer Banks. Sunsets, beach walks, seafood dinners. The usual lineup. I wonder if she'll post pictures from her date with Bourbon? Something tells me he's not fond of public attention.

"Stay safe, Jeanne Williams."

Chapter Fifteen

LANE

Sunday, December 31, 2023
11:15 a.m.

When the front doorbell rings, I've read several pages of Stevie's diary, combed my hair, and changed into clean jeans and a light-blue V-neck sweater. If I've learned anything from my job, it's not to show anger or frustration. I've also had my share of circle members who've railed at me, screaming obscenities, yelling curses, or crying endless tears. But I've never lost my cool. I pride myself on being calm and controlled.

Inhaling, I channel serene energy. I can deal with Detective Becker. I'm innocent and should have nothing to fear from him.

I open the front door and am surprised by Detective Becker's appearance. He's not as buttoned up and formal as he was in Norfolk. No suit and tie now but jeans, a sweater, and a puffer jacket. His hair isn't slicked back, but wind tousled. I can't decide if I hate this version of him less. There's something wild, perhaps unpredictable, about him. Random is never good.

"Detective, please come in." I've not made coffee. Hell, I barely cleared my lunch plates from the counter. The goal is not to entertain but to answer whatever questions he has and send him along.

He steps inside, carrying with him the scents of wind and ocean. "I'm surprised you came back here. I'm sure there was someone to call to retrieve your things."

"I didn't want to wait."

"For the sleepwalking medication?"

"That's right." I decide not to tell him the pills are missing. The less said the better.

"Have you ever walked far in your sleep?"

"A few times when I was little." I don't mention the time I woke up on the side of Shore Drive in Norfolk, ready to cross on a busy Saturday night. I was fourteen. Or the time I turned on the burner in my apartment, cracked a couple of eggs, and went back to sleep. That was last summer. The smoke detector woke me up. "Not anymore."

"Good. That can be very dangerous." For a moment he says nothing, as if gauging his words. "I've heard of some people ending up in other towns."

"Nothing that dramatic has happened to me." My words sound a little breathless.

My comment prompts a smile from the good detective. Friendly, easy, even relaxed. But I've seen him annoyed and frustrated, and that guy can't be too far away.

As I close the door, I glance across the street and spot Reece passing in front of a window. He doesn't look my way, which seems odd given there's a strange car in my driveway.

"What can I do for you, Detective?" I ask.

His gaze shifts to the stairs and lingers as he adjusts from what he must have seen two days ago to now. "Whoever mopped up the place did a hell of a cleanup job."

I slide my hands into my pockets, glance toward the stairs to assure myself there's no blood. "That was Devon. She's the property manager. And yes, she did an amazing job. It's as if the accident never happened."

Reading my glance, he says, "Except Kyle Iverson's body is cooling in Greenville at the medical examiner's office at East Carolina University."

The reminder sounds polite, but it's not. "I haven't forgotten about Kyle." A part of me wishes I could slip into Detective Becker's mind and see what he sees in me. Another part is grateful I can't. "What's bothering you, Detective? What is it you need to hear from me?"

He doesn't respond at first, and then he says, "Must be strange being back. You and Kyle were both here alive and well forty-eight hours ago."

"It's odd." Lies hide best when they're surrounded by the truth.

Detective Becker glances toward the blanket on the couch and the dishes in the sink. "But you look like you've made yourself at home."

"I was trapped by the weather. And this house isn't a crime scene."

"According to who?"

"Devon."

"I see." His footsteps click against the marble floor as he moves toward the stairs. He kneels and runs his fingertips over the floor where Kyle had lain. "Kyle Iverson could have fallen down those stairs a dozen times and survived. But his luck ran out on Friday."

Luck. Some would say I've been unlucky since the day I was born. Maybe the universe saved up all my luck and delivered it at the bottom of those stairs.

"Meaning a crime didn't occur here?" I ask.

He lets the question linger. "If it makes you feel better, we'll call it an incident." He rises, flexes his fingers. "The medics trashed this area as they tried to save you and him. There were a few scuff marks on the stairs midway as if Iverson's shoe caught, but it appears neither one of you tried to catch yourself. Your fingernails aren't torn, and neither were his. Whatever happened was sudden and unexpected."

"You saw Kyle before they took him away?"

"I did. What do you remember?"

Absently, I rub an old scar on my palm. "His neck was twisted, and there was a lot of blood."

His eyes are as relentless as the churning Atlantic Ocean. "I asked the medical examiner to hold Iverson's body for a couple of days until I'm finished with my investigation."

"I didn't realize declaring this an accident was going to be so hard. Is it really that complicated?" Even I hear the bitterness.

He turns toward me. "Sarcasm, Lane? I never thought you were capable. Everyone tells me how nice and sweet you are."

"Everyone?"

"I've asked around. Your neighbor, Shelly, is protective of you."

I can't imagine Shelly talking to this guy. What did he say to even get her to open her door? "You make it sound like a bad thing."

"Not at all. She seems very loyal to you. Drove like a bat out of hell to get away from me in the hospital parking lot. I'd bet she'd say anything to cover for you."

"There's nothing to hide. And Shelly is very literal. She can't lie."

He hesitates. "I'm not so sure about that."

"What do you want?" Annoyance burns through the worry. I'm tired of his questions and unspoken accusations.

He moves toward me, pausing when he's only a foot away. Close enough to make me aware of his height but not quite crossing the edge of my personal space. "You keep rubbing that scar on your palm. Does it calm you?"

I drop my hands to my side. "It's been a long couple of days."

"I'll bet."

"What do you want?"

"Did this house reveal anything to you about Stevie Palmer or Nikki Kane?"

Hearing the names catches me off guard, and I don't recover fast enough to hide my shock. I think about the journal entries Stevie's sent me, her teasing notes, and the name *Stevie* in Kyle's journal. "Could Stevie have been one of Kyle's clients?"

"I asked Kyle's partner, Dr. Romney, but she doesn't remember Stevie. But she also said Kyle blocked out some Friday evenings for people who required more privacy."

I've never met Kyle's partner. Seems Becker knew the man better than me. "Why are you so interested in this missing woman?" I want to know more about her, but he doesn't need to know that. "Women who live on the fringe vanish all the time, and cops don't put this kind of effort into finding them."

He ignores my statements. "Dr. Romney found Kyle's private appointment book when she was cleaning out his office yesterday. I got a look at it. Stevie Palmer had one session with Kyle Iverson on Friday, July 7, 2023. But it appears she never returned after that session, nor did she return to Joey's Bar. She vanished."

His words settle in my stomach. "Do you think she's dead?"

"I don't know."

"I've never met the woman."

His gaze holds me. "Dr. Romney thought it was odd Iverson never created a billing account for Stevie Palmer."

Why is Stevie reaching out to me? What is so important about a one-time client/possible girlfriend of Kyle's?

"I honestly don't know what to say. Stevie is as much a mystery to me as to you."

"Kyle never mentioned her?"

"We only dated a few weeks. And he never discussed any of his patients with me."

"Dr. Romney thinks Stevie Palmer might have been sleeping with Kyle."

It would be incredibly unprofessional if Kyle slept with a patient. "This doesn't sound like the man I knew."

"You barely knew him." He shakes his head. "A man's bedroom escapades aren't my concern until the women around him vanish."

"Any leads on Nikki Kane?"

"Not yet." His gaze travels to the floor-to-ceiling window overlooking the ocean. "This area is really isolated. Plenty of places to hide a body."

"Body? You think Nikki and Stevie's bodies are hidden up here?" The abandoned house in the woods comes to mind.

Detective Becker holds my stare. "I do."

"Who would've hurt them?"

He shakes his head, as if I've asked a stupid question. "Your boyfriend, maybe?"

Blood seeps from my head, leaving me dizzy. The detective's gaze burrows into me, searching for any crack in my demeanor. He's the kind of guy who, once he finds a way in, is impossible to shake. I don't trust him. "Do you have any proof?"

"No. Not yet."

"What is the point of this conversation, Detective? Trying to scare me into babbling something incriminating about Kyle? Because if that's the goal, you aren't winning. Kyle never once tried to hurt me. He was a gentleman."

"He had a reputation for smoothness." His expression softens. "Lane, it's not my intention to scare you. I'm just looking for Stevie and Nikki. Alive or dead, they need to be found."

He sounds sad, slightly defeated. "Did you know Stevie well?"

"A friend told me about her. He says she's brave and was looking for Nikki when she went missing. Stevie had no reason to stick her neck out for Nikki, but she did."

And Stevie had had a counseling session on July 7 with Kyle before she disappeared. But Stevie didn't send her diary to Detective Becker. She sent it to me. She hinted she didn't trust cops. Maybe Detective Becker knows the Sully mentioned in Stevie's diary. Or maybe Detective Becker is not what he seems.

The detective's gaze lingers on me, and then he turns and strides toward the stairs. Slowly he climbs each step. He's relaxed, as if he's already scaled these stairs a dozen times before. I can picture him striding into the bedroom where I'd been with Kyle, going through my weekend bag, touching my clothes and underwear. Someone deleted my pictures and took my pills.

He turns at the second-floor landing and looks down at me. "Reece heard you screaming. Said it sounded like you were in a rage."

I dig inward, pressing through the blackness and trying to grab a thread of a memory that would reveal something about those last seconds. "I've asked him about that, and he has no idea what I allegedly said. I don't agree with him. I wasn't angry or upset."

He shakes his head. "You admitted you don't remember the last few minutes before the fall. Odd that such critical seconds are missing."

"It's trickling back." But those last missing moments dance out of reach. Maybe, if I can reach a little further, dig a little deeper, I'll grab on to them.

"Can you come up the stairs?" It's a command, not a request.

"Why?"

"I want us to share the same view at the same time." His feet are braced, and his hands are curled into loose fists.

The innocent have nothing to hide, and I'm innocent so I climb. He walks to Kyle's bedroom and waits for me at the door. I reluctantly join him. "You two made it to this room, correct?"

I look past him to the rumpled coverlet. "Yes."

"And?"

"I'm not sure."

"How can you not be sure?"

"I . . ."

"What?"

"I don't remember."

"Okay. And then?"

"I went to the stairs."

"Were you upset?"

I draw in a breath. "I just wasn't ready."

He walks toward the stairs, and he turns his back to them. "Kyle was standing here, correct?"

My heartbeat kicks up. "How did you know that?"

"The medical examiner made the assumption based on Kyle's skull fracture." He taps his fist against the back of his head. "His occipital bone was caved in."

His casual tone is off-putting. I clear my throat but say nothing.

Detective Becker waves me closer. I move to within a couple of feet of him. He raises his hands. "Where were your hands before the fall?"

I inhale. "You want to recreate the last few seconds?"

"Might jog the memory. Think of me as Kyle."

Detective Becker is nothing like Kyle. He isn't as tall, and his frame is broader. But if this little exercise will convince him to leave, I'll play. "One hand was on his chest."

"Was it your left, or right?"

Without thinking, I raise my right hand. "Right."

"Good. Keep going."

"I remember his heart thumping under my fingertips."

He takes my hand, tugs me closer, and presses my palm against his chest. His heartbeat is slow, steady whereas Kyle's had been rapid, as if he'd run five miles. "Like this?"

"Yes." My voice is hoarse, barely a whisper.

I try to pull my hand away, but he holds it in place. "How long did the two of you stand here?"

"Seconds, maybe?"

He edges toward the lip of the stairs, pulling me along. His heels teeter on the edge. If he slips, there's nothing to save him, and if he grabs me, we both fall. Pressure builds in my head. "Like this?"

"Yes."

"Wouldn't take much to push a man here. Even if he's stronger and faster, the element of surprise would have been a huge advantage," he says softly.

My face is inches from his. "Why would I push Kyle? We cared about each other."

"You were fighting."

"I don't remember that." I try to pull my hand away again, but his fingers tighten.

"Do you have regular memory lapses, Lane?"

The stairs' steep pitch looms close, and I'm fearful if I look at them, I'll lose my balance. So, I keep looking at him. His blue eyes don't waver from my face. He's looking for a tell, a sign, that I'm lying. "No, of course not. I just have trouble with sleepwalking, and not even that much since I started taking the pills."

This time when I pull against his grasp, he doesn't resist. I take a step back. "Move away from the stairs."

"They bother you?"

"Yes."

He steps closer to me. "Better?"

"Yes."

He cocks his head. "I can't figure out if you're protecting yourself or Kyle."

"There's nothing to protect. Kyle died in a terrible accident."

As if I haven't spoken, he says, "The man valued his reputation, so a woman who cared about him would want to protect his legacy."

I shake my head. "I'm not protecting Kyle."

"Sure? Maybe you fell for him hard in those three weeks. Good looking, well-to-do, attentive. That's a powerful cocktail, Lane. You find out something. You freak out, you two argue at the top of the stairs, and as dumb luck would have it, the guy falls. That what happened, Lane?"

My name sounds intimate when he says it. "I didn't discover anything about Kyle. I liked him."

"See a future with him? Planning on buying a house with the white picket fence?"

"There's no such thing as happily ever after."

He shrugs. "Happy endings happen. Some swear by love at first sight." He sounds a little wistful, making me wonder how many ex-girl-friends or ex-wives he has.

"Not to me."

"How did you meet Kyle?"

The abrupt change forces me to downshift. "I told you, he was a regular at the coffee shop where I work. He asked me out."

"Was he always a regular at the coffee shop?"

"No. He started coming in the shop in late November, early December."

"And he just asked you out, and you said yes?" His voice echoes in the open landing.

"It's not the Dark Ages, Detective. Why wouldn't I go out with a man that asks me out?"

"How long have you worked at that shop?"

"Two months at that location."

"You transferred from the Virginia Beach store, correct?"

His attention to detail is creepy. "This shop is closer to home."

"Tell me about your first meeting with Kyle."

I move farther away from the stairs, deciding I'm safer. "Kyle came in at the end of my Saturday shift. The shop was almost empty. He bought his coffee and came up beside me while I was cleaning up the cream and sugar station. I caught him staring at me."

"Must have creeped you out."

"Maybe. But then he laughed and made a joke about not being able to take his eyes off me. We chatted, and then he left."

"But he came back."

"Yes. He was nice, and I liked the company. Being alone over the holidays isn't always what it's cracked up to be."

"Plus, he made good money."

My patience is thinning. "I didn't get a chance to pull up his online banking account. I'll leave that to you."

"Funny you should mention that, Lane. I did. I discovered that Kyle's finances were a house of cards."

"What do you mean?"

He slowly moves down the stairs, his hands at his sides. I follow, but I hold the railing. "This fancy world he built was smoke and mirrors. That house across the street and this one are almost one hundred percent mortgaged. He owed over two million dollars. Guy lived large and on credit."

Maybe that explains why he didn't do anything to save the woodland house. "I wasn't chasing his money." But maybe I was a little. I'd liked being taken care of.

He rests his foot on the bottom step and draws in a breath, as if mentally regrouping. I can almost hear his mind flipping through questions.

"Okay, he was broke," I say. "That should eliminate one of the motives you're trying to assign to me."

He shakes his head. "I'm not trying to pin anything on you, Lane."

"Then what more do you want?"

Detective Becker turns from the last step and faces me. "You were in foster care, right?"

I don't like the direction of this conversation. "Are you saying foster care kids can only love a big wallet?"

He ignores the challenge. "I looked up your records, too, Lane. You had a rough start. Your mother was a drug addict, she died when you were fourteen. You had to be moved from one home because you were lashing out at the foster parents and vanishing for days at a time."

I can't hide my confusion. "I'm not sure where you're getting your information," I say honestly. "I was in foster care, but I was one of the lucky kids. It was a positive experience. It saved my life."

"Then why were you relocated three times?"

"The first foster family had another child who was acting out, so I was moved to the second home for my protection. I left the second home for a similar reason, and I aged out of the third. For the record, the moves were difficult, but they weren't devastating."

"That's not what the report reads."

"You pulled my reports? They're supposed to be sealed."

"I have friends."

I shake my head. I've built a wall around my past, and to discover it's been breached is deeply unsettling. My discomfort aside, why would he dig deep into my past if he didn't suspect me of something much darker? "One thing I've learned in foster care and in my line of work is that caseworkers are overworked and underpaid, and they don't always record the details correctly. Kids fall through the cracks."

He doesn't appear convinced. "Are you saying the report I received was wrong?"

I fold my arms. "It happens all the time. Did you talk to a caseworker?"

"I did."

"Over the New Year's holiday?" Cops call caseworkers at all hours during an investigation. They try to accommodate, but away from a desk or files, it's easy to make a mistake. "How did you do such a deep dive in less than forty-eight hours?"

"I work fast."

"And sloppy. I'll bet money the social worker is about my age and was hired long after I left the system. She doesn't know me from Adam."

"You're correct. She's about your age."

I don't blame this woman. After long, hard days, I, too, wonder how long I'll be able to stay positive working with so many hopeless people.

"Who could I call that would remember you?" he asks.

I shake my head as my annoyance grows. "No one. Foster kids are issued cloaks of invisibility when we enter the system. Once you're inside and the cape is on, we vanish. No one sees us. No one remembers us."

"Your report documents regular visits by several different caseworkers."

"Okay. Did you call any of them? Or how about my foster parents?" Anger surges. These people were supposed to have been caring for me, yet they don't remember me.

"I tracked down one of your foster parents. We spoke on the phone. She doesn't remember you exactly because you were with her a month," Detective Becker concedes. "Like you said, she was overwhelmed."

His concession brings me no joy. "She made a mistake. It happens. But I can assure you, I didn't have behavioral problems."

"Are you in counseling?" he asks.

Again, he pivots. "That's not your business."

"You said you're on medication."

"For sleepwalking."

"Are you seeing a counselor?"

I haul air into my lungs and then shove it out. Annoyance is warming my face. "I was. I'm out of money right now. My car finally died, and I had to buy a new one. When I get a job with benefits, I'll return."

"No PT, no lawyer, and now no counselor. That's unfortunate, Lane," he says quietly. "All would be good for you."

"I'm well aware."

He holds up a hand. "My observations are not an indictment. Anyone who needs help should get it."

The truth is, I've been in counseling on and off for years. Some therapists have helped, but most were a waste of time and money.

Instead of pressing, he shifts tactics again. "You've had more time to process what happened. Walk me through it one more time."

The extra time hasn't changed much. "We arrived on Friday about noon. Kyle was anxious to give me the grand tour. Show me upstairs."

Becker's face remains blank, but I sense tension moving through him. "Go on."

I look toward the stairs. "I remember climbing, and Kyle was right behind me. I was amazed at the house and said so several times."

"And you made it to the bedroom."

My brow furrows. "We did, but nothing happened."

Detective Becker clears his throat. "Why not? Wasn't that the purpose of the weekend?"

"Like I said, I wasn't ready." The words slip out before I can catch them.

He raises a brow. "How did Kyle feel about that? I mean, the guy brings you all the way up here. Had Devon stock the refrigerator and buy nice wines. He goes all out and you freeze."

"He was annoyed. He didn't want me to leave the bedroom."

"If I were you, I'd not have liked that reaction."

I draw the line at discussing my almost sex life with him. "You can tackle this question from any angle you want, Detective, but the seconds before the fall are blank."

"Anyone else here at the house that afternoon?"

"Devon was supposed to come by that night and cook us dinner, but she hadn't arrived yet."

"She's a house manager and a cook."

"She said Kyle wanted to surprise me with a special dinner."

"Did she tell you what was on the menu?"

"No." A memory flashes of Kyle and me walking past the kitchen. He'd sounded proud that he'd planned every detail of the weekend. My faulty memory is frustrating. "If you want to know more, talk with Devon. She knows more about Kyle than I did."

"They grew up together, right?"

"Yes, about a mile from here. Their family homes were in the woods."

He stills. "I know about this house and the one across the street, but not the one in the woods." He's frowning now.

"Apparently, the title was in his brother Jeb's name. There are back taxes to be paid, so Kyle never took possession. Jeb died midsummer."

Detective Becker rattles change in his pocket. "Did Kyle tell you he was from up here?"

"No. He didn't tell me anything about this life."

"I can see why. Probably worried a city girl like you would think less of him."

"That's not fair."

"You're accomplished. Attractive. I'd be worried if I were him."

I hide my uneasiness. "Is this an attempt to be nice?"

"No. In fact, you look a little like Nikki Kane. She had light-brown hair, too."

"Do you think Kyle was attracted to me because I look like a missing woman?"

"Not saying that at all. Maybe he has a thing for light-brown hair."

Kyle had loved the color and commented on it several times. "Do you always investigate accidents this thoroughly?"

"When they don't smell right, I do."

I sigh. "I didn't cause the accident. I had no reason to hurt Kyle."

"Maybe he had a reason to hurt you," he says quietly.

"Why would he want to hurt me?"

He reaches in his pocket and pulls out a picture. It's Kyle, and he's with a woman with curly hair. His face is visible, but her face is turned away. "I think this is Kyle with Nikki Kane."

I take the picture, almost desperate to search Nikki's face. But it's not visible to the camera. The date stamp at the bottom of the photo is July 2, 2023, 3:00 a.m. "How can you be sure?"

"I'm not."

"You've had this picture for almost six months?"

"Yes."

"Why hold on to it? Why do you care?"

"Good question." He draws in a breath. "Stevie raised the alarm bells about Nikki, but no one believed she'd vanished initially. Everyone thought she'd moved on to another town and guy. She had a history of prostitution. Cops weren't called until July 8, six days after that picture was taken."

"A blurry picture doesn't prove Kyle wanted to hurt me or anyone else. Did you ever ask Kyle about Nikki?" I ask.

"I stopped by his office in early August. We had a short conversation. He didn't say much and insisted he wanted an attorney present going forward. After that, he stonewalled me."

"Did he admit to taking Nikki out?"

"He said he walked her to her car, waited until it started, and watched her drive off." He sighs. "I think he was her client."

"I've met a thousand Nikkis in my group sessions." From this picture, it's hard to gauge her age. "They are lost, sad, and desperate. What do you know about Nikki?"

"Not much. Like I said, she wasn't using her real name."

"I wish I could help you find her. Girls like her vanish too often. Why are you so deep into this case?"

He stares at me hard. "Iverson's been on my radar since July. I've made it my business to learn what I can about him. I've been keeping tabs on him. Thought I was wasting my time, and then Iverson ends up dead at his secluded beach house and the woman with him is a Nikki look-alike. That's too much of a coincidence for me."

I can barely speak. Had Kyle brought me here to hurt me? "Make your point."

"I pulled all missing persons cases between Nags Head and Norfolk for the last fifteen years. There were ten young women who looked like Nikki. I've accounted for nine of the ten. All the others are alive."

"And the name of the missing woman?"

"Amy Grimes. She vanished during a vacation near Nags Head last summer."

"Is Amy Grimes actually Nikki Kane?"

"I'm not sure." Suddenly, he sounds weary. "Kyle is from up here, and now I know he was set to inherit a house in the woods that does not appear on any of his financial statements. It's a good place to hide a kidnapped woman or bury her body."

I feel sick to my stomach.

"Maybe you figured something out when you two were in the bedroom. Maybe he tried something kinky you didn't like."

I remember lying on the bed and Kyle crawling on top of me. The weight of his body had been a little suffocating. Had I panicked?

"Have you seen Kyle's old house in the woods?" he asks.

"Just from the street. It looks like it's falling in on itself. However, no dead bodies lying around."

"This isn't a joke, Lane."

I'm very much aware. "Why don't you get a warrant?"

"No evidence. No probable cause. And anything I find without a warrant won't be admissible."

"I don't know what else to say."

He clears his throat. "Until I know what happened on those stairs or I find Nikki, Stevie, or Amy, I'm sticking close to you. You're my only link to Iverson now."

"If I've learned anything, it's that I barely knew the man."

"Call me if you find out anything." His steps echo in the house as he moves past me toward the front door. He pauses, hand on the doorknob. "See you soon, Lane."

I close and lock the door behind him. There's no relief after he's gone. His energy still hums in the house, leaving me restless and worried. Why is he keying in on me? I was Kyle's friend, maybe even a potential love interest, but that was it. We didn't have a history, and I certainly wasn't his confidant.

That said, I can't believe Kyle would have hurt those women. He never gave me any hint that he was rough.

As I watch Detective Becker back out of the driveway and nose his car south toward the main road, an oily sense of dread slides over my skin.

Chapter Sixteen

LANE

Sunday, December 31, 2023
2:45 p.m.

Minutes after the detective leaves, the front doorbell chimes again as I'm standing at the base of the stairs. The sound echoes through the house, driving chills down my spine. There's no one I want to see, especially Detective Becker. I consider retreating and hiding until the visitor is gone.

A fist bangs on the door. The sound is more urgent. As much as I want to ignore this person, delaying a problem won't make it go away. I know because I've tried.

I move toward the front entrance, ready to confront the cop. But when I open the door, I'm surprised to see Reece standing on the doorstep. He's wearing a thick cable-knit sweater, jeans, and a black rain slicker. "That was the cop, wasn't it?"

Relief floods my system. "Yes."

"What's he doing back here?"

"He's a bulldog. And he's sunk his teeth into something."

"Did he upset you?"

"Nothing that I can't handle." Mentioning Kyle and the missing women in the same sentence feels ludicrous. "I'm sure this is all routine."

His expression softens, and I sense true concern. "Just making sure you're okay."

"I'm fine. I don't like dealing with him, but I'll manage. Have you ever heard of Detective Becker? You live in this county."

"Must be mainland," Reece says. "I know most of the cops in this area, but not as many on the other side. I've never come across him before."

"It's a big county."

"Land-wise, but the population isn't. Maybe he's new."

"He might be new to the area, but he doesn't act like a rookie," I say. I step aside and nod for Reece to enter. He's feeling more like an ally. He wipes his feet on the mat and steps into the foyer. He's taller and broader than the detective. "He's trying to make something out of nothing. It'll be fine."

"Don't underestimate him."

"You grew up with Kyle. You knew him well. Was he ever violent? Did he try to hurt anyone?"

"Where'd that come from? Did the detective bring it up?"

"He was throwing all kinds of theories at me."

Reece regards me. "We all grew up hard. And kids that have it tough aren't always gentle. But even though Kyle could take care of himself, he didn't go out of his way to find trouble."

"Detective Becker said Kyle was struggling financially." Smoke and mirrors, according to the detective.

Reece shakes his head. "Depends on your definition of *struggling*. Kyle came from nothing. No family money backing him up. It was feast or famine with Kyle. And Kyle loved taking risks."

His tone carries hints of disapproval. "You didn't like Kyle's approach to money?"

He rests his hands on his hips. "Look, he's dead and gone. None of that matters."

"It does to me." There are so few people who can talk to me about Kyle, and my window into his world is closing. "Why didn't you approve?"

He hesitates as if searching for words. "Kyle was never satisfied with what he had. He could have a fistful of money in one hand, but it was never enough. He saw money as points in a game. The more risk he took, the higher the potential win."

"Or loss."

"He liked being on the edge. For a long time, he was winning, and then he had several market losses last spring. He took out loans against the houses."

Financial stressors can trigger a variety of negative responses. "What happened when he hit a stumbling block?"

He shakes his head. "No one likes setbacks, and if they say they don't mind them, they're a liar. Kyle made no apologies for his ambition or his frustrations when things went wrong."

"You're defending him, but you two weren't getting along." It's not lost on me that I was just defending Kyle to the detective.

Frown lines deepen. "None of that matters now, Lane. The man is dead. Let him go and leave this place behind."

"Why are you protecting him?"

He studies me closely. "We knew each other since we were kids. He was good to me back in the day. Sent me work the last couple of years. Loyalty matters to me."

"And what if it's misguided?"

A muscle pulses in his jaw. "This isn't a good place for you, Lane. Leave and get on with your life. Kyle is your past."

"He's not my past until I know what we were fighting about and why we fell. How do two people arrive at a getaway weekend, and within an hour it all goes sideways? I have to find those missing moments."

"Maybe be grateful you don't remember the fall."

My hand trembles slightly as I run it over my head. "I'm not making sense."

The lines in his face soften. "You had a trauma. That can scramble a brain."

"I suppose so."

He reaches for the door handle. "If you need anything, call or knock on my door. I'm across the street for a few more days."

"Thanks. I appreciate that."

"The beach is still dicey today. But tomorrow afternoon is clear. I strongly suggest you leave then."

I look toward the tall windows now damp with rain droplets. I'm not sorry I have a reason to stay. "Thanks."

He leaves, moving down the stairs and across the street without looking back once. When he vanishes into his house, my phone dings with a text.

More for you to read, Lane.

The caller's name isn't displayed, and I don't recognize the number. There's a link in the text. My thumb hovers over it. Stupid to open it. Computer viruses. No telling what will happen.

But my yearning for any kind of answer that'll settle this growing disquiet overrules common sense. I press the link before I can think twice.

It opens to scanned written pages. The handwriting matches the initial diary entries from Stevie Palmer.

The small format is difficult to read on my phone, so I move into Kyle's office and flip on the bright lights. There's a printer on the credenza by his desk. It's still powered up, and there's paper in the tray.

It takes me a second or two to configure my phone to the printer, and then I press the "Print" button. The machine remains still, silent. A few seconds pass. Then a few more. "Come on, print."

Finally, internal gears shift, lights blink, and the first page spits out of the machine.

My heart is racing as I watch the second, then third pages of Stevie's diary spill out. The sheets keep rolling, piling up in the paper catcher, until the machine finally goes silent.

I thumb through the still-warm twenty-six pages. "Why me, Stevie Palmer?"

Written on the last page is another personal note.

You can't forget me, Lane.

Chapter Seventeen

STEVIE PALMER'S DIARY

Wednesday, July 5, 2023
5:45 p.m.

Fifteen minutes before closing, I make it to the small gift shop where Nikki's ex-roommate works. I'm hoping that the store is empty, but like most of the retail shops along Route 12, it's bustling. It's high season, vacation time, and everyone's ready to spend money.

The shop is stocked with beach souvenirs, towels, bobbleheads, snow globes, and all the clutter that eventually ends up in the trash or covered in dust on a shelf. There are about a half dozen people in the shop, mostly teens.

The woman behind the counter is young. Her hair is a dark brown, her makeup a tad overdone, and she's wearing a black V-neck T-shirt. Her look is edgy. I'm betting this is Jana.

I've never seen this woman in the bar with Nikki, but just because they shared a trailer for a couple of weeks doesn't mean they hung out together.

I reach for a snow globe that contains a mini version of the Currituck lighthouse and seashells floating among liquid snow. The base is embossed with *Corolla, North Carolina*. I look over the trinkets, killing time until the last customer has left.

"Can I help you?" The clerk eyes me. I don't look like the knick-knack type, so she must be trying to figure out my angle.

"Sorry to bother you, Jana," I say.

Her brow furrows. "Do I know you?"

"We never met formally. I worked with Nikki."

She walks to the front door. It's almost closing time, so she locks it, but she lingers close in case a customer insists on shopping. She might also be worried about me, and I'm not even trying to be scary.

"How can I help you?" Jana asks.

"Glad you asked." I smile, though I'm not sure if it exudes friendliness. "I'm trying to catch up with Nikki."

Jana stiffens. "I moved out of our place last week. Haven't seen her since."

"Why'd you leave?"

"Why do you care?"

"Wondering if your move had anything to do with the blood on Nikki's bed? Maybe you saw the blood and decided to take off."

Her complexion pales. "Are you a cop?"

I laugh, feeling genuine enjoyment. "God, no. My name is Stevie. I worked with Nikki at Joey's Bar. She's a good kid, and I'm a little worried about her. When she unexpectedly missed work, I went by your place and saw the blood on the bed. I also noticed your room was cleaned out."

She crosses to the counter and grabs her purse. "I don't want trouble."

"Neither do I. I want to find Nikki."

"Really? Seems to me you're looking for trouble."

"Nope. Just Nikki."

"I don't know where she is." Keys rattle as she fishes them out of a large brown purse. "Have you asked Pete?"

"Pete with the black truck?"

"That's the guy. She showed up two weeks ago, and Pete was days behind her. I didn't like having him around, so I left."

"I hear what you're saying. He's not one of my favorite people. In fact, I took out his right knee with a baseball bat."

Her gaze pins me with fresh interest. "Then you know he's no good."

"Does Pete have a last name?"

"Griffin."

"He has Virginia plates on his truck."

"That's right. He drives down here for business a few days a week. He's an electrician. Lives in Chesapeake, I think. Beyond that, I don't know anything. I'm not sure how he hooked up with Nikki."

"Was she seeing anyone else?" I ask.

"Not that I know of. She's young and cute, so if she did, I wouldn't be surprised. Why not, right?"

I hold up my hands. "Preaching to the choir, Jana. Was there anyone who maybe wasn't nice to her beyond Pete?"

The woman eyes me. "Sure you're not a cop?"

"Keep that up, and I'm going to think you don't like me." I pick up a shot glass that reads *Corolla*.

"The last guy she brought by the apartment was about July 2. He was older. Seemed to have money. Drove a nice car."

"But this was after you moved out, right?"

"Yeah. But I'd left a few things behind, including a bear that has a nanny cam inside. I got sick of my shit walking out the door, so I set up the camera."

"And you taped Mr. Wonderful?"

"I didn't think much of the recording as I was watching it. Nikki was with a new guy. No big deal. So, I deleted it."

Damn. A tape would have been very helpful. "What did you see on the tape?"

Jana sighs. "The guy looked like a sugar daddy. Money. Possessive. In the last images, he was escorting Nikki out of her bedroom. Had a solid grip on her arm."

"Did she look upset? Was she crying? Laughing?"

"Her head was down, but she wasn't fighting him if that's what you're asking."

"Did you see his car?"

"I did. The camera was on top of the refrigerator and shooting out the front window. The car looked black. Shiny. Pretty. Expensive."

The more I think about the deleted footage, the more pissed I'm getting. What a wasted opportunity. "Know where they were going?"

Jana arches a brow as if my questions are too annoying. "I have no idea. She wasn't carrying her purse or a bag."

Nikki wasn't expecting to be gone long. "And that's the last time you saw her?" I ask.

Jana comes around the counter, jangling her keys. She's ready to get out of here before another customer arrives. "The late arrivals always wander around the store but never buy anything."

I reach the door first and block her exit. "When did you see her in the flesh?"

"June 28, I think. I was moving out."

"When did you retrieve your camera?"

"July 3. That was the last time I've been back. And if I had any doubts about moving, the blood on the bed sealed the deal. I boxed up my remaining stuff and left as fast as I could."

"Have you tried to call Nikki?"

"No."

"Did you call the cops?"

"No." She shakes her head. "I'm on parole, and I don't need the cops in my life. That's why I paid my rent before I split. I don't need that landlord filing a warrant."

I'm no different from Nikki. If I vanished, I'm not sure anyone would come looking for me. "If you hear from her, can you call Joey's Bar?"

"Why?"

I dig a rumpled receipt from my purse and scribble Joey's number. Next, I press her for her number and write it down on another paper scrap. "You can find me at Joey's." For now, anyway.

"Wherever Nikki is, she isn't coming back. She's landed her sugar daddy and is likely living in a swanky apartment and screwing like a rabbit."

"Does that sound like Nikki?"

"We knew each other all of two weeks, and neither one of us was in that trailer much."

"What was your first impression of Nikki?"

Her shoulders slump a little. "She was struggling to get by, and when a gal is tired of working her ass off, she'll do all kinds of crazy shit."

Chapter Eighteen

LANE

Sunday, December 31, 2023
3:00 p.m.

I stare at another note written in the margin.

You can't forget me, Lane.

The repeated command swims on the page. I'm sitting in Kyle's office chair staring at the handwritten words. Whoever is sending me copies of Stevie's journal has an agenda. Someone either cares about Stevie and Nikki or is screwing with me.

But why me? I've never met either woman.

I spend the next hour reading and rereading Stevie's journal. She strikes me as an independent spirit who's loyal to friends, but I still don't recall meeting her once. "Who are you?"

An overwhelming sense of sadness washes over me as I stare at the oddly precise handwriting of a woman who might not even be real.

Bourbon. Who are you? Is Stevie trying to tell me Bourbon is my Kyle? Did Stevie see the notice in the paper about our fall and then decide to reach out to me? It explains why the entries started arriving after the fall.

I thumb through the pages again, trying to create an image of Stevie in my mind. I see someone hard, seasoned, streetwise.

Bang! The noise startles me, and I quickly hurry through the house to my overnight bag. I shove the pages inside and zip it closed before I turn to the side door. It's open. The wind has caught it and is shoving it against the doorframe again and again.

Bang!

Heart racing, I grab the knob and pull the door closed. As I twist the lock, I stare at the boardwalk leading to the beach. On the boardwalk I see wet, sandy footprints running up to this door. I don't see any steps retreating or in the house.

My mind jumps immediately to Earl. I saw him less than a mile from here, and he knows where I'm staying. Rubbing my arms, I scan the first floor for any more signs of sandy footprints. I see none.

But the silence in the house pulses in my chest, squeezing my heart. Who came up on the deck? Are they still around the house? I open the door again and inspect the keypad. There are traces of sand on the numbers. I close the door and throw the dead bolt.

All the doors in the house are keyless entry. According to Kyle, all have the same code. How many other doors lead into the house? There's one at the north end of the deck, one off the laundry room, and the sliding glass doors feeding out to the deck. Plenty of ways to get into the house other than this door. I stand still, listening to the wind beating against the house. No floors creak. But this house has never felt truly empty since I arrived. It's filled with an energy I can't explain.

Gripping my phone, I consider a 9-1-1 call. The rescue squad is close, but a call to them will alert Detective Becker, and I've no desire to see him again. There's something about him that's deeply unsettling.

Rushing to all the main-level doors, I check the locks and discover them all secure. From the kitchen, gears grind, and I move to the kitchen utility room, where I know there's a dumbwaiter that Kyle used to send our luggage up. It's not a huge space, but it's big enough for a small person.

Again, my breath stalls as I turn the handle. The door opens to the empty shaft. The dumbwaiter is supposed to be kept on this floor to prevent anyone from accidentally entering and falling. Kyle warned me about it when we arrived, as he pulled my luggage from the space. *Don't want you to fall,* he said.

The eerie prophecy rattles in my head as my thumb presses the green button. A motor clicks on and wheels grind as the small compartment slowly rises from the carport below. I stand back, watching as the small cage arrives at my floor and then stops. Who sent the dumbwaiter down to the ground-level floor?

Locking the dumbwaiter door, I leave the utility room and cross to the front of the house. Outside I see Reece moving down his front stairs to his truck.

Damsel in distress doesn't suit me. Still, pride aside, he's the closest thing to an ally I have up here. I hurry down the front steps. "Reece."

He looks up, his eyes narrowing. "Everything all right?"

"Not sure." My heart races. "There are footsteps circling the side door. And it was open. And the dumbwaiter was lowered to the ground level. I locked both doors, but now I'm not sure if someone is in the house."

His jaw pulses. "Let me have a look."

"Thanks. I appreciate that."

He moves toward the house, his long strides eating up the distance quickly. He moves in the side door, pauses. "Stay here. I'll check it out."

"I can come with you." I've been alone most of my adult life and can take care of myself, but searching this house alone leaves me deeply unsettled.

"Better you stay put."

Reece's booted footsteps move up the stairs and along the second-floor hallway. I hear him walk into the rooms, opening and closing doors. The longer he searches, the more foolish I feel.

When he descends the stairs, he shakes his head. "Nothing upstairs." He opens and closes more closet doors, and when he moves into Kyle's office, I follow. Having Reece in here feels wrong. I can almost sense Kyle's displeasure oozing from the walls.

He opens the closet behind Kyle's desk, and my heartbeat slams against my ribs. He clicks on the light and stares into the space. Nothing but freshly painted walls and two of Kyle's sweaters dangling from hangers.

"Nothing," he says.

"Why was the closet painted?" I ask.

"The closet? I don't know." The door clicks softly as he closes it.

"You can smell the fresh paint, right?"

"Yes."

"Devon was in the house cleaning after the accident. Would she have rolled paint as well?"

"Maybe. Ask her."

"Seems odd. Everything else is as I remember it."

Reece's brow furrows. "I couldn't say. When I responded to your fall, it was the first time I'd been in the house since the final walk-through after closing. And once the paramedics pronounced Kyle dead and pulled you out of here, Detective Becker chased me off. I haven't been back until now."

Someone took my pills and deleted my pictures. "I'll talk to Devon."

"Show me the footprints." Disbelief hovers under the words.

He's not calling me a liar, but he's now wondering if I'm crazy or just make up stories. "Out back."

We cross through the main room to the door that is still securely locked. Outside the wind blows hard, sweeping across the walkway, swirling sand over the sunbaked wood.

"I don't see footprints," he says.

I move past him to the door and twist the lock. The door opens, and I step out into the wind, searching for traces of the footprints I know I saw not ten minutes ago. "They were here. I saw them."

"Right. I'm sure you did."

"I saw them. The door was open and banging in the wind."

"Okay. Sure." He studies me, but his expression doesn't reveal any of his thoughts.

I glare at the walkway. "I know what I saw."

"The wind is pretty fierce. Footprints don't last."

It feels like Reece is humoring me. He must think I'm a hysterical mess. "You think I'm crazy."

"Not at all, Lane. You've been hurt, and now you're alone in this house. The quiet can get to people. Makes sense you'd be on high alert."

High alert. That's not right. I'm searching for Stevie, Nikki, and the missing seconds. "I know what I saw."

"I hear you."

He's still not sure how to take me, and suddenly I'm annoyed with him and myself. "Right, well, thanks for coming. Didn't mean to sound a false alarm."

His eyes arc full of caution. "No worries. You sure you're okay?"

I twist the lock closed and pull on the doorknob. "I'm fine."

He stands close, and I smell the scents of lumber and salt air on him again.

My annoyance melts. I don't want to be alone. I've had my share of isolation since last summer. Sure, I might have been surrounded by people in the coffee shop or at school, but I've come home to an empty apartment and silence every night. It's by choice. I've had too much on my plate, and there's been no time for anything beyond work and school. But right now, I have no school or work, and I want to have a real conversation that doesn't involve a coffee order or school assignment. I did plenty of talking with Kyle, and I miss that. "Can I at least offer you a coffee? A drink?"

His silence mingles with all the other silences that have been stalking me for months. "Sure, a coffee would be good."

"Terrific."

He glances toward the sparkling espresso machine on the counter. "You know how to use that?"

"I've had a variety of jobs in my life, least of which is a barista." I set the machine up, settle a white cup under the dispenser, and press the button. Coffee hisses out. "Sugar, cream?"

"Just black."

"I would've guessed that if you'd stepped up to my register."

"How can you be so sure? I might have asked for one of those triple vanilla monsters."

I smile, feeling the first sense of normalcy in days. "You develop an eye for people when you serve them coffee all day."

He takes a sip. "It's good." As I turn back to the machine, he asks, "What's your flavor?"

"Hazelnut creamer." I splash in the creamer. "Not exactly a purist."

He studies the cup but doesn't drink. "I never had much of a taste for the flavored stuff."

"Neither did Kyle." I regard him over the rim of my cup. "Hard to believe he's from this area. That fact still doesn't resonate with all that I knew about him."

"He wanted to leave all this behind. Did his best to put distance between himself and the past."

I could buy that if I wasn't standing a half mile from where he grew up. "But he built two houses here."

He reflects. "Hard to let go of our childhood. The good and bad can have a hold on us."

You can let anything go if you want it enough. I've divorced myself from the past. I only look back on rare occasions, and when I do, I search out only the good times. Sometimes the bad finds me, but only rarely. "Do you come up here for old times' sake?"

"I come up here for work, but I don't live here. I wouldn't be on this job now if I had more help, and it wasn't for the holidays. The money was too good to turn down."

I shift, move the weight off my left hip. It's aching now, and I've overdone it walking on sand and climbing stairs. Doubt Dr. Jackson would call this a rest. "I've worked my share of holidays, either at a crisis hotline or at a church food pantry. I've never minded it."

He sips his coffee. He grimaces and sets the cup down. "When you work for yourself, you don't have a choice, especially when you're trying to keep a business afloat."

"How long have you been building?"

"I've had my own business for five years. Before that I worked for three years with another crew."

He must be in his early thirties. "What did you do before?"

"Nothing important."

Unsettled quiet wedges between us. He's not going to answer, and I don't pry. "How does a pipe just come loose?" I think about Earl roaming this area. "Was it really an accident?"

He draws in a breath. "The hose was loosened from the wall."

"Are you saying someone intentionally separated the hose?"

"That's what I think."

"Someone broke into the house? Vandalism?"

He frowns. "The back window was broken. I never had a chance to tell Kyle that detail. We spoke on the phone while he was driving up here."

There was a call when we were passing over the Wright Memorial Bridge onto the Outer Banks. The conversation was brief, and Kyle didn't look happy when it ended. I asked, but he smiled and told me not to worry.

"Who would do that?" I ask.

"I haven't asked around yet, but I'll figure out who broke into that house. Sooner or later, someone up here talks."

"What's the point of destroying that house?"

"I don't know. But I owe it to Kyle to find out who decided to mess his shit up. Some people like to destroy things just for fun."

"Like Earl?"

He stares at me. "Earl wasn't crazy about Kyle, but he's never done something like this."

In this kind of isolation, there could only be so many people who would try to destroy a vacant house. "Does that happen up here a lot?"

"Not that often. Believe it or not, there are enough people around even in the winter to keep an eye out. Hard for an outsider to blend in and not be seen. You screw with someone's stuff, and you'll be found." His words have an ominous ring.

"Have you talked to Devon? She seems pretty dialed in."

He frowns. "I'll catch up with her soon. The last few days have been crazy."

"Should I ask what they do to thieves up here?"

He shakes his head as if an answer isn't necessary, or maybe prudent. "Someone will say something eventually, and then I'll know. Criminals rarely keep their mouths shut for long."

"Kyle didn't say a word about it as we were driving here."

"He had his mind on other things."

Heat rises in my face. He's right. Kyle wasn't focused on the house across the street.

Reece shifts his stance. He's hanging around and not drinking coffee for my benefit. "Are you going to be okay?"

An old heaviness settles on my shoulders. "Sure."

"You're safe up here," he says, sensing my hesitation. "I'm across the street, and everyone in a ten-mile radius knows it."

Knowing he is close is a comfort. "I'll be fine. And thank you for the conversation. And soothing my crazy thoughts."

A light in his eyes softens his features. "Sure thing."

I walk him to the front door and open it. Cold chills race toward me and swirl around.

As he turns, he pauses. "I'm grilling out about six. Join me. Hanging out together will make New Year's a little less lonely."

I swell with anticipation. Seems so odd I should feel this close to a stranger, considering I was here with Kyle two days ago. What's going on with me? This sudden attraction for Reece can't be real and must stem from grief or fear. The plain truth is, Reece is all I have up here.

I smile. "Sure, that sounds nice. What can I bring?"

"Just yourself. Grilling burgers and potato chips. Simple fare."

"Would you rather grill here? I suspect the house across the street is a construction zone."

He looks around the house, and I can't tell if he is saddened, annoyed, or resentful of the space. "Nah, let's do this at my place. It's now habitable."

"Sounds good."

As he moves down the front stairs, his booted feet are oddly nimble. I watch his body move, strong and forceful, and again am surprised by my attraction. What I'm feeling now is different from what I felt for Kyle. More primal. Unrestrained. That realization catches me off guard. I've never done anything that's primitive. Even the kisses I shared with Kyle were restrained. I'm always careful, always controlled. Always thinking about the move that will keep me safe.

And yet, I like Reece Trent. Is there a time limit on watching someone die and then moving on to the next relationship? Shouldn't I be so filled with sorrow that there's no room for anything else? What's wrong with me?

Back inside the foyer, I close the door. Again, the quiet waits for me. Reece has checked all the closets, and he's looked under the beds. I'm alone. I'm safe. Right?

Chapter Nineteen

LANE

Sunday, December 31, 2023
5:00 p.m.

I turn on the shower, and as the steam builds, I lock the bathroom door, double test that it's secure, and then strip down, leaving my clothes in a heap on the floor. Under the spray, the hot water blasts my skin, beads against my face, and melts the chill in my bones as it eases the stiffness in my hip. My bruises are a brutally dark band running along my left side.

I sit on the bed in the main bedroom and slip off my shoes. Kyle enters the room and smiles, moves to the bed, and cups my face in his hands. He kisses me and nudges me back to the mattress.

I'm a little startled by his boldness. I thought we were going to ease into this weekend.

He kisses the side of my neck. "I've wanted this from the moment I first saw you." Champagne lingers on his lips.

My stomach churns, and I blame it on the champagne. "I thought we were going to take this slow."

His eyes are guarding his thoughts. There's something he wants to say but won't or can't. "We have been taking it very slowly, Lane."

He runs his hand up under my sweater, over my belly, and to the crest of my breast. "I know you're shy, but you'll be glad."

His fingers skim down my belly to the waistband of my pants. I've fantasized about this moment, but now that it's racing toward me, I'm scared. Stupid to be frightened, but there it is. I push his hand away, but he traps it in his own and pins it over my head.

There's an awareness in this moment I can't explain. I squirm under him, but he locks my legs in place under his body. He's strong, and I can't move. An overwhelming sense of helplessness squeezes the air from my lungs. Breathing is now difficult. "Kyle, no. I'm not ready."

He unsnaps my pants. "There's a wild woman inside you, I know it, Lane."

I glance over at the nightstand toward a clock. The red numbers read 12:55 p.m. I extend my arm, stretching my fingers until they graze the clock. I nearly knock the lamp over as I try to get ahold of it. But I do, and without thinking, I strike Kyle on the side of the head.

And then . . . nothing.

Where did that memory come from? It can't be real.

In a blink, the hot water turns cold. How did I drain the hot water tank so quickly? I draw in a hard breath and scramble to shut off the water. My skin chills, and I grab a large white towel and wrap it around my body. Wet hair drips on my shoulders and the floor.

When I look down and see the puddles, I'm transfixed by the way the water reflects the overhead lights. My mind jumps back to a moment when I'm much younger. My skin is icy, and I can hear someone telling me to scrub harder. Freezing water burrows into my bones. My teeth chatter.

Stepping out of the bathroom, I rush to my clothes lying on the bed. My hands tremble as I tug on my thick black sweater, undergarments, and jeans. I wrap the towel around my hair and walk to the large mirror in the bedroom to find a cold, drowned rat–like woman staring back. Nothing special to look at here, and I wonder again why a guy like Kyle showed interest in my plain face and unsexy clothes.

"Because he did, Lane. Stop thinking about what can't be changed or explained."

I normally don't wear makeup, but I decide tonight might be a good time to try. I dig through my suitcase and find the drugstore makeup I packed Thursday evening. I apply foundation, a little powder, brown eye shadow, and mascara. Digging through my bag, I search for lipstick. I remember examining all the shades of peach in the drugstore, but realize now I've purchased crimson red. How did I manage such a mistake?

I twist open the lipstick and stare at the very deep red hue. Maybe I'd been overwhelmed by all the makeup choices. Ivory versus light beige. And there'd been dozens of blushes. Cream and powdered. Cinnamon and rose. By the time I'd reached the lipsticks, I'd been impatient, ready to get out of the store. A stupid mistake that's cost me fifteen bucks.

Whatever, I rub the lipstick over my lips, a bit shocked by the bright color. It's not me. Doesn't look like me. But the extra pop of color kind of works.

I glance at the clock, the same clock from my memory. It's not cracked or bent, and shouldn't it be if I hit Kyle with it?

The red numbers blink 5:55 p.m. That can't be right. How could I fall so far behind? I was in the shower for forty-five minutes?

Quickly, I towel dry my hair and apply mascara. Downstairs I slip on my boots, slide on my coat, and grab a bottle of Burgundy from the stocked wine rack and a bottle opener from a drawer. The sun has long since set, shrouding the rows of darkened houses and the street in an inky darkness never seen in Norfolk. No light pollution here.

No one in their right mind would be up here now unless they had a massive deadline and needed extreme quiet, or contractors like Reece with repair work, or women like me working shit out.

The sand squishes under my boots as cold winds gust through my damp hair. I move past a construction dumpster that's already full of discarded drywall. Under the house, there are several piles of lumber stacked neatly in the center, sawhorses, circular saws, and gray plastic trash cans filled with scrap lumber.

I slowly climb the stairs. On the porch, I don't see a doorbell, so I knock. Inside the house, footsteps echo before the door opens. Reece has changed into a clean blue T-shirt and combed back his hair. Drywall particles still dust his jeans and boots. I appreciate the effort.

I hold up the bottle. "My mother said never show up empty-handed." That's not true. My mother couldn't afford to give anything away.

"Thanks." He looks at the bottle as if he's not sure what to do with it. "I might have a wine opener here somewhere."

I pull mine from my coat pocket. "Girl Scouts are always prepared." That's not even a correct analogy, and the closest I've ever come to the Girl Scouts is a box of cookies in the break room at the coffee shop.

He smiles.

"And if wine is not your thing, there's beer in the fridge back at the house." I have a pleasing personality, which Kyle pointed out when I agreed with him.

"I have beer. Not the fancy craft kind," he says.

"How about we start with that?"

"This wine looks like it's expensive."

"If Kyle bought it, it likely is. But I don't know much about wine. For the record, I like regular beer."

He closes the door behind me. "Then it's settled."

I look toward the open great room to a vaulted ceiling and the skylights that reveal bright stars in the sky. The furniture is herded into the room's center and covered with a clear plastic tarp. The rugs are rolled up, and only silhouettes of art remain on the white walls.

A huge swatch of drywall on the west side of the room has been cut out, creating a hole that's ten feet high and twenty feet wide. Through the studs and wiring I can see the newly installed metal hoses waiting to be hooked to the washer.

"Wow. Looks like a river flooded this place."

"It did."

"I had no idea water could do this."

"Water is as destructive as fire."

I move toward the open wall that smells faintly of mold. "This was done on purpose?"

"It was." He moves toward the kitchen island and sets the wine bottle down before reaching in the refrigerator for two bottles of beer. He twists the tops off and hands me a bottle.

"Will insurance cover this?" I sip the beer and savor the malty flavor.

"Kyle said he'd file a claim on January 2. I took plenty of pictures for him."

"All this because someone acted out." I understand how fury can foster the urge to break or destroy, but I've never acted on it. It stays locked tight inside me. "What a waste."

He's studying me, contemplating. "I've seen you limping a little. That from the fall?"

"It is. I pulled a few muscles in my hip when I hit the floor. Also have several big bruises. It'll all heal over time if I take it easy. And for the record, I'm not good at taking it easy. Sitting still is more painful than the hip."

"I never would've put you with Kyle," he says.

Devon had said the same thing. I picture them huddling close, discussing Lane, the odd chick who saw their friend die. "How so?"

He shrugs, frowns. "I shouldn't have said that."

"It's no big deal. Devon said the same. I'm just as curious as you are. What do you think Kyle saw in me?"

"In the last few years, Devon tells me Kyle went for the rich, untouchable type of woman. The kind who gets spray tans and manicures. You're more down-to-earth."

I sip my beer. "I don't come with social points or money."

"Maybe he saw a bright young woman who came from nothing and is making her way like he did."

"I reminded him of himself?" Or Nikki, as Detective Becker suggested. I gulp another swig of beer.

"Or maybe the kind of woman he grew up with. No one put on airs around here."

"He left his past behind." Some men did gravitate back to their roots as they neared their mid- to late thirties.

"He'd started reconnecting the last few years."

Would reminders of his youth have sustained us? I'll never know if we'd have gone the distance. Eventually, I suspect he'd have grown tired of my crazy work hours, constant budgeting, circle groups, and school schedule. Poor and struggling gets old even for me sometimes.

"Did you love him?" Reece asks.

The question catches me off guard. Kyle and I had never spoken of love. "After three weeks?"

He shrugs. "It happens."

"I'm not sure there's such a thing as love. The best any of us can do is find someone that fits into our life and then build from there."

He raises a brow. "That sounds good to me."

"Maybe." I think back to the last moment Kyle and I shared in the bedroom. If it's a true memory, then it's cast a shadow over the entire three weeks we were together.

He clears his throat. "Let me turn on the grill. Help me carry plates downstairs."

From the fridge he grabs a box of burgers on a plate and hands it to me before snagging a metal spatula and a sleeve of buns. "Follow me."

He opens a back door and leads me down a rear staircase to the concrete parking pad under the house. We both weave through the construction supplies to a covered gas grill. He pulls off the plastic cover, opens the lid, and presses the starter button.

I shift the plate to my right hand so I can burrow my left hand in my pocket. "Is this how you eat?"

"No takeout up here unless I'm willing to drive thirty miles south. But I'm ready to get out of the house. The grill is my compromise for both. Just a few more days, and I'll return to the mainland." He takes the plate from me and sets it on a strip of plywood resting on two sawhorses.

I shove my right hand in my pocket. Despite the chill, I feel less constrained with the air blowing around us.

"Any more footprints or open doors?" He closes the gas grill lid and sips his beer.

"All quiet." But I remain rattled and uncomfortable in the house. "I have no idea what happened."

He opens the grill and drops raw burger patties on the hot grate. They sizzle.

"Think whoever might be lurking around my house could've done the damage here?" I ask.

"I suppose that's possible."

"Maybe they were scoping out my place, realized I was there, and backed off." *My place.* I've become too acquainted with Kyle's beach house. It's not mine. Not ours. Not anything.

"Maybe Devon came up to the house to see if you were still here," he offered. "She realized you were, and then she left."

"That's very plausible." I take a long pull on the beer. "What do you remember from Friday?"

He regards me for a long beat. "I wasn't paying that close attention to you two. I had my hands full dealing with the flooding in this house."

He reaches for the spatula and flips the burgers. Melting fat sizzles. My gaze is drawn to his hands and the way his watch encircles his wrist. So few guys wear a watch anymore, which is a shame. It's kind of sexy. No wedding band on those long, calloused fingers. Which doesn't mean anything. Lots of guys in construction don't wear rings for safety reasons.

I clear my throat. "But you spoke to Kyle. You knew each other."

"It was a quick greeting," he says. "He said we'd talk later. He wanted to get you settled in the house."

"I don't remember you."

"You were already up on the deck headed toward the ocean. You looked lost in thought."

"I was admiring the view." I had no idea he'd been watching me. Who else had noticed my arrival?

He presses the spatula into a burger, squeezing blood out the top and sides. "You looked lost in thought, worried even."

"I can be pensive. Kyle didn't love that trait. Said he could see my mind drifting to a far-off place."

"Don't we all at times. I'm not judging."

"If you do judge, you can join a large, esteemed group of people. I doubt Kyle's business partner approved of me. I'm not exactly in their league. Detective Becker doesn't like me. And Devon is nice, but she sees me as an outsider."

He laughs. "Everyone is an outsider to Devon. And what league is the best kind? The hoity-toity crew?"

"Educated. Multiple degrees from the right universities. Major life plans already in play. Not me. Up until now, I've barely been able to see one step in front of me."

"You have no big plans?"

"I've got plans. But they won't make me rich. Social workers don't generally hit the high net worth lists."

"Who knows? Nothing says you won't make it big one day."

"Fingers crossed. I'm not sure I'd know how to live with lots of extra money in my pocket. It's a good month when I make the rent on time."

"Back at you."

"Whatever Kyle and I were is already fading into the shadows. There aren't even pictures that prove *we* existed. Maybe if we'd been together longer, I'd feel this loss deeper."

His eyes linger on me. Brutal honesty rarely sits well with most people. He raises the beer to his lips, watching me, and then he sets the bottle down carefully on the grill's side table.

"No pictures?" he asks.

"I thought I had a few on my phone, but they're gone. No evidence that we existed."

His gaze fills with questions and something else. What am I seeing now? Longing? Yearning? On too many levels I hope it's desire. My thoughts shift to his lips. They won't taste like champagne, but maybe salty hints of beer? Even before I speculate, I halt this line of thought. What the hell is happening to me? I did not return to the beach house for this.

Reece moves behind the grill and drops his head. He removes the burgers from the grill and places them on a clean plate. "Let's get you back inside. You look half-frozen."

My skin feels hot, not cold. "Sorry. Too much information."

"Naw. I've heard a lot worse."

I follow him inside, and the heat in the house eases the bunched tension activated by the cold. He sets two barstools in front of the large kitchen island. "Not super fancy."

"Works for me," I say.

He plates the burgers and sets one in front of me. He opens a large bag of sour cream and onion potato chips. "Another beer?"

I finish my first one. I don't drink much, but right now I want to take the edge off this restless energy humming inside me. "Sure."

He sets two fresh beers on the island, and we eat in silence. The burger is good and is complemented by the salty chips.

"Thanks for dinner," I say. "You didn't have to do this."

"I like the company. I know it gets lonely up here sometimes."

I glance at his hands wrapped around the beer bottle. I imagine them running over my skin. Human contact. I've been craving it for months, and then when Kyle kissed me on the bed, I freaked. Was it him or some other weirdness about me?

What would it be like if I touch Reece now? Just a brush of my fingertips over his hand? A hug? A kiss? Would I melt into it or run screaming from the house?

I turn my body until I'm facing him. My knees brush the side of his leg. For a moment, he doesn't look at me, but I really want him to look at me. Finally, his head turns. I moisten my lips. I want him to kiss me, and his darkening eyes tell me he knows that. But he doesn't lean toward me.

I tip in toward him, praying he'll meet me halfway and not leave me hanging. A muscle pulses in his jaw, and then slowly he closes the narrow gap between us.

When our lips touch, I do taste beer, as well as the salt from the chips. He has an earth energy. Solid, stable. Patient. Whereas Kyle was fire. Hot, intense.

Feeling no sense of panic, I tilt more into the kiss. He cups the side of my face. He's enjoying the kiss, too. I rise off my stool, and step between his legs. His hand skims over the base of my spine. Something sparks deep inside me, and I can almost feel myself floating over my body.

I reach for the hem of my sweater and pull it over my head. My full breasts spill over a simple white bra trimmed in delicate lace. He presses me against him.

I glide my hand down his belly and slide it under his waistband. He's hard. He wants this as much as I do. He grabs my hand, and for a moment our eyes lock. He wants me. But a part of him needs to remain loyal to Kyle.

Finally, he rises and pulls me toward a midsize sofa tucked in a corner by the windows. It's one of the few pieces not covered in plastic. I lower to the plush fabric. He pulls off his shirt and straddles me.

This is going to happen. And I'm not scared. I want this.

Outside, a gust of wind slams into the side of the house, rattling one of the storm shutters. The loud bang startles us both, and we jerk back. The moment is broken.

He draws away, his back stiffening as if he realizes he's betrayed something sacred. "I don't know where that came from."

Without him close, a breeze cools my warm skin. "Me either. But it was nice."

"We got carried away." His voice is rusty. "I don't think it's a good idea."

He grabs his shirt and yanks it over his head. It's as if someone dumped an ice bucket on him.

I swallow my disappointment as I sit up. I stand and cross to my sweater. It takes a moment to turn my sleeves right side out. He's looking away.

"You're right." That's a lie. I'm attracted to him, and I needed to prove I'm not a crazy woman who loses it when a man touches her. Tears tighten my throat. "Do you hate me?"

"What?" His brow furrows. "No. I don't hate you."

"I was with your friend when he died." My voice is uneven and ragged. "Do you blame me?"

He looks at me. There's pain and certainly regret in his eyes. "It wasn't your fault."

Does he believe that? Does Devon? Do I?

Suddenly, I feel like a fool. It's as if I'm trapped in my body. I can see the world outside, but it's unattainable and a million miles away.

"Thanks again for dinner, but I better get back." I don't want to leave but staying now is impossible. I can't tell if he notices my unease, but it doesn't matter.

I'm starting to believe my own loneliness and fear pushed me toward Kyle. He was kind, and he made me feel safe. Maybe he liked the idea of rescuing me. And part of me really wanted to be saved.

Reece's features look carved in stone. "You're going back to an empty house?"

"It's not that bad. There are books." I've barely scanned the titles but mentioning them makes me feel a little less lame. "And I need the rest. I'm leaving tomorrow if the weather cooperates."

A slight smile softens some of the hard lines etched in his face. He's close enough to touch me, take my hand, and pull me toward him. He doesn't. "I'm sorry."

"Don't be." I step away. I'm not sure why I'm drawn to him or his apparent strength. Still, the added distance solidifies my isolation.

He leans forward a fraction as if ready to kiss me. "Stay a little longer, and I'll tell you a story about Kyle and me."

"Why?"

"I like talking to you."

But not kissing me? Still, I'm curious and ready to latch on to any excuse not to be alone. Yes, I want to know about Kyle, but I also want to know something more about Reece. "Is this a Huck Finn kind of adventure?"

He grins. "Not even close."

Chapter Twenty

Lane

Sunday, December 31, 2023
7:30 p.m.

"Our adventure began at the fence on the beach between North Carolina and Virginia," Reece says.

"Fence?"

"The one that keeps the wild horses on the preserve," he says.

"I saw two black horses yesterday. I thought I was imagining them for a moment."

"You're not. There are about a hundred horses in the herd. They mostly live on this side of the dunes in the winter and hang out in the woods. They travel toward the ocean in the summer when it's hot or when the wind shifts and blows out of the west and brings the black flies."

"Black flies?"

"They bite."

"Another day in paradise."

"It can be at times."

I'd seen hints of it on Friday, but it vanished almost immediately. The weather's version of bait and switch. "So, what did you and Kyle do?"

"We borrowed a truck." He used air quotes around the word *bor-rowed*. "His brother's truck."

"Devon said Kyle had two brothers."

"Correct. But they weren't close."

"Kyle never mentioned brothers when we were together. I guess neither one of us was ready for that conversation. Was this the brother who died or the one who went to prison?" Everything I knew about Kyle is falling apart. But people are complicated, messy. He presented an image that wasn't much better than a magician's illusion.

Reece draws in a breath. "Jeb, the one that went to prison."

"That must have been hard on the family." I've worked with families torn apart by prison sentencing. The inmate isn't the only one sentenced to purgatory. "Why was Jeb sent to prison?"

He pauses. "Jeb kidnapped a woman in Nags Head. Messed her up pretty good. He was seventeen at the time, but old enough to be tried as an adult."

The words chill into my bones. I don't need to ask what happened to the girl. Several of the women in my group have suffered sexual assault. Though some have grown comfortable enough to discuss it, others keep their ghastly experiences buried deep. "What happened to the girl?"

"She filed charges. There was enough DNA and surveillance footage to back up everything she said."

Did the truck parked under the woodland house belong to Jeb? My mouth dries. "Kyle never once said a word to me."

"The three Iverson brothers were tight at one time. But as they got older, they started to go their separate ways. Kyle wanted a different life." He shakes his head. "And now they're all united again."

This conversation strikes something deep inside me.

Nervous, defensive laughter bubbles up. "How did we get from 'borrowed' truck to kidnapping?"

A half smile tips the edges of his lips. "Most of the stories featuring Kyle take a turn for the worse. This was supposed to be one of the good ones."

I'm not ready to press for more details about Jeb or Zeke, but I want Reece to keep talking. "What did you and Kyle do in that truck when you drove into Virginia?"

He takes a long pull on his beer. "Nothing that extreme. No real laws broken like with Jeb if that's what you mean."

I'm not so sure of anything anymore. "What happened?"

"We went through the gate in the fence. It's locked to most, but Kyle got hold of a key to the lock. Don't ask me how, I have no idea. Anyway, we drove the thirty miles into Virginia Beach. There's a bar on Chic's Beach."

I saw the fence at the Virginia border on the beach. I didn't realize it extended into the woods or had an access gate, but I know the Chic's Beach area well. "I waitressed in a few restaurants around there."

"We got pretty drunk. We needed to sober up before the drive home, so we went to the bay, stripped, and went for a swim."

"That's hardly shocking," I say. "You two wouldn't be the first."

"Someone stole our clothes. No shirt, no shoes, no pants, no service. Cut the evening short, and we had to drive back here."

"Naked?"

"As the day we were born."

I never saw any hints of this young rule breaker in Kyle. Until those last moments with me in his room, he was slightly rigid, almost prudish. I reach for my beer and gulp down the rest. "The Kyle I knew kept his shirt buttons fastened to the collar."

But I also would never have pictured Kyle living in the woodland house or having a brother who did jail time for kidnapping.

The inky specks in Reece's eyes darken. "When he left here for good after his sophomore year, he put it all behind him. He put up some high walls between the man he became and the kid he was. I think Kyle was afraid of turning out like Jeb. Their daddy could get violent when he was drunk. Jeb gave in to his urges. Kyle decided he would always be in control."

"Was Kyle ever violent?"

He hesitates. "Not that I ever saw."

"But . . ."

"But nothing." He shakes his head as if he senses this conversation took a wrong turn. "I was trying to be amusing, but it looks like I've botched that, too."

"You opened the door to the past," I point out. "Based on the work I've done with my patients, that always leads to stormy waters."

His gaze lingers on me as if there is more he wants to say. "And now I'm closing that door."

"Why tell me anything about Kyle?" I press.

Secrets, if kept hidden long enough, can take on a life of their own. Reece might not want to talk about the past, but that doesn't matter if the secrets want to be heard.

He grabs his empty plate and mine and walks both to the trash can. "I don't know. I shouldn't have. I shouldn't have kissed you."

"I liked the story and the kisses."

He doesn't respond but pulls two cold beers from the refrigerator. He sets one in front of me.

Was Kyle prone to violence like his brother and father? Even tight lids could boil over occasionally. "Did Kyle ever mention a woman named Nikki Kane?"

The bottle pauses close to his lips before he takes a long swallow. Dark eyes narrow. "No."

"What about Stevie Palmer?"

"No. Why are you asking?"

I dig my fingernail into the beer bottle label. "Stevie or someone else is sending me her diary entries via mail and a texted PDF file."

"Why you?"

"I've no idea."

Reece looks as if he wants to say something but remains silent.

"According to her diary, Stevie was looking for Nikki Kane. She vanished in early July."

Reece's jaw pulses. "What's that have to do with you?"

"I don't know."

I'm not sure why I feel like I can talk to him or trust him, but I do. "I started receiving her diary entries after the fall." I try to shrug off my growing dismay, but it clings to my skin. If Stevie was trying to warn me about Kyle, her timing sucked.

"Think Stevie was having an affair with Kyle?" Reece asks.

The question doesn't sting. Kyle had lived a full life before me. What worries me is Stevie's retelling of Nikki and Bourbon. Could Kyle be Bourbon? Was Kyle one of the last people to see her? "Maybe. Maybe she is a jealous ex-girlfriend who wants to get back at me or him and is screwing with me." Honestly, that would be the most welcome option.

"Have you tried to find her?" Reece asks.

"I searched her name, but nothing popped on the web or on social media. Whoever she is, she's a ghost."

"Hard to be a ghost in today's world." Reece frowns.

"I don't think she's using her real name." Even I can be found with a quick internet search.

"All correspondences addressed to you?"

"Home address and then texted to my phone. Whoever she is, she certainly knows me."

"After the write-up in the Outer Banks online local paper."

"Yes, but I wasn't named in that." I swirl the remaining beer in the bottle. I'm almost sorry I mentioned Stevie to Reece. If I didn't know Kyle, I certainly don't know Reece. "Never mind. She's likely someone I know through school or work, and she's messing with me. That happens."

"If that's true, it's a hell of a bad joke."

"You're right. It's not funny."

"And it bothered you enough to bring it up to me."

I hold up my beer bottle. "It's the beer talking."

"You've only had two and a half."

"Already over my limit." I summon a smile. "Thanks for the meal, the stories, and letting me bend your ear about nothing important. I better get back."

"To your dark house."

"Are you trying to scare me?"

White teeth flash. "No. I'm just giving you a hard time."

The teasing light in his eyes returns. Reminds me of why I wanted to kiss him. "Duly noted. Now, the plan is to get a full night's sleep."

"It's nine."

"I'm a terrible sleeper, so I start early each night knowing three a.m. is coming fast." And without my medication, who knows how the night is going to go.

He sets his bottle down. "3:33. Halfway to hell."

"Very true."

"I'll walk you home."

I find his offer very charming. "It's right across the street."

"And dark." He grabs a large flashlight and clicks it on. "I'll see you to your front door."

His determination is oddly comforting. "Lead the way."

As I slide on my jacket, he opens the front door and steps into the cold darkness as if he's accustomed to it. He grasps my elbow as we move down the dark steps. I'm more gun-shy than expected on stairs, and it's nice to have backup.

We move slowly as my hand skims over the cold metal railing. The last riser on the steps feels slightly higher than the rest, and I stumble toward the wooden sidewalk. My grip tightens on the rail as his arm shoots out and grabs mine. I right myself, but when I'm steady on my feet, his hand doesn't drop away. We follow the beam of light along the wooden sidewalk and across the sandy street toward my house. The porch light glows.

"Thanks for the assist," I say. "I'm normally not so . . ." I don't know who I've been tonight.

"No problem." His deep voice reverberates in my chest, and I'm very aware of his height, and his fingers still gripping my elbow. "Glad to be of service."

I like the feel of his hands on me. His touch isn't sexual now, but I want it to be. What the hell is wrong with me? I just survived a fall, I saw a man die, and I am nursing an injury. I should be in full-on hermit mode. The last thing I should care about is sexual attraction. Still, my pulse remains quick.

"Good night, Reece."

He eases his grip on my elbow until it finally releases. I miss the connection. And I think he does, too. "Call me if you need anything."

"As soon as the weather clears, I'll leave, and then I won't be here to drive you crazy."

He chuckles. "It's a bold move for you to come back to this house. It can't be easy."

"Easier than I thought. Weird, right?"

He nods. "Better get inside."

As I walk up the stairs, I can feel his gaze trailing me. I fumble to press in the key code. I enter the numbers incorrectly, and a red *X* appears. Quickly I retype the code, and this time am rewarded with the green check. I glance back at Reece, raise my hand.

He smiles, turns, and follows the beam of light back to his house.

Inside, I close the door and turn on more lights until the entire space is as bright as high noon. The silence settles around me as I shrug off my jacket. I move to the kitchen and pull a water bottle from the refrigerator. I take a long gulp, surprised my mouth feels so dry.

Glancing toward the stairs, I find I've no desire to sleep in the main bedroom or any other on the second floor. The sofa wasn't ideal last night, but I'd rather stay there again. Here I can stare out the skylights and enjoy the stars.

Kicking off my shoes, I recline on the couch and pull a throw blanket over me. Lying back, I expect to stare at the ceiling for hours. But my eyes are heavy, and soon they close.

I want to ignore Stevie Palmer's diary. I don't know who she is or why anyone wants me to peek into her life. But I appreciate that she cared about Nikki Kane. The girl was a forgettable, like me. When our kind falls in the cracks, few come searching for us.

But I sense there's something more embedded in Stevie's written words, and that unspoken truth is unsettling. I rise from the couch and dig the printout from my bag. Jeb went to prison for kidnapping and rape. Stevie had been taken from Nags Head and been the victim of that exact crime. Kyle hadn't been accused of any crime, but violence runs along family bloodlines. Sometimes it skips a generation, and sometimes it rises out of the family tree's roots and poisons all the fruit. Maybe Stevie thought Kyle might be another bad apple. *God, Stevie, were the two men who raped you Jeb and Kyle?*

Maybe Stevie saw Kyle's picture and read my name in the Saturday morning article. Maybe she was triggered. Reece said the brothers looked a great deal alike.

As much as I would like to hide and get on with my life, Stevie is reaching out to me and goading me to help her find Nikki and maybe solve the injustice done to her.

"Stevie, I want to find you, but you're going to have to give me more. And while you're at it, explain to me who the hell are you, Stevie Palmer?"

My phone dings with a new text.

Chapter
Twenty-One

Stevie Palmer's Diary

Thursday, July 6, 2023
2:30 p.m.

I wish I could say that I spent the day looking for Nikki, but I didn't. Like I often do, I let the abyss take me. I found a quiet place to park, pulled my blanket over my head, and fell asleep. In the inky blackness there was peace and rest from a constant shameful feeling that I was somehow failing.

But I finally wake up, and when I see the sun blazing in the sky, I realize I need to get my act together. I owe Nikki my attention. She has been lured into the shadows and now is trapped in the cracks. She needs me to reach in and pull her out. As much as I want to run from that truth, I can't.

I grab my phone and search White Wine, a.k.a. Jeanne Williams, a.k.a. last seen with Bourbon at Joey's Bar. She owns and operates a home care agency in Virginia.

The drive to Chesapeake takes ninety minutes. Traffic is light, and I find Jeanne's office in a strip mall. There's a sign in her storefront window that reads, WILLIAMS FAMILY HOME CARE. WE'RE HERE FOR YOU, MOM AND DAD.

"Here for Mom and Dad? Right." The last thing I would do for my mother is pay hard-earned cash to prop her up when she barely bothered to do the same for me when I was a kid. Fortunately for me, Mommie Dearest is in a better—hopefully, hotter than hell—place.

I see Jeanne through the storefront window. She's on the phone, looking very prim and proper. Not the chick with her horns up in the bar. But hey, not judging. All girls want to have fun.

Out of the car, I move to her front door and open it. She glances up at me, and I can tell by the vacant look on her face that she doesn't recognize me from the bar. Most people don't recognize me when they see me outside the bar. For most, I'm invisible when I'm serving them.

She hangs up, stands, smiles. "Can I help you?"

I adjust my purse on my shoulder and offer a tentative smile. "I'm looking for a caregiver for my mother." The simplest lies are the best.

"Well, you've come to the right place. I'm Jeanne. Why don't you have a seat?" Jeanne smiles as I sit in front of her fancy mahogany desk. "How did you hear about us?"

"Social media." Everyone's on it, so it stands to reason so is she.

"Great. We try to stay active online."

"It worked for me."

"How old is your mother?"

How old would Mom have been? Fifty? I can't picture her that old, and she'd have hated aging. Maybe it's too bad she did die so young. A life sentence in an old and failing body vulnerable to predators would be a just reward. "Mom is seventy."

"That's young."

"I know. She has cancer. It's been several tough years."

She pulls out a notepad and pen. "It's a story I've heard too much."

I sit back and regard her as if seeing her for the first time. "Do I know you?"

Her smile is bemused. "I don't think so."

I point an index finger at her. "Do you ever come in Joey's Bar on the Outer Banks?"

Confusion turns wary. "From time to time."

"I work there as a bartender. I thought I saw you there Tuesday night."

She shifts. "That's a good memory."

"Helps with the job if you can remember a person's face and their drink. White wine, right?"

She clears her throat. "That's right."

I hold up my hands and lean back. "Sorry, I don't mean to bring up your personal life. It's just weird, us seeing each other again."

"What are you doing in Virginia?"

"This is where Mom lives. I work part-time at Joey's. But don't worry about the money. Dad set up a trust for Mom."

Her eyes brighten a fraction. "That's fortunate for your mother."

"Do you get down to Joey's often? I remember seeing you with Bourbon. He's a regular."

"Bourbon?" Something clicks behind her eyes. "Do you mean Kyle?"

Kyle. Finally, I have a first name. "That's him. He comes in often enough for me to remember him, but he always pays cash. Not everyone wants to share their names, if you know what I mean. I guess that's why I remember you. Because you were with Kyle."

Jeanne sits straighter and tucks a strand of hair behind her ear. "Can we get back to your mother?"

I've struck a nerve. If I were smart, I'd back off. But I sense with Jeanne it's now or never. "I don't suppose you know how I can find Kyle? Guy left behind a jacket. It's currently stashed in lost and found, but it's really nice and won't last much longer."

Jeanne's eyes narrow. "I don't know much about Kyle."

I toss her a slight grin. "I get ya. A one and done. We've all been there."

Her face reddens. "Are you here to talk about your mother or not?"

"Sure. I want to talk about her. Kyle have a last name?"

"I'm sure he does." She taps a manicured finger on the desk. "But I don't know it."

"No worries. Didn't mean to bring up a sore subject. Gosh, don't know how I got so far off course. I can be too much of a talker. Drives my boss nuts."

"It's fine. I like to keep my private and professional lives separate."

"Preaching to the choir."

We settle into the details about my dear old mom. After making up a half hour's worth of bull about a mother who's been dead for fourteen years, Jeanne seems to relax. She appears excited about a trust fund client who might need extended care. I take Jeanne Williams's card and leave her store.

I now at least have a first name for Bourbon. Kyle. Too bad there are like a billion of them in the world.

It takes me over an hour and a half to get to Joey's, and when I push through the swinging door connecting the kitchen and bar, I have a half sandwich in hand and an apron wrapped around my waist.

Joey glares at me as he pulls the tap on a beer and fills a mug. "So, you think you can just waltz in here and expect me to give you work?"

I eat the last of the sandwich. Joey growls like a bear, but he just makes noise. I've been around enough to know the good guys from the bad, and he's one of the good ones.

My grin spreads across my face and I wink. "You're glad to see me, aren't you, Joey? I can tell."

His eyes narrow. "Really, how can you tell?"

"I read people really well."

"And what do you know about me?"

"You're a teddy bear."

I grab a damp glass from the steamer and dry it off. Say what you want about me, but I'm good at this job. With me serving he'll rake in an extra 20 percent tonight. I set the glass down and reach for another.

"Shit," he mutters.

"Have you seen Nikki?" I ask.

"No." Genuine worry darkens his gaze. "I thought if I gave her a chance and taught her bartending, she could make a different life. Can't save everyone."

"Who says?" I challenge.

"Says me. I learned that lesson the hard way, kid."

"Stevie!" a man shouts.

As I turn, I see a regular at the end of the bar. Dave. Tax accountant. Trouble with the wife. Gin and tonic. I allow a sly grin. "Dave, my man. Can I get you another gin and tonic, baby?"

He holds up his glass filled with melting ice cubes. "You're one of the few people that understands me."

Dave, as with most of the guys, likes it when I call him *baby*. I pour the gin in the glass and wave tonic over it. A couple of these, and then I'll cut him back until his sixth or seventh glass is pure tonic. "Baby, you know Stevie loves you."

Placing a fresh napkin and his new drink in front of him, I grin and lean a little forward so he gets a better glimpse of the girls. I've got nice tits and am not afraid to use them for tips. I swipe away the old glass and damp napkin.

"I wish all women were like you," Dave says.

"They broke the mold with me, baby. Broke the mold."

When I turn around, Joey has vanished into the kitchen, likely to deal with another issue. That's the thing about a place like this. There's always a problem, whether it's the plumbing, a customer, or an employee. But Joey knows that, at least for tonight, he doesn't have to worry about the bar. Stevie is in charge.

The night falls into a regular routine. It fills with the usual suspects who look ready to escape the heat and whatever holiday/vacation disappointments trouble them. Within the hour, Dave is pleasantly drunk, and I help him call an Uber so he can get home to the wife and kids. As I return to my post behind the bar, I see Bourbon step up to the end. I'm a little stunned. Did Jeanne call him? She said she didn't know his last name, and I thought I covered with her well, but maybe I'm losing my touch.

Bourbon stands in the same spot each night. We all tend to have a familiar chair or spot and without realizing it stake our claim.

I set a clean glass in front of Bourbon and pour in two fingers of top-shelf bourbon.

A grin tips the edges of his lips. "You know me too well, Stevie."

"I do try." I meet his gaze. "Glad to have you back."

"Whenever I get the chance to talk to my favorite bartender, I take it."

"You're a real charmer."

His grin is very engaging. "I'll take that as a compliment."

I'm immediately distracted by a waitress who orders five beers. Her name is Brenda, and she's in her late twenties, tall, thin, and for the most part quick on her feet. I fill the iced mugs and set them on her tray.

"Stevie, glad to have you at the helm," Brenda says. "My tips are always better when you're here. Tell me you're going to make this a permanent gig."

"Can't make any promises, but I do love it here." Brenda has worked at the bar for a year and knows the politics of the place. "Have you heard from Nikki? I've been trying to catch her."

"Haven't seen her for a bit. I thought she quit."

No, she didn't quit. Her trailer is splashed in blood, and she's vanished. And the more I think about that kid, the more I question if she's still alive. Maybe Joey is right. You can't save them all.

"Everything okay with Nikki?" Brenda asks.

I've been here six days. I'm not in the inner circle, but the waitresses know I work my ass off when I'm here, and that helps their tips. There's now a begrudging respect. "I hope so. Did you see her hanging out with anyone in particular?"

"She flirted with everyone," Brenda said. "She liked to tease the guys. No sense of boundaries or filters. A magnet for the bad ones."

And Nikki had a body to die for.

Brenda settles fresh napkins on her tray. "Not saying she can't do what she wants, but a girl has to be smart."

"Any guys that struck you as odd?"

Brenda laughs as she hoists the tray. "Easier to point out the ones that don't have major issues." She catches the gaze of a waiting customer and without a word walks toward him.

I move down the bar, check the beer for a couple of guys, and finally make my way to Bourbon. His glass is half-full. Not enough for a top off, but I still reach for the bourbon bottle to refill his glass.

"You're spoiling me," Bourbon says.

"You deserve to be spoiled." I almost call him *baby* but sense he won't like that. He likes power.

"Do I?" He's intrigued by the comment.

"Of course. I can tell you work hard."

He sips. "Really? How can you tell that?"

"The eyes," I say. "They say it all."

"And what do mine say?" His voice drops a notch, signaling both interest and hesitance.

I remember how he stared at Nikki. It was a hunter's gaze. Love and hate. Pleasure and pain. They're tightly linked in this guy. "You take on a lot of everyone else's problems." A fact true for many successful people.

He sips his bourbon. "What kind of work do you think I do?"

"Your suits, shoes, and haircut say you do very well." His nails are buffed and his hands smooth, uncalloused. A professional. Asking questions comes easily to him. This is the kind of bar where a professional won't run into his peers. He doesn't want his clients seeing him in public while he blows off steam. I teeter between lawyer and doctor. "A doctor."

An unspoken emotion sharpens his gaze. Eyes widen slightly. I've caught him off guard, as if he's not accustomed to being in the hot seat. Bingo. "Correct. What kind of doctor am I?"

He's got an edge, which doesn't jibe with family doctor. In my experience, those doctors don't dress as well. Bourbon is good at asking questions and seems to parse my answers, searching for any kind of angle. Surgeon might fit, but where's the fun when the patient is under anesthesia most of the time. "Psychologist. Shrink."

He sits back and softly claps his hands. "You should be a detective."

"I don't think the police force wants me among their ranks."

"Why is that?"

My laughter is genuine. "You're the shrink, you tell me."

He regards me as he leans forward. "Drilling into that would take several counseling sessions."

I wonder if he used that line on Nikki. "What happens in these meetings?"

"We sit, talk. You tell me what's bothering you."

"That would definitely take a few sessions."

"I can already tell you had a tough childhood." His confidence is unnerving.

I grab the bar rag and wipe up a dry, clean spot. "That so?"

"Absent parents."

Getting closer to the root from which all my shit stems. "Why do you say that?"

"You're the mother hen here. I see the way you talk to the waitresses, the way you hover over Nikki, the way you watch your customers and White Wine. Do you really have a mother who's in need of care?"

Jeanne did call him. "Of course."

"Sorry to hear that."

"Thanks."

He's made his point and seems to quickly grow bored with it. "Is there a problem with Nikki?"

"Missing." I picture her locked in a box screaming for help or buried in a shallow grave. "I don't suppose you've seen Nikki after your date?"

He raises his glass to his lips, pauses. "*Dating* is a bit formal for our arrangement."

"When's the last time you saw her?"

"It was a one-night stand, Stevie. My guess is she's run off with a new boyfriend or high on drugs."

"Maybe."

"Is she a friend of yours?"

"Coworker."

"So why do you care?" His gaze sharpens, telling me he's not just tossing out questions but seriously wants to know.

"I guess my damaged childhood makes me care too much."

"Was there a time when you were lost?" He delivers the question with calculated compassion.

Fake or not, it hits a nerve in me. My chest tightens, and something deep inside me claws, as if it's hauling itself out of the primordial ooze. "Maybe."

"Ever talk to anyone about your life? You could talk to me. This is what I do for a living."

"No. I've done just fine. But thanks for asking." The tables are flipping, and I don't like it.

"I don't make these offers lightly."

"You don't randomly ask women to stop by your office for a one on one?"

"No."

"Did you ask Nikki?"

He turns his glass a quarter turn. "I asked, but she said no. Too bad really. I could help her."

Why is Nikki missing and Jeanne isn't? Maybe Jeanne was someone people would miss, and cops would care about. "If I come by, what happens?"

"We talk."

"About my terrible childhood?" I laugh. "That could take a while."

"That's a good place to start. That's where most trauma stems."

Talking to anyone about my past is a risk that I've never been willing to take. I vowed a long time ago to shut the door on the good old days. But for Nikki, I could crack it very slightly for a second or two. Show just enough to him for dramatic effect.

A slow smile curves my lips. "Okay, I'll bite, Dr. Bourbon. Do you have a card?"

"You'll call?" He's not as surprised as he seems. He's wondering what angle I'm working. He might be a lot of things, but he's not stupid. I'm on his radar.

"If I say I'm going to do something, then I will," I say.

He reaches in his pocket and hands me a white card with raised black lettering. The address is in a nice part of Virginia Beach. His name is *Dr. Kyle Iverson.*

Chapter Twenty-Two

LANE

Sunday, December 31, 2023
9:30 p.m.

My heart is pumping when I read Kyle's full name underlined in bold black ink. There's no mistaking who Stevie was talking about now.

Stevie had met Kyle in a Nags Head bar and agreed to meet him at his office.

Clearly Stevie is (or was) a false name. She isn't the first woman to hide her identity, work for cash tips, and avoid using social security numbers or ID cards.

"Who are you, Stevie Palmer?"

The front doorbell rings and startles me. I grab my phone, rise, and look toward the tall windows bracketing the front door. The shadows shift. I move to within ten feet of the door and pause. My heart pulses. Then the shadows move again, and I see Devon staring back. Her smile is fixed and broad, her eyes wide. She's always so cheerful. She waves, holds up a bottle of wine.

"I saw your lights on," she shouts. "Shame to spend New Year's alone. It might even be bad luck. So here I am!"

All I can think about is Stevie and Kyle.

Devon is grinning. Normally, I would send her away. But she's ready to drink and maybe talk more about Kyle.

I unlock the front door and open it. "Devon."

She holds up her bottle in an I-come-in-peace kind of way. Mascara smudges under her eyes, and she's wearing bright-red lipstick that looks freshly applied. The red is like mine. "Hoping you'll share a couple of glasses with me. And for the record, *no* is not an option."

I laugh quietly. "Maybe one drink. I've already had a couple of beers."

"A couple of beers?" She laughs. "Girl, that's barely a warmup."

"I'm a lightweight when it comes to booze."

"It's New Year's Eve. What better time to have fun, even if it hurts tomorrow?"

As she moves past, I see the lights in Reece's house. I scan the windows, hoping to see him pass in front of one, but there's no sign of him.

"Looking for Reece?" Devon asks.

I close the door. "I see his lights are still on."

"He's been working nonstop since he arrived on Friday." She shakes her head, drops her voice a fraction as if we are coconspirators. "Kind of a crazy guy. In more ways than one. But mostly good."

And I'd been ready to do God-knows-what with him a half hour ago. "I guess that's true for most of us."

She raises the bottle in a toast. "No truer words."

Devon is bubbly, upbeat as she moves toward the kitchen, clearly very comfortable with the house. She knows it better than I do, maybe even Kyle.

But I'm so curious about Kyle and Jeb now. "There are degrees of crazy. Define Reece's brand of crazy."

Devon sets her bottle on the counter, then shrugs off her coat and lets it fall on a barstool. "He's a good guy. Don't get me wrong. But he marches to his own drummer."

I suppose she assumes I'm clued-in on more than I really am. "I still don't understand."

"When we were growing up, he was always in fights. Drugs got ahold of him, and he did some time in jail. Kyle tried to help him, but Reece pushed Kyle and everyone else away. Finally, he reappeared about eight years ago. Clean and sober-ish and ready to make amends for his past. He's really gotten his act together."

Telling Devon about the beers Reece and I shared or how fast we got seminaked feels akin to snitching.

And I'm only interested in pressing Devon for more details about Kyle and his family. Devon, I suspect, won't need much prodding. She's primed to talk. "I hear a *but*."

Devon reaches for a towel and wraps it around the top of the champagne bottle. She twists. *Pop.* "Kyle and Reece shook hands a few years ago and said bygones and shit, but Kyle kept his distance from Reece. Whatever happened between them must have been bad."

"Did it have anything to do with Jeb?"

"Why do you ask that?" she asks.

"I don't know. I understand he died last summer. Kyle never said anything to me, but it must have been hard to lose his brother."

"Yeah, it was. Kyle took that hard. Hell of a way to kick off the July Fourth holiday."

"Reece said he overdosed."

"That's about all Kyle would say. He didn't like to talk about Jeb. He was the family black sheep. His stunt could've cost Kyle his college career."

"His stunt?"

"Taking that girl, doing what he did to her. Lucky for Kyle, Jeb confessed to it all. Swore he acted alone and had never done anything like that before. Jeb stood before a judge, heard his sentence, and the case barely made the papers."

"When was all this?"

"Fourteen years ago."

The same year Stevie was attacked. Stevie had been clear that two men had taken her. It could have been Jeb and Kyle, but what about the other brother, Zeke? Or Earl? According to Stevie, she never filed a police report.

"Tell me about Jeb."

Devon sets the bottle down, retrieves two flutes from a cabinet. She fills each with liquid bubbles. "Champagne makes one hell of a hangover, but what's one glass, right?" She holds out a glass for me.

I accept it, and when she raises hers, I lift mine and we clink flutes. "Thank you."

"To Kyle." Her voice loses some of its vibrance, which I suspect is a cover for stinging grief. "May he rest in peace."

A part of me doesn't want to toast this man. Fragments of me are inexplicably angry. Does he deserve peace or to burn in hell? The anger behind that question throws me off.

I catch myself. There's no evidence that proves Kyle did anything wrong. Knowing a woman does not mean he hurt her. He was a human being who died in a tragic accident and deserves the benefit of the doubt. "To Kyle."

Our glasses *clink*.

I sip and savor the cool, dry bubbles. "Nice."

Devon nods toward me and grins. "Only the best for you."

The comment feels odd, but she's that way, right? Super friendly. A little too well acquainted.

"Want to get in the hot tub?"

"No, I'm fine inside."

"It's super fun. Has all the bells and whistles." She takes a liberal sip. "Just between us girls, when no one is here, I get in it."

"I didn't bring a suit."

She grins. "Who needs a suit?"

"Thanks, but let's stay inside."

"Suit yourself."

I settle on an overstuffed side chair, and she takes the couch, slipping off her shoes and tucking her feet under her. She's right at home here.

Devon sets the bottle on the coffee table. "Jeb was the best looking of the Iverson brothers. I had a crush on him. But he was not good at looking ahead. He wanted what he wanted and didn't consider the consequences."

"He saw that girl, and decided he could just take her?"

She shrugs. "He wasn't that bright, and he had a mean streak. The more successful Kyle became, the more Jeb lashed out. He and Reece were getting into a lot of fights then. The summer Jeb did what he did, Kyle was back home. It was between his sophomore and junior years of college. Kyle was the conquering hero. Everyone wanted to see Kyle and congratulate him. Jeb was seventeen, failing high school, and smoking meth. He had no plans to do anything with his life. Seeing everyone fawn over Kyle made it all worse. He got pissed, drove into Nags Head, found that poor girl, and did what he did."

"He acted alone?"

"That's what he said."

"What do you think?"

"I don't know. He had friends up here who might have been willing to help. All the guys that grew up together were super tight. Stands to reason Jeb would take the blame to save a buddy."

Or one of his brothers.

"He gets out of prison and dies almost immediately," I say. "No one will ever know if there was someone else."

She traces the rim of her flute with her finger. "Probably for the best. What's past is past. And Jeb's life wasn't going anywhere, and he knew it."

"Did Kyle reach out to him while he was in prison?"

"No. He had a life that was taking off. He didn't need that kind of drama."

"What about after Jeb's release? Did they connect?"

"I don't know."

According to Stevie, Kyle had been drinking in Joey's Bar around the time of Jeb's death. And then Nikki had vanished.

"Kyle wasn't anything like Jeb?" I ask.

"Kyle was smarter. More ambitious."

"But he would never act out like Jeb, right?"

Devon laughs. "No. Why would you say that?"

"I don't know. Champagne makes me stupid." The more layers of Kyle's life I peel back, the more unsavory the findings.

"Can I be honest with you?" Devon asks. "I mean, I can be nosy, so tell me to butt out if you don't want to answer."

I suspect she'll ask no matter what I say. "Sure, tell me what you're thinking."

"When Kyle found you, it was like a missing piece fell into place. The last time I talked to him was Friday morning. He was packing at his apartment and getting ready to pick you up. He sounded so happy. He couldn't wait to show you this place and share his world with you."

Would he have mentioned the house in the woods, his shaky finances, or the brother who'd done time for rape? "I'm not so sure."

"He might have been complicated, but his feelings for you were simple." She cocks a brow. "Did you love him?"

I clear my throat of unnamed emotions tightening it. "I cared for him. I thought it could grow into love."

Devon's gaze spears me. "Are you doing okay, Lane?"

"I'm hanging in there."

"As terrible as dying is, sometimes dying is better than living with a tragedy. Jeb knew that."

"I'm sad, but I'll find a way to live with this." I've no desire to talk about living or dying. "I walked up toward the woods today. I wanted to see where Kyle grew up."

Devon frowns. "I told you it wasn't safe."

I know the streets of Norfolk can be dangerous. I'm always looking around corners and into shadows. But up here, it feels so far removed from danger. "You mean Earl?"

Devon sips her champagne. "You met him?"

"Briefly."

Her gaze turns serious. "Stay clear of him. He might seem nice, but he's not going to be nice if he gets you alone. Avoid him. He used to run with Jeb and Zeke."

"What was Zeke like?"

"Moody. Kept to himself."

"He ever hurt anyone?" I ask.

"He had a temper, but he kept it in check."

"What about Earl? I mean, what's his story?"

"He doesn't have a job but gets by dealing drugs. Nothing big-time, but enough to make him very protective of his stuff."

I'm not going to psychoanalyze Earl. He's mean. Stay clear. End of story. "Could you take me up to the forest and woodlands? I'd like to really see the house where Kyle grew up."

She shakes her head as she finishes off her glass, reaches for the bottle, tops off mine, and refills hers. "The house is falling in on itself. I'm not sure it's even safe."

It hadn't looked sturdy, but it's still standing, and there's something about it that stirs questions I can't put into words. "Agreed."

"Why do you want to see it?" she asks. "It's nothing special."

"All this is a piece of Kyle. I need all the pieces to see the man."

"Why?"

"I saw him die," I say softly. "That's a connection I can't break."

Devon sips, staring at me. "I don't think you'll ever know Kyle. None of us did."

"You must have known him better than most."

"We had a connection when he was up on the 4x4, but once he left for the city, he forgot all about me. We've not spent any real time together in the last decade. He did hire me when I needed the work, so I guess that's saying something."

I can feel her sadness. Kyle had moved on from her, and she hated being left behind. "That couldn't have felt good."

"It's my fault, not his." She raises her chin. "He asked me so many times to join him in the city, but I've no use for crowded streets and gridlock."

"You dated Kyle?"

She draws in a deep breath. "That was a long time ago. When we were practically kids."

This is a small community, and romantic relationships are bound to form. Still, I've no desire to hear the details, which I suspect Devon would share with a little prodding. "How often did Kyle come up here?"

"At least once a month, sometimes twice. He loved the solitude."

"He must have loved this place during the summer." I think about Stevie seeing him on July Fourth weekend. "He only mentioned this place to me a day before we left."

Devon sips her champagne, and bubbles rise to the top of the glass. "Ask me anything about Kyle, us, or growing up here. I'll tell you everything I know."

I raise the glass to my lips, pretend to sip. "Did he ever mention a woman named Stevie Palmer?"

She stills. "He mentioned her once or twice. How do you know her?"

That's not the answer I'm expecting. Reece had never heard of her, but Devon has. "I don't know anything about her. That's why I'm asking. She's a mystery."

Devon studies me a beat longer, as if she's trying to figure out if I have an angle. "She's kind of . . . complicated."

I told Reece about Stevie's journal, but telling Devon doesn't feel right. "What does that mean?"

Devon chuckles, finishes off her glass, and reaches for the bottle. "She's batshit crazy."

I think back to another entry. Is Stevie crazy? Have I missed something in her diary?

Chapter Twenty-Three

STEVIE PALMER'S DIARY

Friday, July 7, 2023
10:00 a.m.

When I wake up, I'm in the back seat of my car, curled on my side, my pillow tucked under my neck. My mouth is dry as I try to push up on my elbows. But as I struggle to rise, my body freezes as if imaginary hands press me flat against the worn cloth seat.

Panic rises in me. I push harder, but my muscles refuse to work. A heaviness weighs down on my body as hot, sour breath brushes my neck. *I can do whatever I want to you. I own you.*

Gritting my teeth, I push away the memory as I buck free of the past. "You don't own me anymore, shithead," I hiss.

Heart beating fast and sweat pooling at the base of my spine, I draw in several deep breaths as I swing my legs onto the car's floor. I look around the back seat, scanning the discarded dirty shirts, jeans, and the extra pair of boots. I'd been exhausted when I parked last night, and I could barely summon the energy to kick my shoes off and pull the blanket over me.

I am alone in the car. There's no one lurking in the corner. No one is restraining me. Nothing bad is going to happen to me today or ever again. I'm safe.

I can do whatever I want to you. Those echoing words, like coiling tentacles, spiral around me. "No, you can't! No, you can't!"

I can do whatever I want to you. Whatever. I. Want.

My fists clench as adrenaline pumps through my veins. I'm ready to fight whatever comes at me, real or imagined. I've been fighting since I was a kid, and combat is my superpower. Few people challenge me on the streets because there's a look in my eye that signals I'm crazy enough to do anything.

Maybe that's why I'm so worried about Nikki. She looked past all the damage and offered a brand of kindness that I've experienced so rarely in my life.

I climb over the seat and slide behind the steering wheel, fire up the engine, and drive to the YMCA. I wait until the man behind the desk is distracted, and then I hustle into the women's locker room.

I strip, pull a towel from my backpack, and head into the showers. A twist of the knob and hot water splashes my body. When the steam rises, I step into the heat, willing it to chase the chill from my bones. I wash and scrub my skin until it's pink.

Drawing in a breath, I towel off and make my way back to the changing area. A glance in the full-length mirror reflects bloodshot eyes ringed with dark circles. My cheeks are more hollow than usual, and the color in my hair is fading.

Yeah, surviving is my superpower. Still, in this moment, I'm shaken.

Toweling off, I dig clean jeans from my backpack and a black V-neck T-shirt. I slid on my brown leather boots. Most people are knocking around in flip-flops and shorts at the beach this time of year, but my wardrobe rarely wavers. Covered skin and boots are my protective shell.

I drag a brush through my damp darkish hair and bind it back in a small ponytail. The spray of freckles across my nose makes me look uncomfortably younger. Without makeup, my version of battle paint, I feel vulnerable. I detest this bare, childish face.

"I'm not weak." I grab foundation and dab a liberal portion over my nose. With each pass, I rub harder, erasing traces of the girl who'd once been too weak, too small to save herself. By the time I've lined my eyes, painted on eye shadow, and brushed on mascara, that girl is gone, and I feel in control. I am me again.

On the way out, I wave to the guy behind the counter, who seems to wonder who I am. I keep moving. I drive north, and my first stop is a quirky coffee shop with a vine-covered trellis. There's a mural on the side of the building and benches outside that on a cool day would be nice. Inside the store, I scrounge a rumpled ten from my pocket and buy a double espresso and then dump the remaining singles in the tip jar.

The caffeine chases away some of the cobwebs and sharpens my focus as it juices me up. I am feeling more like myself. Less emotional. Detachment is like a muscle, and mine is well used.

It's still midmorning. Joey will be looking for me at the bar by six, which gives me plenty of time to visit Nikki's trailer one more time. Criminals do return to the scene of the crime to retrieve evidence or maybe even gloat. There will be a different crop of people stirring around this time of day, and there could be someone new who's seen a stranger lurking around. Daylight will also offer a different perspective on everything.

The only lead I have to Nikki now is Bourbon. Kyle. Kyle Iverson. I don't believe in coincidence, and Kyle Iverson was with Nikki the last time I saw her. He also hooked up with Jeanne for a night. And now he's my new therapist. Kyle. Kyle. Kyle. The three faces of Kyle.

In midday beach traffic, the drive across the bridge to the mainland takes less than twenty before I pull onto the dirt road dividing the twin rows of beige trailers. There are plenty of jobs on the Outer Banks, but finding an affordable place to live is another matter. Few who visit here look beyond the sunny beaches and trendy shops. No one wants to see where their servers live. Sort of like finding out how the sausage is made.

I park and move toward Nikki's place, and as I approach her door, I realize it's open.

As I slow my pace, a man's deep voice drifts out of the room, and when I look inside, I see a man with broad shoulders standing with his back to me, phone to his ear. He's wearing jeans, a black T-shirt, and boots.

My foot nudges a beer can, and the man turns with startling speed. His hand goes to his hip and the grip of a gun holstered on his belt. His eyes meet mine, and after a beat, we both relax.

Something in his expression suggests he's not surprised to see me here. He ends the call. "What are you doing here?"

"I'm still looking for Nikki. She hasn't shown up for work, and no one has seen her."

He moves toward me with even, steady strides. In the light of day, he's composed, and the armor that slips when people get naked in bed is in place. Bulletproof comes to mind.

"When's the last time you saw Nikki?" he asks.

"July 2, give or take."

As this near stranger stares at me, I realize he also saw Nikki the night she vanished. Sure, he doesn't have the income to afford a fancy car, but police impound all kinds of vehicles ready for borrowing.

"Have you found out anything?" he asks.

"Me first. What are you doing here? Why are you suddenly concerned about Nikki?"

"Joey called. He asked me to ask around. Said you were looking, and it might not end well."

I can't decide who I love more in that moment. Joey or Sully. My two antiheroes. "I thought you were in construction, Sully."

"I am. Now."

"Now? But not always?"

Sully holds my gaze. "No."

"Let me guess, military police?"

"That's right. Retired. Marines."

"Did Joey file a missing persons report for Nikki?"

"No. He knows any investigation will have a low priority," Sully says. "Nikki was over twenty-one, had been in the area less than two weeks, and was seen with various men." He draws in a breath. "Now it's your turn. How about you show me your driver's license. I'd like to know who I'm dealing with." He trusts me about as much as I trust him.

"I'd love to, but I lost it along with my phone," I lie. "Been meaning to get a new one, but the lines at DMV are murder."

"Lost it?" A smile teases his lips. "Where?"

"It's a long story that'll bore you to tears."

"What about registration on your car?" He glances toward the silver four-door with Virginia plates. No doubt he's committing the plates to memory.

"In the wallet I lost."

Tension simmers under Sully's direct gaze. "You didn't say wallet."

"All ID lost. Credit cards. All the stuff that makes a person a real person. I don't even have a cell."

His latex-gloved hands flex slightly. He knows I'm fucking with him, but he's not a real cop, so I don't care. "I can have you arrested."

I'm smart enough not to smile. "Not my idea of foreplay."

"I'm not screwing around, Stevie." His voice deepens, sharpens. "What do you know about Nikki?"

Best not to keep poking the bear. "The night you and I met in Joey's, I spotted Nikki in the back seat of a customer's car. She was trying to get free, and he was forcing her down on the back seat."

"Joey told me. He said the guy's name is Pete. Do you remember the vehicle?"

"Pete Griffin, by the way. Drove a big black truck. Supposedly he lives in Chesapeake, Virginia." I rattle off his plate.

"I've already checked into Pete Griffin," Sully says. "He had an alibi the following night. Apparently, he was in the ER with a shattered knee."

"That was a little memento from me."

He ignores my passing confession of assault. "Why are you here, Stevie? You barely knew the kid."

"Call it a weakness for the underdog," I say. "Nikki is a nice kid. And if she's hurt and suffering somewhere, I'd like to help her. I came by this place the other night and saw the blood. Something is really wrong."

"Why didn't you call it in?"

"Because then there'd be questions for me. And seeing as I lost my wallet . . ."

He stares at me, and the cop he used to be is champing at the bit. "Joey said she flaked a lot in the two weeks she was at the bar."

I hear the implication. She wasn't reliable so it'll be easier to forget her. Out of sight. Out of mind. "Why are you here?"

"Would she have run off with someone?" he asks.

"Maybe. But whoever she's with is not a good guy."

"She wouldn't be the first woman to stick with an abuser," he says.

I think about her leaving willingly with the suit after he splattered her blood on that bed. "You're right. She might be her own worst enemy. But I liked her. I want to find her. Help her."

"I remember a preppy-looking guy, overdressed for the crowd in the bar that night," Sully says. "He always ordered top-shelf."

Powers of observation are so sexy. "You always remember random guys in a bar?" I ask.

"Old habits die hard."

That I know well. "For the record, his real name is Kyle Iverson. A doctor. Not the medical kind but the mind kind."

"And you know this how? He paid with cash."

"He had a date who used a credit card. I tracked her down. She told me his first name. And then last night, he came in the bar. We played twenty questions. I got his business card, in case I need some counseling."

His stare turns into a glare. "Why would he care if you're asking around about him?"

I smile and lean slightly toward him. "Because I hit a nerve."

He mutters *shit*. "You're not considering seeing him for a counseling session, are you?"

"I don't know." I shrug. "Maybe. You never know what you'll learn. Secrets have a way of revealing themselves."

Frown lines on his face furrow deeper. "Let me ask around and dig into his past before you lock yourself in a room alone with him." His eyes blaze.

"Sure. Ask around."

"Does that mean you'll stand down?" He's leaning so close I can feel the energy radiating off him.

"Does that look make men shake in their boots?"

"Yes."

"I can't be scared. Seeing hell will do that to a person."

His expression softens a fraction. "Stevie, I'm just looking out for you."

"Don't worry about me, Sully. Nikki needs all boots on the ground looking for her." Chasing Kyle Iverson has become very personal to me.

"If you get into trouble, who will save you?" he asks.

"I'll leave that to you, Sully. I suspect you're up to the challenge."

Those comments seem to douse some of the fire blazing in his blue eyes. "Does Iverson come into Joey's Bar regularly?"

"Not according to Joey. I've only been working there a week."

"How often have you seen him?"

"Three times. That's a lot of visits for a professional man from Virginia."

"Maybe he has a house nearby."

"Maybe."

I draw in a breath. "Okay, well, if you find her let me know," I say. "The bar is the best place to get in touch with me. I'll be around a few more days."

"You're leaving?"

"Never know with me."

He scribbles his number on the back of a hardware store receipt. "Call me if you need anything."

I hesitate before I reach for it. I'm careful not to touch him because I wouldn't mind feeling those hands again on my body. "You think the cops could get some kind of crime scene unit in here?"

"I have a friend in the sheriff's department. I'll call him. But it's not going to be on anyone's priority list."

Girls like Nikki never are. I watch him closely. "Don't forget her."

"I won't." He rubs his hand over his clean-shaven chin as he walks into the bedroom and studies the space. "The blood patterns suggest someone was hit in the face. See the stipple on the sheets?"

I follow and my gaze is immediately drawn to the red droplets scattered on the grayish-white sheets. "How can you tell?"

"I've looked at my share of scenes." He studies the dingy carpet stained with blood. "Facial wounds can bleed a lot." He moves toward the small bathroom. "It's in here as well."

"What do you think happened?"

"I imagine someone hitting Nikki, her clutching her mouth and running to the tiny bathroom. Her attacker follows her and watches her clean up."

"No one heard screams." I tell him what Jana saw on the now-deleted tape.

"Whatever he said to her in that bathroom charmed and calmed her. He's slick. Knows how to manipulate."

"Nikki told me she was used to violence."

He frowns. "I can poke around and see what I can find about Kyle Iverson. If he does have property down here, it might be the ideal place to take Nikki. This time of year, hotels are packed. And not very private."

"Thanks, Sully. Nice someone cares."

He studies me, and I sense he has so many questions for me, but instead he shakes his head.

Sully strikes me as one of the good guys, but he's different from Joey. This one has secrets. But who doesn't, right? "Back at you."

As I turn, he clears his throat. "Call me."

He's said it twice now. Is twice enough? "I'll call if I find out something about Nikki."

His hand slides to his pocket. Change rattles. "Call me even if you don't."

"And do what? A repeat performance?" A buzz rushes me. Easy to say yes to more time with him. But what's the fun if I don't tease a little? "Or just chat?"

Sully cocks a brow. "Whatever you want. I like to talk, and I bet money you have lots to say."

That makes me laugh. "My life's a hornet's nest, Mr. Not-a-Detective-Any-Longer."

He's a man in full who doesn't need to push a woman, but he's not above suggesting. "I'm not looking for a white picket fence," he says.

I grin. "In that case, I just might be in touch."

Chapter Twenty-Four

LANE

Monday, January 1, 2024
7:00 a.m.

I wake to the sound of a text pinging on my phone. The *beep* burrows deep into my brain, dragging me up toward consciousness. The instant I sit up, I regret it. My head pounds. The champagne that tasted so good last night is now chiseling its way through my head, carving out pieces of gray matter as it also churns my gut. Happy New Year to me.

Devon and I finished the bottle last night, and then she opened a second bottle of wine and then a third. By the time Devon left around midnight, she didn't appear affected. I was barely able to follow her to the front door, wave, and lock the door behind me before I collapsed on the sofa. Now my entire body aches.

Devon and I talked some about Kyle, but she talked mostly about the houses she manages and the people who own and rent them. She never lacked for things to chatter about as she refilled my glass over and over.

Six hours of sleep. That should be enough for me. I've gotten by on far less when I had a paper due or a double shift to work at the coffee shop. But my eyes feel as if they're filled with sand and were closed for seconds, not hours.

Pushing off the couch, I rise and walk to the window that faces Reece's house. The lights on the second and first floors are on. I see him pass by a window, and then his front door opens. He steps out and Devon follows. Her hair is tangled, and she burrows deep in her jacket. Reece is wearing his jeans, a pull-on shirt, and boots that don't appear to be laced.

Devon pauses, rises on tiptoes, and kisses Reece on the lips. His hand comes to the base of her back, but he makes no move to pull her closer.

I angle my body so I'm out of their view, but I keep watching them. She clings to him and then cups his ass with her hand.

Am I jealous, angry, or disappointed that I'm not the one walking home smelling of sex? My emotions roll around like a game show wheel. Finally, the wheel stops on angry.

Devon knew I had dinner with Reece, and last night she returned to stake her claim. She's as familiar and relaxed with touching his body as she is in Kyle's kitchen. I don't belong. And she's showing me.

Devon releases Reece, and then she shoves her hands in her coat pockets and trots down the stairs. She's smiling when she turns west on the dirt road and quickly vanishes into the thicket of trees.

Reece pushes fingers through his hair and then rubs the back of his neck. He's not smiling, and his expression is grim. I hope he has regrets.

My phone dings with a text.

I cross the room and check the text. **Did you see the morning show? Any doubt in your mind who Reece belongs to now?**

The text sounds as if it could be from Devon, but the number isn't the one I have for her. It's the number linked to the original PDF containing Stevie's diary. There's a new attachment. Could this be Devon using a different phone? Or is there someone else watching me?

I open the attachment and find Stevie's now-familiar handwriting. Whoever is connecting us, she's become my partner in crime. And I don't feel so alone now.

In the kitchen, I set up the coffee maker as the printer spits out pages in Kyle's office. As the coffee maker hisses, I move into the office and take the ten pages off the tray.

Back in the kitchen, I reach for the coffee, dress it with hazelnut creamer. Hot and strong.

Cup cradled in my hands, I carry the pages to the front window, where the light is better, and begin to read. Again, a stranger is pulling me into her world. She has more to tell me about the man she's been hunting. Judging by Kyle's notebook with her name scrawled in it, she did visit his office.

My phone dings with another text.

Shelly here on a borrowed smartphone. That cop came by yesterday, or the day before. He was asking about you. Asked about Stevie. I told him I haven't seen her in a while.

The text stares back at me. Shelly, my neighbor, knew Stevie? I text back: Shelly, what do you remember about Stevie?

There's no response. I know Shelly well enough to know she's returned the phone and is now sleeping. She rarely rises before twelve noon.

Tucking the phone in my back pocket, I finish the coffee. I don't see Reece's truck in the driveway. No idea where he'd go this early on New Year's Day. Maybe he needed a break after a night with Devon. I do. Devon is likely back home, curled up under the covers.

It's where I should be. I need to wrap this visit up and get the hell out of here. But this place has sunk hooks into me. And what I want doesn't seem to matter right now.

I grab my coat, hat, and gloves and step out into the cold wind. Down the front steps, I stare at Kyle's oceanfront house. Kyle and I stood in this spot days ago. Our arms were locked, but he made no mention of Reece's presence, the crushing water damage, or that it was his property. *I've always loved this area.*

Curious, I move toward the house and climb the front steps as I had last night. I try the front door and discover it's open. Hinges squeak as I step inside. The interior is cold, and shadows weigh heavy as the morning sun's orange rays bounce off the walls.

I glance toward the large beige couch in the corner of the room and remember how lost I felt when Reece was kissing me. If not for the distraction of the shutter, who knows what would have happened.

I cross through the kitchen. On the marble counter is a pair of worn work gloves. Reece. I pick up the gloves and clench my fingers around them. The leather is soft, made even more buttery by endless hours of work. I raise the gloves to my nose and smell him. So different from Kyle.

Moving up the central staircase, I realize the house's interior mirrors the larger one across the street on the beach. I suspect Kyle had had a vision with this house, but he wasn't happy with what he created. So, he started again across the street. He remade his dream, only bigger and grander.

I climb the stairs. The second floor is intact. Carpet, walls, even the artwork on the walls is in place. In the largest bedroom, the rumpled sheets on a king-size bed remind me again of Reece, but this time I picture him kissing Devon. Why do I care that they screwed last night? I mean nothing to them, and they even less to me.

I run my fingers over the white sheets. As I turn, I see a trail of red leading into the bathroom. I follow and step into the bathroom. There's a spray of blood on the counter and pools of it in the sink. The mirror is cracked in the center, as if someone slammed a fist into it. The blood wasn't leading into the bathroom but out of it.

My stomach tightens. What the hell happened?

There's no blood downstairs or on the steps, so whatever happened, it occurred up here. Did Reece return upstairs, see himself in the mirror, and strike?

Back in the bedroom, I move to the side table and open it. There's a holstered gun settled in the center and several single condom packets. The gun is not secure, and the house is unlocked. That doesn't seem like something Reece would do. Whatever happened here must've been fast and unexpected.

I call Reece. It rings four times, and the call lands in voice mail. As I stare at the gun, I find I'm at a loss for words. I end the call and close the drawer.

Out of the main room, I move to each of the three other bedrooms. They are all neat, clean, and untouched.

Downstairs I search for any signs of blood. There's nothing. Whatever happened upstairs was contained there.

Outside a truck rumbles down the street. It slows and pulls into this driveway. I freeze. And then finding my legs, I hurry toward the back door, open it, and slip outside. Carefully, I close the door and wait as footsteps thud on the front deck.

I rush down the stairs, careful to keep my footsteps light. When I reach the sandy soil, I run away from the beach toward the woods. My hip complains bitterly, and I beg it to hold steady. Just a little bit longer.

I finally stop running when my lungs and hip both are burning. It's ice in my lungs and fire in my hip, but I've put at least a half mile between myself and the house.

Pressing my palm against the joint, I rub and pray I've not torn my labrum. Pushing the clutch when I drive out of here might be a challenge, but I'll manage.

I jam my hands into my coat pockets and realize I still have Reece's gloves. I hold them up, wondering how I could have made such a stupid mistake. I am not only a snoop but also a thief.

How do I return these without an awkward explanation? *Hey, looking around in your house. Picked these up on a lark. Didn't mean to take them. By the way, what's the deal with the blood? And did you have sex with Devon?*

Why don't I get in the car and leave this entire place behind?

There are no other houses on this packed-sand road, and as I walk closer to the woods, I feel as if I'm again leaving what remains of my world behind. Thick trees line both sides of the road. Wind blows down the street, snaking under the open folds of my jacket. I zip up the front and burrow my hands into Reece's gloves. They're surprisingly soft and warm.

It takes ten minutes to reach the old, graying house that had been Kyle's as a child. All the while, I'm on the lookout for Earl. If we cross paths now, I doubt there'd be anyone around to help if I scream.

The house is as I remember it. Sun-bleached gray siding, overgrown bushes and vines, and a roof that sags in on itself. It's as if this land resents the house and is doing its best to retake the timbers, swallow the entire structure back into the earth, and erase traces of all things made by human hands.

I follow the overgrown, narrow graveled path that snakes across the sandy soil toward the house's stairs. Weeds and vines brush my legs and several grab hold, forcing me to pull free.

At the house, the railing is shaky, and several steps are broken. It's a fall waiting to happen.

Gingerly, I place a foot on the bottom step. It's sturdy enough. I climb up another and another. I'm halfway up when the boards under my feet splinter and crack. The railing wobbles, and for a moment I'm certain I'm going to fall. I stagger a step forward. Time stops.

This time I see our fall happening in real time. Kyle is facing me. My hand is pressed to his chest. The thump, thump of his heart flutters under my fingers. I lose my footing, fall forward, and my body tilts into his. He tries to steady us, but he teeters off balance. And we fall. One instant we're on the top step, and the next we're lying on the marble floor covered in blood.

Did I cause the fall? Did I stumble, trip, or misstep? The remaining missing seconds are winnowing down. Just a few beats, and I'll have the full picture.

I grip the railing. Another good shake proves it still holds well enough, so I step over the broken tread. I hurry to the porch.

There's a screen door, and it opens with a hard tug. However, the interior door is locked. There are three windows at the top, but they're above my head. I move along the exterior deck toward the first window. The glass is covered in grime, but the interior curtains are open.

I open the flashlight app on my phone. The house is dark, but light from the exposed roof leaks morning sunlight into the central room. There's water puddling on the floor from the rains we've had in the last couple of days. I see a small kitchen off to the left, and a living room outfitted with cargo furniture. It feels like a time capsule dating back fifty years. I try to imagine the house full of children, parents, and laughter. But there's nothing here but gloom, dust dancing in the morning light, and an eerie silence.

A kitchen table is surrounded by six chairs. One of the chairs is equipped with arms, and that chair has been pulled away from the table. It's alone and isolated. There's something dangling from one of the arms. When I shine the light through the window and squint to hone my gaze, I realize that it's a red nylon rope.

If someone wanted to hide a woman from the world, this would be the place to do it. Stevie said she was taken to a remote area. But that rope isn't fourteen years old. It appears new.

My phone rings. Startled, I glance at the number. Reece. I tug off his gloves and shove them in my coat pockets. Adrenaline rockets through my veins as I look around, half expecting to see him standing at the bottom of the stairs.

When I don't see him, I answer the call. "Reece."

"You called?"

I look inside the window toward the chair, and the single strand of rope hanging from the chair's arm. "Ah, yeah. Sorry. I didn't see your truck. Thought you'd taken off."

"I had to run into town. Thankfully, I know the guy who owns the hardware store, and he met me there."

"Everything all right?" I ask.

"Sure, why do you ask?"

I stare at the still rope. "Just checking."

"Where are you?"

I turn and look toward the street. There's no one there. "What do you mean?"

"I'm on your front porch. You didn't answer the door."

He's already back. How did he get into Corolla, which is a good fifteen miles from here, and return so quickly? Because he never left. If he needed a bandage, the volunteers at the fire station could have patched him up. We're both lying.

"Oh, I'm out walking on the beach." Boards creak under my feet as I take a step back. I wince, freeze.

"Where?"

"Not far from the house," I lie. "I woke up early. Needed to clear my mind. Devon's champagne did a number on my head."

"You drank with Devon?" Caution blends with amusement.

"She came by and wanted to toast the New Year. One drink turned into several."

He chuckles. "She can drink me under the table."

I bet. "I'm the first to admit I can't hold my liquor." I ease toward the stairs, careful to step over the spot that creaks. "Better get going. I'll see you in a bit."

"It's going to rain. Clouds are getting thick."

"I can see that," I lie. "On my way. See you soon."

As I end the call, my gaze scans the western view from the house. Woods, grasslands, and marshes reach toward Currituck Sound. There's a small dock at the end of the dead-end road and moored to the pylons is a flat-bottom boat. The road is not the only way to reach this section of beach.

I move down the stairs, gingerly stepping and gripping the rail. The boards under my feet moan. Bend. Groan. When my foot touches the ground, I'm relieved. Down the narrow path, overgrown vines brush against my legs.

"Where are you going, little girl?"

The question comes from the woods. I recognize Earl's voice, but I can't see him. I walk faster.

"What were you doing peeking in that old house, little girl?" His voice isn't much more than a whisper, but it sounds closer. "Poking into things you shouldn't?"

Gripping my phone, I fold the fingers of my other hand into a fist. I start a jog, wincing almost immediately as I put the stress on my injured hip. I slow to a fast walk. I can hear the reeds and woods around me rustling as if I'm being tracked.

"What are you doing in the house?" Earl asks.

The dunes are getting closer. I can't outrun anyone, but I keep moving, my teeth gritting against the discomfort. My heart hammers in my chest.

"I was looking for Stevie and Nikki, Earl. Have you seen them?"

The rustling stops, but I can feel him staring at me. I face him. "Were you with Jeb when he took that girl?"

"You don't know what you're talking about." He's in the woods, surrounded by the thick trees, and it's hard to know exactly where he is. I'm moving slowly now. "I never hurt nobody," he says.

"Someone was hurt in that house. And not a long time ago but recently. Did Kyle bring a woman up here last summer?"

Branches rustle.

I look back and see him on the road. He's walking toward me, but his pace is slow and steady. "I don't know Nikki or Stevie. And Jeb and Kyle are dead."

"Did they hurt girls?"

"You ask too many questions. No one up here likes questions. And there are plenty of places to hide a woman like you. Leave while you can."

I start moving again toward the dunes. Blood rushes my body and pounds against my eardrums, deafening me to anything around me.

When I reach the dunes, I look back. There's no sign of Earl. I haul in a breath and then shove it out.

I walk quickly toward the ocean. The wind gets stronger, colder as I get closer. The clouds have thickened, and portions are shaded with dark grays and streaked with black. Soon the storm hovering in the east will hit the shore.

Reece's gloves feel bulky and out of place in my pockets, and I'm not sure how I'm going to return them without explaining. Maybe I can drop them by his truck or at the base of the stairs.

As I approach the row of houses, a black horse appears on the dunes. He studies me, snorts, and begins to move toward me. I back up, holding my hands up. "I don't want trouble, pal."

He's large, and his muscled legs are built for power. If he charges me, I'm powerless to stop him. I still, hold my breath. Finally, the creature stops, paws at the sand, and then walks away as if I'm of no interest.

Shoving out a breath, I limp over the dunes and return via the beach. If I'm spotted by Devon or Reece, my story will at least match my location now.

I don't want Reece to know I was in the woods or at Kyle's old home. No one here needs to know my business. The only reason I'm staying now is because of Stevie and Nikki.

Jeb, Earl, Zeke, Reece, or even Kyle kidnapped and raped a young girl. Kyle had met Stevie in the bar where Nikki worked. Nikki vanished. Nikki looks like me. Stevie asked hard questions. Now she's gone.

Every person is a creature of habit. Maybe Kyle had a thing for working-class women. He had the perfect house to tuck a woman away for as long as he wanted. And if a woman were to die up here, it would be easy to hide her body.

Blood rushes my head, pounding alongside the champagne hangover. Maybe I'm alive because I'm just damn lucky.

Chapter Twenty-Five

LANE

Monday, January 1, 2024
8:30 a.m.

I'm limping by the time I climb over the dunes and walk toward Kyle's house. The nerves in my left leg are burning as I climb up the beach house's back stairs. Across the street I hear Reece's truck door slam closed.

I toss him a wave. He looks frustrated. "Everything all right?"

"Misplaced my gloves," he says. "They were my favorite pair."

Climbing down the stairs, I notice the bandage on his hand. "Do you have another set?"

"Sure." He sounds pissed. "Took me six months to break in those gloves."

I shift the weight from my left hip to my right. "They'll turn up."

He shakes his head as his gaze takes in my flushed cheeks and windswept hair. His frown softens. "You look a little off. The hip bothering you?"

"I walked too much." I nod toward his hand. "What happened?"

He doesn't spare his hand a passing glance. "Stupid accident. Not a big deal."

The spiral fracture in the mirror says otherwise. "What's on your agenda today?" I ask.

"Ripping up the flooring in the laundry room."

"Progress?"

"Yeah. What about you? You finished with that house?"

I'm out of reasons to stay, but the longer I linger, the more questions appear. Footprints. Blood. Rope. Even Earl. Questions are piling on top of questions. "The weather is closing in fast, but I should have clear skies tomorrow."

"Back to Norfolk?" he asks.

"That's right."

He nods, his gaze holding me a long beat that warms my chilled skin. "I'm sorry about last night."

"What do you have to be sorry about?"

"I kind of blew you off."

His loyalty to Kyle, Devon, and this world outweighs his desire for me. "This feels weird for you. I get it."

"I like you, Lane."

I think about the rope dangling from the chair. What does he know about that house? "I get it."

"I'm sorry."

"Don't be." My smile is wan. "Good luck finding your gloves."

That startles loose a smile. "Thanks."

I climb the stairs to the house, and when I close the door behind me, I lean against it. I'm drained from a bad night's sleep, the morning adrenaline dump, and walking on a bad hip.

I pull Reece's gloves from my pockets and turn them over in my hands before raising them to my nose. My attraction to him is now drowning in suspicion. Very little happens up here without Devon knowing it, and Devon and Reece are clearly tight. How much do they share with each other about me?

Tucking the gloves back in my pockets, I shrug off my jacket. I'll find a way to drop them by his car or the house sooner or later.

I dig a couple of slices of bread out of the plastic sleeve. I don't bother with toasting or butter. Just plain white bread to settle my stomach.

"What happened at that house, Kyle? Who was tied up?" My thoughts go to Nikki and Stevie. Both vanished six months ago around the Fourth of July weekend. And if I can believe what I've heard about Jeb, he was dead by then.

According to the diary, Sully told Stevie he was going to run down local addresses for Kyle. I wonder if the woodland house showed up in his search.

I walk into Kyle's office, pausing at the threshold before flipping on the light. Slowly I move behind his desk and toward the closet behind it. I open the door, drink in the faintest scent of new paint, and stare at the plain white walls.

Why was the closet painted? I don't remember the scent when I stood in this office with Kyle, but I'd been distracted and more interested in his diplomas.

I pull the sweaters off the hangers and toss them on Kyle's desk. I smooth my hands over the walls, pressing against the drywall as if I expect to find a secret wall or panel. I move up and down the walls pushing and prodding, hoping that something will give and prove to me that I'm not losing my mind. But each section is solid, secure.

Dropping to my knees, I shift my attention to the carpeted floor. It's beige, like the carpet in Kyle's office, but the shade is slightly different. No one would notice unless you're looking for it.

I reach for the corner and pull and pluck at the carpet strands, hoping to lift the section. But it doesn't budge. I grab a letter opener from Kyle's desk and burrow it into the corner, scraping the baseboard as I tunnel the metal tip between the carpet's edge and floor. Finally, the smallest edge breaks away from the floor.

This bit of success fuels me. My heart pounds hard as I continue down the baseboard, not caring that I'm marring the baseboard's fresh paint. When I reach the end, enough carpet is lifted so I can grab the frayed edges and pull. The carpet tears away from the floor as I yank until the four-by-four strip is free of the baseboard. I'm a little breathless when I lean back on my heels and toss the carpet piece into the office.

The floorboard is intact and has been sealed with a coat of polyurethane. But under the shiny coating is a dark-brown stain that stretches out toward all the corners. The blemish reminds me of a darkened version of the bloodstains in Reece's bathroom. The blood, if that's what it was, must've soaked through the old carpet and splashed on the walls. What kind of injury would cause this?

My cheeks flush as heat floods my face. I was alone in this house with Kyle for one hour. We ended up at the top of the stairs. I was standing nose to nose with him. His back was to the stairs.

Closing my eyes, I trail back to that moment.

"Don't be like that, Lane," Kyle says.

I stop at the top step, blink as my vision shifts and my head swirls. Panic cuts through my body.

"It's a beautiful afternoon." He approaches me like I'm a skittish colt. "Let's have a drink on the back deck."

I grip the railing. I need to leave here now.

"Come on, don't pout. I thought you wanted to make love." He holds up his hands. "Look, we'll have a drink, loosen up, and just relax. Take it slow like you want."

My fingers curl tighter around the metal.

"A drink will loosen you up, turn the tide," he insists. He takes me by the arm and pulls me away from the stairs. We're standing face-to-face. And I'm mad.

"You're treating me like a child."

He shrugs. "Did I hurt you? Did I do anything that upset you?"

"No." Having him on top of me set off a flurry of panic. "You're putting this all on me."

"Because you're not being reasonable."

The doorbell rings, chiming through the house. On its heels a fist pounds. Stiffening, I pick up the carpet and sweaters, toss them back in the closet, and close the door.

Rising, I push back my hair and close the office door behind me. I move toward the front door, and through the glass panels I see Devon. Shit. Girl talk is the last thing I need now.

Smiling, I force my shoulders to relax and open the door. "Devon."

She holds up a plate sporting coffee cake covered in clear cling wrap. "I brought a peace offering."

"A peace offering. I don't understand."

"I saw Reece. He said you're moving a little slow." Her grimace teeters toward amused. "That's my fault."

The two are talking about me. Great, I'm now the subject of their pillow talk. "No one forced me to drink."

Smiling, she moves past me inside. I'm tempted to ask her to leave, but I'm curious about what she and Reece were saying about me. I give her the space to enter.

"You do look a little pale," she says.

"What can I say? I'm a lightweight."

She walks into the kitchen with the authority of an owner. She shrugs off her jacket. She's wearing a faded blue T-shirt that reads BLINK IF YOU WANT ME.

She opens the correct drawer immediately, selecting a long knife, and then from the cabinet above grabs two plates.

I sit on a barstool by the kitchen island. The cake does look rich and delicious. "How did you make this so quickly?"

"Made it yesterday. It's my defense against the January 1 hangover." She slices two pieces from the cake and sets a plate in front of me with a fork.

I take a small bite. It's too sweet for me. "Thank you. It's delicious."

She raises a fork with cake to her mouth but pauses. "I saw you out walking this morning. You were in the woods."

Cake in my mouth forces me to chew faster and swallow before I can speak. "Really?"

She winks. "Not much happens in the woods without me seeing it."

During my walk, I'd kept my head on a swivel and didn't see houses, only thick green woods. "Where do you live exactly?"

"It's a trailer. Tucked in the woods across from Kyle's old house. It's very hard to see from the road."

"I didn't notice it."

"Few do." She pops cake in her mouth and grins.

"I was trying to clear my head. I'll be leaving tomorrow, so I wanted one last look around the area."

Her body tenses a little. "That's why you climbed the steps and peeked in the window?"

Ah, the real reason for the coffee cake. "I'm curious about Kyle. This is my chance to get to know him a little."

She arches a brow. "And what did you learn?"

The chair and rope flash in my mind. "He was a self-made man. Well liked and loved. Accomplished. I respect that."

"He was the whole package," Devon says. "Smart, good looking, successful. I don't know where I'd be now if it wasn't for him."

"I can see you were very fond of him," I say. Under years of sun damage, drinking, and drugging, she's still a striking woman. While Devon and Kyle were young, I imagine her skin was likely sun kissed and her blond hair was smooth and soft, not brittle as straw. Life has not been easy for Devon.

"Yeah, of course," she rushes to say. "I loved him. It hit me this morning that he's really gone. Even when I was cleaning up his blood on Friday night, I kept telling myself he was alive and being airlifted to the hospital in Norfolk. I kept saying the doctors were fixing him up."

I can hear her sorrow. "I'm sorry."

Tears well in her eyes and slide down her cheeks as she plucks a string off her flannel cuff. "I don't know what's going to happen to me now. I'm not sure I know how to live knowing he's gone." Her words carry a raw, naked truth that she quickly covers up with a smile. "That sounds very dark. I didn't mean that."

Devon meant exactly what she's said. She's terrified of a life without him. I've seen the fear in the girls in my circle when they break up with an abusive boyfriend. I've seen it in my own eyes when I'm telling myself I'm doing okay.

"I'm sure he was grateful for your love and devotion," I say.

"Sometimes he was. Sometimes he wasn't."

I let silence coax her into speaking more.

"I was jealous when he told me he was bringing you up here. He's not had a woman up here since the summer." She stabs another piece of cake. "We had such a fun fall, and I was beginning to think he had figured out I loved him."

My mind races to last summer, Stevie and Nikki. "He couldn't have been serious about whoever he brought here last summer. I mean, she's not in the picture now."

"I think he liked her," Devon said. "He was definitely obsessed with her."

I struggle to keep my voice light. "Did they break up?"

"I guess. The next time he came, she didn't." Her voice is full of triumph.

Without her saying, I sense Kyle and Devon have been lovers on and off since they were teens. Kyle might've seen Devon as a convenience, but she saw him as her everything. "I'm glad you two had a nice time."

She takes a big bite of cake and chews it slowly. "Jealous? I mean, does it bother you knowing I loved Kyle?"

"No."

Only someone who was dedicated to Kyle would have been in that closet sealing the floor, painting the walls, and laying down new carpet. A woman who desperately loved a man would go to great lengths to protect his legacy. "All this must be very hard for you. I can't imagine what it was like to clean up after the fall."

She sniffs, stabs another piece but doesn't eat it. "I had to. I couldn't bear to see Kyle's blood on the floor. I owed it to him to put things right. He hated it when the house wasn't perfect."

"You kept this place going. I bet Kyle never had to worry about cleaning, pest control, plumbing, or a million other things while he was in Norfolk."

"It takes a lot to maintain a place like this." A knowing smile tips the edge of her lips. "The earth in these parts does all it can to reclaim what humans think they've claimed."

I think about the thick vines snaking around the woodland house, choking the pilings and climbing toward the first floor. In a couple more years, it will fall in on itself.

There's a question in Devon's eyes, but it has nothing to do with maintaining houses. "You're trying to get at something, Lane, but I'm not sure what it is."

I force a smile. "I'm not sure, either." I cut off another bite but find my stomach has soured. "I came here to make peace with what happened, and it's gotten complicated."

She shakes her head as she stares. "You came for more than that."

"I wanted to know Kyle."

"You never will." Devon's brow furrows. "I'm the only one who really knew him—the real him."

If Kyle had brought Stevie or Nikki up here and killed them, would Devon call the cops or help him bury the bodies? I suspect the latter is true.

"Maybe you should leave today," she says. "Best to forget about all this and get back to your life. You came, honored Kyle, but you aren't a part of our world."

She's right. I don't belong here. But I still don't know what happened to Nikki and Stevie, why there was a rope dangling from the chair at the house, or what stained the closet floor. The questions are piling up. "You might be right," I lie.

Devon smiles and eats the cake bite. "Maybe I can come see you sometime in Norfolk. On a clear night I can see the lights from the city on the horizon, but I've never been there. Silly that it's so close, but I've never bothered to go there."

"I'm surprised you didn't visit Kyle."

A brow arches. "I didn't fit in that world."

I try to imagine Devon on the busy streets, skirting dark alleys. "I bet you'd do really well in the city."

That seems to please her. "Think so? I'm not used to the crowds and people."

"You'd do just fine. You're tough and a survivor."

She smiles. "Kyle used to say I'm a cockroach. Can't stop me."

Kyle's backhanded compliment surely stung a little.

Her head cocks slightly. "I'm not crazy about cities. All the people make my skin crawl. But it could be nice to see those lights up close once."

"Someday soon."

Her grin broadens. "I think we could be real good friends, Lane McCord."

My mouth is dry. "So do I."

She rises and moves to the sink. She rinses off her plate. "I need to get this place put right."

"Don't worry about that. I'll make sure I run the dishwasher before I go." I've been doing for myself for so long that having her here, waiting on me, is beyond uncomfortable.

I pull her gently away from the sink. "Please, don't worry over me."

"It feels wrong leaving dishes in the sink," she says.

I walk her to the door and open it. "I'll get it before I leave. Thank you for everything."

She stops and wraps her arms around my neck and hugs me with surprising strength. She smells of grease and cinnamon.

"I'm going to miss you, Lane."

"Thanks, Devon."

She peels herself off me, but her gaze lingers on my face. "Don't be a stranger, Lane."

I smile, wave as she sets out on the road toward the marshes. When she vanishes around the corner, I close and lock the door.

For the next hour, I search all the closets in the house. I open Kyle's weekend bag and dump the contents on the bed. Clothes, shoes, shaving kit, and a box of condoms. Nothing out of the ordinary.

I open all the dresser drawers, look under all the beds. I pull back the coverlets and sheets on all the beds, looking for what, I don't know. When I finally stop, I'm breathless. There's nothing that tells me anything about Kyle, Nikki, or Stevie.

Back in Kyle's office I open the closet door and pull out the carpet. I sit and stare at the stain on the floor. "I'm here because of you, Stevie and Nikki. What do I do next?"

I don't need Stevie sitting beside me or another diary entry to know exactly what I must do next. I need to return to the woodland house, search it just like I combed this house. That house has secrets that are waiting for me.

When I head west toward the woods, Reece will easily notice me as I pass the house he's repairing. Devon will be watching from her invisible trailer in the woods.

I could wait until dark, but the inky blackness will make the journey more difficult. A flashlight would help, but up here, the light will draw attention like a lighthouse beacon.

Rubbing my hip, I look out toward the rolling ocean. I'll walk up the beach, cut across the dunes, and tackle the house from the back side. But before I go, I want to read Stevie's latest diary entry. I enter Kyle's office and pick up the printed pages off the printer.

Chapter
Twenty-Six

STEVIE PALMER'S DIARY

Friday, July 7, 2023
7:00 p.m.

I call Kyle, Bourbon, Dr. Iverson to schedule an appointment. He has an opening tonight and tells me to arrive at his office at seven. The number he's given me goes directly to his private line. No receptionist. Feels a little squirrelly, but he's totally professional. The quick turnaround feels off, especially on a Friday night, but no time like the present, right?

When I arrive at the building, it's ten after seven. I'm late thanks to summer beach traffic. Normally, I don't care, but I do this time. Kyle is my only lead on Nikki, and I'm not letting him off the hook.

The front door is open, and a guard at reception directs me to the fifth floor. When I enter the waiting area of the office, I see no one. There's a receptionist's desk, a couch, a coffee table, and two closed doors. I sit on the couch and prop my feet on the coffee table. Leaning back, I close my eyes. It feels good to sit. I rarely stop moving, but occasionally nature forces it.

A door opens, and I raise an eyelid. Kyle, Dr. Iverson, is staring at me. He looks annoyed that my feet are on his coffee table, and I take pleasure in the knowledge. I want to be under his skin. I want him to show me the man hiding behind the smiling mask.

"I've seen patients like you before," he says. "They go out of their way to look like they don't care. You're hoping I react, so you won't have to."

"If I didn't care, I wouldn't be here." Feet off the table, I roll my shoulders and stand as I brush bangs from my forehead. "Dr. Kyle Iverson. You look different in your office."

"How so?"

"Maybe less or more dangerous? I can't decide."

He grins. "Hopefully less. It's important to me that you have a positive experience."

"Me too."

It's after hours, and the office is quiet. We're the only ones here. I thread fingers through my hair. Thick chained bracelets, multiple rings, and hoop earrings clatter. Easy to pass me on the street and assume I'm trouble, but I'm not. Leave me and mine alone, and I got no problems with anybody.

"Please come into my office," he says.

He waits, allows me to pass. I catch the scent of aftershave and mints. I glance left and right as I move into his office. Hanging behind his desk is a large-print photo of a beach cottage. The house is a modern sculpture set in what looks like a remote setting. My breath hitches, but I force it out slowly.

I trail a finger over one of the two chairs that angle toward each other in front of his desk. I cross toward a collection of framed diplomas and certificates on the wall. No denying the guy is educated, if all these framed diplomas can be believed.

"I've always been on the fence about displaying those," he says. "Feels like I'm bragging, but many folks want to see proof of my education."

"You must be pretty smart." I face him and summon a mild smile.

He slides his hands into his pockets. "I hold my own."

"What does it take to earn a PhD in psychology?" Do you have to be a little crazy to get one?

"Our time today isn't about me. It's about you." He motions toward one of the chairs and then closes his office door. "Would you like to have a seat?"

I rub palms over my thighs. We're alone. I've walked into the lion's den, but I've no plans. He's certainly not going to drop to his knees and bare his soul. "Is that how this works? I've never done anything like this before."

"I don't want you to be intimidated. All we do is sit and talk." His voice is soothing and soft, whereas in the bar his vibe is aloof and a little dangerous. The two faces of Kyle Iverson.

"About me?" I ask.

"About whatever you want to talk about." He motions to the chair again, and when I finally sit, he moves to the other side of the desk. I'm grateful for the distance and the barrier between us.

"Nice beach house," I say.

"Thanks."

"It yours?"

"Yes. It's located on the northern Outer Banks near the Virginia line."

A knot forms in my belly. I remember that long ago bumpy, hot ride up the beach in a truck's back seat. My hands were tied behind my back, and one of my captors kept his hand on the back of my neck. When he finally pulled me up, I was surprised by the utter darkness and desolation. If not for the crashing waves, I'd have sworn I'd been dragged into a crater.

"Pretty secluded up there." My voice has an eerie calm.

He's watching me closely. "That's its appeal."

I force myself to relax my shoulders and melt into the chair. There's a notepad and pencil on his desk, but he doesn't reach for it. "What do we do now?"

"We talk," he says.

"About me?"

"This session is for you, Stevie." He appears to be in no rush. "What do you want to talk about?"

I glance toward the air vent behind him and see a small red light. Of course. He's recording me.

I smile. "I don't know what to say."

His body is relaxed, but I sense he's keenly aware of me. "You reached out to me. There must be something."

I cross, uncross, and then recross my legs. I don't speak for nearly a minute as I stare at him. He's not someone I can trust. I know this in my bones. But I need to create the impression I'm willing to accept therapy.

"I've been feeling really lost," I say.

"Okay. Tell me about that."

I draw in a breath, angle my head from side to side. That beach house would be the place to hide someone. "I've had some issues with drugs and booze," I say honestly. "But I've been working a program for several months. Ninety-six days to be exact."

"That's a terrific accomplishment."

I draw in a shaky breath. "Feels pretty fragile right now."

"You work in a bar."

I hold his gaze. "Got to be willing to look the devil in the eye, right?"

"But constant exposure raises your chances of drinking."

He's right. Some nights are harder than others. As my brain has cleared, the demons, who'd been suppressed by the booze, have crawled toward the edge of the shadows. "I thought it would get easier the longer I was sober, but it's getting harder."

"How so?"

My left foot jangles up and down. How much of myself am I willing to give? "I'm remembering."

He doesn't ask me to explain as his gaze lingers on me. He's leaving it up to me to translate my trauma into words.

"My childhood wasn't exactly *Leave It to Beaver*." That's true, and if I'm going to sell myself to him, I'll have to use some truth. This kind of guy can sniff out bullshit.

He isn't surprised. "I'm sorry."

"It was just my sister and me. Well, it didn't start that way. My parents weren't happy. Dad drank. Then he started hitting Mom. She finally threw him out. I can still remember him packing a suitcase. I asked him where he was going, and he said he was making a quick trip to see his mother. I didn't even know he had a mother. He promised he'd be back. He didn't come back. You've heard this story a million times, I bet."

"Doesn't make it any less painful."

I fish a pack of cigarettes out of the front pocket of my jacket. It's a nasty habit, but since I arrived at the beach, I've been craving them, so I'd picked up a pack at the drugstore on my way here. Now the hunger is insatiable. "Can I smoke? I know it's not PC or allowed in most businesses."

"Normally, no, but I'll make an exception for you."

"Why am I so special?"

"I've been at this long enough to know when a patient needs something extra to calm themselves."

I was unruffled when I entered the office, and then I saw the picture. Now I'm nervous. "I bet you've sat in a lot of smoke-filled rooms."

"A few."

I raise a red plastic lighter to the raw edge. It flames. I inhale. When I've taken several puffs, I relax. The ritual of lighting up and the slow inhale and exhale elevate the dopamine in my brain. Smoking calms me. "Thanks. I thought you'd say no."

"I try to be helpful." He rises, crosses to a shelf, and retrieves a marble ashtray. He sets it on the desk in front of me.

I flick an ash into it.

He takes his seat behind the desk. "What happened after your father left?"

"I'm sure you can guess."

"I want you to tell me."

Another pause. "I'm spilling my guts to you a lot faster than I normally do."

What's brewing under his calm reserve? "Because you're ready to speak your truth."

"Maybe." That's not far off the mark. It would be nice to drop the walls. Of course, I've chosen a potential monster as my confessor.

"Where's your sister these days?"

"She's doing well. Better than me. Has her life on track. Job. School. Wouldn't be surprised if she ends up married with the white picket fence one day, two and a half kids and a dog."

"Is that a bad thing?"

"No, it's not bad. Not bad at all." Two more deep inhales. "If she hadn't turned out so great, then there'd have been no point to it all."

"What is *all*? Can you explain?"

"The sacrifices I made. For her," I say honestly. I'm not bitter, but that realization doesn't always ease the memories. I crush the end of the cigarette into the white marble ashtray, painting the center with black ash.

"How did your mother behave after your father left?" he asks.

My brow cocks. "Three guesses and the first two don't count."

He sits back, lays knitted fingers over his chest. "Tell me."

"She left us alone a lot. The parade of boyfriends began." I sniff. "And then other things happened."

"Other things?"

My chest is tight with anger when I glance at the picture of the beach cottage. I don't want to do this, but I need to show him some of me before he'll reveal his true self. "I don't know you well enough to get into that."

"Did any of these boyfriends hurt you or your sister?"

"Not her. Just me. I made sure of it." Pride and sadness drift under the last words. "Whenever a boyfriend had my sister in his sights, I found a way to get his attention. It always worked. I'm good at getting attention."

His gaze hasn't strayed. "You have my attention."

"Good."

"How old were you?"

"I was three when my parents divorced." A moody silence is oozing through me. I'm sailing into dangerous territory. And in this moment, Kyle Iverson is not the threat. I am. I'm convinced there's a darkness in him, and he's hurt Nikki, maybe even me. Am I transferring my rape onto him? I've done it with other men before. Still, with him the feeling is so strong, and I fantasize about picking up the ashtray and bashing in the side of his head.

"When did the assaults stop?" he asks.

I shove out a breath and any violent thoughts as I meet his gaze. "The last happened when I was fifteen. A couple of guys picked me up, took me to a house, and, well, fill in the blanks. But I survived."

His breathing slows as he stares at me. He flexes his fingers and grips a pencil so tightly, I think it's going to snap. Somehow, I doubt this is righteous indignation for my suffering. My story has triggered something in him, but I can't tell if it's fear, worry, or excitement.

He clears his throat. "Do you want to talk about that last incident?"

I'm watching him closely now. I first saw him in Joey's Bar, which is less than twenty feet from where I'd been taken. Like I've said, predators, like the rest of the world, love the familiar. We are all creatures of habit.

"It's a hard time to forget." My voice sounds shaky as I scramble through old memories I've locked tightly in my brain. The men who took me were young. They had thick beards and were dressed like they worked construction. Shit. After all these years of returning to Nags Head . . .

I drop my gaze and regroup. "It happened right outside Joey's."

He stills. "And yet you take a job within feet of where you were taken."

"Maybe I get a little thrill when I relive the trauma."

"That's not too far off the mark. Reexperiencing a trauma and walking away from it reinforces that you're a survivor. Overcoming fear is an accomplishment, and successes trigger dopamine hits."

"Is that why criminals return to the scene of the crime?"

"Yes. Reliving the moment is also a thrill for them."

Is that what we're both doing in Joey's Bar? Is he remembering a young girl he and his buddy took? Does that make him excited or horny? It makes me angry, and I carry a baseball bat. "We're all trying to find the magic in that moment." Anger drips from my words.

"What do you want from me?" he asks. "What do you need?"

"That's a good question, Dr. Iverson." I think about the baseball bat in my car. "As soon as I've figured it out, I'll let you know."

"What's prompted this session, Stevie?"

"I don't know. My friend Nikki has vanished, and it's stirred up a lot of the old fears. When those two guys took me, I thought I'd vanish, and no one would ever bother to look for me."

His expression remains calm, placid. "Are you looking for Nikki because no one looked for you?"

I smile and point at him. "That PhD wasn't a waste."

He doesn't speak, but his gaze lingers on me. He's searching, but for what, I don't know. "I've asked around about Nikki, but there's no sign of her." I shake my head. "I'm clearly dealing with shit that I thought I'd put in the past forever. Now because of Nikki it's all front and center."

He studies me a long beat. "I can't help you with your friend, but I might be able to help you. Is this a one-time session, or are you coming back, Stevie?"

I lean back in my seat, fingering the packet of cigarettes. "Do you want me back?"

"Therapy has to be voluntary, or it really doesn't work. But I would like to get to know you better. Hear what you have to say."

"Therapy." A half smile tugs my lips. "Sure, I'll come back."

Chapter Twenty-Seven

Lane

Monday, January 1, 2024
1:30 p.m.

That lone strand of rope teases me. Is it trying to tell me something about Stevie or Nikki? Did Kyle take both women? Did Kyle see Nikki on the day his brother died and decide to recreate the good old days? Was he doing that when he met me in the coffee shop?

When I walk out onto the beach, I notice a black four-wheel-drive truck parked on the sand. It faces the ocean. The plates are from North Carolina, and the driver is sitting in a foldable chair facing the ocean. A fishing rod rises out of a holder burrowed deep in the sand. The air on the beach feels ten to fifteen degrees colder than on the other side of the dunes.

I jam my hands in my pockets, and my fingers collide into the worn leather of Reece's gloves crumpled on the bottom. As isolated as this area feels, it's clear someone is always watching.

Moving down the beach, I know there's another turnoff about a hundred feet ahead. Once over the dunes, it should be a straight shot down the dirt road to the woodland house.

I'm not worried about getting into the old house. I've been locked out of my apartment enough over the years to find my way through a jimmied back door or window. I'll get into the house. It's just a matter of how.

I walk a hundred yards up the beach before crossing over the dunes. I'm well beyond all of Kyle's houses. I hustle up a different side street, hoping I'm moving parallel to the right one. The woodland house should be twenty yards up ahead on the left. When I cross the side street, I look toward the thick woods to my left.

As I step into the land smothered in live oak trees bent by years of wind, my foot immediately sinks into the soft soil. There's a sucking sound when I pull out my foot. I keep moving, trying to keep my footfalls quick and light. The brush and bramble grab the fabric of my coat, forcing me to constantly pull free. Several times fabric rips. I'm glad I have Reece's work gloves. They're sturdy enough to clamp down on the bramble.

Movement through the woods is slow going, and once or twice I lose track of where I am. Several times I swear I hear footsteps behind me, and I stop, expecting to see Devon, Earl, or Reece. Heart hammering, I stand still, waiting for the silence. There's the whinny of a horse and the pawing of ground. I'll take a herd of charging wild horses over Earl or Devon.

I move forward. I hope I'm walking in a straight line, but I fear my trajectory is angled, and I'm simply moving parallel to the road.

"Stevie, I don't know why the hell you picked me," I whisper. "But this is feeling really crazy right about now."

I push through the next thicket and discover I've reached the dirt road. Breathless, I look left and right. I see the woodland house to my left. I've overshot it. But not by much.

Aware that Devon doesn't miss much, I stick to the woods as I move closer to the house. When I reach the overgrown yard, I walk toward a set of stairs on the back side of the house.

As I get ready to climb, I glance under the house. I move toward the truck covered in the tarp. I raise the brittle plastic and a small animal scrambles under the vehicle. I drop the tarp and step back. My heart kicks into high gear.

Drawing in a deep breath, I grab hold of the tarp's slippery corner and pull hard. At first the tarp resists, as if someone on the other end is pulling against me. A racoon scrambles out from under the truck and runs toward the brush around the house. I jump back, my breathing fast, as adrenaline rushes my body. Wincing, I take hold of the tarp again and pull it the rest of the way off.

The truck is a faded black Ford. The tires aren't flat, but low, and the windows are covered in caked-on dirt. I clean off a section of the driver's-side window and raise my phone light. The brown seats are torn and mended with duct tape in a couple of places. There's a nest on the passenger-side floor, and there are several crushed old beer cans on the front seat. A faint scent of rot drifts around the vehicle, and I wonder what animal crawled in a vent, got stuck, and died.

There's an unsettling familiarity about the truck. I think about Nikki trying to escape Pete's truck behind Joey's Bar. Stevie was able to save her that night. But there was no one to save Stevie when she was thrown in the back of a truck. No one noticed she'd vanished then, but she has my full attention now.

I try the truck's door handle. It's unlocked. Hinges groan as I open the door. More foul smells assail me.

Stevie had been driven to a house like this one. In Stevie's mind, when she saw the picture in Kyle's office, she believed he was not only Nikki's attacker but hers.

Criminals return to the scene of the crime.

A wind blows under the house, sending a chill around me. The hairs on the back of my neck rise.

I close the door and move around to the tailgate. My gaze is drawn to a large toolbox mounted behind the cab. I open the tailgate, haul myself up into the bed, and walk carefully to the box. I pull, and when the top begins to lift, I pause and brace, half fearing and half hoping I've found Stevie or Nikki. I raise the top. The box is empty, save for a handful of rusted nails. Staring into the confined space makes my chest tighten, and suddenly I must close it. Quickly, I cross the bed, ease down, and back away from the truck, not sure why it unsettles me so badly.

I move toward the staircase on the back side of the house. I test the railing. It's wobbly, but not as badly as the front set. The stairs creak under my feet as I climb toward the deck. When I reach the top landing, the wood cracks and fractures. I pull my foot back quickly and shift my weight to a section that appears more stable.

There's no door on this side of the house, but there's a window. Looking left and right, I don't see any houses within eyeshot of this portion of the house. I cross to the window and push up. It's locked.

I ball up my fist, curling Reece's gloves around my fingers. Raising my arm, I hit the glass with the meaty side of my fist. The glass cracks. I flex my fingers. The strike hurts, but my hand is intact.

A second strike shatters the brittle glass. Some of the shards fall inward into the house, but several remain dangling, ready to slice through my jacket and skin. Carefully, I take the first sharp sliver in hand and wiggle it back and forth until it breaks free. I set it aside and turn my attention to the next one. Ten minutes later, I've cleared an opening wide enough for me to climb through.

I hike up my leg and lift it over the sill. I push up and settle the first foot inside, then lift my second leg. As I pull myself into the house, my left calf catches on a small shard that cuts into my jeans. I try to lift it, but it snags. I struggle to maintain my balance, but it's off just enough, and I topple. I fall hard onto the floor. The glass shard cuts my jeans and scratches my skin.

I've landed on my right side, but my hip is pulsing as I lie on the floor. For several seconds I breathe in and out, praying I've not done any new damage. Finally, the pain eases, I catch my breath, and I sit up.

I've landed in the cottage's kitchen. It's dark, grim, and the countertop is covered in grime and spiderwebs. The avocado-green stove is coated in grease, the sink is full of unwashed dishes crusted with dried food, and the refrigerator sports a calendar from 2009. I open the refrigerator and release a fetid smell. Gagging, I slam the door.

"Damn it." I press my arm against my nose and turn away.

I move out of the kitchen into the central room with the vaulted ceiling. Light seeps in from holes in the ceiling and falls on a wooden floor covered in a faded red industrial-grade rug. I move past the dining table and notice immediately the chair with arms has been replaced at the table. The rope that was dangling from the arm hours ago is gone.

Unease slides along my nerves. Devon knew I was here, and I wouldn't be shocked to learn she's been behind me and cleaned up anything out of place. I scan the cargo furniture, windows covered in threadbare curtains, and a brick fireplace covered in years' worth of soot.

On the first floor there are two doors. Bracing, I open the first and find a small bathroom. I cross to a moldy plastic shower curtain and open it. It's filthy but clear. The next door leads to a bedroom outfitted with twin beds. The bedding has been stripped, leaving behind sagging, stained mattresses.

I turn toward the stairs and slowly climb, gripping the banister. The stairs creak.

There are two more bedrooms on the top floor. The first has a double bed, again stripped and bare. On the dresser is a collection of pictures tucked in a plastic discount frame. The first features young boys who appear to be about ten and eleven. I recognize Kyle's wide, charming grin. He's thin, and his brown hair skims a striped T-shirt. The boy next to him must be his brother. Is it Jeb or Zeke? This boy is shorter, and he's not grinning as he stares blankly at the camera.

There's another picture featuring a twenty-plus-year-old bearded Kyle with his arms around two guys about his age. Like Kyle, they all have thick, dark beards. The guy on the left must be Reece. His face is fuller, and his cheekbones less etched, but there's no missing those forlorn eyes.

While Kyle and Reece are grinning, the third guy isn't. I lift the picture and study his face. Is this Jeb? All three of them fit the description Stevie gave of her attackers. Which, of course, wouldn't mean anything in a court of law. Lots of young men drive pickups and have beards.

Still, something dark roils inside me, and from the maelstrom an old fear rises and clogs my throat. I grieve for Stevie, Nikki, and the other young girl Jeb kidnapped.

The more I study Kyle's smile, the less jovial it appears. Instead of warmth, his eyes reflect a feral edge.

According to Reece, Kyle returned home after his sophomore year. That's the same year Jeb was arrested and went to prison. Was this that summer?

My gaze remains transfixed on the trio as I tug my phone from my back pocket and center the camera lens on the image. I snap several pictures before turning toward the bed.

The bed is covered in rumpled, graying sheets. They don't look clean, but they're also not old or threadbare. I move closer to the bed and catch the scent of urine. My stomach tumbles, but I don't dare draw in a deep breath to calm my nerves.

My gaze rises to the headboard. There are no ropes, but each post is ringed with worn marks on the left and right. Absently, I run my fingers over the smooth skin of my left wrist.

Stevie had keyed in on Kyle because Nikki had last been seen with him, which led to dark suspicions about her own past. And then Stevie had also vanished.

All those bits of information certainly aren't proof of any misdeeds. Maybe Kyle slept with Nikki. Maybe he even paid for her time, but that didn't mean he killed her or Stevie. But if Stevie is right, Kyle took her here as a teen and Nikki fourteen years later.

As I stare at the scored marks on the bedposts, frost chills my blood. I glance toward the footposts and see similar marks on each. How hard and long would a woman have to struggle to make these marks?

I run my fingers over the rough edges of the wood. Time would have discolored the scarred wood, but these marks are light. Stevie and Nikki had been in this area six months ago.

My hands tremble when I lower them to the bedsheets and touch the rough polyester fabric. I glance toward the ceiling and see faded gold star stickers. I count the stars. Seventeen. How many times had the person tied to this bed counted those stars?

Sweat pools at the base of my spine.

"Kyle, who were you?"

My chest tightens as a memory, maybe from one of Stevie's diary entries, bubbles through my subconscious.

She's tied to a bed like this. She's cold, wet, and so scared. It feels as if her body is being split in two.

"You like this, don't you?" he asks.

"No!" she screams.

I step back as if I've been hit by lightning. Where the hell did that come from? Did Stevie write about it in her entries? I can't remember. Must check.

Nothing like that has ever happened to me, and I struggle to pull in a deep breath. That memory is not mine and makes me wonder if I'm channeling the energy in this room.

I back away from the bed and out of the room. My heart throbs. This entire house resonates evil.

I move carefully and swiftly down the stairs. As I reach the bottom step, I sense that someone is behind me, watching. Stevie. Nikki. Kyle. All ghosts. I turn, look up the stairs, but there's no one there. The wind blows outside. I'm alone.

I take several pictures of the living room, open the broken window, and climb out onto the deck. I draw in a deep breath and stare at the overcast, gray sky. The salty air smells sweet, but it doesn't chase away the house's stale, musty scent that's invaded me. I close the back window, leaving it unlocked.

Down the steps, I retrace my path through the bramble, and when I emerge on the road, I know I need to leave. I didn't like Detective Becker, but it's time to call him. Maybe he can get a forensic team up here. They can sample the bedsheets, and the stain in Kyle's beach cottage.

Rain taps against the house's metal roof as I move down the pathway toward the beach road. I cross over the dunes and repeat my steps. The ocean is churning, and the waves are crashing close to the dunes, leaving only a narrow path for me. The black truck is gone; likely he saw the tide coming in and took off. As I stand here alone, invisible bands wrap around me, squeezing my body tight.

When I turn the corner, I'm relieved to see the cottage and my Jeep parked next to the Range Rover. The waves are hitting so high, the cold, salty spray splashes my face. High tide or not, I'll leave for Norfolk as soon as I am packed.

Nearing the house, I hear a circular saw buzzing in the house across the street. The first-floor lights are ablaze, and Reece's large frame passes in front of the window. He doesn't pause or look in my direction, and I'm relieved. The less contact I have with him and Devon the better.

As I approach my Jeep, my gaze lands on the front tire. It looks off. When I kneel, I realize in the fading light that it's flat. I look toward the Range Rover. Both back tires are flat. As I run my hand over the tire, I think about Stevie's last entry. We're both chasing after Kyle Iverson.

She's now missing. And I'm trapped.

Chapter Twenty-Eight

STEVIE PALMER'S DIARY

Friday, July 7, 2023
8:30 p.m.

As I drive back to Joey's, I'm certain getting information out of Kyle Iverson is not going to be easy. He's smart, and after our meeting I wonder if I'm chasing him or he's now chasing me. He's clearly not convinced I want therapy.

I consider making a flyer with Nikki's face on it. But I don't have a picture of her, and I don't have access to a computer. And how will my paltry collection of facts inspire anyone to find her? Nikki Kane, age twenty-five-ish, light-brown hair, is missing. Last seen in a nice car maybe with Kyle Iverson.

I park in the alley beside Joey's, and as I get out of my car, I notice a couple of the women standing on the corner staring at me. I've seen them before in Joey's. I suspect both deal drugs in between various dates each evening. I don't judge. We all got to get by.

I smile and move toward them. "Ladies. How are you doing this evening?"

One woman is tall, wafer thin with long black hair that falls over her shoulders. She's wearing a mesh jacket, a miniskirt, and low-heel boots. I think her name is Kit. The other woman, Delores, is shorter, more buxom with a fuller waist. She wears a tank that hugs her midsize breasts, a miniskirt as short as Kit's, hiking boots that look ideal for running—a skill a gal like her needs from time to time.

"Stevie," Delores says.

"Gals, I'm looking for Nikki. She bartended with me on July 1 and 2. No one has seen her."

Delores frowns. "I know the kid. Perky. Doesn't always make the best decisions." She shakes her head. "I haven't seen her."

"You haven't been here that long, right?" Kit asks. "Why do you care?"

"Someone has to, right?" I ask. "Word is she was seen with a guy named Kyle Iverson. Drives a fancy car."

Delores nods. "I know him. Been with him once or twice. He doesn't live around here. Likes to shop in other neighborhoods so he doesn't get recognized."

"I hear ya," I say. "What was he like?"

Kit studies me. "You show up out of nowhere and take a job bartending. Now you're asking questions like a cop."

"You're the second person this week who's accused me of that," I say. "I bartend, sleep in my car, and do my best not to give a shit about people because when I do, I end up where I am right now."

Each woman nods, as if they understand, though I bet both still think I'm a cop, wearing a wire, or I'm a confidential informant. "No agenda, ladies. Just looking for Nikki."

"Your boy was okay," Kit says. "Paid cash."

"Not overly rough?" I ask.

"What's your definition?" Kit asks.

"I don't know, you tell me."

"He had a thing about control. Made me hold my arms over my head like they were tied. Not the weirdest thing I've done."

"You think it got out of hand with Nikki?" Delores asks.

"I can't prove anything, but it's starting to feel like that." I shift. "Did he mention a beach house?"

Kit shakes her head. "Nope? All my business was handled in the back seat of his Cadillac."

"If either of you ladies hear something, would you let Joey know? He's easier to find than me."

"Don't you have a phone?" Kit asks.

"No. I've never been good at keeping up with them." That's not true. But again, what's the point in explaining?

"Are you sure you're not a cop?" Delores asks. "You're asking just enough questions."

My laugh is genuine. "No. I really do my best to avoid them."

"That's what a cop would say," Kit says.

"Ladies, not looking for a fight. Just want to find Nikki. If you can call Joey's with any tips, I'd appreciate it."

Kit snaps her fingers. "Now I remember you."

"Do you?"

"You're the one that took the baseball bat to that john here last week."

"Good old Pete," I say. "Have you seen him?"

"I saw him in a bar down the road later that night. He was one hurting cowboy," Kit said. "Since then, there's been no sign of him. Likely licking his wounds. But when he mends, be careful. He's going to come looking for you."

The last thing I need is someone else gunning for me. "I hear ya. Thanks," I say.

Delores chuckles. "I like you, Stevie. Nice to cross paths with someone who cares."

"I'm no saint," I say.

"All the better," Kit says.

"Think Pete caught up to Nikki?" Delores asks.

"I don't think so. Rumor has it he has a shattered kneecap. And like I said, she was last seen with Iverson," I say honestly. "Thanks, ladies. Call Joey's if you hear from Nikki."

As I turn and walk away, Delores says, "If you vanish, who comes looking for you?"

I shake my head. "Who knows, Nikki might've asked questions and looked for me. She's that kind of person."

When I arrive at Joey's, it's nearly nine and not super busy. There are a half dozen folks huddled over their drinks, but most of the table rounds are empty. Joey's pushing through the swinging door with a rack of clean glasses as I'm wrapping my apron around my waist.

He glances in my direction but keeps moving. Glasses rattle when he sets them on the bar. "Glad you could join us."

"Running late." I make it a habit not to apologize.

He looks around the thinning crowd. "Doesn't look like I'm going to need you tonight."

Some nights are slow even in midsummer. Hot, raining, traffic, or folks are just burning out toward the end of vacation week. The tips will be lean.

"Go home and sleep," he says.

It's too early to curl up in the back of my car. "Sleep and I have a passing acquaintance." I walk around the bar and wash my hands.

"Do you ever listen to me?" Joey growls.

"I listen." I toss him a rare genuine smile.

"Any luck with Nikki?" he asks.

"Vanished off the face of the earth."

"What about the cops?"

"Sully is asking around."

Joey nods. "He said that he would. He's a good guy."

"What's his story?"

"Military police for fifteen years. Finally decided he'd had enough and didn't reenlist. Working construction with his brother part-time now."

I refill a bowl with peanuts. "Nikki was nice to me."

"She was nice to everyone."

Was that supposed to make me feel less special? "All the more reason to find her."

"Keep at it. Stick with Sully."

"Speaking of help, I told a couple of girls who work around here to call the bar if they hear anything."

"Seriously?" Joey's expression is a blend of shock and annoyance. "Am I the tip line now?"

"You're lucky I don't have a picture of Nikki. I'd have made flyers, and your phone would've been ringing off the hook."

"You're going to break me," he mutters.

The futility of my search grows by the hour. I know searching for her is as much about me as her. Someone needs to care. Someone needs to sound the alarm bell. The problem is, both Nikki and I are running out of time.

A customer catches my eye and holds up an empty mug. I refill it for him. The phone rings, and before Joey can grab it, I do. "Tip line."

"Is Joey there? This is his sister."

I hand the phone to Joey. "For you."

His brow arches. "Imagine that."

He takes the handheld in the back room, and I oversee the bar, refilling a few drinks, chatting up the customers. This goes on for an hour, and then Sully walks in and takes a seat at the end of the bar.

I fill a mug with beer and set it in front of him. I'm glad to see him. "Sully."

"I hear you've been asking around," he says.

I grab a rag and wipe the bar around him. "You know what they say about idle hands. They're the devil's plaything."

"Every time I see you, you're in constant motion."

"Make hay while the sun is out."

He stares at me over the rim of his mug. "Any leads on Nikki?"

"No."

His skin is a deep tan with hints of red on his cheeks, a sign he was in the sun all day. I imagine him on a rooftop, shirtless. Glistening with sweat.

"Sorry to hear that," he says. "I asked a buddy in Virginia State Police to check in on Pete. His knee is in a cast. He can't drive for the next six to eight weeks."

"Too bad."

I meet his gaze. "I had my first session with Kyle Iverson tonight. He kindly worked time in his schedule for me."

His features harden. "What?"

"Went by his office and had a counseling session."

He leans forward, his eyes narrowing. "You were alone with him?"

"I was. Guy has a huge print behind his desk of a house on the northern beaches. Says he owns it."

Silent, he's staring at me and considering what he's heard.

"And I booked a second session with him for next week."

"That's not smart, Stevie." It's a restrained, dangerous statement.

I force a smile. "I even brought up Nikki, so if there's any doubt in his mind about my motives, I cleared that up."

His gaze is fixed on my face, studying and analyzing every expression. "Stay away from him, Stevie," he warns.

Stubbornness is my greatest asset and my worst enemy. "Not until I find Nikki."

He sips his beer and sets the mug down precisely in the center of the napkin. "Stay away from him."

I don't want to talk about Iverson or the past or the future. Now is such a good place to be. "Ah, Sully, do you care about me?"

His eyes blaze. "I don't want to add you to the missing persons list."

"I'll be fine." I lean forward, deciding I might find this man very acceptable. "It's a slow night, Detective. Why don't we get out of here? If memory serves, you live nearby."

He's frustrated or maybe puzzled by me. Not sure why he cares so much about my lost soul, but he does. Maybe he's like me, or maybe he has a thing for underdogs, or maybe he's just a detective to his core and peeling back the layers is habit for him.

But under all that, I sense his desire for me. We've already proven we know our way around the sheets.

Normally, I run from anyone who gets too close, but not tonight. It could be my attraction to him, or I might like to believe that someone would miss Stevie Palmer if she were gone.

Sully tosses a twenty on the bar. "I do live close."

My body warms. Sully is about to be the exception to my no-second-date rule. I untie my apron and toss it under the bar. "Want to get out of here?"

"Do you?" he asks hoarsely.

My heart shifts a fraction. "I do. Very much."

He stands. "Let's get out of here."

***

The drive to Sully's small house takes fifteen minutes in summer traffic. He lives in Kill Devil Hills on a back road that tourists aren't likely to find. The yard is neat, and the siding a light gray. The house backs up to woods. Even on the Outer Banks there are places that are off the beaten path. He parks in his driveway, and I slide in behind him.

Without hormones fueling us blindly toward one another, I'm oddly edgy. I follow him up to the front porch and watch as he unlocks the door. His body is stiff.

"Are you nervous?" I tease.

He chuckles. "Maybe a little."

We step inside, and in the darkness, I take his face in my hands. The shadow of his beard feels rough under my fingers as I kiss him on the lips. He hesitates a moment, and then a low growl rumbles in his chest. He cups my butt and hauls me closer to him.

"I've wanted to do this since I walked into the bar tonight," he says.

"Really?" I'm not shocked. Half the guys in the bar were likely thinking the same thing.

"Yeah." He takes me by the hand, turns on a small light, and leads me to his back bedroom. Like before, his space is neat, organized. The last time I was here, I didn't pay a lot of attention, but this time I search for family photos or mementos that tell me about him. We pass a spare room that's set up as an office. The marine flag hangs behind the desk, and the room is lined with bookshelves filled with hundreds of hardback and paperback books.

When we reach his bedroom, I kick off my shoes and pull off my shirt. No reason to be coy. We both know what we want.

His gaze darkens as it drops to my cleavage, and he shrugs off his shirt. He has several tattoos. On his chest, there's a list of five names on the left pec, and on the right the Marine Corps eagle standing on top of the world and Semper Fi. Along his ribs there's some quote, and on his bicep a wild horse ensnared in thick vines. There's also a woman's name on his arm. JENNIFER. I'm guessing that's the ex-wife who remarried two weeks ago.

I smooth my fingers over tanned skin and swirl them around Jennifer's name. He's lean, muscled, but he's not the kind of guy who struts.

"Do you miss her?" I ask.

"Sometimes. Not as much." He frees a heavy sigh. "Jealous?"

"No."

"Who the hell are you?"

I shake my head. "Just me." I kiss him, and in less than a minute, I'm shimmying out of my jeans and we're both getting naked. He tosses back the blue-and-red spread on a double bed.

I meet his gaze, still filled with lingering assessment. My gut twists. I don't want him looking too closely. "Tell me there are more condoms in that nightstand."

"There are."

I settle on the bed and lean against the pillows. He opens the drawer and removes a condom. He's erect, ready, but seems to be in no rush.

Anticipation builds in me. I'm more than ready. I smooth my hand over his back and over his backside. He flinches, rolls on his back, and slides on the condom. I kiss his belly and smile when I feel him tense.

"Slow down. Or this is going to be over before it starts," he groans.

"It's only been a few days, cowboy."

"Feels like a few years."

"Years?" I kiss his chest and then settle back against the pillows beside him. I'm giving him control, which is no small feat for me. When he settles on top of me, I close my eyes, wanting to be lost in the primitive sensation.

I feel him settle between my legs as his hands gently rub the insides of my thighs. "Stevie, open your eyes."

When I look at him, his expression is focused, stern. He leans forward and kisses me on the lips. He tastes salty, like the on-tap beer I serve at Joey's. "Are you sure you want this?"

"I do."

"Why do I feel the tension in your body?"

I'm never totally honest or candid, but in this moment the truth slips past the barriers. "Sex hasn't always been pleasant for me. A lot of pain. But you proved that wrong before and you will again."

"I sure as hell will."

I nod, finding no words, but sensing I can trust this guy.

His kisses skim along my neck and then move to my breast. I draw in a breath. His touch is so gentle, but I feel his restrained intensity.

I want to make a smart-ass comment, but I can't summon one. Very slowly he slides into me. I rest my hands on his hips, tensing a little. He's concentrating on me. He'll stop if I ask. Which is why I don't want him to stop. I relax. The sensation takes my breath away.

Maybe a guy like Sully just might come looking for a gal like me if I vanish.

Chapter Twenty-Nine

LANE

Monday, January 1, 2024
2:00 p.m.

Again I smooth my hand over the tire, but still don't feel any puncture, nail, or wood fragment. I don't think I hit anything on the beach, but the ride was very bumpy in several spots. Besides, Kyle's tires are flat. What are the chances both of us damaged our tires?

I check the air cap on the flat tire. It's in place, but when I check the tension, the cap is loose. The same is true for Kyle's tires. Someone has deliberately removed the caps and bled air out of the tires.

"Someone is screwing with me," I mutter. "Everyone wants me to leave, so why do this now?" I think about Earl, the house in the woods, the stained closet floorboards, and the ropes. Maybe I've now seen too much. Fear churns in my belly, and a whimper rises in my throat before I calm myself.

Storm clouds are gathering overhead, and soon the sky is going to open. Changing a tire now is possible, but it won't be easy when the rain falls.

I could pack my stuff and just drive out of here on my deflated tire. Assuming the beach is even passable, I'll probably destroy the tire, but if I make it to the hard surface road, it would be worth it, right? I can change the tire there. Walking back to the main road is also an option. But eleven miles of rough beach on foot in the cold rain will ensure I screw up my hip joint.

Staying put in the house until the rain passes makes the best sense. I can lock the doors, barricade them if need be, and wait out the rain. Then I'll change the tire and leave.

"What's going on?"

Reece's deep voice catches me off guard, and I'm surprised to see that he's so close to me. How could such a big man move so silently?

I face him. "I have a flat tire."

He moves closer to inspect the tire, and I automatically step back. As of this moment, I have no idea who I can trust. "You must've picked something up on the beach. Happens all the time."

"The two back tires on Kyle's car are also flat."

He looks at the flat tires of the Range Rover. "He could have done the same."

"What are the chances?"

"Near a construction site like the one across the street? Pretty good."

And what about the loose valve caps? But I don't mention the caps because I don't know who's behind this, though my guess is Reece might have a good idea.

"You okay?"

"Yeah, other than I have a flat and the skies are about to open up."

"And when they do, the beaches will be swamped with high tide. Leave it for today. I'll change your tire first thing in the morning. You can drive out when the tides are calmer."

"Can you drive me out tonight?"

"I'm in the middle of more demo. If I push through, I'll be finished by midnight. Unless it's an emergency, you're going to have to wait."

Another night here. "I'll work on the tire myself."

"We've got one hell of a storm coming." He glances toward the sound and the blackening skies. "It'll be here in less than fifteen minutes."

I shove back my hair. "How do you know that?"

"I've seen my share of storms."

In answer, several fat raindrops land on my head. One more night isn't the end of the world. And I can barricade the doors inside. This time tomorrow, I'll be out of here, and I'll have spoken to the local police and shown them the pictures of the woodland house. "How long does it take to change a tire?"

"Longer than fifteen minutes."

"So I'm stuck."

"Until the morning. That's not a big deal, is it?"

"No." I don't want to explain why I want to leave now.

"Okay. Call if you need anything. Have your flashlight close and phone charged. We're going to lose electricity."

"Terrific."

"Are you okay? You look off." The raindrops grow larger and drop faster.

I think about the house in the woods and the bedframe posts marred by old rope, and the picture of the three boys—Kyle, Jeb, and Reece. Did they know what Jeb had done? If Jeb did take Stevie, then one of them could have helped him. She also said there was someone in the shadows who didn't try to stop her escape. Who was who? "Do you miss him?"

"What?"

"Kyle. You two have been friends for so long." My voice is quiet. "You must miss him."

"I told you we had a falling-out years ago. We've barely spoken since."

"Why did you two fight?"

I expect him to blow me off. Most would see this as none of my business. "He was never the same after his brother went to prison. He blamed himself for Jeb's incarceration. After that, he wanted nothing more to do with me."

"Why did he blame himself? Jeb made his own choices."

"Maybe Kyle felt he let Jeb down. We knew he was struggling with the drugs. But I was tired of cleaning up Jeb's messes while making a run at a different life. Kyle had been away at college for two years. The way Jeb saw it, we'd ditched him for better lives. His rage spilled out."

"Onto a girl who had done nothing wrong other than let him get close enough to snatch her."

"Yeah."

"Did Jeb act alone?"

The question dangles between us. "Why do you ask?"

"I don't know. Did Jeb ever hint that there was someone else working with him?"

"He never said anything to me. And if he told Kyle, Kyle never said. Loyalty means something up here."

"Jeb overdosed right after he was released from prison. He had his freedom, and he tossed it away."

"I think he killed himself," he says. "Dying was Jeb's way of ensuring he never screwed up Kyle's life again."

"Jeb or Zeke didn't screw up Kyle's life."

"Both came damn close." He shakes his head. "All three brothers are gone, so whatever Kyle knew or didn't know about Jeb or Zeke really doesn't matter now. Let it go, Lane. It's all in the past now."

The topic is closed for him. But if there was a second man, and he escaped the law, there will be no justice for Stevie, or any other girl hurt by them.

The rain begins to fall faster, and the droplets grow thicker and heavier.

"What was her name?" I ask. "The girl Jeb kidnapped and raped. She has a name."

"I don't know."

"How can you not know? You must have heard her name during the trial."

"There was no trial. DNA proved Jeb did what he did, the cops arrested Jeb at his job in Nags Head, and he confessed." The rain grows heavier. My hair and coat are getting soaked. "Go inside, Lane. Wait out the storm."

I walk up the stairs. Under the porch cover, I strip off my soaked jacket and kick off my shoes.

As I step inside, the black skies open, and the wind picks up. Pelting rain hits the roof and echoes in the house. Inside, I lock the door. From the downstairs bath, I grab a towel and dry off as I move toward the kitchen.

I flip on the lights and scroll through the pictures that I took at the woodland house. "What the hell happened in that house, in this house?"

Bad things. The words echo in my head and sound so real I could swear someone is behind me.

I grab a water bottle from the refrigerator and drink almost half before my thirst feels even partly quenched. As I glance at my phone, I fish Detective Becker's card from my back pocket. I dial his number.

He answers on the second ring. "Detective Becker."

"This is Lane."

"Lane. Everything all right?"

"I don't know." I sit on the living room couch. "I've found things while I've been here."

"What kind of things?" His voice is deep, intense.

Why am I trusting this guy? I barely know him. He says he's a cop, but do I really know that? The temptation to run and hide is real, but I stand my ground. "The house near Kyle's beachfront property in the woods."

"The one that belonged to his brother."

"Yes."

"I drove by it. I know where it is."

I shove fingers through my damp hair. "I broke in and looked around."

Fuck rolls softly out on a breath. "Why did you do that?"

Adrenaline is still pumping through my body, tightening muscles and stretching nerves. How can I explain my intense need to see the inside of that house? "A feeling."

Silence stretches between us. "What did you see?"

"The first time I only looked in the window."

"The first time." Each word has a sharp edge. "Okay."

"I saw a chair, and there was a rope dangling from the armrest. When I went back the second time, I got inside the house." He doesn't ask how. I was trespassing, and whatever I saw likely won't be usable in court. "The rope was gone, and the chair was put back at the dining table. I went upstairs and found a four-poster bed. There were worn marks around the wood spindles, like someone had been tied to them and was trying to get free. I took pictures of the bed."

"You broke into his house." He speaks the words more to himself, as if he's playing out the ramifications and how they'd affect an investigation. "Can you text me the pictures?"

"Sure. I'll send them." Stevie's texts are proof my cell signal is strong enough.

"Does anyone know you went to the woodland house?" he asks.

"Devon saw me the first time. And a guy named Earl. He's a backwoods kind of guy."

Another whispered oath drifts over the line. "Earl Mason."

"How do you know him?"

"I've done a deep dive into Iverson's life. I missed the woodland house because it wasn't listed in Kyle Iverson's name."

"How did you do all this since Friday?"

"We'll talk about that later. Right now, you should leave that house, Lane."

"Detective Becker, one other thing. I lied."

He doesn't speak.

"You asked me if I know Stevie Palmer? I don't. But she's been sending me her diary entries."

"You can show them to me when I see you." He doesn't sound surprised, but he's a cop and people lie to him all the time. "Get out of the house, Lane."

"That was the plan, but my front tire is flat, and the sky just opened up. Even if I could change the tire, the beach is impassable now."

"I'll come get you."

"In the rain on a beach." Lightning cracks across the sky. "It'll take you hours from the mainland."

"You're assuming I'm on the mainland."

"Where are you?"

"Close enough."

A part of me doesn't want a rescue. Until this moment, I've always rescued myself. "Okay."

"Text me those pictures, Lane. Hang tight."

I end the call and send him five pictures. The texts appear to go, but seconds later I receive an *Undeliverable* message. I try again, this time sending one image at a time. I don't get a bounce message, but I'm not sure if they've made it. Time will tell. Lightning cracks outside.

I move to the kitchen and set up coffee to brew. My hands are shaking, and I spill coffee grounds on the counter. It takes three ties to lock the grounds holder into the coffee maker. Finally, the machine begins to hiss. I lay my head on the counter and wait as the cup slowly fills. When the machine goes silent, I splash creamer into the cup and drink. My hip is throbbing, and it's uncomfortable to stand. I shift my stance, hoping to find a pain-free spot. I don't.

The caffeine blunts the fatigue, so I cradle the coffee in my hands and drain the contents before making a second cup. Moving to the downstairs shower, I finish the second cup. I turn on the hot water, strip down, and step under the stream. The heat hits my body, sending a molten jolt. I tip my face upward, shuddering as the chill leaves my bones.

The water helps some, but I'm still in pain. I step out of the shower and reach for a towel. When I'm dry, I dig aspirin from my overnight bag and swallow three. I need more coffee. I need to keep moving. Keep the hip lubricated.

I dress in an oversize nightshirt, which doesn't require anything of my hip. Barefoot, I move steadily to the kitchen. I set up another cup to brew.

"You're limping. Are you in pain?"

The sound of Devon's voice startles me, and I whip around. She's standing on the other side of the kitchen island. Her hair and clothes are soaked and dripping water on the marble floor. She looks more like a ghost than a living, breathing person. "Devon."

She smiles. "Everything all right, Lane?"

The machine hisses behind me. "What are you doing here?"

"Just checking in. The storm is bad." She looks toward the ocean-front windows as lightning slices the dark sky. "I was afraid you might be scared to be alone. Are you scared?"

I feel not fear but anger. Who the hell does she think she is? "Get out of here," I demand.

She smiles. "It's not your house."

"It's not yours, either!" I shout.

"It's more mine than it'll ever be yours. Just like Reece belongs to me. You took Kyle, but you don't get Reece."

I remember how the shutter slammed so hard against the house when Reece and I were half-naked. "You slammed the shutter against the house."

"That's right. I saw you pawing him like a mare in heat."

Color warms my face as I remember how much I wanted Reece in that moment. It was humiliating when he sent me away. And Devon saw it all. "Get the hell out of here, Devon."

She shakes her head and smiles. "You're upset. I saw how he pushed you away, and you don't like it."

"Leave."

She cocks her head. "Why are we fighting, Lane? We are friends."

I don't respond as my fingers clench into tight fists.

"Maybe we should get in that hot tub now. I can open a bottle of wine for us."

Is she even hearing herself? "No."

"You should get into the hot tub. Best way to relax and ease some of the pressure on that hip. It's got to be hurting with all the walking you've done today." She motions toward the door leading to the porch. "I turned the hot tub on for you. It's nice and warm and bubbly."

Whatever grip she appeared to have on reality has completely slipped. "I don't want to get into the hot tub." When she reaches out toward me, I step back. "Get the fuck out of here, Devon!" I'm surprised by the fury that's spilling out of me. I stagger another step and steady myself with a hand on the counter.

She puckers her lips into a pout. "It's a miracle you haven't had another bad fall, Lane. You're so unsteady on your feet, sweetie."

I shift, wince at her pathetic grin. "I'm fine."

She shoots her arm out and tries to grab me, but misses. "It wouldn't take much for you to slip and fall. And without your meds, I bet you're really feeling off your game."

I struggle to maintain my balance. "You took my pills."

She nods. "I did."

"And the photos on my phone?"

She looks offended. "That wasn't me. That was Kyle when you were in the bathroom. He didn't want any traces of you and him anywhere."

"How do you know that?"

"Kyle is smart. He thinks about all the little details like that."

Kyle teased that he could guess my phone password last week. He rightly assumed I'd used my birthday. "God, I fell for everything he threw at me."

"Don't let that trouble you one bit. Kyle was smart. There isn't anyone who could outthink him. Now, let's get you into the hot tub on the porch. It'll warm you right up."

"Why do you care about the damn hot tub?" I stumble back and bump into the counter behind me, knocking the coffee maker with my elbow. Hot coffee sloshes, burns my skin.

"It's what you need."

Devon moves toward me. I hobble from the kitchen toward the front door. I don't have shoes, my hip is on fire, and I'm barely dressed. But I don't care. I just need to get out of this house and away from her. I've reached the door when fingers tangle in my hair and pull me backward. My neck cranes, my scalp burns as the hair strains against the pressure. I stagger backward and fall to the floor. I cry out in pain.

She straddles me and shoves me back as I struggle to sit up. "Poor Lane. Too tired to fight."

"Get the hell off me!" I scream.

Devon presses her hands against my shoulders. "I can't wait to watch you drown in that water."

I blink, struggling to keep my eyes open and praying the adrenaline dumping into my system is enough to keep me awake. "Why are you doing this?"

Devon laughs, but there's no hint of humor. "Because you ruined everything. *Everything.* Kyle would still be alive now if it wasn't for you."

"It was an accident."

"No, it wasn't." Her face is next to mine, and I can smell beer on her breath. "You pushed him."

"I did not."

"I'd let myself into the house because I was curious about you. I heard you two fighting, and I saw you both at the top of the stairs. I watched you push him."

Devon had been in the house watching Kyle and me. Tension tightens in my belly. "Why were you here?"

"Kyle told me he'd found a special woman from the old days. That he was bringing you back here. I wanted to see you."

"What does that mean, *the old days?*" I need to keep talking until I can get to my feet.

"I don't know. But Kyle said you were special. When Kyle says a woman is special, all kinds of things happen."

The ropes. The bed. "What things?"

She smiles. "You know. You saw the chair. And I know you went back to the house." Her smile widens. "Nikki was special."

"Nikki." Stevie's friend.

"Yep." Her eyes narrow as she grabs the sides of my face with her hands. "I still can't figure out how you knew about Nikki. Did she find you after she got away?"

"Nikki escaped?"

Devon ignores my question. She grips my hair tighter, pulls my head back, and exposes my neck. "How did you know about Nikki?"

I refuse to give her an answer. "What did you do to Nikki?"

"I didn't do anything. But Kyle . . . he'd have done more if he had his way."

"The closet." The faded rusty stains under the new patch of carpet.

"Boy, you have been busy," she says.

My scalp burns as Devon twists her hands. "Did Kyle and Jeb rape Stevie?"

"Aren't you a smart one."

"What did they do to Stevie when she was just a kid?"

"Kyle and Jeb took her up to the woodland house, but she got away. Jeb was so mad he found another girl. He didn't bring her up here where it's safe, but he did rape that other girl in town. And he got caught. Kyle was so pissed. He was afraid Jeb's foolishness would circle back to him, and he'd lose his scholarship."

As I stare into her eyes, fear, rage, and fury collide inside me. "Jeb confessed to the second crime to protect Kyle."

"Jeb idolized Kyle. None of us wanted to ruin Kyle's future, including Jeb."

Something deep inside me stirs, scrapes at the underside of my skin. "I saw marks on the bedposts."

Devon's gaze cools for a moment. "Kyle liked ropes. I told him to keep that between us, otherwise it would get him in trouble. But Jeb had just died, and Kyle couldn't stop himself. He was so stressed, so he drove into town to that bar he liked."

"Why do you keep his secrets?"

Devon raises her chin a notch. "He was always good to me, and I would never turn on him. I'm loyal." Her gaze flares with renewed anger. "And none of those women matter. They are all less than nothing."

"I care about them."

"Who are *you?*" Devon sneers. "You're Kyle's girlfriend who came back to his house and have been living out some kind of creepy fantasy for the last few days."

She hauls me to my feet, and I don't fight her. Easier to throw a swing standing. I stagger. I hear the hot tub bubbling. She wants to drown me.

"Does Reece know that you covered for Kyle?" I ask. The more I talk, the more time I buy. Detective Becker said he was close, but he didn't say how far away. And in this weather, a few miles could make the difference.

"He thought Kyle had stopped after Zeke died. Zeke's death hit Kyle hard."

"But Kyle didn't stop."

Her brow furrows. "I shouldn't have asked Reece to fix the carpet in the closet. I told him the stains on the wall were paint, but he knew right away Kyle hadn't kept his promise."

"Reece has known all along?" The realization coils in my belly.

She smiles as if she's enjoying my shock. "Since the very beginning."

This woman has lied about so much, but for the first time, I sense she's being honest. I intentionally challenge her to keep talking. "I don't believe you."

Devon removes a gun from her pocket and points it at me. "Why would I lie?"

A chill crawls up my back as I stare into the barrel of the gun. My head spins. I blink. "Why would you be honest? It only hurts Kyle's memory."

Her body tilts slightly toward me. "Feels good to tell someone. It's hard keeping all this bottled up."

I did a prison rotation last spring, and many of the women were ready to confess sins family or law enforcement weren't aware of. "When did Reece realize what Kyle had done? Did he help with that first girl?"

"No, he didn't help. I think Reece was the one who let her go. He's a soft touch, and she was tougher than anyone thought. No one ever saw her again."

It's common with criminals who've been silent for so long to open up when they've been discovered. For them, it's a relief. "The girl they kidnapped and raped didn't file charges."

"She was smart enough to keep her mouth shut."

Thinking about young Stevie stumbling out of the old cottage, battered and bruised, stokes fury in me. I need to squeeze every last detail out of Devon. "Did he ever wonder what happened to her?"

"Kyle never fretted much about the past. He was all about building a better life."

And that better life involved me—a woman who looks like Nikki. "Did you tell Reece that Kyle was bringing me here?"

"I did. Didn't think much of it at the time. Pillow talk, you know." She frowns. "That was a mistake."

Reece had no reason to be up here when Kyle and I arrived. "He unhooked the water pipe to the washer and flooded the house across the street. He knew you would call him to fix it. The project gave him reason to be around. He was worried about what Kyle would do."

"Yeah, he was worried. Thought he could protect Kyle from himself."

But what about the other women Kyle hurt? Did Reece ever consider his silence gave Kyle a license to keep hunting? "I guess that makes me lucky."

Devon smiles. "But Reece didn't need to be here to save you. You found it in yourself to kill Kyle, didn't you?"

"What's Reece going to do when he finds me drowned in the hot tub? Won't he suspect you?" Will he continue to stay silent? Will he help bury my body?

"He won't have any proof that I did anything wrong. And I know how to make him happy and forget. He's not Kyle, but he'll do."

I'm struggling to keep my brain working. Lack of sleep and raw nerves are tangling around Devon's words now, but I won't let them pull me off track. "I went back to the woodland house and took pictures. I texted them to Detective Becker."

As the weight of what I've done settles, anger smears Devon's face. Her thoughts must be racing now. "Won't matter once you drown. I'll clean up the woodland house and this one. I'll make it right, like I do everything else."

As long as I'm talking, I'm awake and have a chance. "Are Stevie and Nikki alive?"

She ignores the question. "Get in the hot tub."

"What happened to them?"

"It doesn't matter."

"It does to me." I fist my fingers. "You'll have to shoot me where I stand." I sway as my hip burns. "I'm not helping you."

She points the gun at my legs. "I won't kill you right away. I'll take out your knees, and as you're howling in pain, I'll drag you to the woods and bury you alive."

I lean toward her, resisting the urge to lunge. I need to hear her entire confession. "Did you bury Nikki and Stevie up here somewhere?"

"You don't get all your questions answered. That's not how this works. It'll give me satisfaction knowing you go to your grave with questions buried in you." She fires the gun into the floor, inches from my bare feet.

I stagger, then move toward the screened porch and push open the door. Cold air races into the house, and my wet hair and bare feet drink up the ice.

Devon digs pills from her pocket. "Recognize these?"

"My pills?"

"Exactly. I ground up a few and put them in your favorite hazelnut creamer."

The hot tub is bubbling, and steam rises into the cold air. The story she'll tell about me will be very simple: *Lane was anxious, and the remaining pieces of her broken heart shattered. She wasn't thinking about killing herself when she climbed into the hot tub. But she slipped under the water.*

"The medical examiner will do a tox screen," I say.

She shakes the bottle, rattling the pills. "And they'll find traces of the medicine you take every night."

"No."

This is bullshit.

The gruff words echo in my head.

Devon shoves me toward the hot tub, and it's enough to throw my weakened hip off balance. I stagger against the side of the hot tub, and the hard surface catches my knee.

This is bullshit! Do not let this happen!

Fury bubbles up again, and rage roils inside me. My fingers curl into fists. Stevie and Nikki deserve justice. And I'm the last person left to give it to them.

I size up Devon. She's tall. But I'm desperate. Desperate for . . . revenge.

"Take your T-shirt off," she orders.

As I stare at her, I pull off my T-shirt and fist it in my hand. I don't feel humbled or vulnerable as I stand here naked. Fury fuels me. And the cold air offers a welcome jolt.

Approaching the hot tub, I drop my T-shirt into the water and swirl the fabric in the warm water. The fabric grows heavy.

I raise my leg as if I'm going to climb inside. In the corner of my eye, I see Devon's smile reappear. She believes she has won. She believes I have given up. But I've never wanted to harm anyone as much as I want to hurt her now. She's carried Kyle's sins all these years, and she can now pay for them all.

My shoulders slump, but instead of climbing in, I grip the edge of the waterlogged fabric in my fist. Using my body weight, I snap it as if it's a whip.

Warm water splashes over me as the tip of the waterlogged fabric hits Devon in the face. It's enough to leave a red mark and startle her. She staggers back and lowers the gun a fraction. I lunge toward her, slinging the T-shirt around the gun like a bullwhip. The end wraps around her arm, and I quickly coil the moist fabric around the gun still clasped in her hand.

The shock on Devon's face is almost comical. We are practically nose to nose and bonded by wet fabric and hatred.

Her confusion contorts with rage. She tries to jerk up the gun, but my bone-deep determination fuels my strength. My fingers dig into the shirt and twist the gun's muzzle toward Devon and away from me.

"You bitch!" Devon screams.

Within the wet bundle, her index finger must still be near the trigger guard. I can feel her muscles and arm moving as she struggles to reach the trigger. I don't know how long I can hold her, but I know as soon as I release my grip, she's going to shoot me dead.

Whatever shock she suffered after my initial attack wanes quickly, and she regains her focus. I use the last of my strength and press my body into her, inching the muzzle closer to her face. She pushes back. A moment of satisfaction flickers on her face, and I know she's found the trigger. I shove my body into her.

In the next second, the gun fires. The sound explodes by my head, and the *bang* is deafening. The ringing in my ears sounds like emergency sirens.

Fresh, bright red blood splashes Devon's face. She stares at me with utter disbelief. I brace for a countermove, but her legs give out slowly, and she drops to her knees. I'm still gripping her hands, forcing me to lower with her.

Our faces are inches apart, and I can see now that the bullet struck the side of her face. The flesh covering her jaw is torn and jagged. The bullet has entered her jaw, likely torn into bone and teeth, however, I don't see an exit wound. The pain must be excruciating.

Eyes locking, I see raw hatred reflected in her eyes. She can't speak, but she's not letting go. I wait, wondering which of us will pass out first.

Pressing my face against hers, I know I'm sending searing pain through her body. She immediately releases her hold on the gun as her eyes roll back in her head. I tug the gun free of her hands and the wet, blood-soaked shirt.

Slowly, her eyes glaze. Crimson trails down her face and seeps into her flannel shirt. She must be in terrible pain. Good.

I stagger to my feet, grimacing as I step back. The moans rising out of Devon sound more animal than human, but I fully expect her to rally and come after me.

Her confession has answered many questions, but it's left several unanswered.

Where is Nikki?

Where is Stevie?

And why do I feel like Stevie is alive and very close?

Chapter Thirty

LANE

Monday, January 1, 2024
3:00 p.m.

My ears are ringing loudly, and I can't really hear anything but the buzzing. But the noise is fueling me, prodding me to reenter the house. My naked body is covered with gooseflesh and blood that splashes my face, breasts, and belly.

I check my body for wounds. There's so much blood. Pain on my left side. God, have I been shot, too? But I slowly realize there are no injuries beyond the ones I suffered on Friday.

Devon has not risen. The flesh of her face is torn, her lip a fleshy mess. As I pull back, she grabs my arm with more strength than seems possible. She can't speak, but I feel her fury.

Nausea rolls over me. I jerk free, hobble into the house, and rush to my phone on the counter. I set the gun down as I snatch up my phone. My hands are shaking, and the heat in the house doesn't touch the cold burrowing deep in my bones.

"Where are you, Detective Becker?" Has the weather slowed his progress? I focus on the phone and press the 9. Before I can hit 1-1, the front door bursts open. It's Reece.

He takes one look at me, and his fury turns to concern. "What happened?"

Three days ago, he found me bloodied and broken at the bottom of the stairs. He'd been close to save me then, knowing Kyle was a monster. Is he here to save me from Devon?

"I'm calling 9-1-1."

He takes the phone and ends the call. "What happened?"

"Devon tried to kill me." Whatever fear and anger that was fueling me is fading. My teeth are chattering. I don't know how much longer I can stand on my feet.

He removes his flannel shirt and drapes it around my shoulders. I thread my arms through the sleeves and clutch the flannel folds over my chest.

Reece's shirt smells of sawdust, sea air, and him. It's such a comforting scent. It makes me feel safe. My gaze drops to his bandaged hand. Blood is seeping through the white gauze.

"What did Devon tell you?" he asks.

"There were two missing women. Devon said Kyle and Jeb raped a girl a long time ago. She said you let the girl go."

Disgust hardens his face. "Devon drinks too much. She gets confused. And she's not right in the head."

"She wouldn't tell me what happened to Stevie." I swallow the rising fear and shock. "I don't know what happened to Stevie."

He cups my chin in his calloused hands, smearing the blood over my jaw. "Where is Devon?"

"On the porch. She's shot, but she's alive."

"You shot her?"

"I was fighting her for the gun when it went off. She was ready to shoot me if I didn't get in the hot tub. She wanted to drown me."

He nods slowly as he picks up the gun and tucks it into his waistband. "I need to go to her."

"Did you hear what I said? She tried to kill me. She has covered for Kyle for years. You've covered for Kyle."

He grips my arm. "I heard you. Let me check her."

As he moves toward the porch, I clutch the folds of his shirt around me. "Were you the one that let Stevie go all those years ago?"

He stops, turns, faces me. "I don't know any woman named Stevie."

My throat tightens with a silent scream. "Did you let her escape?"

"There was no one to free." His voice is soft, but there's no conviction shoring up his words.

Tears well in my eyes. I liked him. Kissed him. Had been ready to have sex with him. How could I be drawn to two men who hid such terrible secrets? "You all knew each other for so long. Devon was devoted to him. Loved him. She said you were up here on Friday because you thought he was going to kill me."

A muscle pulses in his jaw. "I was here to fix the water damage. That's all."

"You said yourself someone disconnected the hose from the wall."

His strong fingers bite into my arm. "I didn't know anything about Kyle's plans. Devon called me." Reece is repeating the words as if saying them again will convince us both.

"Devon said you arrived here so quickly."

"Luck. I had another job close by."

He's looking at me as if I'm crazy, but I'm not. He's lied to the world and himself for so long, he believes all the stories he's told. "You fixed the closet floor and carpet in Kyle's office. Someone was locked in the closet of his office, and somebody covered up the evidence."

"You're reaching for random pieces and putting them together all wrong. None of what you're saying is making sense."

A cold current rises under the shirt, chilling my skin. I want to believe he's innocent in all this. I want to believe he didn't know Kyle's true nature. "We need to call the cops."

"Let me check on Devon first."

"And do what?"

"Help her."

"The cops and rescue squad can help her. She'll need professional help, pain meds. The bullet struck her in the face."

He squeezes my shoulders, reminding me of how strong he is. If he shifted those hands to my throat, I wouldn't be able to stop him from strangling me.

Taking me by the hand, he pulls me out to the porch. I resist, but his grip tightens, and he tugs me forward. Out on the porch, I shiver against the cold that quickly shoots more energy into my system.

I stand barefooted on the cold, wet wood as he kneels and tenderly touches Devon's face. "Devon? Can you hear me?"

Her eyes flutter open, and a painful moan escapes through lips soaked in blood and torn flesh. Her eyes roll toward me and narrow. Even in this much pain, she wants to kill me.

Those eyes shift to Reece, and she stares directly at him. The look is intimate, the kind shared by people who've known—no, loved—each other for years. He brushes back a strand of bloodstained hair from her face and nods. She can't smile, but even with all the agony racking her body, she relaxes a fraction.

Reece rises and turns toward me, the gun at his side. "I can't let her go to jail."

I grip the folds of the shirt as I back up toward the house. "She tried to kill me."

He shakes his head as his shoulders slump slightly. "She's always been crazy when it came to Kyle."

"She's insane."

He studies me closely. "You look so much like her. When I first saw you, I thought you were her."

"Who?"

"It doesn't matter."

Maybe that's why Kyle approached me initially. Why he was hell-bent on us having a relationship. "I reminded him of someone else."

"I didn't know about the others."

"How could you not know? You knew what Kyle was capable of."

"I spent a lot of time away. I didn't reconnect with Devon until a few years ago."

"When did she tell you what Kyle had done?"

"We were in bed. She was drunk. I was annoyed with Kyle because he was late paying a construction bill he owed me. She figured I'd feel better if she confessed Kyle had done it again."

"Did you press her for details?"

"I didn't have to ask to know what she meant."

"And when she said I was coming here, was she drunk then?"

"Yes."

"You knew it was my turn." I'm clutching flannel folds, wondering why he never called the cops. One phone call would have changed the trajectory of Kyle's plans.

"I didn't know that for sure."

"Come on, you knew. I wasn't supposed to go home, was I?"

His eyes close for a moment. He radiates shame. "I wasn't going to let him hurt you. That's why I was here. I thought if I was around, it would be different this time."

Devon had protected Kyle and so had Reece. The picture of the three boys flashes in my mind. Reece had said loyalty mattered to him. Clearly, he was devoted to Kyle, Jeb, Zeke, and Devon. He had no allegiance to the women they'd hurt.

He raises the gun toward me. "I'm sorry."

Chapter Thirty-One

LANE

Monday, January 1, 2024
3:30 p.m.

Reece might've seen himself as a savior, but we both witness the facade crumble to dust.

Knowing what I'm now facing, I don't linger but hobble into the house, praying he won't shoot me. I'm in the kitchen in seconds and begin opening drawers, searching for a knife or scissors.

"Stop, Lane," Reece says as he follows.

"Reece." It's a struggle to keep my voice calm. His eyes are wide, filled with anger tinged with sadness and worry. I don't see the driven fury that blazed from Devon's gaze.

If I can get him to work with me to help her, he might lower his guard, and I can escape. If I can get outside, I can find a place to hide. I'll worry about my bare feet when I have the time. "We need to help Devon," I say.

"You shot her. Hurt her." His jaw is clenched, and tension has tightened all the muscles in his body.

I see a slow change overtake him. He's not hearing me anymore. He's loyal to those he grew up with.

How can logic combat alliances that were formed decades ago? "I didn't want to hurt Devon. Hurting people is not what I do."

"You pulled the trigger."

"She pulled the trigger." Genuine tears well in my eyes. "We were both desperate and afraid."

There's a deep sadness in his eyes. He's now faced with a choice that he'll hate to make. "She's hurt. You're not. Kyle's dead. You're not."

"You're not Kyle. Or Devon. You are a kind man, Reece."

He shakes his head. "I'm not who you think I am."

I back away until I bump into a counter and feel the heat from the coffee maker behind me. "Who are you?"

"I'm a ghost. I died a long time ago."

His soul did die when he became an accessory to Kyle's violence. But pointing that out now could get me killed. "You made mistakes, but you've rebuilt your life." Reece is still talking to me and that's what matters.

"I'm nothing without Kyle. He sent all the best jobs my way, even after our fights. He was loyal to me. All I wanted to do was protect him from himself. Without him and Devon, I'm a dead man walking."

Is Reece even hearing his lunacy? "Is that what Kyle told you?"

"He said we all were still alive and living well because of him. He's right. We're nothing without Kyle."

"That's not true. You knew he was going to hurt me like Nikki and Stevie, and you didn't want that to happen."

"I thought if I were nearby, he'd find a better way to deal with whatever it was inside him." He draws in a deep breath and releases it slowly, as if the secrets haven't allowed him to draw in a deep breath for years.

There's a bizarre current running between us now. In this moment we are united by blood and death. "I know you loved Kyle and worried about what he was doing. You and Devon fought about it. I saw her coming out of your house. I saw the broken mirror in your bathroom."

He looks at me, his face tight with grief. "How do you know about the mirror?"

"I was in your house. I saw it."

"You were in the house?" He shakes his head. "Devon is right. You're trouble." He doesn't sound reasonable now. He's angry. "Did you push Kyle down the stairs?"

"No."

"Devon says you did." His gaze spears me. "Did you kill him?"

"No." My conviction straddles shaky ground.

"You couldn't have kissed me if you loved him."

Reece stands between me and the door. My Jeep is disabled, but drivable if I don't care about flat tires and rain.

"Reece, let me help Devon," I say. "It's going to take us both to save her."

He shakes his head. "We're not a team, Lane. Devon kept reminding me of that. I didn't want to believe her. But she's right. You're an outsider."

"You don't live here anymore. You clearly want something different."

Devon's faint moans drift from the porch. "It doesn't matter what I want. Now I need to help Devon."

"Reece, help Devon and let me go. I don't want trouble."

"You came back here. You asked too many questions. You snooped. You wanted trouble." Reece shakes his head. "When you kissed me, I thought you liked me, but you were using me."

My head pounds. "I did—*do*—care about you. You have a good heart, Reece."

"Devon said you'd say something like that." He studies me closely. "She was right about it all."

"She doesn't know me. She doesn't understand." Images of the rope marks on the bedposts flash in my mind. I imagine the ropes cutting skin and rubbing wrists raw as desperation builds into a scream.

I whirl around and grab the coffee, and I rush him. I throw the cup's contents. It's not as hot as it was, but the liquid strikes him directly in the eyes. He winces, wipes his eyes. I strike him on the side of the head with the cup so hard the stoneware breaks. He stumbles and howls. I run.

I reach the front door and race into the cold rain. I'm disoriented. I have no idea where I'm going or where I'll hide.

Headlights glow on the street and I tense, wondering if help has arrived or the driver is another local who loved Kyle. Up here, I can't trust anyone.

The sandy soil grinds under my bare feet as I rush down the stairs. Rain soaks the flannel shirt and my naked legs as a black truck pulls into the driveway. The headlights catch my frame, but I'm too desperate to care who it is.

My heart hammers, and I struggle in the glare of the headlights. I'm torn between asking for help and running. Footsteps thunder in the house. Reece is coming for me.

The front driver's-side door opens, and a man gets out. For a moment, his face is shrouded in shadows, and then he steps into the headlights. It's Detective Becker. Relief floods my system as he races up toward me.

When he sees Reece rushing the front door, he pulls me behind him and draws his weapon. He shouts, "Drop it! Now!"

Reece snarls and levels his gun at Detective Becker. I stumble back, searching for a rock or something I can use to stop Reece.

Detective Becker's training kicks in, and he fires twice, the bullets catching Reece in the chest. The sounds make me flinch, and I look up in time to see Reece drop to the ground, his gun falling from his hand.

Detective Becker takes the stairs two at a time and makes quick work of kicking the gun out of Reece's reach and rolling him on his back. He handcuffs his hands and pats down his body for other weapons. He raises his phone to his ear and instructs the sheriff's office and rescue squad he needs assistance.

My hands tremble as I climb the stairs. Relief and fear carve into my sinew and bone, and my body begins to tremble. "Where did you come from?"

His gaze raises to me, and I can feel it trailing over my body, assessing damage. He shrugs off his coat and lays it on my shoulders. "I've been hanging out at the fire station. Are you okay?"

His coat cloaks me in his warm scent. "I'm okay. Devon tried to kill me. We struggled for the gun, and it went off. She's still alive by the hot tub."

Detective Becker pulls me past Reece, and I struggle to make my feet work. We move into the house and toward the side porch, where Devon is barely conscious. He removes rubber gloves from his pocket, dons them, and checks the pulse in her neck. He doesn't try to move her.

"Help," Devon whispers as her eyes roll toward me. "She tried to kill me."

"Rescue squad and cops are on the way," Detective Becker says.

"Reece?" Devon asks.

"Down."

A scream rises in Devon's chest but trickles out as a sorrowful moan. "No."

Detective Becker pulls me into the house and grabs a throw blanket from the couch. He wraps it around me, and for a moment his hands linger on my shoulders. "You're crazy."

"No argument," I say.

"Are you injured?"

"No. Other than the hip."

A silence settles us as we wait for the rescue squad. Within minutes, the local rescue crew's sirens wail in the darkness.

"I didn't want to hurt her," I say. "She forced me."

He nods. "I know. It's okay."

I want Devon to live. I want her to confess to the police what Kyle has done. I want her to tell everyone where Nikki and Stevie can be found.

Rescue vehicles roll into the driveway, and seconds later the emergency crews thud up the stairs. Three days ago, they'd arrived for Kyle and me.

Detective Becker holsters his gun. "You sure you're okay?"

Jitters rock my body. "I'm fine."

"You don't look fine."

"Not my first rodeo." The casual comment surprises me. I can't believe I'm holding it all together so well.

He cocks his head. "That's something Stevie would say."

"You know Stevie? She never mentioned you." I think back over the diary entries. Sully had mentioned a nameless detective friend of his. Was he referencing Becker? And then a tumbler clicks into place. "Are you Sully?"

He nods. "Donald Sullivan Becker."

"You two were together."

His eyes meet mine.

Heat warms my cheeks.

"Yeah, I knew her." His voice sounds ragged.

"Knew. Past tense. Is she okay?"

He holds my gaze, but it's impossible to read his stony expression. He clears his throat. "She sent her diary to me. She wanted me to give it to you when the time was right."

The first entry arrived after the fall. "What was so right about that time?"

"I didn't realize Kyle had planned a weekend away with you up here. I fucked that up. And then I received a call from the responding officer up here. Seemed a thousand years passed between the moment he told me about the fall and that you were alive."

"Were you working with Stevie? Was she a cop?" But before he can answer, more questions tumble out. "In her last entry, she suggested she might vanish. What does that mean?"

His gaze lingers on my face. "This isn't the place to have this discussion."

"Later," I insist.

Lights flash outside, spraying the interior with blue and red. "I need to talk to them. We'll finish this later."

Detective Becker opens the front door, and the paramedics push through carrying their equipment and a stretcher.

After that, we are swept up in chaos.

Chapter Thirty-Two

LANE

Tuesday, January 2, 2024
10:00 a.m.

When I open the front door of my apartment, a relentless sense of exhaustion overtakes me. I am physically and mentally spent.

Once the paramedics and cops arrived on scene, Detective Becker and I were separated, his gun and Devon's confiscated, and we were both questioned individually. The EMTs hauled Devon out on a stretcher and declared Reece dead. He was loaded into a body bag, and I stared at the black bag that must mirror the one they used for Kyle on Friday.

I told the sheriff about the woodland house and what I'd found. He said little as he listened and took notes. He promised to dispatch officers to Kyle's old family home.

Detective Becker made sure I had my purse and phone before I was transported to Norfolk and checked out by doctors. My hip ached, and I was nearly breathless with the pain. Barry, the EMT who'd helped me on Friday, saw me, shook his head, and checked me for injuries.

As luck would have it, I ended up with Dr. Jackson, who was not happy to see me. "This isn't my idea of taking it easy, Lane."

After he checked me out, I swore I'd rest this time. No more beach trips. No more anything for a couple of days. The nurse wheeled me out to the hospital's front entrance, where my Uber was waiting. There was no sign of Detective Becker.

I now gratefully peel off my clothes and turn on my shower's hot tap. I stand under the spray, willing the water to wash away the smell of the hospital, Devon's blood, and that house in the woods.

My body clean, I towel off and dress. The memories of the last few days still linger, but beyond them are Stevie's words. They've been replaying over and over in my head.

I should lie down and rest as I promised Dr. Jackson, but I'm too wired. I need to talk to Detective Becker before I can consider shutting my eyes. I'm in the kitchen drinking a fresh cup of coffee when the front doorbell rings. With my hand on the doorknob, I hesitate before I open the door to Detective Becker.

Dark circles ring under his eyes, but his hair is damp, as if he's freshly showered. "Good, you're back home," he says.

"Arrived home about an hour ago." I glance past him and spot my white Jeep parked in front of the building. "You brought my Jeep back. Thank you."

He hands me my keys. "No reason for you to return to that house."

"Never." I jangle the keys. "Thanks."

"I just wanted to make sure you were okay." He stares at me. "Are you okay?"

"I'll be fine." To prove it, I attempt a smile. "How will you get home?"

"A buddy is picking me up. He'll be here in fifteen minutes."

Good, we have time to talk. There's too much that remains unsaid. "Come inside."

"If this isn't a good time . . ."

I step aside. "There's no better time."

As he moves past me, his gaze swivels over the main room, taking in the furniture, the layout, and the art on the walls. "Nice. I never would have made you out as a neat freak."

I close the door. "My therapist would say it's a form of control. Maybe true, but I like to think extreme organization is simply efficient."

A smile tweaks the edges of his mouth. "If you say so."

"I just made coffee. Want some?"

"God, yes." He takes one of the barstools at the kitchen island.

I fill a white mug and set it in front of him. "Cream, sugar?"

"I'll take both."

That's a little surprising. He looks like a black coffee kind of guy. Intense. Strong. I set the milk and sugar in front of him. He lumps two sugars and a large splash of milk in his cup. "The one time I dressed my coffee in front of Stevie, she gave me shit for it."

"Why is that?"

He takes a long sip. "I guess she thought everyone drank their coffee black." A smile plays on his lips. "I think she liked to get under my skin. Her way of showing me she cared, I guess."

"Liked. Past tense." I feel an unexplainable pull to him, as if I know him. "Who was Stevie to you?"

He sets his cup down. "That's a big question with a complicated answer."

"Why is it complicated? It's very simple."

He reaches in his coat pocket and pulls out a page torn from a notebook. I recognize Stevie's bold, dark handwriting. "These are the last pages of her journal. She told me not to send them unless you were ready to read all. I think you are."

"Why did you send the pages to me? It all feels so random."

"It's not." A sigh leaks through his lips. "Read the pages. And if you have questions, we'll talk."

I drop my gaze to the page.

> Dear Lane,
> Here's the thing, I know you better than you do your-self. I have since we were kids. This is going to sound crazy, but I swear it's all true.
>
> See, you and I are the same person. Two sides of the same coin.

I draw in a sharp breath. The claim is insane.

> I stepped forward when we were kids, so I could take the abuse from Mom's boyfriend when we were very little. I took on the pain so you wouldn't have to, so we could survive. And I got good at it. Maybe too good.
>
> You must've sensed there was something wrong with you, because you started seeing the therapist a couple of years ago. Your journey to wholeness was the beginning of my demise. I realized last summer that when I "got out," my time was limited. Like I always do when I'm out, I go to Nags Head to the place where Kyle and Jeb grabbed me fourteen years ago. Criminals are creatures of habit, too. And I hoped I'd find one of them eventually.
>
> You don't remember, but I do. They took me to the woodland house, and well, safe to say, I thought I was going to die. They tied me to the bed for hours. I screamed until I was hoarse. And then they left, and Reece arrived. He let me go. I could barely walk,

but I got dressed and ran. When I made it back to the hard-surface road in Virginia, I called your foster mother. She picked me up and took me to the hospital. The cops asked me over and over who did this to us, but I wouldn't say who. When I arrived back at the foster home, I melted away into you.

I can tell you now, if not for Reece, I'm sure Kyle or Jeb would have killed me. I—we—would've been swallowed up for good, and no one would have cared.

Anyway, I was in Nags Head during this summer when I met Nikki. When I walked into Joey's, I saw Kyle. I didn't recognize him at first. I sensed he was off, but he was so polished, so not like the grungy young man who I'd crossed paths with fourteen years ago. And then I saw him flirting with Nikki before she vanished. And as you now know, the trail kept circling back to him. It wasn't until that "counseling" session I had with him that the dots connected for me. I know he took me, and he killed Nikki. I can't prove anything, but maybe that's where you'll come in.

This last night with Sully, I can feel myself slipping. I have so many reasons to stay, but you've never allowed me more than a week or two. I don't expect picket fences for Sully and me. I doubt he does, either. But go easy on him, he's a good guy.

I hope you can figure out what Kyle did. I'm not worried about me, but maybe it would all be worth it if you found Nikki. Don't let her vanish into the cracks.

Take care of yourself. Stevie.

I sit back, look at Detective Becker, and search my memory for any of the moments he shared with Stevie. The sex. The affection. But there's nothing. No sign of us. Them.

"I don't know what to say."

"It's something, isn't it?" Detective Becker says.

I clear my throat. I don't know how to process all this. My first reaction is that it's an insane piece of fiction. I've another personality in me. And she/I slept with Sully . . . Becker. I can't tell by his expression how he feels.

"I don't recall any of Stevie's life," I say carefully.

"Yeah, I get that." He's trying not to sound frustrated as he reaches for his phone and pulls up a picture. "The one picture Stevie allowed me to take of us. I think she said yes because she knew a moment like this might happen."

I stare at a face that looks like me, but the expression, body language, dark-rinsed hair, and entire demeanor are not me. The eyes staring back are street savvy, hardened, and vulnerable. I have no memory of any of it.

"A personality split," I say. There have been occasions when I've lost time. "The doctor at the urgent care thought I had an issue with sleepwalking, so he prescribed pills to help me sleep. He blamed it on anxiety."

He clears his throat. "You weren't sleepwalking last summer."

Last summer. I took off the week of the Fourth of July to work on my dissertation. I remember I accomplished precious little and slept most of the time. I chalked it up to burning the candle at both ends. "Why didn't you tell me?"

He sips his coffee as if he needs something to do. "I'd read Stevie's diary a dozen times but didn't really believe her story, so I ran her car license plates. Your name popped. I wasn't surprised she wasn't using her real name, but I was irritated she left me with a diary full of what I thought was fiction. It wasn't hard to gather facts on Lane McCord.

Finally, I visited your coffee shop, and you didn't even bat an eye when you looked at me. You were either one hell of an actress, or you really didn't have a clue."

"I don't remember seeing you."

"The shop was packed. You were moving at full steam. Reminded me of Stevie at Joey's Bar."

"Why didn't you say something?"

He shakes his head. "What was I supposed to say? Tell you about Stevie? Us?"

"Maybe. I don't know." I shove fingers through my hair. "You know how crazy this sounds, right?" I meet his gaze, hoping he'll start laughing and say this has been an elaborate hoax.

"Then I realized Iverson was sniffing around you."

"You came back to the coffee shop again?"

"I hung around outside."

"Why?"

He sighed. "Because I realized he knew exactly who you were. Stevie had been on his radar since that counseling session. He must have figured out you had a dual personality when he saw you in the Norfolk coffee shop."

"I was pictured in an article in late November. He could have seen it."

"How did you end up working in the shop near his office?"

"I transferred from the Virginia Beach store to the one located on Kyle's office block. I kept telling myself the new location would be a nice change."

"Maybe that was Stevie."

I shake my head. This all sounds so far-fetched.

"At first, I thought Stevie was working an angle," he says. "So, I returned to the coffee shop again. There were no traces of Stevie in you."

"Did you know what Kyle was planning?"

"I knew he was at that shop a lot, but I didn't realize he was taking you to the beach house until after you two left. I was almost at the beach house when I got the call you two had fallen. Like I said. The last few miles were hell until I saw you were alive."

I stare into eyes so filled with worry and guilt. "I don't remember you. I'm sorry."

He clears his throat. "Don't be."

I swallow and fall back to all that I've read about personality splits. "A dual personality is created generally when the patient is under the age of five. It occurs after extreme trauma and is a survival tactic."

"That's what I've been able to piece together. I've done my share of reading on it in the last month."

I glance at his hands, but don't remember them on my body. "Why did you start sending me her journal after the fall?"

He sips his coffee as if he needs a moment. "I wanted you to remember. I figured this was going to be the last chance to find Nikki."

Is he here for me or Stevie? Or is he here to determine if I had anything to do with Kyle's death? "You're a cop. How do I know this isn't your way of figuring out if I killed Kyle?" I shake my head to release tension in my neck and shoulders. "The medical examiner ruled Kyle's death *undetermined*. Did you say something to him?"

"First, I'm not a cop anymore."

"I saw your badge."

"It's from back in the day. It looked official enough, so I pulled it out when you asked to see it."

"You said the medical examiner ruled Kyle's death *undetermined*."

"I have buddies in the sheriff's department. I told them what I thought about Kyle and asked for a few more days."

"So, Kyle's death was not ruled *undetermined*."

"It was. If I hadn't cracked this, the sheriff's office would have been paying you a visit."

"Do you think Stevie pushed him?" I'm speaking about myself in the third person.

"What I think is that Kyle wanted to kill you. With you—and Stevie—gone, there'd be no one asking questions about Nikki again. And whatever he did to Stevie would be erased."

"But you think I got to him first. That's what all this was about?"

He shakes his head. "I don't know what happened, Lane. I truly don't."

I sip my coffee, taking a moment to think. "Kyle wanted to have sex." As I speak, he stiffens. "I should've been fine with it. I knew that was the purpose of the weekend. But when he touched me so intimately, I panicked. I ran out of the bedroom. He was right behind me and caught up to me at the top of the stairs."

"What do you remember?"

"I remember him facing me. I was yelling at him. He was trying to calm me. He kept acting like my worries were all my fault." I close my eyes. "Kyle knew Reece was across the street and likely watching. He didn't want a problem because he feared Reece would turn him in." Though I realize now that Reece, if put to the test, likely wouldn't have betrayed Kyle.

I tread carefully now. Becker might be an ex-cop, but we're now talking about homicide.

Those last seconds at the top of the stairs come into focus. Kyle's back is to the stairs. I'm so upset my body is trembling. *You need to calm down, Lane. Nothing has happened. You're overreacting.*

But it had felt so wrong. Even dirty. "I needed to put distance between us. I wanted him away from me."

I placed my hands on his chest. He was breathing fast. The next move was reflex. No different from a hand violently jerking away from a hot stove. But instead of pulling away, I shoved my hands hard into his chest. The sudden move caught him off guard. He stumbled backward. Lost his footing and grabbed me.

Color drains from my face as I realize what I've done. I can't blame that moment on Stevie. It was all Lane, reacting to a trauma she didn't even know existed.

I clear my throat and meet his gaze.

Becker stares at me a long moment, as if his mind has been trailing mine all along. "Kyle Iverson lost his footing, grabbed you to stop his fall, and you both went down. His death was a freak accident."

"Devon said she saw me shove Kyle."

"The woman who tried to kill you? The woman who knew Kyle killed Nikki?" He shakes his head. "She has no proof, so she'll sound vengeful."

"What about Stevie's diary?"

"The only copies that exist now are on your phone. I destroyed the original."

"There were printouts in my overnight bag."

"Not anymore."

"Why are you doing this for me?" I ask.

A slight shrug raises his shoulder. "It's time to close this. You've suffered enough."

If all this is true, terrible things have happened to me. "But I didn't absorb the suffering, Stevie did."

"You suffered plenty."

Tears glisten in my eyes. "I don't remember any of it. Doesn't seem fair."

He nods toward my overnight bag. "I pulled strings and got ahold of your full juvenile file."

"I told you the reports on me were wrong."

He shakes his head. "They're not wrong."

Do I want to read the reports? Maybe ignorance is bliss.

"The report is in your overnight bag," Becker says. "Read it or not, but you deserve to have the facts, good and bad. It might explain why you created Stevie."

"What happened to me?"

"Read it. It'll give you better perspective, especially if you decide to see that therapist again."

I'm quiet for a long moment. "Have they found Nikki?"

"Cadaver dogs are on the woodland property as we speak. The sheriff walked the property, and they've found a few spots with broken soil and sparse vegetation."

"What does that mean?"

"When a body is buried in the ground, it bloats with decomposition gases, pressing against the soil on top of it. When the skin finally pops, everything drops, including the topsoil. It leaves cracks. Kills grass. Sheriff thinks there might be more bodies. He's bringing in an excavation team."

I try to imagine my own body lifeless and trapped under the soil for eternity. My chest tightens, and I force a deep breath in my lungs. "I hope they find Nikki."

"Me too."

Slowly I nod. "You tried to warn Stevie to be careful. She didn't listen."

"Stevie could be stubborn. Like you."

It's easier to talk about Stevie as if she's another person. "She sounds like she's pretty tough."

"Yeah."

My gaze drops to his hands resting on the coffee cup. My pulse speeds up. "I still don't remember us."

"I know." Sadness lingers under the words. He clearly cared for Stevie.

"I'd like to remember us," I say. "You were important to Stevie." And somewhere in me, I guess, Stevie is there along with all the pain and suffering. Finding her is touching true darkness. "I'm sorry."

"Don't be." He sets his cup down. "Look, I better get going."

"You don't have to go."

"You're exhausted and so am I. And I came to deliver Stevie's last message, your car, and your suitcase. I've fulfilled my promise."

I follow him to the door. "Can I see you again sometime? I'd like to talk to you about Stevie."

He holds my gaze for a long beat. "Anytime, Lane. My door is always open."

Epilogue

LANE

A lot has happened in the last five months. Kyle Iverson's death was ruled an accident. I'm officially graduated. PhD. Dr. Lane McCord. Devon is out of the hospital and in jail awaiting trial. She has trouble talking, and her face will always be disfigured. Reece was buried in a public cemetery next to Jeb and Zeke.

The sheriff found two bodies on the woodland property. One has been identified as Marsha Davis, a.k.a. Nikki Kane. She was from Raleigh, North Carolina, and was twenty-five when she died.

The second set of remains doesn't belong to Amy Grimes, the other missing woman Becker hoped to find, and had to be declared unknown. The cops believe the female victim has been dead about five years and are hoping DNA pulled from her bones and teeth will match someone eventually. I think about Amy and that unidentified woman often. Is anyone searching for them, or are they so deeply wedged in the cracks they've been forgotten?

I've found a new therapist. I can't afford lots of sessions, but the hope is a new job with benefits will present itself soon. I've had several job interviews. Fingers crossed.

I was afraid to tell my therapist about Stevie. It sounded so crazy, and I know dissociative identity disorder is a rare condition. After a few sessions, however, I was finally able to tell her about the possibility of an alter personality. As expected, she didn't buy it. And for a couple more sessions, I doubted it myself. I didn't want to believe Stevie and I are the same. After all, all this is based on a letter Sully gave me.

But each time I told myself Stevie didn't exist, I felt a surge of rage.

Finally, I showed my therapist Stevie's journal, and I also presented her with my pediatric medical records. Those records contained reports describing bruises on my legs, a broken wrist, and phrases like *vaginal tearing*. I still can't speak about those injuries without crying or flying into a rage. Jesus, how could anyone assault such a young child?

My therapist accepted both and spent the next week reading it all. She still isn't 100 percent convinced that I might have an alter, but she's researching the subject. That's a sign to me—she suspects I could be right.

Just the fact that she might believe me is a relief, but I'm still struggling with it all. I think about all the sleepwalking and missing time. Was that all Stevie? And what had she been doing?

I know how treatment for this kind of disorder goes. I have to integrate and accept Stevie as part of me. But that'll mean knowing all her memories and experiencing her fury and anger.

As much as I don't want to peer into the darkness, I owe it to Stevie to try. She stepped forward to protect me and shield me from so much pain. Maybe it's time for me to share her burden. Maybe then we can be whole.

Today I'm driving to Nags Head. It's a beautiful day and I've texted Becker, but not heard back. I'm not sure if he wants to see me. We've not communicated since he told me about the discovery of the bodies.

Either way, I need this trip. I'm making the drive right before the summer season kicks off, so tourist traffic isn't terrible. My first stop is Joey's. Kyle and Jeb first saw Stevie beside Joey's, and that's where they grabbed her. It explains why Stevie returned here over and over.

I've scanned a decade's worth of old calendars and found blocks of days in July that I can't account for. Maybe I was here in Norfolk working, and there was no reason to indicate the day's agenda. Maybe I was Stevie, searching for the men who'd assaulted her. Since January, I've been making daily video logs of me as a way of proving I'm here. So far, no messages from Stevie of any kind.

I park outside Joey's and don't move for several long minutes as I watch patrons coming and going. Do I remember the place or the streets around it? Maybe not specific details, but the longer I stare at the freshly painted aqua cinder block building, the tighter my chest feels. I'm really tempted to leave and forget about all this. Maybe best to leave well enough alone.

But if Stevie has taught me anything, it's not to hide or run from trouble. I can almost imagine her now telling me not to be a baby.

I take several deep breaths and get out of the car. As I push into the dimly lit bar, I feel a strong sense of familiarity. The waitress scrambling from table to table, the music, and the neon BEER sign behind the bar are echoes of a different life. This moment is akin to a sort of coming home, maybe not for me but for Stevie. It's a closing of a circle.

I see a large man moving behind the bar serving drinks. He wears a black T-shirt that reads JOEY's on the back. His muscled arms sport tattoos that start at his wrist and snake up under his shirtsleeves. Deeply tanned skin sets off gray hair bound back in a thinning ponytail. Without anyone telling me, I know that's Joey.

"You should go talk to him." Becker's voice is right behind me.

I face him. His hair is sun streaked, has grown longer, and now brushes the top of his shirt collar. He looks like he's lived here forever.

It's good to see him, and I can't help but smile. "You got my text."

His stony features seem to soften despite whatever he thinks or doesn't think about me. "Just read it an hour ago. I was kayaking on the sound and didn't have my phone with me."

"You've never looked better." It feels oddly natural to tease him. "What's with the hair? That's not regulation."

He stabs fingers through his hair. "I decided it's time to let my past life go."

"Change is good sometimes, isn't it, Sully?"

His head cocks slightly at the sound of his name. "Sully?"

"In this bar, it feels like I should be calling you Sully. But for the record, I'm still Lane," I say.

He leans a little closer, as if he's sharing a secret. "I know. And it doesn't matter."

Becker is tied to Kyle's death. Sully connects with something better, more positive. "You okay? Are you doing well?"

"I'm more than okay." He's standing close to me but makes no move to touch. He clears his throat. "I really can introduce you to Joey."

"No, that's okay. I didn't come here to see him per se. I just wanted to walk in Stevie's steps at least once."

"So, what do you want, Lane?" Disquiet echoes in his tone.

"I thought we could grab dinner." I'm amazed how easily I suggest it. "I mean, unless you have something else to do." It's been five months since I've seen this guy, and I'm stepping back into his life like it's been five minutes. "If this is too weird, I get it."

He shakes his head slowly, a slight smile tugging his lips. "It's not weird at all."

I laugh. "Really? Because I think on the weird scale, it's ten out of ten."

He grins. "Like I told Stevie once, white picket fences don't interest me."

I lean in and kiss him. His hand comes to the base of my spine. He doesn't press, but he wants me to know he's there. His lips feel good, familiar, but no memories jog loose.

"Why'd you do that?" he asks.

"I'm not sure. The kiss was mine, but maybe I did it hoping to connect to Stevie."

"If you're worried about remembering, don't," he says. "Let's just focus on now."

"I'd like that."

ABOUT THE AUTHOR

Mary Burton is the *New York Times* and *USA Today* bestselling author of more than thirty-five romance and suspense novels, including *The Lies I Told*, *Don't Look Now*, *Near You*, *Burn You Twice*, and *Never Look Back*, as well as five novellas. She currently lives in North Carolina, with her husband and three miniature dachshunds. For more information, visit www.maryburton.com.